Lindsay Buroker's

the Emperor's edge

A High Fantasy Novel in an Era of Steam

CHAPTER 1

CORPORAL AMARANTHE LOKDON PACED. HER short sword, night stick, and handcuffs bumped and clanked at her thighs with each impatient step. Enforcer Headquarters frowned down at her, an ominous gray cliff of a building that glowered at the neighborhood like a turkey vulture, except with less charisma.

Amaranthe drew her pocket watch and checked the time. Where *was* her partner?

At the soft squeak of boots on snow, she looked up. A narrow side street expelled a squat, burly man in enforcer grays. Morning light glinted against the large brass rank pins crowding his collar: four bars under two crossed swords, the mark of a district chief.

Amaranthe fought back a grimace and straightened, heels clicking together. The chief's dark gaze latched onto her from beneath shaggy gray eyebrows that crashed in the middle when he scowled. He was scowling now.

She swallowed. "Good morning, Chief Gunarth."

"Lokdon," he growled. "Does the city pay you to loiter in front of headquarters? Because if the capital city of the Turgonian Empire, the most powerful nation in the world, pays its enforcers to loiter uselessly in front of *my* headquarters building, I'd think somebody would have mentioned it to me."

Amaranthe opened her mouth to give him an obedient "yes, sir." Or was it a "no, sir"? She had lost the question in his diatribe. "I'm waiting for my partner, sir."

"It's five minutes into your shift. Where is he?"

"He's..." *Hung over, still asleep, trying vainly to find a uniform that isn't wrinkled....* "Investigating some suspicious activity at Curi's Bakery."

The chief's already-lowered eyebrows descended further. "Let me explain something to you, Lokdon."

"Sir?" Amaranthe tried to look attentive.

"Your first loyalty is to the emperor." He reached above his head, demonstrating a lofty plateau. "Your second is to the city, and your third is to everyone above you in the chain of command." His hand descended in increments as he spoke until he finished with, "Way down there by your boot is your loyalty to your partner. Understood?"

"Emperor, city, you, boot. Got it, sir."

"Is that a joke, Lokdon?" His tone made it clear it had better not be. She sighed. "No, sir."

"If you can't remember where your loyalties lie, better you take up a shop like the rest of the women in Turgonia."

Amaranthe forced her face to stay neutral, ignoring the heat warming her cheeks. "Yes, sir."

"Now, I ask you again, where is your partner?" The chief's tone had grown soft, dangerous.

She lifted her chin. "Investigating suspicious activity at Curi's."

Furrows like canyons formed across the chief's forehead as his scowl deepened. "I see. I'll remember this when I'm filling out the extra duty roster."

"Yes, sir."

"Start your patrol without him. And when he catches up, tell him if he can't arrive at work on time, you can both sleep here. In one of the cells."

"I will, sir."

Amaranthe trotted away before the chief could spout further threats. She crossed the wide boulevard in front of headquarters and jogged around a lumbering steam tractor obscuring ice with sheets of salt. Snow piles framed the ancient cobblestone alley she entered, its walls close enough to touch with outstretched arms. She almost bumped into a man and woman coming out of a temple that had been turned into a bookstore. Bundled in fur caps and parkas, they saw her uniform and stepped out of the way, joining a headless statue in one of the recessed

nooks by the door. At the turn of the last century, Mad Emperor Motash had declared atheism the state religion and ordered all statues depicting deities beheaded. A hundred years later, the locals still called the seat of the empire, "Stumps."

Amaranthe smelled the scrumptious scents of Curi's Bakery as she came onto the next boulevard, and she cast a longing gaze at the building. Paintings of apple pastries, glazed fruits, and spiced breads adorned the windows for those unable to read the sign. A gangly university student ambled out with a pastry stuffed in his mouth. Warm frosting dribbled down his chin.

Someone tapped Amaranthe's shoulder. "Buy one. The city won't catch on fire if you indulge occasionally."

"Can't." She glanced at her partner, Corporal Wholt, as he fell into step beside her. She wanted to yell at him for being late again, but it would change little, and she had yet to meet the man who appreciated unsolicited criticism. "Enforcers are supposed to be fit. I'd have to run the whole lake trail tonight if I ate one of those pastries."

"You probably will anyway. To punish yourself for being tempted."

Amaranthe did not consider diet advice from Wholt worth much. Though he stood several inches taller than her five and a half feet, his slouch made the difference negligible. A fledgling pot belly slumped over the belt of his rumpled gray uniform. The double-bar rank pin on his left collar flap was skewed at a different angle than the pin on his right. She reached up, unfastened the backs, and adjusted the pins so both sides matched.

"Thanks," Wholt said dryly. "You know you're the most grandmotherly twenty-five-year-old woman I've met, right?"

"That's because most of the women you know work at brothels."

"The best kind. Very amenable ladies."

"You missed a spot shaving." Amaranthe's hand dropped to her utility knife. "Want me to...?"

"No!" Wholt sidled away. "Don't you ever grow weary of being the ideal enforcer? Perfectly pressed uniform, gleaming weapons, not a single hair out of place in that unflattering brown bun."

Frowning, Amaranthe touched her hair. It was neat and out of the way. That counted more than beauty.

"You come to work early," Wholt continued, "stay late, precisely follow every regulation, and where's it gotten you? You're still a corporal after six years."

"You're still a corporal after six years too," she said.

"Actually," he said, tone growing calm, and a smile coming to his lips, "I came up on the list for promotion. It'll be sergeant next month."

"You? You're going to make sergeant? You don't know half the regulations and you're late for work every other day."

Wholt looked away. "You're my partner, Amaranthe. I figured you'd be happy for me."

She stared at the snow edging the cracks in the sidewalk. He was right. She should be happy for him, but it was all too unfair. "Congratulations," she managed, though she doubted it sounded sincere.

"I'm sure it'll be your turn next month," Wholt said.

Amaranthe was sure it would not, even if the chief forgot to mark her file with a demerit for that morning's lie. She knew of no female sergeants in the Stumps force. The empire did not permit women to join its armies, and it was only in the last generation that it had begun allowing them to join the city law enforcers—grudgingly.

"Wholt." Amaranthe looked him in the eyes and touched his arm. "Try to...be a good sergeant. You represent the empire when you wear that uniform. And you represent yourself. That should matter."

He actually stood taller. "I will. I know. It does."

"Good."

His attention shifted over her shoulder. "Is that smoke?" He pointed toward the blocky buildings crouched alongside the lake. "Or just factory haze?"

Down the hill, dozens of men and machines toiled on the frozen water, hacking out blocks of ice that would be stored for summer use, but smoke blurred the scene. Amaranthe pinpointed the source.

"There's not a factory there." She grabbed Wholt's arm and tugged him forward. "Fire!"

They took a trolley toward the waterfront and hopped off at the nearest stop. Smoke thickened the air, and they slipped and skidded as they negotiated the slick sidewalks. They ran around a corner, almost crashing into the back ranks of a gathering crowd.

In a residential district, where wooden structures were more common, people might have raced back and forth with buckets to help, but this dilapidated wooden building was an island surrounded by brick, stone, and cement. The onlookers appeared more fascinated than concerned about the flames spreading, and the Imperial Fire Brigade had already arrived with one of the city's self-propelled fire pumps. Black smoke poured from the stack, mingling with the plumes rising from the building. A thick hose was attached to the pump and to a fireplug up the street. Water streamed onto the flames flickering through the broken windows of the old building. Only one corner, which was dominated by a multistory brick kiln, was not burning.

"You mentioned something about the city not catching on fire today?" Amaranthe asked as she and Wholt pushed their way through the onlookers.

"Did I say that?"

Heat flooded over them, dry and powerful. Charred flakes of wood and paper floated through the air.

"We better help with crowd control," Amaranthe said, but as they advanced, she glimpsed a merchant standing at her counter in a tea-and-coffee import store. Other shop owners had joined the gawking crowd. Two men loomed in front of this woman. Customers? Given the proximity of the fire, shopping seemed unlikely. "Or we could help this lady who I believe is being robbed."

"Huh?" Wholt turned his head. "Oh. It wouldn't hurt these businesses to be looted once in a while. Merchants are practically running things around here anyway." But he drew his sword.

"I'll go in the front," Amaranthe said. "You go around back."

"Be careful." Wholt trotted down the street toward an alley where he could cut over.

Amaranthe strode through the front door. Barrels and canisters cluttered the aisles, and stuffed shelves rose from floor to ceiling on each wall. The scent of tea leaves and coffee beans from distant parts of the world soared above the pervading smell of smoke. Her strongbox open, the merchant was clutching a stack of bills. Her eyes brightened when she saw Amaranthe's uniform.

Amaranthe focused on the two men towering over the shopkeeper. The huge brutes were only a couple feet shorter than the floor-to-ceiling stack of coffee tins fronting the aisle behind them.

"Well, well," one man said, nudging his cohort, "it looks like a girl enforcer. We're very concerned."

His comrade snickered. Scars lined the faces of both men. Swords hung in belt scabbards, the hilts' sweat-stained leather wrappings evidence of frequent use. One thug shifted to reveal a flintlock pistol aimed at the merchant. Apparently, he did not consider Amaranthe enough of a threat to warrant switching his target. Indignation flared and her hand twitched toward her sword. She caught herself before she acted foolishly. After all, it was better not to have a weapon pointed at her chest.

"Gentlemen," Amaranthe said, "this robbery is over. If you put down your weapons and submit to being detained, perhaps I can speak to the magistrate on your behalf. Your possession of firearms, which, according to Imperial City Code seven-four-three dash A, are for military use only, will elevate your crime from simple theft to aggressive larceny."

"Darn." The thug waved a negligent hand at her, then leered at the merchant. "Give us the money, lady."

Amaranthe drew her sword. The thugs displayed less concern than men chattered at by irate chipmunks. Probably rightfully so. They outnumbered her, and they had the miens of ex-soldiers. While she had undergone weapons and unarmed combat training at the Enforcer Academy, that was mediocre compared to the constant drilling military men endured. And they knew it. One of the robbers assumed a bored ready stance, lips canted in a knowing smirk.

A glance at the back of the building revealed no one charging in to help. What was keeping Wholt?

The thug shifted his weight to advance.

Amaranthe bent her legs, drew her shoulder back, and hurled her sword with all her strength. Reflexively, both men lifted their blades to block. As soon as they realized her weapon would not touch them, they burst into chortles.

The men were not her targets.

Her sword crashed into the ceiling-high collection of coffee tins behind them. The stack exploded, full canisters pummeling the robbers. Metal thudded against skin and bone, and the men cursed as they flailed, tripped, and inevitably toppled. One hit his head on the counter as he went down and did not move when he landed. The other fell, scrambled to rise, slipped on a canister, and cracked his chin on the tile floor.

Amaranthe picked her way through the mess, stepped on one man's back, and collected their weapons. She handed the pistol to the merchant who pointed the weapon gleefully at the prone robbers while Amaranthe cuffed one and found twine to tie the other.

"Nicely done, Corporal," a quiet voice said from the direction of the front door.

"Thanks." She started to look up to identify the speaker when Wholt burst in through the back. "Where have you been?" she demanded. "Did you get lost?"

"There was a third one out back. I had to...uh...uhm..." Wholt's mouth dropped open as he stared past Amaranthe. "Good morning, Sire," he finally managed.

Sire? Amaranthe slowly stood and turned. Crowded at the entrance, six tall broad men wearing black gold-trimmed uniforms—the color of the emperor's elite bodyguard—framed a smaller man of eighteen or nineteen. He had pale brown hair, gentle dark brown eyes, and yes, his *was* the same face that adorned the currency in the merchant's strongbox. Emperor Sespian Savarsin, in power this last year since reaching his majority.

"Good morning," the emperor answered.

Amaranthe stammered a greeting. What's the emperor doing down here? Shouldn't he be somewhere safe, doing emperorly *things?* She ransacked her memory for the proper protocol and found...nothing. Emperors did not traditionally saunter through the waterfront shops. They certainly did not mingle with people of the labor class.

The merchant, equally flustered, curtseyed deeply and said, "Sire, I must apologize for the state of disarray infecting my store."

The emperor arched his eyebrows. "I should be apologizing to you, madam. For allowing this—" he gestured toward the fallen thugs, "—in the city. Fortunately, our enforcers are quite competent." He bounced a little at this and smiled at Amaranthe, more like a young man hungering for a friend than a leader over millions. Don't be presumptuous, Amaranthe.

"Yes, Sire," she said. It felt like a safe answer.

"What's your name?" he asked. "Both of your names?" He waved to include Wholt.

"Corporal Lokdon," Amaranthe said. "And this is soon-to-be Sergeant Wholt," she added when Wholt did not manage to utter anything intelligible.

A ponderous man with flapping jowls thundered through the doorway. Beads of sweat gleamed on his face. The emperor sighed like a boy whose tutor had caught up with him.

"Sire, there you are. They've got the fire under control. Do you want to finish the inspection now?"

"Not really." The emperor smiled wistfully.

"Commander of the Armies Hollowcrest will be expecting our punctual return."

"I suppose." The emperor cast a mournful gaze at Amaranthe as he trooped out the door flanked by his guards.

When the entourage had departed, Wholt shuffled through the tins and elbowed Amaranthe. "I think he liked you."

She snorted. "Yes, I'm surely destined to be the next empress."

"That might be ambitious, but you could have asked him for a promotion."

For a moment, Wholt's words enticed her. If the emperor told the chief someone should be promoted to sergeant, surely it would happen. And she deserved it, didn't she? She worked harder than Wholt. But no.... "If I get promoted, it'll be because I earned it, the same as everyone else. Not because I begged someone for a favor."

"You *have* earned it."

* * * * *

The bodies were charred into anonymity and still smoldering. Eight, Amaranthe counted as she walked around the pile, sodden floorboards creaking ominously beneath her feet. It was a dangerous spot, since the fire had also charred the support posts and beams in the basement. Several boards had already given way and plunged below. A great hole in the floor marked the spot where a worktable had stood. Yet she stayed, breathing air thick with the stench of fire and death, seeking answers from the carnage.

The corpses had been there, piled just like this, when the first firemen walked in. They had left the bodies untouched for the enforcers. The flames had seared facial features, clothing, skin and hair color into indistinguishable black lumps. Amaranthe could not even tell gender for certain.

"Definitely arson, sir," a rookie enforcer reported to Wholt, who stood near a window. The flooring was more stable next to the walls. "We found empty kerosene tins downstairs."

"Thank you, ah..."

"Quets," Amaranthe supplied the name, looking up from the bodies to focus on the younger enforcer. He and his partner had been nearby and had also responded early to the fire. "What else is down there?"

"Just some tools, a bunch of pots stored on shelves, and the biggest kiln I've ever seen," Quets said.

"One wonders why they didn't just cremate the bodies in the kiln," Amaranthe mused. "Why torch the whole building?"

"They?" Wholt asked.

She could only shrug, having no idea yet who 'they' were nor why anyone would choose a pottery studio for a mass murder. Of course, the corpses could have come from anywhere and been brought here and arranged like this for...what? She shook her head.

"Quets," Amaranthe said, "take the trolley back to HQ, tell the chief what we've found and that we need a steam wagon. The Sawbones will want to take a look at these corpses."

The smell of singed flesh was turning her stomach. Amaranthe picked a path around puddles and over to the window where Wholt stood. Soot stained the panes that were not broken. Snowflakes flitted in through burned holes in the ceiling, mingling with water dripping from the rafters.

"What do you think?" she asked.

"It's a mess."

"Very perceptive, thank you."

"It's obvious, isn't it?" Wholt asked. "Someone killed a bunch of people and wanted to cover it up by rendering the bodies unidentifiable. They probably meant for them and the floor to burn completely. The Fire Brigade was just too good."

"Hm," Amaranthe said. "I want to look in the basement. Then we'll have to interview the artists who work here, see if anybody—eight anybodies—are known to be missing and if anything odd has been going on around here. We should find out who owns the building too."

"We?" Wholt raised his eyebrows. "We're patrollers, not detectives. The chief will send a lieutenant down to oversee the investigation."

Amaranthe grimaced. He was right, of course. This case would make the papers, though, probably the front page. Working on it might be just the opportunity she needed to stand out and earn her promotion. Maybe she could get herself put on the investigation team.

"I bet it's Sicarius," Wholt said.

Amaranthe blinked. "What?"

Wholt was staring at the charred corpses. "You know, Sicarius, the assassin, the only criminal with a million-ranmya bounty on his head. The only criminal with a bounty signed by Emperor Sespian himself."

"I know who Sicarius is," Amaranthe said. Thanks to that bounty, everyone in the empire knew who he was. "But why would you think he's responsible for this?"

"He's back in town. I just heard last night. One of the gymnasium pickpockets we've been after all winter turned himself in. Seems he was in the baths, doing his looting circuit, and he touched Sicarius's towel before realizing whose stuff he was trolling through. The thief spent half the day looking over his shoulder and then showed up at HQ wanting to be arrested so he could hide out in a cell."

"Did the chief send some men to the gym?" Amaranthe asked, annoyed at the idea of a criminal daring to exercise and bathe in public facilities.

"He claims he doesn't believe the pickpocket," Wholt said. "I don't blame him. The last time Sicarius was in Stumps, we lost thirty men trying to get him."

"I remember." A couple of men from her class at the Academy had been among the slain. Still, the idea of looking the other way for a criminal did not sit well with her. Throwing men at someone so dangerous might not be the answer, but surely there were alternatives. If she were chief, there was much she would do differently. Amaranthe sighed. "I'm checking the basement."

Several of the blackened wooden stair treads were broken where the big rookie's foot had gone through. For once, being smaller than all the men was helpful, for she made it to the bottom unscathed.

Fallen boards, broken tables, and other detritus from above littered the cement floor. When she spotted a soot-covered broom in the corner, she almost went over to grab it. Alas, whoever came to investigate officially would not appreciate her cleaning the crime scene.

Her foot crunched on ceramic as she walked toward the kiln entrance. None of the pots on the back shelves were broken. Why were there shards all over the floor?

She knelt for a closer look.

The first piece she picked up didn't look like part of a pot at all. Cone-shaped, it reminded her of a cup, but since it couldn't be set flat, it seemed fairly useless in that capacity. She turned it sideways and then upside down. In the last position it looked a bit like a perked dog or cat ear, though it was far too large to be either.

Other shards she picked up were even less identifiable. It would take someone with a lot of time and devotion to piece together the puzzle.

"There are fresh ashes in here," Amaranthe called when she reached the firebox.

Wholt dared a few steps down the precarious staircase. "You may not have noticed, but there are fresh ashes *everywhere*."

"These are from the kiln, not the building fire." Amaranthe held her hand above the embers. "They're still warm."

"Again, you may not have noticed, but *everything* is still warm here."

"You're not being very helpful, Wholt. I'm saying the kiln was used recently."

"I imagine people fire pots here every day."

She grabbed a poker and overturned gray coal to find still-red embers. "How about in the middle of the night?"

Wholt had no sarcastic answer for that question.

"What if..." Amaranthe chomped on her lip and eyed the broken pieces of ceramic on the floor. "What if the fire wasn't about covering up the bodies at all? Or maybe that was a secondary reason. What if someone was down here, trying to destroy something in the kiln, but there wasn't enough room?" That seemed unlikely given its massive two-story size. "Or maybe they were *making* something in the kiln, something they didn't want anyone to see. Or what if—"

"Emperor's balls, Amaranthe. What nefarious thing could you possibly make in a kiln?"

"I, well, you're probably right. I'm just thinking out loud."

"Well, quit it. The steam wagon is here, and, yup, there's a lieutenant from the NoDoc District. Better get up here before he yells at you for disturbing things."

Sighing, Amaranthe climbed the stairs. She eyed the pile of corpses again as she headed for the knot of enforcers gathering inside the front door. Who *were* those people? Victims? Cohorts? Innocents? Colluders?

As soon as she spotted the lieutenant, Amaranthe jogged over and came to attention before him. "Sir, I'm Corporal Lokdon, and I've been looking around here. I've got some ideas. Are you choosing people for your investigation team?"

"I've heard of you, corporal," the tall, slender graying man said.

He had? She raised her eyebrows. In a good way?

"You have a reputation for fastidiousness," he said.

Blighted ancestors. *That* was what enforcers in other districts knew about her?

"Why don't you and your partner head up the cleanup team out here. The whole block is a mess."

Amaranthe stared. That was a task for a couple of rookies! If she was going to earn her promotion, she'd have to distinguish herself by arresting villains and solving crimes, not poking around on the street with a broom and dustpan.

"Is there a problem, Corporal?" the lieutenant asked.

She stifled the first response that came to mind, one that would only get her in trouble. "The...cleanup team, sir?" she said instead. "I have a good eye for detail. I believe I could—"

"Yes, the cleanup team," the lieutenant said, a warning in his eyes. "It's a more appropriate assignment. Young ladies shouldn't be surrounding themselves with gory bodies." He walked toward the stairs, patting her on the shoulder on the way by. "You'll do fine."

Just barely, Amaranthe had the discipline to walk outside, where the crowd had dissipated, before ripping her sword out and hurling it at the closest wall. The point glanced off instead of sinking in with a satisfying

thunk, and the weapon clattered onto the frosty sidewalk. She stalked over, grabbed it, and thought about throwing it again. She really wanted to skewer something.

Wholt, who had just come outside, lifted his arms, stepped back, and wisely kept his mouth shut.

Amaranthe stuffed the blade back into its sheath, nicking her hand in the process. "Lovely," she muttered at the stab of pain.

She would oversee the street cleanup, but then she was going to get herself put on the investigation team. One way or another.

CHAPTER 2

B Y THE TIME AMARANTHE REACHED ENFORCER
Headquarters that evening, she had mentally organized a
neat list of reasons she ought to be placed on the investigation. With chin lifted, she thrust open the front door and almost crashed
into Chief Gunarth, who was pacing in the hallway.

"What did you do, Corporal?" he demanded before she could mention the arson or her list.

"Sir?"

"Commander of the Armies Hollowcrest wants to see you," the
chief said.

The list evaporated from her mind, and she put her hand on the
hallway's cool limestone wall for support. Commander of the Armies
Hollowcrest was the highest ranking military officer in the empire. Each
of the eight satrapies' Commander Lords General answered to him personally. He had also been the closest advisor of Emperor Raumesys for
forty years and Sespian's regent for three. Due to Sespian's youth, many
still considered him the ultimate authority in the empire.

"He wants to see *me*?" Amaranthe cleared her throat to hide the
squeak underlying her last word.

"You," Chief Gunarth said. "Requested by name. You are to go to
the Imperial Barracks immediately. Actually the messenger came two
hours ago, but you weren't on your assigned route." He gave her a cool
look.

That was hardly fair. "Sir, Wholt and I were responding to the fire
on—"

"Give me your report later. It's already dark. You better get your arse up to the Barracks before you inconvenience Hollowcrest by delaying his dinner."

"Yes, sir."

Crisp twilight air swirled about her cheeks as Amaranthe caught a trolley uptown. She shivered and moved closer to the hissing boiler and the heat radiating through its walls.

Poised at the crown of Arakan Hill, the Imperial Barracks overlooked the city, the frozen lake, and dwarfed even the largest homes on the Ridge. The emperor's ancestors had rejected the idea of a "palace" and chosen the ancient fortress atop the hill for the imperial seat.

There was no trolley stop near the gate—apparently casual visits to gawk were not encouraged—so Amaranthe jumped off as it rumbled by the outer walls. She had performed similar moves dozens of times before, but the combination of slick pavement and watching sentries probably made the slip inevitable. Her feet skidded on ice and she flailed before recovering her balance, if not her dignity.

Snickers came from above. Atop the high stone walls, two musketeers lounged against a cannon, their silhouettes black against the starry sky. Amaranthe limited herself to a brief upward glower as she walked toward the entrance.

In a formidable display of redundancy, two towering soldiers blocked the barred gate. Amaranthe could not help but feel that as an enforcer she only played at being a warrior. Imperial soldiers were intimidating enough; the elite men privileged to protect the emperor's home represented the best.

"Uhm, hello," she said, then cursed herself for sounding like a scared child. "I'm Corporal Amaranthe Lokdon. Commander of the Armies Hollowcrest requested to see me."

"It's late," one of the guards said in a voice reminiscent of boots grinding into gravel.

"I realize that. Could you check to see if I'm on the list?" She had no idea if there *was* a list, but it seemed like the right thing to say.

Both guards offered flat unfriendly stares. Their humorless expressions were so similar Amaranthe wondered if it was part of the training. Disapproving Stares, the Advanced Course. Finally, one reached his arm through the bars and withdrew a clipboard from some inner hook.

He stepped beneath one of the two gas lamps spreading wan globes of light on either side of the gate.

Amaranthe fidgeted while he read. Anticipation wrestled with unease in her gut. What was this meeting about? Would it bode well for her, or ill? Either way, why would someone as important as the Commander of the Armies bother with her? The emperor must have said something after seeing her that afternoon. Did he have some reward in mind? It seemed unlikely—she had done nothing beyond what the job called for. Still, the fledgling hope thrived, and she thought of Wholt's words. Maybe she should ask Hollowcrest for a promotion. No, she decided. The possibility of a reward thrilled her, but she would not ask for a favor.

"Huh," the guard said. "You're listed."

The other one said, "Looks like the old man wants someone to keep his toes warm tonight."

Amaranthe fluctuated between anger at their assumption and anxiety at the insinuation. She settled for a curt, "Can I go in, now?"

One of the soldiers shouted to someone in the courtyard. Another man appeared and assumed his post, and the first relieved Amaranthe of her weapons and led her through the gate.

Walkways lined with lampposts sliced through snow-blanketed lawns. Numerous outbuildings adorned the installation, but the guard led her to the main structure. When they reached the polished marble stairs, she had to take exaggerated steps to climb them. On either side of the landing, gold-laced statues of bare-chested men grappled with each other.

"Pretentious architect," Amaranthe muttered.

"What did you say?" the guard asked.

"Such beautiful artwork."

The guard grunted dubiously.

The gold-gilded double doors groaned open of their own accord, powered by some hidden machinery. A single hallway stretched away to a distant exit point with dozens of doors lining either side. The decorating style continued on the inside—gaudy but consistent in its reverence toward the warrior. Periodic alcoves featured more statues of ancient heroes, some naked and locked in wrestling matches, others wearing the weapons and armor of their times. They all had clunky, unrealistic

features. Her people might be peerless engineers, but great artists they were not.

Weapons from different epochs perched between gas lamps on the walls. Amaranthe's fingers twitched toward her handkerchief when she noticed one still exhibiting bloodstains. Yes, let's erase eight hundred years of history with a swipe of a rag. She stuffed her hands into her pockets and resolutely stared straight ahead as she walked.

Her escort led her a long way before stairs branched off, one set leading up, another down. They climbed to the third floor and stopped before a guarded door. Amaranthe's guide left her to deal with the soldier alone. Fortunately, he must have had orders to admit her, for he pushed the door open wordlessly and gestured for her to enter.

"Thank you," Amaranthe murmured, though she hesitated before going in. A bead of sweat snaked down her ribcage.

Show some fortitude, girl.

Shoulders back, she strode into the office. Her boots thudded on a cold hardwood floor. The room's utilitarian furniture was neatly arranged, but the crooked and curling maps papering the walls made Amaranthe want to start rearranging tacks. A coal-burning stove glowed cherry in one corner. It was the only warm thing in the room.

The white-haired man behind the desk had easily seen seventy years, but he still possessed the fit frame of a soldier. His sharp features were humorless. His black eyes glittered behind glasses that did nothing to distort their iciness.

So, this is the one who teaches the Disapproving Stare class. Amaranthe dropped her gaze to the folders and papers stacked haphazardly on his desk. She clasped her hands behind her back to keep from tidying the clutter. He probably did not approve of people touching his belongings. *He probably doesn't approve of people breathing.* No wonder such gloom had draped the emperor; with this man as an adviser, there were probably not many laughs at meetings.

"Corporal Lokdon," Commander of the Armies Hollowcrest said.

"Yes, sir."

"Good of you to come so promptly." Spoken by another, the words might have sounded friendly, but the man's sarcastic edge dulled the effect.

Amaranthe shifted her weight. A floorboard creaked.

"You're wondering why I called you here," Hollowcrest said.

"Yes, sir."

He shuffled papers, then opened a folder. "I've been looking over your records. You have a halfway decent education, though you didn't finish the last term at the Mildawn Business School for Women." He pushed the top page over to look at another. "That's the year your coal miner father died of Black Lung Disease. All that money he must have scrimped to send you to that school, and you didn't finish. Instead you lied about your age, took the enforcer entrance exam, and signed up for the academy. Have I got it right, so far?"

"I couldn't afford to finish school, sir," Amaranthe said stiffly. "My father was sick for months before he died, and he didn't get any pay during that time. I worked, and took care of him, and went to school until he passed away, but I couldn't afford to pay the tuition and rent on a flat after that."

"I see."

Amaranthe felt as if she were balancing on the frozen lake. Might a hole open up beneath her and suck her in? It wasn't surprising that Hollowcrest had access to all her background information, but it alarmed her that he had bothered to look into it. What had she done to warrant such scrutiny? Surely she was not here because she had lied about her age seven years ago.

"You chose a hard road," Hollowcrest said. "A female enforcer is rare, even if it's allowed now. Why not work for someone in business or start your own? It seems to be the trend for educated women these days." His last sentence came with a faint sneer.

She supposed a man of Hollowcrest's age remembered the time when women had been free of ambition beyond birthing future soldiers. She knew their growing financial clout alarmed the conservatives, but her ambitions were not business-related. Why would he bring it up now?

"I went to that school because it was what my father wanted," she said. "I never cared much for business."

"No? Your marks suggest otherwise."

"I didn't mind the lessons. Just the ultimate goal seemed...shallow. I want to serve the throne, not my own pockets. I want to be the first female enforcer chief in the empire, sir, to be somebody that history remembers."

Hollowcrest frowned. Wrong answer, but why? Amaranthe shifted her weight again, still struggling to gain her balance in this conversation.

The old man flipped a few more pages on his desk, tendons jumping on the backs of his creased bronze hands. Coals shifted in the stove. Surreptitiously, Amaranthe wiped moist hands on the sides of her trousers.

"Would you be interested in an independent assignment?" Hollowcrest finally asked. "Something that would challenge you?"

The breath caught in Amaranthe's throat. Had all these questions been not an interrogation but an interview? She found herself balancing on her toes. "Sir?"

Hollowcrest leaned back in his chair. "Have you ever heard of an outlaw named Sicarius?"

"Yes, sir. He's an assassin, wanted for crimes against the empire."

"An understatement. In the last five years, he's been responsible for the deaths of some three hundred imperial soldiers, two hundred enforcers from various cities around the empire, half a dozen patriarchs from the warrior caste, thirteen city officials..."

As the list continued, Amaranthe's jaw went slack. Neither the number nor depth of these crimes were listed on the wanted bulletin. Likely it was in his enforcer record, but assassins weren't something a patroller dealt with, and she had never been asked to look him up.

"He's suspected of collusion with both the Kendorians and the Nurians," Hollowcrest said. "And just two months ago, he assassinated Satrap Governor Lumous."

"I'd heard about that death, sir. The papers said it was an accident."

"Yes, Lumous *accidentally* earned someone's wrath and had a dagger stuck in his back," Hollowcrest said. "Our enemies read our papers. Naturally we don't confess details that could make the Turgonian Empire appear weak."

"Naturally, sir," Amaranthe said, trying not to look too appalled. "What was he doing before?"

"What?" Hollowcrest asked.

"You said Sicarius had done all this in the last five years. What was he doing before then? All those nefarious accomplishments don't sound like the work of someone young and up-and-coming."

For a moment, Hollowcrest considered her through half-lidded eyes. Perhaps deciding if she were worthy of some secret he might have to divulge? But all he said was, "I believe he's in his mid-thirties. His origins are unknown."

Amaranthe opened her mouth to ask another question, but Hollowcrest cut her off.

"You may have heard he's recently arrived in the city," he said. "He's known to be hirable for assassinations, so his presence here is disturbing. Sespian's nineteenth birthday celebration is coming up in a few weeks, a massive event with guests and diplomats from all over the world. I fear it might also provide a venue for a showy assassination."

Amaranthe grimaced. The young man she had met in that shop had been so gentle and inoffensive, especially given the number of tyrannical warlords who had preceded him. He had not even had a chance to come into his own authority yet.

"Sespian set a prodigious bounty on Sicarius's head," Hollowcrest said, "but the more soldiers we send after him, the more he kills."

"And enforcers. I know, sir." What Amaranthe did not know was how this related to her. What could she do?

"Clearly, we need to pursue a new tact," Hollowcrest continued. "You are an attractive woman, and according to your record, quite capable. All you have to do is locate Sicarius, seduce him, and lead him to some dark room. Once there a feminine smile will allow you to slip in close, draw your dagger, and accomplish what platoons of soldiers have not been able to do over the last few years."

Amaranthe took a step back before she could catch herself. All she would have to do was *seduce someone*? She was an enforcer, not a prostitute. Besides, she had spent her entire adult life trying to act as tough, strong, and confident as her male counterparts. What did *she* know about seduction? And assassination? She captured criminals and took them to the magistrate for justice. She didn't kill them. To deliberately seek someone out for that purpose... That was despicable.

"Sir, I'm not—" Amaranthe started.

"Such an accomplishment," Hollowcrest interrupted, "would gain you great recognition...a promotion."

She sucked in a breath.

"In fact," Hollowcrest went on, "Someone who could handle Sicarius would doubtlessly be officer material."

He was offering her a chance to jump straight to lieutenant? Emperor's ancestors almighty.

Hollowcrest watched her intently. He was manipulating her, luring her into doing something she found distasteful. Any fool could see that, but what he offered was everything she wanted.

Surely she could eliminate somebody who was a proven criminal. True, assassinations circumvented justice, which made them undeniably wrong, but if this Sicarius was brought in, the magistrate would assign him the death penalty anyway. By killing him in the field, she would save the department time and manpower. It would be for the good of the empire.

Amaranthe rubbed her face. The need to justify her decision was trampling all over her thinking. Still, was this really that bad? Would it truly be a blemish on her integrity? Even if it was, every day people sacrificed a lot more than integrity to get what they wanted. Besides, this was the Commander of the Armies, not a man it would be smart to refuse. She didn't even know if refusal was permitted.

"I'll do it, sir," Amaranthe said.

"Excellent," he said simply, though she caught a predatory gleam of satisfaction in those dark eyes.

Hollowcrest slid a folder out of a drawer and withdrew a single paper. "A sketch of Sicarius. It's fairly accurate, at least as of five years ago."

Amaranthe accepted the sketch and studied it. She admired the precision of the crisp portrait. The artist was surely not related to the unsubtle sculptors responsible for the statues on the first floor. In the black ink drawing, the criminal's features appeared cruel and menacing. Military-style short hair topped an angular face above a lean, muscular torso.

"It's blond," Hollowcrest said, startling her.

"What?"

"His hair. It's hard to tell in the drawing."

"Oh," she said. Blond hair was rare in the empire, a nation of people whose blood had been mixed and mixed again via generations of conquering and expansion; most citizens shared Amaranthe's bronze skin and dark locks.

"Where should I look for him, sir?" She thought of Wholt's suggestion that Sicarius might be behind the pottery shop arson, but that had been groundless speculation. The man could be anywhere in the city.

"I'll leave that to your ingenuity," Hollowcrest said. "Finding him is a feasible task. Sicarius doesn't travel in disguise and, though discreet, he goes where he pleases. He does have a knack for knowing when our soldiers or enforcers are trying to spring a trap on him though. Then he disappears." Hollowcrest grimaced. "Or doesn't. The results are less devastating when he does."

"I understand, sir. When should I start?"

"Immediately. Speak to no one about this mission. It's imperative the criminal not find out we're aware of, and angling for, him."

"What about my regular duties, sir? I'll need to report to my superior."

"I'll see to it that your district chief is informed. You don't even need to go home; I have a soldier waiting with money for you. If you decide to buy new clothes—" A crinkle of his nose at her soot-stained uniform implied this was more than a suggestion, "—don't attend shops you usually visit."

Not a problem. The shops she visited leaned more toward uniforms and utilitarian clothing rather than whatever it was women wore to seduce men. Not much, she guessed.

"Avoid all your typical haunts until the mission is complete," Hollowcrest finished. "Likewise, don't return home until you've reported back to me."

Amaranthe wondered why was it so imperative she not interact with anyone she knew. Corporal Wholt certainly was not going to find Sicarius and inform him of her intentions if she told him.

"Sir, what—"

"You may go now," Hollowcrest said. "The soldier outside my door will escort you."

Amaranthe longed to question the man further. But Hollowcrest had already turned to the papers on his desk. She stared at him for a moment, then turned on her heel and strode out the door. She was not an imbecile; she could find the answers to her own questions.

As promised, a soldier waited in the hallway, an envelope filled with bills in his hand. She followed him through the corridor, toward the stairs that would lead her back to the first floor.

"Corporal Lokdon," a voice called before they entered the stairwell.

The young emperor jogged down the hallway in his socks. He carried a pad of paper clutched under one arm. His guards, fully armed and armored despite the hour, trailed dutifully behind.

"Hello," the emperor said brightly. "What are you doing here?" Before Amaranthe could answer, he burbled on. "Are you on duty? Will you be working at the Barracks?"

"I've just received a mission, Sire."

"Really? That sounds exciting." He smiled hopefully, eyes eager for details.

"It's going to be...challenging." Amaranthe found herself reluctant to provide more information. She had the feeling he might be the type to put a person's safety above the possibility of achievement, and cancel her mission. If anyone could countermand Hollowcrest, it would be the emperor. *A minute ago, you were dreading the idea of an assassination, and now you don't want to give up the chance of this assignment?*

Amaranthe was saved from further accusing statements from the back of her mind, when the emperor dug something out of his pocket and extended it to her. She accepted it curiously. It was one of the chain bracelets soldiers wore into battle. A flattened side left room for inscribing one's name in case the body was unrecognizable when it was recovered. This particular bracelet was far more ornate—and valuable—than any Amaranthe had seen. The golden chain was woven in a complex pattern one might expect in thread but not metal.

"Take it for luck," the emperor said, smiling.

She blinked. "Sire, I can't—"

"Would you like to see what I'm working on?" He thrust his pad of paper toward her. "It's the design for an art wing at the University."

Though she knew little about architecture, the detailed blueprint impressed Amaranthe.

"Until now," he continued, "there has been no place for students to gather and study sculpture, writing, and painting." His mouth twisted wryly. "Four military academies in each satrapy though. I'm planning a new science wing too."

Though his passion spilled out like a refreshing fountain, the differ-ences in their stations left Amaranthe staring awkwardly. What was she allowed to say to him?

The emperor shook his head. "I'm sorry, I'm babbling. What sort of mission are you going on? Who assigned it? Why are you starting here? Not that I mind. It's nice seeing a new face. These halls are so drab, like a prison." The wry smile returned. "Babbling again, aren't I?"

"I...think it's allowed, Sire," Amaranthe said. "I just had an appoint-ment with—"

Commander of the Armies Hollowcrest appeared, moving with sur-prising alacrity for an older man. He draped an arm across the emperor's shoulders. "Ah, Sire. There you are. Would you mind coming into my office for a few moments? I have some documents I'd like to discuss with you."

The emperor removed Hollowcrest's arm and stepped away. He tucked his pad under his arm and turned a frank stare onto the older man. "Documents to discuss this late at night? More dedicated to your work than usual, aren't you, Hollow?"

If the emperor had seemed a tad simple while speaking to Ama-ranthe, she realized it probably had more to do with her belonging to the opposite sex than any dullness on his part.

"It's important, Sire," Hollowcrest said with a smile that did not reach his eyes. "It'll only take a few moments."

The emperor lifted his gaze toward the ceiling, bade Amaranthe goodnight, then trundled back down the hallway in the opposite direc-tion. She frowned at her hand, realizing she still held his bracelet.

"Artonis," Hollowcrest said.

One of the last of the emperor's guards dropped out of line and stepped into place before Hollowcrest.

"See that the emperor has his tea. He seems too...perky tonight."

"Yes, sir." The guard trotted after the others, mail jangling.

Amaranthe frowned after him. Tea?

Hollowcrest noticed she was still there and waved her toward the door. "I believe you have someone to hunt."

"Yes, sir," Amaranthe said.

She allowed her guide to usher her out of the building. This time, with thoughts spinning in her head, she didn't notice the scenery. That

meeting had left her doubting Hollowcrest's veracity, though it hadn't been surprising. She had no reason to believe the Commander of the Armies would tell a common enforcer everything. But if he was keeping secrets from the emperor.... It sounded like the old relic was sedating Sespian. Maybe more. How could she accept a mission from someone who might be betraying the empire?

Yet what could she do? If she made a fuss or disobeyed Hollowcrest, he could destroy her career. Or worse.

If, on the other hand, she cooperated, assassinated Sicarius, and earned her promotion... Well, she could investigate her concerns later, when Hollowcrest didn't have his eye on her. Yes, that's how it had to be. First, she had to complete the mission.

She paused beneath a lamp in the courtyard and eyed the outlaw's picture again. The cold face made her uneasy, and the idea of seduction seemed ludicrous, possibly suicidal. If she was going to take an experienced assassin down, she'd have to do something he wouldn't expect.

CHAPTER 3

A S SOON AS HE ENTERED HIS SUITE, SESPIAN SA-
varsin, emperor of the most powerful nation in the world,
slapped himself on the forehead.

"Babbling idiot." He paced the rug in the antechamber. "She thinks
I'm a babbling idiot."

A soft thud came from the bedroom, and an elegant tan-colored cat
with a deep brown mask and paws padded into the anteroom. He hopped
onto a desk abutting the window.

Too agitated to give the cat his usual pats, Sespian continued pacing.
"The most serene, competent, beautiful girl—no, woman—I've met
shows up in my hall, and I babble." He pushed his hand through his hair
hard enough to dislodge several strands. "And then I let Hollowcrest
chase me off like a five-year-old child told to go to bed without supper.
Although maybe I should thank him. He probably saved me from further embarrassing myself." Sespian faced the cat. "It was bad, Trog.
Very bad."

Trog sat on the desk and swished his tail back and forth. A cobweb
hung from his ear. Not surprising. His name was short for troglodyte,
a label received due to a penchant for exploring dusty old ducts and
passages in the Barracks. The swishing tail sent a sketch fluttering to the
rug. Trog had no respect for artistic endeavors, but at least he listened.

"You should have seen her," Sespian said. "She was so unflappable
but not arrogant, not at all. An enforcer. Not some stodgy matron de-
voted to holding up the values of the warrior caste and not some ma-
nipulative businesswoman intent on selling you something. Someone
who looks out for people. What a wonderful friend and ally she would

make. Maybe more." He smiled wistfully. "I made her uncomfortable though. Because I'm the emperor. Stupid social rules. I wonder what it would have been like if I were just some man off the street. What would she have said? Do you think I'm her type?"

Trog yawned and flopped down on his side, tail twitching.

Sespian raised an eyebrow. "It's as if you're trying to tell me that my piddling romantic ramblings, while of vast interest to me, are inconsequential to anyone else." He sat in the chair in front of the desk and ran his fingers through Trog's thick fur. "You're probably right."

Trog purred and stretched his legs out. He always liked being told he was right.

As Sespian stroked the cat, he gazed out the window, where falling snow blanketed the grounds. Amaranthe had been a delightful distraction, but with the event fading, his headache returned. Sespian sighed and tried to ignore it.

"I shouldn't let him push me around anymore."

Trog rotated an ear.

"Hollowcrest. When Father died, I had so many ideas. But after three years with Hollowcrest as regent... I guess I got used to following his orders." Sespian grimaced. "And so did everyone else. I need to change that. *I'm* in charge now, and I need to be someone who can lead an empire—and maybe be someone Amaranthe would like, eh?"

A knock sounded.

"Come in," Sespian called.

The familiar scent of apple herb tea accompanied the servant, Jeddah, into the suite. Steam rose from a porcelain cup on a silver platter. The man set the tray down on an ottoman.

"Thank you, Jeddah," Sespian said.

The man bowed and walked out.

When Sespian stood, his headache intensified. He winced. The pain came every day now, a constant and loathed companion.

At least the tea seemed to help. It had been his mother's favorite. More than a decade had passed since she died, but he still missed her. Father, the great warrior emperor, had been an obstacle to overcome— or avoid—but Mother had loved him and never failed to support him. Every night, when he drank the tea, he felt close to her, as if he were honoring her memory.

Sespian picked up the cup. He inhaled deeply, the pleasant blend of herbs tickling his nose. Not so sweet as spiced cider, it warmed and soothed as it flowed down his throat.

He soon finished the cup.

*   *   *   *   *

The next evening, Amaranthe visited the Maze. From the outside, it looked like little more than a warehouse, but the long line she stepped into promised something more entertaining. The establishment had only been around for a few years, but it was already more popular than any other gambling venue in the city. It was more profitable, too, though the question of the place's legality had come up in more than one enforcer report. This was not her district, though, so she had never visited.

Dressed in parka, ankle-length skirt, leggings, and the fitted jacket of a businesswoman, she was a little out of place amongst the jostling folks wearing factory coveralls or labor uniforms under their coats. She hoped to meet with the owner, though, not mingle with the gamblers.

When the bouncer let her in, a moment of claustrophobia swallowed her. Hundreds of cheering men and women pressed from all sides. Thick tobacco and warkus weed smoke did not quite obliterate the stench of stale sweat and alcohol-swathed bodies.

Since the crowd kept Amaranthe from seeing the layout, she found a support pillar and climbed onto its concrete base. Rows of benches formed descending squares around a fifty-meter-wide pit filled with the ever-changing maze that gave the establishment its name. Even as she watched, a section of the wall detached and started moving. It slid along one of myriad tracks in the floor and clanked into a new slot on the far side of the pit. Two more walls began a different journey before the first finished. Within the maze, a stout fellow wearing a white tunic turned out of a dead-end and hunted for a new path. Four clackers, mechanical constructs with crab-like pinchers, rolled through the maze on treads. In the center of the labyrinth, a tiny alcove held a dais. A small chest rested on top, its lid open to display a pile of gold coins. Spectators cheered or booed for the lone player, depending on which way they had bet.

Amaranthe dropped off her perch. She had not come to watch the game but to see the owner. She slipped through the crowd until she found the betting cage near the back wall. Several bouncers with the prerequisite prodigious muscles kept the gamblers peaceful. The backs of their hands sported brands, inelegant feline faces with pointed ears and fat whiskers. The marks showed allegiance with the Panthers, one of the larger gangs in the city.

Amaranthe approached the closest bouncer, a man with a cleft chin and wavy black hair. Without the scowl, he might have been handsome.

Before she could speak to him, he turned and yelled at a little man tugging on his sleeve. "I already told you, bets are final! You can't change your mind in the middle. Go away!"

The man scampered into the crowd. The bouncer turned on Amaranthe.

"*What?*" he roared.

She stifled the instinct to step back. Instead she met his eyes and asked, "Rough day?"

"Huh?"

She added a sympathetic smile. "It looks like you're having a rough day."

The irritation bled away from the bouncer's face. "Actually, yes."

"I'm Amaranthe. What's your name?"

"Ragos."

"It must be trying dealing with the same silly questions day in and day out," she said.

"That, I'm used to. But today, two of the bookmakers didn't show up. The potatoes for our vendors' potato cakes didn't come. The furnace that powers the Maze decided to break down, and who do you think got to fix it?" Ragos pulled a wrench out of a back pocket and waved it.

"I didn't realize bouncers had so many responsibilities," Amaranthe said.

Another bouncer sidled up to Ragos and grinned. "Most don't. Unless they're the boss's pet."

Ragos glowered at his comrade. "Your section is over *there*, isn't it?"

The man's grin never left, but he returned to his post.

"The boss? Is that the owner?" Amaranthe asked. "I came to see her about some business."

"Do you have an appointment?"

"No, but she knows me. We went to school together."

"Is that the school that makes her sound like she's swallowing spikes when she talks about it?" Ragos asked.

"I believe so. She didn't get along well with the teachers. Or the students."

"I'm sure she'll love to see you then."

"Probably not," Amaranthe admitted.

Ragos smiled mischievously. "In that case, I'll show you right up."

He unlocked a door behind the betting cage, and they climbed a metal staircase to a catwalk that passed over the Maze. They stopped before an office built against the rafters. A name plaque on the door read: The Boss. Ragos raised a finger for Amaranthe to wait before ambling inside.

"No!" came a woman's voice almost immediately.

Ragos ambled back out and winked. "Go right in."

"Thank you, Ragos."

Amaranthe waited until he descended the stairs. She was tempted to leave as well, but she had already asked every pawnbroker, bar keeper, weapons smith, and loan shark in the city how to get a message to Sicarius, all with no luck. Either they did not know, or they were not willing to risk the infamous criminal's ire by bothering him.

She knocked.

"Oh, come in already," the woman growled.

Amaranthe stepped inside. The magnificent, floor-to-ceiling window overlooking the Maze was not quite enough to distract her from the old clutter, new clutter, and nascent clutter swamping the office. At first, the mess overshadowed the woman lounging behind a desk overflowing with boxes, ledger books, and discarded men's clothing. She wore tight-fitting leather that emphasized lush curves. Maybe Hollowcrest should have hired *her* to seduce Sicarius.

"Amaranthe Lokdon?" the woman said. "I never expected you to show up here. And look. You're still wearing your hair in that unimaginative bun."

"Mitsy Masters." Amaranthe forced a smile. *Be friendly. If anyone has the right contacts to get in touch with Sicarius, it's her.* "I like to keep my hair neat, out of the way."

"Yes, I remember your neatness, my dear. The way teachers gloated over your pretty penmanship and ingratiatingly perfect papers."

"That didn't keep you from copying them, as I recall." Easy, Amaranthe. Remember you're being nice.

"I never believed in wasting time doing something you could get someone else to do for you. That's what business is all about, isn't it?"

Mitsy yawned, took out a file, and began working on her fingernails. A gang mark identical to the bouncers' branded the back of one of her hands. As of the latest enforcer reports, Mitsy was the Panthers' leader.

"I'm not sure that's quite the philosophy our teachers tried to instill," Amaranthe said. "Though your tactics must be working. It looks like you've done well since, ah..."

"Being kicked out of school? Yes. You? I assume you went on to become a model entrepreneur, though I admit I haven't heard anything of you."

Good. Since female enforcers were rare, Amaranthe had feared Mitsy would have heard about her career. "You wouldn't. I've been... discreet. I have an...export business."

Mitsy leaned forward, eyes narrowed, interest kindling for the first time. "Oh ho, what illegal commodities are you sending out of the empire?"

"Parts," Amaranthe said, intentionally vague. "That's why I'm here."

"Dear Amaranthe, do you mayhap need a favor?" Calculation glittered in Mitsy's eyes.

"Nothing that would require much effort on your part, I assure you. I have a shipment that I need to get from my warehouse in Itansa across the border to Kendor. I need someone reliable to accompany it, to make sure it reaches its destination. Someone who can handle any imperial soldiers or Kendorian shamans who might snoop too closely."

"I must say, Amaranthe dear, I'm impressed by these nefarious allusions. You always acted so insufferably noble. If I'd known devious streaks lay beneath that façade, I would have teased you and your prissy cohorts less frequently in school."

"Only three times a week instead of five?"

Mitsy flashed a lupine grin. "Precisely."

"Sicarius," Amaranthe said, anxious to end the meeting and leave. "I've heard he's in town. I've heard he's good. Do you know of him?"

"Certainly, he's the best."

"Do you know what he charges?" Amaranthe asked, trying to add a hint of verisimilitude. She was supposed to be a businesswoman after all.

"Whatever it is, he's worth it."

"Oh? Have you met him?"

Anything more Amaranthe could learn about the assassin would be invaluable. Before running the lake trail that morning, she had sneaked into Enforcer Headquarters to retrieve Sicarius's record, but it contained no personal information, and the arm-long list of kills had done little to bolster her confidence.

"Not personally, no," Mitsy said. "They say he never fails an assignment though. They also say..." She shrugged, deliberately mysterious. "Let's just say you'd do best to take care with him."

"Temper?"

"No, he's a cold one by all accounts. I know a fellow in Iskland—or rather I *knew* a fellow—who hired Sicarius for a retrieval operation, then decided he didn't want to pay the agreed upon price."

"I assume Sicarius got the money from him," Amaranthe said.

"Cut his throat, actually. Left the money."

"I see."

"And then there's that merchant in Komar who paid Sicarius but thought he would recoup his losses by tipping the local garrison to the assassin's whereabouts. Sicarius killed the merchant and the soldiers who came after him."

Mitsy smiled as she spoke, intentionally trying to rattle her guest, Amaranthe suspected.

"As much as I'm appreciating story hour," she said, "I really just need to know how to get in touch with him. Can you get word to him for me? I've heard you have a vast network of contacts in the city."

"I can get it out to my people. Whether it'll reach his ears or not..." Mitsy shrugged.

"Good enough. Have them tell him the job won't take long, but I'll pay well. If he's interested, he should meet me tomorrow at midnight in Pyramid Park."

"Got it."

Amaranthe thought about insisting Mitsy write it down but changed her mind after a brief survey of the clutter—Amaranthe could swear some of it was oozing toward her like a lava flow.

"What do I owe you?" she asked instead.

She reached into her purse and thumbed the bills Hollowcrest had given her. There were not a lot. If Sicarius demanded partial payment up front, she would have to sneak back to her flat and delve into her savings.

"Nothing, my dear," Mitsy said. "I'll do this favor for you, and someday mayhap, you'll be in a position to do a favor for me."

Amaranthe winced. She would rather have paid.

* * * * *

The gargantuan stone structure that gave Pyramid Park its name hogged four city blocks in the middle of the business district. Thousands of years old, the pyramid had been confounding city planners throughout imperial history. Various administrations had attempted everything from dismantling it to selling storage space inside. It had taken a graduate from Amaranthe's school to make the structure profitable. The woman had bought the land and turned the old pyramid, with its labyrinthine tunnels and burial chambers, into a tourist destination replete with guides, food stands, and shops hawking tacky replicas. That was in the summer. In the winter, the pyramid stood silent and abandoned, locked steel grates barring the interior from the curious.

Amaranthe arrived at the park an hour before midnight. On the chance Sicarius was the type to likewise arrive early, she wanted to out-early him. More, she wanted to see him coming, and the top of the pyramid was the one place in Stumps that assured that opportunity. Thanks to previous vandalism problems, it was also well lit, with gas lamps lining the walkways and even the steps of the looming structure.

Though she had debated on a public meeting spot, she doubted a room full of people would keep Sicarius from killing her if things went badly. No, she would meet him alone, without distractions. The better to analyze him.

Nodding to herself, she strode toward the base of the pyramid. Stairs on the west side, slick from snow that had melted during the day and re-

frozen, led to the top. The steps were high but shallow, as if their makers had possessed tiny feet and abnormally long strides. The steepness and the lack of a railing made Amaranthe's ascent cautious.

A single gas lamp burned at the top. She could cross the platform in five strides and see the lights of the city sprawled out in all three directions. Only to the west, where the frozen lake stretched, lay darkness. Four columns supported a flat stone roof adorned with a foot of snow. In the center of the platform, an altar held a headless statue. Two wings, clawed feet, and the suggestion of a furry chest remained. People had worshipped some odd things in those days.

Amaranthe slipped a mitten-clad hand into her parka and withdrew the thin stiletto that had replaced her enforcer-issue knife and sword. She examined the blade without enthusiasm. It was a believable weapon for a businesswoman to carry, but it felt flimsy to her.

"An infamous assassin is coming to meet me and I'm armed with a letter opener," she muttered.

Amaranthe hid the weapon. If she got into a fight with him, it meant she had already fouled up beyond redemption anyway. *Comforting thought.*

She checked her pocket watch. Midnight.

Not a single person walked the streets near the park. She made a fist and dropped her chin on it. What if he didn't come? What if Mitsy had not believed Amaranthe's story and hadn't sent the message? What if Sicarius had received the message but had seen through it?

She turned to check the view from the other side of the platform.

He was there.

Amaranthe jumped, dropping her watch. It clanked against the frozen stone and skidded into the base of the pedestal. Sicarius's eyes never left her face. He was leaning against one of the back pillars, his arms folded across his chest.

Unlucky fallen ancestors, she cursed silently. How had he gotten up here without using the stairs? How long had he been there? Had he seen her checking the knife?

To give herself a moment to recover her composure, Amaranthe bent to pick up the watch. She wondered if her mittens hid how much her fingers shook as she grasped it.

As she slowly stood, her gaze traveled up his black boots, fitted black trousers, tucked-in black shirt, an armory's worth of daggers and throwing knives, and came to rest on his face. He was the person from the sketch, no doubt, but unlike the menacing image Hollowcrest had given her, this man's face bore no emotion at all. By the flames of the lamp, his eyes appeared black, and they gave no indication of feeling— or humanity.

He had the bronze skin of a Turgonian, but that pale blond hair was rare in the empire. It was short and damp around the edges. Whoever had cut it looked to have used hedge clippers instead of scissors.

"Thank you for being prompt," Amaranthe said, relieved her voice didn't waver or crack.

He said nothing. His eyes never left hers.

It was unnerving, though she dared not show it. It was time to play the role she had designed for herself. If he agreed to the job, they would travel together to Amaranthe's fictitious warehouse in Itansa, which would involve a four-day locomotive ride. He would sleep sometime, and she would fulfill Hollowcrest's mission then. Assassinate the assassin.

She remembered a piece of advice from a marketing class. *Start out asking potential customers questions they have to answer with yes. Consistency is your ally. People are more likely to say yes to a sale after a string of positive responses. Just don't let them start out saying no.*

She cleared her throat. "I'm Amaranthe Lokdon. You are Sicarius, correct?"

"You know who I am."

"Are you as good as they say?"

"You asked for me by name. Frequently."

Amaranthe tried to decide if his words implied suspicion. His tone never fluctuated. Like his face, his voice betrayed nothing of his thoughts.

"That doesn't answer my question." She smiled.

"You have work to propose. Do so."

So much for the get-them-to-say-yes strategy.

"Very well," Amaranthe said. "I need to move some machinery across the border to buyers in Kendor. Since sharing technology with outsiders is illegal, I anticipate trouble from the soldiers who inspect the

ports. I've tried bribes before with little luck. I need someone who can handle them, in whatever way deemed best, should they try to block the shipment. I've heard you're not squeamish about such things."

Sicarius stared at her, eyes hard and unwavering. Amaranthe forced herself to meet his gaze, lest he suspect her of dishonesty.

"I decline," Sicarius said.

"What? Why?"

"You are lying," he said and passed her, heading for the stairs.

Desperation dawned—this was her only chance!—but she kept herself from reaching for the stiletto. There was no way someone with his experience would fail to anticipate a stab in the back at this moment.

She noticed something that made her freeze: a small smudge of red dirt on the back of his boot. Not dirt, finely crushed brick, and there was only one place in Stumps where one might walk in that. She knew the stuff intimately because she wiped it off her shoes every morning after a run. Then she remembered his damp hair. By the time Sicarius reached the bottom and glided into the darkness, she had a new plan.

"I may be a liar," she muttered to herself, "but I know where you spend your evenings."

CHAPTER 4

THE NEXT NIGHT FOUND AMARANTHE HUNKERED in the shadows between two snowy hills overlooking the lake trail. Beyond the banks, elevated fire pits illuminated men sawing blocks of ice out of the frozen water. Their clinks and clanks carried to the shore. Since their harvest season was short, they would work through the night, but Amaranthe did not think she needed to worry about the men. As long as things didn't get too noisy, they were too far out to notice an assassination on the trail.

Just as she started to rise, a trio of soldiers jogged around the bend. They wore black fatigues, boots, and heavy rucksacks with muskets and swords strapped to their backs.

She crouched low again, hugging the shadows.

Fort Urgot stood sentinel a couple miles north of the city, and it wasn't uncommon to see soldiers training after dark during the short winter days. If they saw her, they would stop to ask her about the repeating crossbow strapped to her back. Carrying weapons wasn't illegal, but using them outside of practice or a duel was, and this wasn't a likely spot for either.

The soldiers jogged into a tunnel carved through a granite outcropping.

Once she was sure they were gone, Amaranthe skidded down the slope and over a mound of crusty snow left by the steam plows. Sand coated the icy trail, offering traction for her boots. Everyone from soldiers to enforcers to athletes training for the rings used the twenty-mile lake route, and the city maintained it year around.

She trotted into the tunnel, the crossbow bumping against her back. A gas lamp on the wall illuminated the interior. This was the only covered spot on the trail, and no ice obscured the surface. She knelt and ran a gloved finger across the packed red earth.

The bracelet the emperor had given her slipped from beneath her parka sleeve. He had suggested she wear it for luck. She could use more than luck, but she was wearing it—and had etched her name on the plaque—so whoever found her body could identify it.

"All right, girl," she whispered to herself. "No thinking like that."

She lifted her hand and examined the red dust on the finger of the glove. Yes, it was exactly like the smudge on Sicarius's boot.

The thought sent a jolt of anxiety through her body. If he showed up tonight, she was supposed to kill him.

Not 'supposed to,' Amaranthe, you will *kill him.*

She grimaced. She wasn't a killer, not even close. She had never even fatally wounded a criminal in the line of duty. Yet, she was planning to intentionally shoot a crossbow quarrel into someone's chest, in cold blood. Without a doubt, Sicarius deserved it, but...

"Why couldn't he have been an ass to me last night?" Amaranthe muttered.

The man had been a thousand miles from friendly, but he hadn't hurt her, threatened her, or even sniffed disdainfully at her. This would have been easier if he had.

"Maybe it's not supposed to be easy," she said, adjusting her crossbow and walking out of the tunnel on the other side. "Maybe my chance for promotion is meant to be a great test. Maybe Hollowcrest isn't doing anything nefarious to the emperor, and I'm *not* a fool for doing his bidding. And maybe, I shouldn't be talking to myself."

Shaking her head, Amaranthe climbed off the trail, following one of dozens of narrow foot paths packed into the snow. If it was possible Sicarius was in town to assassinate the emperor, she would not be doing the world a disservice to kill him tonight. She had to believe that.

Her path ran parallel to the main trail, leading up a hill overlooking the tunnel. The elevated position offered a clear line to someone exiting.

Beyond the hill, apple trees rose, icicles draping skeletal branches, but she stopped before she reached them. Several snow-blanketed bushes dotted the top of the incline, offering good cover. Someone running out

of the lit tunnel would already have trouble seeing into the dark, and the shrubbery would doubly hide her.

Amaranthe knelt down and carved a level shelf into the snow. After tugging off her gloves, she slid a slender metal case out of her pocket, from which she removed five poisoned crossbow quarrels. She laid them out, an inch apart, perfectly parallel. Five quarrels; five seconds; five chances.

There was little point in laying out enough for a second round. In the time reloading would take, Sicarius would either run back into the tunnel—she doubted it—or close the distance and tackle her. In truth, she suspected the first quarrel would be the only real chance she had.

With that grim thought, she loaded the five quarrels into the top of the magazine. She pulled the lever to draw back the string and lock the first into place. Then she wriggled into a prone firing position, her elbows supported by the ground and the crossbow in her hands. She sighted down the shaft to the trail and the tunnel exit. Her finger found the trigger. She was ready.

Now she just had to wait for him to come. If he did.

This was a hunch, and she knew it. That he had been here, she was sure of, but that he would return was more of a question. Even if he was a runner, there was no guarantee he came out every night. She might not get her chance to...

What, Amaranthe?

Do something she didn't really want to do? Kill a man? Not honorably in battle, but while hiding behind a bush. Without allowing him the opportunity to speak to the magistrate, without giving him a chance to defend himself. Murder.

Cold seeped through her parka and into her stomach. Amaranthe dropped her forehead onto the stock of the crossbow. She couldn't do this.

Someone grabbed her hair.

Her head was yanked back, her torso torn from the ground. An arm snaked around her neck.

Sicarius.

He jerked her head to the side. Amaranthe threw her arm up in an attempt to grab his, knowing it would be too late.

He paused.

Her neck twisted nearly to snapping, Amaranthe froze. She could not breathe. Tears of pain stabbed her eyes. Her instincts screamed for her to struggle, try to escape. But if she fought, he might finish the motion.

Then he dropped her.

Amaranthe took the fall on her forearms, head turning to keep from smashing her face into the ground. Pain sprang from her neck, lancing into her skull and down her spine.

A moment passed. Snow chilled her cheek. Slowly, very slowly, she rose to hands and knees and turned toward him.

First, she saw the black boots. Next came the pants of the same hue. As she sat up—no tilting her head back just now, thank you—she saw the black shirt, and finally the blond head.

"Who sent you?" Sicarius asked.

Amaranthe considered carefully before answering. If he simply meant to scare her into providing information, he could have started with a knife against her throat. No, he had almost broken her neck. He had intended to kill her but stopped mid-motion. Why? And would he continue where he had left off if she answered incorrectly?

"Commander of the Armies Hollowcrest." Given the previous demonstration of how he could see through lies, the truth seemed a safer choice. Besides, she found herself reluctant to die to protect Hollowcrest's anonymity.

"Why?"

"To kill you."

"That I gathered. Why did he send *you*? What did you do to anger him?"

"I... Uhm, what?"

"It was a suicide mission. You must have suspected."

Amaranthe started to shake her head, but stopped at the pain. "No, that doesn't make sense. If Hollowcrest wanted me dead, he could have arranged it without ever bothering to meet me. He could have paid someone to assassinate me at work or at home."

"Why pay someone when he knew I'd do it for free?"

"You didn't though." Amaranthe stood so she could look at his face. "Why not?"

He did not answer, but his gaze flickered downward for a moment, resting briefly on her wrist. She lifted it for a better look, and the gold bracelet caught the light of a gas lamp on the trail below. Had it done so when she tried to grab his arm to stop him? It was the only thing she could imagine. But why would a name bracelet keep him from killing her? Surely, he couldn't know it had belonged to the emperor. The golden threads created a handsome pattern, but there were no imperial symbols slipped into the weave. Even if Sicarius did somehow recognize it in the darkness, why would the emperor's bracelet stop him? This man had been a burr in the empire's paw during the years since Emperor Raumesys died. And young Sespian was the one who had placed the bounty on his head.

"Hollowcrest thought you might be in town to kill the emperor," Amaranthe said.

"I am not."

He could be lying to her. Who would admit to such a plot?

"How'd you find me?" she asked, trying to keep him talking while she puzzled through the situation.

"I've been following you."

"Oh."

Of course. After she lied to him, he must have been suspicious. She had allowed his lack of emotion to lull her into believing he lacked interest as well. She sighed. As an enforcer, she should have been prepared for that. *Stupid, Amaranthe. Very stupid. People die for mistakes like this.*

"I do run the lake though," Sicarius said.

For the first time, she detected a hint of something in his voice. Curiosity? He was wondering how she guessed perhaps. Given the situation, Amaranthe could hardly feel triumphant at her deduction. Was it truly possible Hollowcrest had planned for her demise? Assumed her death at this man's hands? And, if so, why? As an enforcer, she had done everything her superiors ever asked—more!

"What now?" she asked.

Again, he glanced at her wrist. It *was* the bracelet that had stopped him—she was sure of it.

"You leave me alone; I leave you alone." Sicarius turned and headed back to the trail, keeping her in his peripheral vision.

"Wait," Amaranthe blurted. "I think the emperor..."

He stopped.

She hesitated. If the emperor had nothing to do with why Sicarius was letting her live, this next statement could be considered treasonous. Dare she let an assassin know Sespian might be an easier target than ever right now? But if Sicarius cared for some reason, he could be an ally.

"The emperor is in trouble," Amaranthe said.

Sicarius turned around. "How so?"

Amaranthe rubbed her neck. "I believe Commander of the Armies Hollowcrest is controlling Sespian by unnatural means." She had little to base theories on, but she had found that comment Hollowcrest made about fixing the emperor's tea insidious. Belatedly, she thought it odd he had risked giving the order in front of her. Maybe he wasn't expecting me to live to *tell anyone*. Yes, now that Sicarius had started her mind down that path, she had a hard time veering.

Sicarius closed the distance between them. Amaranthe fought the urge to skitter backward.

"Such as?" he asked.

"I think he's putting something in Sespian's tea. Maybe it's not all that deleterious, but maybe it's the reason..." She lifted a hand, palm up. "Emperor Sespian is enthusiastic about art and science, but no major policy changes have come down since he reached his majority and assumed power last year. Until I met him, I didn't think anything of it— we've had seven-hundred years of conquering warrior emperors—but now that I've seen what a peaceful, gentle fellow he is, I can't imagine him following in his father's footsteps." She had a hard time even imagining Sespian holding a sword. "I didn't dare refuse Hollowcrest's mission to, ah, kill you, but I had hoped for a chance to find out more about Sespian and the tea when I reported back."

"You won't live long enough to report back if you choose to return."

Amaranthe frowned. "How can you be so sure he wants me dead?"

"Hollowcrest knows me, knows my capabilities. He also knows a pretty smile wouldn't distract me."

Maybe it was good she had avoided the seduction scenario then. "Look, maybe it's suicidal, but I have to go back and get an explanation. I can't just walk away from...from *my life*. If Hollowcrest wants

me dead, where could I even hide that would be beyond his reach?" She gulped. Only now were the full ramifications spinning through her mind. "And if I can get back into the Imperial Barracks, maybe I'll have an opportunity to find out more about the emperor's situation. I can tell you what I learn if..." She raised her eyebrows. "Can you help me?"

He stared at her without expression. Amaranthe shifted her weight, and snow compacted beneath her boots.

"I understand you probably don't get asked that often," she said, "but the expected responses are yes and no. Stony silence is not helpful, though if it was accompanied by a nod or head shake it would be decipherable. And, yes, I realize I'm being cocky considering you almost killed me five minutes ago, but you changed your mind for some reason that I suspect has nothing to do with me, so I figure I've got little to lose."

Amaranthe was beginning to see the strategy behind that silent, unresponsive face. It made her uncomfortable and had her babbling like an idiot.

Sicarius drew a black dagger. She tensed, but he simply held it out.

The curving blade was edged only on one side. At first, she thought it had been painted, but the metal itself was black. A dye? Or some uncommon alloy?

"Take it with you to the Barracks," Sicarius said. "Tell the guards you succeeded in killing me. Show them this as proof. Hollowcrest will recognize it, and he will take your meeting out of curiosity. What happens after that is for you to determine."

Amaranthe accepted the weapon. She held the exotic blade across the palm of her hand. Expecting the icy bite of metal, she was surprised by its warmth, like a rock basking in the sun. She brushed her thumb along the edge. Even the faint touch drew blood.

"I'll bring this back to you," Amaranthe said, "and let you know what I learned."

He twitched an indifferent shoulder.

She met Sicarius's eyes. *You don't think I'm coming back, do you?* She lifted her chin. "Where would you like to meet?"

She *was* going to come back.

"The trail. Choose a spot. I'll find you."

"What time?"

"Dusk. I'll look for you for the next three days. If you don't come, I'll assume you're dead."

"Thanks," Amaranthe said dryly.

Sicarius started to walk away again. This time he paused of his own accord. Over his shoulder, he said, "There are hidden exits in the dungeons beneath the Imperial Barracks. Follow the drafts to find them."

Amaranthe watched him disappear into the darkness.

CHAPTER 5

T HE IMPERIAL BARRACKS WERE STILL IMPOSING, maybe more so. The black walls loomed taller than Amaranthe remembered, the cannons larger. The guards at the gate were much bigger. Maybe the runty ones—less than six and a half feet—had been on shift for her previous visit.

She strode toward the gate, more nervous than she had been the first time. Her breathing sounded quick and shallow in her ears. She had changed back into her enforcer uniform and exchanged the crossbow for her service-issue sword and knife. Sicarius's dagger was tucked into her belt. Hairpins she could open her handcuffs with secured her bun. She had no idea if she could pick a dungeon cell lock with them but hoped she would get a chance to talk to Sespian before Hollowcrest condemned her to that fate—or a worse one.

The two guards watched her approach, one a corporal, one a private, both with disdainful eyes. Their mail jingled as they moved to block her way.

"State your purpose."

Amaranthe drew a deep breath, exhaled, and watched it form a cloud. "I'm Corporal Lokdon, an enforcer from the Commercial District. I'm here to see Commander of the Armies Hollowcrest."

"It's late, and he doesn't see people without an appointment."

Which she did not have this time.

"Corporal." What were the odds she could cow him? It was not likely; imperial guards were not intimidated by enforcers, less so by women. It would be Hollowcrest's name that swayed them, if anything.

"I have been on a mission assigned by the Commander himself. He instructed me to report back to him immediately upon its completion."

"What mission?"

"To kill the assassin, Sicarius." Before they could start laughing, she tapped the hilt of the black dagger. "I brought the criminal's favorite weapon as proof of his demise."

Their eyes narrowed. One man extended his hand, palm up. She hesitated. Dare she give up her only evidence? Hollowcrest might take the dagger and send her away without a meeting. Or have her killed at the doorstep. But surely he would want to know how she succeeded—especially if he intended her to fail. With that not-exactly-hopeful thought, Amaranthe handed the dagger to the guard.

He studied it. "Interesting metal, but this could belong to anybody."

"Commander of the Armies Hollowcrest said he would know Sicarius's foul blade if he saw it." Not exactly true, but she could hardly admit Sicarius had been the one to suggest the idea.

The corporal handed the weapon to his comrade. "Run this up to his office and check."

The lower-ranking man paled, obviously not enthused about disturbing Hollowcrest. He accepted the dagger as if it were a venomous snake, unlocked the gate, and trotted into the courtyard.

Neither Amaranthe nor the corporal spoke while his comrade was gone, though he sent numerous suspicious glances her direction. She leaned against the wall and did her best to ignore him. A nearby clock tower tolled ten times.

The waiting gave her time to think—and doubt. She had no leverage to hold over Hollowcrest to make him answer her questions. She was walking naked into the grimbal's den, hoping chance gave her a weapon before the fearsome predator ate her. It was the sort of 'plan' she would have chastised a rookie for presenting. If Hollowcrest wanted her dead, it would be more logical to flee fast and far. She could go back to her flat, collect her savings, and leave the city forever. Of course, she would spend her whole life wondering if there might be an assassin on her trail. And then there was that niggling comment about the emperor and the tea. If she left now, she would not only be running away from her life, but she would be abandoning Sespian, the emperor she had sworn to honor and protect the day she became an enforcer.

When the soldier returned, he no longer carried Sicarius's dagger. Amaranthe's stomach lurched.

"Hollowcrest will see her," he told his superior, voice laced with surprise. "I'm to relieve her of weapons and escort her to his office."

"Very well." The corporal tilted his chin toward Amaranthe as if he were granting some vast favor. "You may pass."

Amaranthe decided against saying anything lippy or smug. She might pass this way again and had no idea what terms she would be on with Hollowcrest on the return trip. The guard searched her and confiscated her weapons.

"Come with me," he said.

The same guard stood outside Hollowcrest's door, though he regarded her with curious eyes this time.

"You killed Sicarius?" he asked as Amaranthe's escort left without a word.

"Yes."

"That's...impressive."

"Thank you."

The guard straightened and seemed to remember his lines: "The Commander of the Armies isn't here yet, but you may wait inside. He'll be there shortly."

Amaranthe entered and closed the door behind her. The office remained the same, though without Hollowcrest's cool presence, it felt less imposing.

She inched forward. Maybe she had time to snoop.

On the desk, next to Sicarius's dagger, a fat book hung precariously over the edge, one inadvertent nudge from landing in the trash can. Leave it be. It's snooping time, not desk-tidying time. Amaranthe stared at the crooked tome for a few heartbeats before disobeying her inner voice.

She crossed the room and straightened the book so its edges precisely lined up with the edges of the desk. She noticed a piece of paper tucked—hidden?—between the pages. After a moment of hesitation, she stuck her thumb into the book to mark the spot and plucked the unattached sheet free.

Hollowcrest, it read, you said the emperor was under your control. Your puppet hasn't made any of the changes we—

A thump sounded behind the wall to Amaranthe's right. She jumped back from the desk. A vertical crack appeared—a hidden door. She stuffed the note into her pocket.

Hollowcrest emerged from the passage.

Don't notice the book, don't notice the book....

His glare never left her face as he moved around the desk to sit. Hostility gleamed in those eyes. That verified Sicarius's supposition more thoroughly than any words could. No, sir, you didn't expect me to succeed, did you?

"Corporal Lokdon, it's good that you've returned unharmed. And so soon. Remarkable results." His smile was as icy as the frost gathered on the panes of the window behind his desk.

"Thank you, sir."

"This is indeed Sicarius's dagger." Hollowcrest ticked a fingernail against the dark metal. A conflagration of emotions swarmed across his face; in the mix, she thought she detected both anger and regret, neither of which seemed right. The cold facade returned quickly, masking further emotion. Much like Sicarius, she mused, except the assassin did it better.

"Yes, sir."

"How did you manage to kill him?"

"Actually, sir, I'd like to start with a question of my own." Tension coursed through her body, and she felt like a trap poised to spring. She had never questioned a superior officer. It was not done. "Why did you send me to die?"

"I don't know what you mean."

"Sicarius is a professional at a deadly game I've little experience in. He appears out of the dark and moves across snow without making a sound. If he's interested at all in women, I doubt he'd let it interfere with business. I no longer believe you expected me to defeat him."

"Obviously, you did. The details, please."

Amaranthe considered that cool face. Hollowcrest was not going to give anything away, and he certainly wasn't going to answer her questions. She would be hauled off to a dungeon—or the gallows—never knowing why. Her only hope was to try and surprise him, startle the answers out of him.

"Sicarius isn't dead," she said. "He gave me the knife. We reached an agreement."

"No!" Hollowcrest surged to his feet, upending his chair.

Amaranthe reacted without thinking. She grabbed the dagger from his desk and held it defensively before her.

"You conniving bitch," Hollowcrest growled. "I don't believe you seduced him too."

What? How had he come up with that? Her mind caught up to her surprise, and she asked the more pertinent question: "Too?"

Hollowcrest seemed to notice the dagger in her hand for the first time. Amaranthe lowered it but made no move to return it.

"What do you mean, 'too'?" she asked. "You can't possibly be talking about..."

"Sespian." Hollowcrest never took his eyes from the dagger, though calculation, not concern, showed on his face.

"How could I have seduced him? I haven't—"

"Spare me your meager denials. He came back the day he met you, gushing about a fabulous enforcer woman. How competent and pretty she was. What a wonderful mother she'd make. I couldn't risk Sespian courting someone so—" Hollowcrest's sneer took in the dagger, "—inappropriate. It was easier to get rid of you than to turn his interests elsewhere."

"You sent me off to my death so that I wouldn't inconvenience your marriage plans for the emperor?"

"Precisely. A shame you weren't considerate enough to die."

"I spoke to him twice." Amaranthe spread her arms. "I assure you I have no designs on the emperor."

"You lie. I saw the ambition on your face when I spoke of a promotion. But why settle for being a lieutenant when you could be an empress? A seat next to the most powerful man in the empire, whispering in his ear, influencing him, having everything you ever dreamed of."

"I can see why that would concern you, since you currently occupy that position." Her audacity surprised her, but it hardly mattered if she offended Hollowcrest now. If he was telling her all this, he had already decided to have her killed. She frowned. Actually, there was no reason for him to explain anything, even if he *did* plan to kill her. It was almost as if he was stalling.

"I deserve the position," Hollowcrest said. "I have the experience. I'm the one who worked with his father for more than thirty years."

"What would the emperor say about that?" she asked. "I assume he doesn't know you're drugging him."

"And he's not going to know." Hollowcrest opened a drawer.

Before Amaranthe could reply, the door swung open. She turned, and she abruptly knew why Hollowcrest had been stalling.

The emperor and his six bodyguards crowded the hallway. At first he appeared delighted to see her, but a startled question flashed across his eyes when he spotted the dagger in her hand. Then he looked harder at it. Those eyes widened and his jaw sagged open.

Amaranthe winced. *Sicarius, you didn't tell me the emperor would recognize your dagger too.*

"Sire," she started, "I can—"

Papers rustled behind her. She whirled. Hollowcrest lunged at her with a knife. Instinctively, she sidestepped and lifted Sicarius's dagger. Going over the desk made Hollowcrest's attack awkward, and she blocked it with her own stab. Her blade raked across his forearm. Hollowcrest cursed and dropped the knife.

"She's a traitor," he yelled. "Kill her!"

Steel rasped from scabbards, and the guards charged.

"No!" Sespian grabbed at the closest, but none of the men paused. They were following Hollowcrest's orders, not his.

Amaranthe jumped onto the desk, flung her arms over her face, and leaped through the window.

* * * * *

Sespian grabbed the doorjamb, stunned. The sound of shattering glass echoed through the room. Swords in hand, the guards started to run for the door.

"Nobody leaves!" Sespian blocked the exit with his body, trapping them inside.

The guards looked at Hollowcrest. Sespian noticed they were more concerned about his advisor's orders than his, but he could only stare at the window.

Had Amaranthe survived? Broken an arm? A leg? Sespian swallowed. Her neck?

Torn between needing to know and being afraid to find out, he hesitated before going to the window. Finally he started across the room. He had to know.

Hollowcrest intercepted him. Sespian tried to push past, but the older man gripped his arm with surprising strength.

"Let go," Sespian said.

Hollowcrest did not. Blood ran down his arm and dripped onto Sespian's wrist.

"She's a traitor," Hollowcrest said. "She attacked me."

"You attacked her first. Do you think I don't have eyes? She was defending herself."

"She came to kill me, and you as well. I *know* you recognized that knife!"

Hollowcrest so rarely raised his voice, so rarely showed any emotion at all. His tone made Sespian pause. But, no. It could not be true.

"There's an explanation," Sespian said. "There must be. You're the one who brought her here, sent her on a mission."

"One which she did not complete. She's allied with Sicarius."

Sespian pushed past him to the window. Footprints trampled the snow below. Even from the third floor, the spots of blood were visible. But the courtyard was empty, Amaranthe nowhere to be seen. The front gate was locked, the guards in place. She had not fled that way.

"Where is she?" Sespian whispered.

"Sire—"

Sespian waved Hollowcrest to silence and charged out the door. He raced through the halls and down the stairs. More than once he skidded on the polished marble floors and banged into the walls, but he did not slow.

When he ran out the front door, cold air wrapped around him, but he hardly noticed it. He veered off the walkway and followed the wall of the building. Only when he reached the spot below Hollowcrest's office did he slow.

The gas lights in the courtyard provided little illumination this far from the walkways. Blood spattered the snow, but only under the window. There was no trail leading away. The darkness, and dozens of boot prints, thwarted Sespian's attempts to pinpoint Amaranthe's tracks.

A shard of blackness against the white ground demanded his attention. He bent and brushed aside snow, revealing the midnight black dagger.

A twinge of old fear wound through his gut. What had she been doing with Sicarius's weapon? Hollowcrest couldn't be right, could he?

Voices at the front of the building returned him to the moment. Feeling dizzy, Sespian staggered back to find Hollowcrest and two guards talking on the stairs. When Sespian approached, Hollowcrest sent the men inside.

"What happened?" Sespian asked.

Hollowcrest met his gaze. "She broke her neck in the fall. The guards have taken her body away for incineration."

"No. She's too good. She wouldn't... I don't believe it." The headache that always lurked behind Sespian's eyes intensified. Perhaps all that running had been too much. He put a hand on one of the statues for support.

"Sespian," Hollowcrest said, "she wasn't what you wanted her to be. She was a traitor. I brought her here because I suspected she was not the loyal enforcer she appeared to be." He reached out and touched the knife in Sespian's hands. "She was in league with Sicarius."

"No," Sespian whispered.

He leaned forward, panting. The running had strained him more than it should have. Spots floated across his vision, and blackness probed the edges. The constant pain in his head intensified. He hunched over, clutching at his temples—and collapsed into unconsciousness.

CHAPTER 6

SHACKLES BOUND AMARANTHE'S WRISTS BEHIND her back. Two guards dragged her through dark narrow hall-ways and down a dank stairway framed by walls of roughly quarried stone. Lanterns burned at distant intervals, hanging from old torch sconces. As the group moved in and out of the shadows, Amaranthe felt as if she had stepped back hundreds of years in time.

Warm blood trickled down her temple. Numerous glass cuts afflicted her face and scalp. Worse pain came from her battered muscles, courtesy of the pummeling they received in the three-story fall. This discomfort was only the beginning, she knew. *I can survive this. Whatever torture they inflict on me, I will survive, and I will plan, and I will escape.*

Then she entered the dungeon.

She was expecting shackles, instruments of pain, and moldy, blood-stained walls. The archaic atmosphere ended at the doorway, however. Inside, a honeycomb of whitewashed tunnels and chambers spread out. They were brightly lit by gas jets and smelled of lye soap. The first man she saw likewise did not meet expectations.

Amaranthe had anticipated towering, monosyllabic guards led by a sadistic, whip-cracking overseer who had not seen the sun in twenty years. Instead, a gray-haired man in crisp black military fatigues greeted her with a smile.

"Ah!" he said cheerfully. "A female. You're our first. Excellent."

The pin on the left side of his collar proclaimed him a colonel; the pin on the right bore a needle, the symbol for a surgeon.

A shiver raised the hair along her arms. "First for what?"

"I'll show you." The surgeon hummed and tapped his clipboard against his thigh as he led the way down the stark, white corridor. "Come along, come along."

The guards forced Amaranthe to follow. If her hands had not been bound behind her, she might have tried for one of the swords or pistols hanging from their belts, but she had no hope of reaching them.

Cells lined either side of the corridor, each secured by steel bars and locked gates. Male prisoners occupied most. Some stood and watched her pass, but most lay prone and unresponsive. One had black fingers and toes, symptoms of the advanced stages of frostbite. Another had pox marks all over his skin. Occasionally, medics in military fatigues surrounded the prisoners. One would hold a clipboard and pen while others stabbed and prodded at their victims.

In one cell, a man was stretched facedown on a metal table with a surgeon poking around several inches of exposed vertebrae. He screamed with each prod, and blood flowed from his back. It splashed the floor, ran down a slight slope, and poured into a central drain. Amaranthe experienced the unwelcome insight that someone had angled the floors and placed the drains with exactly that purpose in mind.

Torture, but more methodical than the simple cuts and burns designed to extract information. They were performing medical experiments on these people. She shuddered.

"The emperor might not like the idea of a lady being dissected in his dungeon," one of the guards holding Amaranthe whispered to the other as they traveled deeper into the tunnels.

"This was *his* idea," the other said. "He wanted more money to go into medical research, right?"

"He has no idea what's going on down here, and I'm sure this isn't the kind of research he meant."

"That's 'cause he's soft, and you are too if you listen to him. Hollowcrest is smart to keep his thumb on the boy. The Nurians would be mauling us if they had any idea how weak-minded our supposed emperor is."

Amaranthe wondered how many men in the Imperial Barracks were loyal to Sespian and how many to Hollowcrest. If these two were representative of the whole, Hollowcrest's supporters were more vocal.

The surgeon turned into a large room with four occupied cots against the back wall. A counter with upper and lower cabinets stood along one side and a coal stove along the other. No fire burned in it, and the room was cold. The men on the cots were inert, flushed faces and wheezing breaths the only indications of life. A bumpy red rash covered their skin.

The surgeon paused by a cot. "Ah, good. This one's dead. Take him to my examination room. A few more dissections and we ought to make some headway." He rapped his knuckles on his clipboard. "It's not right that those magic-throwing Kendorian shamans can cure this while sound imperial medicine lags behind."

The guard who had spoken up for Sespian left Amaranthe to obey the surgeon's orders. He touched her shoulder briefly, eyes sad, before he dragged the corpse away. The pity unnerved her more than the callous attitudes of the others.

"Magic-throwing shamans?" Amaranthe asked. The empire's stance was that magic did not exist. Of course, the empire also forbade its use, so one tended to wonder about the truth of the first statement. Either way, she had never seen any evidence of magic in her life.

"Yes, their healers sacrifice chickens, wave their hands, and cure the disease." The surgeon sniffed disdainfully. "Fear not. Your sacrifice will help us find a legitimate cure and distribute it to our troops along the southern border."

"Oh, good." Amaranthe swallowed. "What is the disease?"

"Hysintunga."

"And it's always deadly?"

"Oh, yes."

"How long does it take to ah..." She nodded in the direction the corpse had been taken.

The surgeon unlocked a cabinet and rummaged inside. "Three to four days from infection to death, at least based on the cases we've had so far. Perhaps it'll be faster for you, since you're smaller than the men."

A locomotive trip to Kendor took over a week. I'm dead if I let them infect me.

She flexed her shoulders and tried to work her wrists free of the manacles. The remaining guard clamped his hand tighter around her biceps and gave her a warning frown. The hilt of his sword dug into her side. If she could somehow get his weapon, maybe she could hold it to the surgeon's throat and bargain her way free. She would need her hands free first.

"I don't suppose you'd—" she started, but a shadow fell across the doorway.

Hollowcrest entered the room, and four guards came in on his heels. Amaranthe slumped.

He regarded her coolly, hefting his right arm. A bandage wrapped it from wrist to elbow.

"You are a tedious pain, woman. In more ways than one."

"You attacked *me*," she said, seeing no reason to bother with honorifics at this point. "After you sent me on a suicide mission. I'm the one who's a pain?"

He snorted. "Don't put this on me, girl. It seemed a shame to waste a bright enforcer; it's not like they're a common breed. Your ambition is what made you dangerous. I couldn't let you at the emperor."

A shame? Vanquished ancestors, was he actually regretting what he had done? Did he feel guilty? Or was she imagining it? Maybe he had just come down to gloat. It didn't seem that he had noticed the missing note yet, though she was not sure how that helped. She could not read it with her hands behind her back.

The surgeon removed a jar from a cabinet, one of several on a shelf. A large, winged insect buzzed inside, its droning ominous. Amaranthe made herself focus on Hollowcrest. As long as he was talking, she had to learn as much as she could in case she had the opportunity to do something with that information later.

"Does the emperor know you've got me locked up down here?"

"Unfortunately, he is mourning your tragic death," Hollowcrest said. "Killed falling out the window. You should be pleased; Sespian appeared quite distraught by the news."

"What are you doing to him anyway? What does the drug you're putting in his tea do?"

Amaranthe glanced at the surgeon and the guards, hoping the news would come as a surprise to them. If she could trick Hollowcrest into answering in the affirmative, maybe it would shock them, coerce them to do something to defend the rightful leader of the empire.

"It's a herb that dulls the intellect and renders the drinker susceptible to manipulation," Hollowcrest said calmly.

No one in the room reacted. *They know. They all know and they don't care.*

"Why?" Amaranthe asked. "When you were sworn to act as his regent, you made a promise to him and the empire that you would step down when he reached his majority. That was last year."

"Do you think I wanted to break my word? I'm no power-hungry tyrant. I have always been content to advise. But the boy would destroy the empire." He cleaned his eyeglasses with a handkerchief. "In his first week on the throne, he vowed to make peace with all the nations we've ever warred with, cut military spending in half, funnel the money to education, and...oh, yes, and phase out the empire itself, instating some ridiculous people's republic with elected officials."

"They sound like noble goals."

"You're as naïve and idealistic as he is. Yes, let us announce to all the nations we've conquered over the last seven hundred years that now we wish for peace. I'm sure they'll embrace us with heartfelt brotherhood and forget about all the men slain, the land taken, the freedoms stolen, the laws imposed. Please. They would send diplomats on the one hand and secretly build their armies for revenge on the other. And dissolving the empire? Since religion fell out of fashion, faith in Turgonia is the only thing that gives our people a sense of meaning. The empire is not just a government; it's a way of life. Our citizens know they're a part of something greater than them. Without the empire to define an ideology for them, they would be lost. Take that away and the next zealot with a vision would end up creating something with all of the tyranny and none of the benefits. Sespian's idealistic world doesn't exist. It can never exist as long as men live in it." Hollowcrest returned his glasses to his nose and curled his lip. "Nineteen year olds. They shouldn't be allowed to tie their own shoes much less rule a nation."

Amaranthe groped for an argument that would sway the old man. It was hard because she wasn't sure he was entirely wrong. But Sespian wasn't wrong either. These two stubborn men ought to be working together to find a middle ground, not trying to force their visions on each other.

"I'm ready, sir," the surgeon announced.

"It's not too late," Amaranthe said, forcing herself to meet Hollowcrest's now-withdrawn gaze. "You don't have to do this. I'm loyal to the emperor, but have no designs on his future. You don't need to kill me, and you could stop drugging him—involve him in his own rule. You make some good points. Maybe his enthusiasm just needs to be tempered with your experience, not stifled by it. He's smart. He'll learn in time. You have to give him a chance."

Hollowcrest did not immediately reply. Amaranthe had no reason to think her words would mean anything to him, but she found herself hoping anyway, for her own life and for the emperor's.

"Once battle has been engaged," Hollowcrest said, "you cannot call back your armies and say never mind. You are committed. There can be only victory or defeat." He nodded to the surgeon and said, "Go ahead," before leaving.

"The emperor's not an enemy to be made war upon," Amaranthe called after him. "He's a man."

Hollowcrest's soldiers stayed behind. That left five guards plus the surgeon. Not good.

Two men forced her to her knees. One unlocked her shackles to free her arm for the surgeon. Though she had no hope of escaping, she elbowed the guard in the gut and lunged for the gate. Another simply caught her and threw her down, forcing her back against the cold floor.

"This will go easier if you relax," the surgeon said.

Amaranthe eyed the jar in his hands. Inside, the malignant black bug bounced around, reminiscent of both wasp and lizard. Its wings flapped, and its agitated tail hammered at the glass with audible ticks. Strange that such a healthy-looking bug could carry a disease that would kill her.

"What is it?" she asked morbidly.

The surgeon loosened the jar's lid. "The desert nomads call them Fangs. They transmit the infection with their bite." He cocked his head and studied her as if she were an exotic fungus growing on a damp wall. "It will be interesting to examine your cadaver and see if the disease affects women differently than men."

"Interesting. Right."

The surgeon pushed up her sleeve. A part of Amaranthe wanted to face the moment with dignity, but when he removed the lid and set the mouth of the jar against her skin, fear surged through her. She twisted and jerked her arm away.

The surgeon cursed and flung the lid back on before the insect could escape. "Hold her!"

"Sorry, sir. She's stronger than she looks."

Another joined the first two, leaving a guard on her legs and one on each arm. The surgeon descended, ready with the jar again.

She tried to thrash free, all sense of strategy forgotten in pure desperation. Despite her frenzied struggle, Amaranthe felt the bite of the insect.

At that point, she deflated. Tears formed in her eyes.

"You can let her go." The surgeon screwed the lid back on and returned the jar to the cupboard. "She won't fight now. There's no point, eh?"

He was right. Amaranthe became as inert as the wheezing forms on the cots. When the guards released her and backed up, she made no lunge to her feet. Their heads receded, and she only stared up at the reinforced concrete ceiling.

"I'll be back in the morning," the surgeon said in parting. "There's water in a jug over there."

Amaranthe did not move her eyes to follow his pointing arm. A part of her mind registered the clank of the steel gate shutting, the throwing of the lock. The insect bite burned, and a hot tingle spread toward her shoulder.

So, this was defeat.

She had always imagined death would come at the end of some criminal's sword during a battle for a worthwhile cause. Never had she pictured dying amongst strangers, forgotten by the world. Was anyone even wondering where she was? She had no family in the city, but surely some of her enforcer comrades would be curious why she had disappeared from work without a word.

What about Sicarius? Would he wonder what was happening to her? No, he had predicted she would end up in the dungeon. And why not? She was an amateur next to him. She had walked into Hollowcrest's office without any sort of plan. What had she expected would happen? That she would talk her way out of a death sentence and get Hollowcrest to stop drugging Sespian while she was at it?

After a time, Amaranthe grew bored of staring at the ceiling and feeling sorry for herself. She still had a reason to escape. Even if she was going to die, she could tell Sicarius what she had learned.

She staggered to her feet and plucked her hairpins from her sagging bun. The lock was set into the corridor-side of the door, which made it awkward to probe. It only took a moment to discover her pins were too large to reach the tumblers in the back. Opening that door would take a key or a professional set of lockpicks. She had neither.

While mulling her next act, she took some water to the men on the cots.

They smelled of urine and sweat, and cracks like canyons marred their lips. The men were an unsettling preview of her own last hours, and she wanted to crawl into the corner as far from them as possible. Instead, she tried to get them to drink. One opened his eyes briefly, but stared through her, not at her. She took his hand. With the splotchy rashes covering his skin, it felt like rust-licked metal under a summer sun. She fumbled for something comforting to say. All she could think of was how soon this would be her.

A smooth patch on the man's hand drew her attention. She rotated his arm. A gang brand marked his skin. The Panthers. He was one of Mitsy's. Amaranthe checked the other two men. They bore brands for the Black Arrows, another gang in the city.

"They're using our own people," she whispered, chilled.

One of the men sighed, exuding tangible pain.

"I'm sorry I can't do anything for you," Amaranthe said.

She wished for a book or something to read aloud to them. The thought triggered the memory of the note she had stolen from Hollowcrest's office. She dug it from her pocket.

Hollowcrest, you said the emperor was under your control. Your puppet hasn't made any of the changes we discussed, primarily to exempt key businesses from taxes in order to foster growth. Forge also demands a voice in the government. The empire is a defunct warrior aristocracy out of touch with the modern world. Your recalcitrance forces us to make threats. If the emperor does not pass the laws we have requested, he will be eliminated during his birthday celebration. The people will not accept you as a ruler. Since Sespian is the only Savarsin

left who claims royal blood through both paternal and maternal lines, he is the only legitimate heir. His death will create civil war, giving us the opportunity to back a more amenable prospect.

How do we go forward? The choice is yours.

—Forge

Amaranthe slowly folded the note and returned it to her pocket. She dropped her chin to her chest. Not only was Sespian being drugged, but his very life was at stake.

She could not imagine Hollowcrest giving in to those demands, not after that lecture he had given her. He was warrior caste through and through, and he would only raise his hackles at the idea of government power for businesses. But if he did not give in to this Forge group, the emperor's life could be forfeit.

Amaranthe slammed her palm against the wall. I can't die now.

More than ever, she had to escape and warn Sicarius. If the emperor truly meant something to him, perhaps he could be counted on to pass on this information to someone with clout. Even if she died, perhaps the ripples from the pebble she tossed in the lake would create change by the time they reached the shore.

But first, escape.

Footsteps in the hallway spurred hope. She slid her hairpins under a cot, and edged close to the gate, poised if an opportunity came.

Unfortunately, there were a lot of footsteps. Hollowcrest came into view first, and then the four guards crowded behind him. Too many.

Hollowcrest unlocked the gate. "Search her."

Guards flowed in. Two grabbed her arms, while the other two rummaged through her pockets and more personal places. They found the note. Amaranthe sighed as they took it. Now, even if she escaped, she had lost the only physical evidence that Hollowcrest was manipulating the emperor and that Sespian was in danger.

"Is there anything you don't have your fingers in?" Hollowcrest asked.

"I've been trying to broaden my interests of late," she said. "Since I've learned how dangerous it can be to blindly follow the orders of men you grew up thinking you could trust."

"Take anything else she could use to escape," Hollowcrest said.

They took her enforcer identification, her money, Sespian's bracelet, and the key to her flat. She watched Hollowcrest to see if that bracelet would mean anything to him, but he let the guards remove it without an eye flicker.

He shut the gate with a clang. The lock clicked, and Hollowcrest led his men away.

Amaranthe threw her back against the bars and glared about the room. "All right," she whispered to herself. "Nothing's changed. I still have to escape."

She checked the stove, but only a useless layer of ash lined the firebox. A narrow pipe exited the top and disappeared into the ceiling. The hole would not be wide enough to crawl through if she dismantled the stovepipe.

The cabinets were locked, but the mechanisms were simpler than the ones securing the door. She found a hairpin and soon defeated them. Empty canisters, a spool of surgical thread, and stacks of papers rested on shelves inside. Nothing particularly useful.

Her hand brushed against one of the jars holding the odious bugs. She jerked her arm away with a horrified yank. Then she snorted and relaxed. No reason to be afraid of them now.

Amaranthe paused. "No reason for *me* to be afraid of them."

The beginnings of an idea percolated through her mind. There were a total of four glass jars, each with a wing-flapping, tail-flicking bug inside. Amaranthe spun out some thread and tied the jars together, leaving a long leash dangling. She placed them on top of the cabinet near the cell door. Next, she found an empty canister with a lid and scooped ashes from the stove into it. Thus prepared, she pushed herself up to sit on the counter under the jars. She clutched the thread leash in one hand and rested the canister next to her thigh, where it could not be seen from the gate.

Several hours would pass before the surgeon returned. She could only hope she retained the ability to act when the time came.

The awkward position and the knowledge of impending death made sleep inaccessible. Waiting had none of the distracting qualities of plotting an escape or trying to draw information out of Hollowcrest. One of the sick men stopped breathing during the night. The pained wheezing of the others finally cracked Amaranthe's stoicism, and she wept quietly.

Whether for them or herself or both, she did not know. The tears felt strangely cool on her cheeks. I have a fever already, she realized numbly.

In the morning, the surgeon's voice drifted down the corridor. She checked the thread wound around her hand.

Two men stopped before the gate. Amaranthe, staring at the floor, saw them at the edge of her vision. The surgeon and a single guard, carrying a repeating crossbow. She feigned a stupor. She was not a threat; at least, that's what she wanted them to think.

Amaranthe waited until the surgeon unlocked the gate and pushed it open.

She yanked on the thread.

The jars crashed down, and glass shattered as they hit the concrete floor. The surgeon and the guard blinked in confusion at first. Then an angry buzz educated the silence. Realization came to the surgeon first, and she smiled with grim satisfaction as a bug flew at his face. His eyes widened and he leaped backwards, smashing into the guards who did not yet understand the ramifications of the broken glass.

Amaranthe jumped to her feet and lunged for the exit. She grabbed a fistful of ash from her canister and threw it at their faces. The surgeon paid her little heed except to swat at the ash and run back the way he had come.

"The bugs are out, you idiots!" he called over his shoulder.

The guards, finally realizing the danger, raced after the surgeon.

Amaranthe paused only long enough to slam the lid onto the canister, then ran the other way. She headed deeper into the dungeon, hoping her captors would expect her to go up instead of down. Numerous shouts rang from the direction of the stairs. No, she would never escape that way. She wished she could stop to free the other prisoners, but she had neither keys nor time. The virus-laden insects might delay pursuit, but only temporarily.

After a few turns, ancient stone replaced the whitewashed concrete walls. The gas lamps ended, but a rack with a few lanterns provided a means to travel deeper. She grabbed one and considered destroying the others, but figured the task would take her more time than it bought.

Deeper she went, the lantern doing little to drive back the shadows. Perhaps it was for the best. The glimpses of ancient torture implements, rusty wall shackles, and rat feces did nothing to hearten her. Staleness competed with mildew to taint the damp air.

Under what circumstances, she wondered, had Sicarius spent time down here?

At each intersection, Amaranthe tilted her head and tried to feel breezes that might indicate an outside exit. She was putting a lot of trust in Sicarius, a man she barely knew and whose deeds hardly spoke well of him. Whether he had been lying, or her fever-befuddled senses were betraying her, she reached a dead-end before she felt any hint of a draft.

She sniffed liberally around the walls, trying to detect some hint of the outdoors amongst the must and mold. Nothing.

Amaranthe backtracked and tried other passages. The exercise fatigued her. She came to two more dead-ends before a faint breeze brushed her cheek. Voices sounded, not far enough away for comfort. She removed the lid from her canister of ash, yanked her shirt over her mouth and nose, then threw handfuls of the fine gray powder in the air. It assaulted her eyes, and she stepped back, bumping into the wall.

"Hear something?" a man asked nearby.

"She's down here somewhere."

"Don't see why we have to bother searching. Can just wait until the corpse starts to stink and find her then."

They laughed, and armor and weapons clanked. There might only be two of them, but they were armed. Amaranthe had nothing, not even Sicarius's dagger. Besides, she doubted she could best a five-year-old in her present condition. This *had* to work.

She held her breath and squinted through blurry eyes into the cloud of ash, looking for a disturbance.

There.

A draft coming from the floor swirled the cloud at foot level. She groped around the area, searching for a switch or button.

At chest level on the left side, she found a crease in the mortar that depressed when touched. A mechanism ground behind the wall. She winced, sure the guards would hear.

In front of her, a jagged edge detached like two pieces of a jigsaw puzzle coming apart. Amaranthe had to set down the lantern and use both hands to open the heavy stone door.

She threw more ash behind her to obscure her footprints. She grabbed her light, stepped inside, and pulled the door shut.

Cobwebs and dust owned the tunnel she entered. Too tired to swat at them, she ran—no, stumbled—straight through. Her clumsy gait evoked resentment; already, this disease was sapping her muscles. Her breath whistled as if she were at the end of a hard run around the lake. She doubted she had much time left where she could do anything useful.

The tunnel ended at a steel grille blocking the passage. Outside, a pink sky filtered through bare, tangled limbs that screened the exit. Amaranthe found a lever to open the grate, and she pushed past the brambles. Thorns clawed at her hands and cheeks. A nearby sign read SEWER ACCESS POINT.

She snorted. Sure.

She stumbled forward, looking for a path out, and hoping she could make it to the lake without running into the enforcers. Strange to think those who should have been her allies would now be foes. When Hollowcrest learned of her escape, he would surely place a reward on her head. What crime would he make up to put on her wanted poster? Releaser of Deadly Bugs, reward 5,000 ranmyas. Cutter of Hollowcrest's Arm, reward 10,000 ranmyas. Although, since he knew she was destined to die from the disease, he might not bother sending out search parties or alerting the enforcers. Too bad. She would rather be wanted than dead.

All she could do was make it to the lake and hope Sicarius would be there so she could deliver her message. After that...

She swallowed grimly. After that, it would not matter.

* * * * *

Dusk found Amaranthe curled on her side on a park bench beside the lake. Fevered and numb, breathing shallow, she didn't recognized the black boots at first. Sicarius squatted on his heels beside her head. She had wanted to tell him something. What was it? Shattered pieces of thought flitted through her mind, too elusive a puzzle to fit together. She just remembered they were important.

"Emperor...Hollow—" She licked cracked lips. Speaking was too hard. She drew a shuddering breath between each word. "Forge...assassin...ation. Can't...celebration. Tell...someone."

Amaranthe panted, fighting to get out more words. The effort devoured her remaining strength. Darkness crept into her vision. She tried to push it back, but it overwhelmed her, and she lost consciousness.

CHAPTER 7

PAIN PULSED BEHIND SESPIAN'S EYES. THE WORDS on the page blurred and danced. The medical journal from the Kyatt Islands was written in a language he wasn't fluent in, but Kyattese used the same alphabet as Turgonian, and he had a language dictionary to reference. The translating should not be so hard.

Sespian slammed his pen down and grabbed his hair. What was wrong with him?

"Problem, Sire?" came a voice from the doorway.

Hollowcrest strolled into the library with a handful of papers. He stopped next to the table. Under his feet sprawled a massive floor medallion that depicted the muscled bulk of Agroth, the founder of Turgonia and the first emperor. From Sespian's viewpoint, it looked like the ancient warrior's sword tip was poking Hollowcrest in the ass—a rather pleasant notion.

"No," Sespian said.

"Why are you reading that?" Hollowcrest frowned down at the book.

"I'm trying to figure out what's wrong with me. When I woke up, the surgeon said nothing, but people my age aren't supposed to collapse on the steps of their homes for no reason." Now, if Hollowcrest pitched down some stairs, that'd be more understandable, but the lean old gargoyle would probably live forever.

"Yes, we should discuss that." Hollowcrest slid into the chair across the table. "Surgeon Darrik was reluctant to speak his findings to you, but he confided in me."

"Did he." Sespian leaned back in his chair, folded his arms across his chest, and eyed Hollowcrest.

"He was concerned you might not take his findings well and didn't want to deliver them himself."

A flutter vexed Sespian's stomach. "What findings?"

Hollowcrest set down his papers, propped his elbows on the desk, and steepled his fingers. "There is a possibility—we don't know for certain, mind you—that you have a brain tumor."

The utter silence in the library made it possible for Sespian to hear his breaths quicken. "No." He stared at his notes without seeing them. "No, I don't believe that. I'm not that sick. I'll be fine. I'm sure it's just..."

What? He had no idea. That was the problem.

"We're not certain, so there's always hope it'll be something less problematic." An attempt at a sympathetic smile creased Hollowcrest's weathered face. "It would explain your headaches, though, and your fainting episode."

"I didn't faint, I passed out in a manly way," Sespian muttered. "I'm probably not getting enough exercise or the right kind of food. Or something. I'm sure it's not a tumor. The whole idea is just ludicrous. I'm too young. I haven't done anything I wanted to do yet. I..." He barely heard his own words. He couldn't believe this.

"There is, perhaps, still time to leave a legacy." Hollowcrest pushed the sheets of paper across the table.

"What's this?" Sespian grabbed them and looked at the top page. His hands were trembling. "A picture of a woman? What is this supposed to—"

"A suitable prospect for marriage," Hollowcrest said. "There are several ladies there, all of flawless warrior caste bloodlines, all of child-bearing age."

Sespian stared at the old man. "You just told me I'm going to die soon, and now you want me to get married?"

"As you've said, Sire, you've had little time to fulfill your desires as emperor. Do you not, before you die, want to at least produce an heir to carry on your blood and one day rule the empire?"

Sespian started to respond but stopped. Something was very wrong here. He needed to think before he spoke. Why were his thoughts so fuzzy? It seemed like a child's puzzle was before him, but someone had blown out the lamps, and he had to assemble it in the dark.

He took the papers, stood, and walked to a window overlooking the snowy banks piled against the courtyard walls. If he died, leaving a babe behind, Hollowcrest could end up as regent for the next eighteen years. Theoretically, Sespian could name another regent, but would anyone listen to his mandates? As Sespian had so recently seen, Hollowcrest had the full support of the guards. Everyone else snapped to obey his orders as well.

I'm just a figurehead. It was so obvious; why had it eluded him all year? He kept trying to insinuate his ideas, but he crashed against walls everywhere he turned. It was as if Hollowcrest had never really stepped down as regent.

How had Sespian let it all come to pass?

He could feel Hollowcrest's eyes boring into his back, so he pretended to peruse the papers. It was time to do some snooping and figure out exactly what Hollowcrest was doing.

"Take your time, Sire." A chair scraped as Hollowcrest stood. "Let me know if you wish to speak further, or please talk to the surgeon anytime if you have questions."

"I will." Sespian had no doubt the surgeon was ready with just the answers Hollowcrest wanted him to have.

Once he was alone, Sespian lowered the papers and returned to the table. The book and his notes were gone.

* * * * *

Dreams and reality meshed for Amaranthe, creating a fevered realm of fear and confusion. Nightmares of Hollowcrest, enforcers, and those dreadful bugs mingled in her head. Sometimes she saw a tiny room with wooden plank walls and metal beams on the ceiling. Perhaps those were her waking moments. During them, she was alone and afraid.

In one of her dreams, Sicarius appeared, accompanied by a pale-skinned man with tattoos and long braids of gray hair. They spoke in a foreign language. The stranger touched her forehead, chanting as he traced symbols on her skin with a gnarled finger. Confused and alarmed, she tried to pull away, but Sicarius held her down. The ritual had the feel of an ancient death ceremony done by a priest to send her spirit off to some hypothetical afterworld. Amaranthe struggled to retain con-

sciousness, afraid every slip into blackness would be permanent, but it swallowed her again.

* * * * *

She woke alert and fever-free in the wooden room she had seen in her dream. Surprised, she struggled to prop herself up on her elbow. The effort made her heartbeat leap to double time.

A kerosene lantern squatting on a desk provided dim illumination. She was lying on a cot against a wall opposite a closed door. The only other pieces of furniture were a wooden chair and a stove burning next to a stocked coal bin.

A sickly odor permeated the air. Amaranthe lifted the scratchy wool blanket draping her and sniffed. Great. She was the source. Someone had removed her soiled clothing, but she badly needed a bath.

Abruptly, she laughed. Who cared if she reeked? She was alive!

But where was she?

On the nearest wall, a large rectangular panel of wood hung from hinges like some makeshift shutter. Curiosity won out over fatigue. She wrapped the blanket about herself and sloughed off the cot. Despite the heat radiating from the stove, the scuffed and dented wood floor wept coldness. She propped the panel open with a stick apparently there for the purpose. An optimist would have called the rectangular opening underneath a window. She decided "ragged hole sawed in the planks" was more accurate.

She looked out upon an enormous icehouse. One- to two-foot wide blocks formed a frozen mountain that stretched into the rafters. Her room was almost as high. A metal staircase to her right led down to the sawdust-strewn floor.

Motion drew her eye. Sicarius. He had pulled out a few blocks and was practicing kicks and punches from atop them. With agility that would have embarrassed a cat, he hopped from one slick perch to the next. Sometimes he spun and kicked midair, yet he never slipped when he landed. She expected him to look up and acknowledge her—without a doubt he had heard that panel creak up—but he continued his routine without pause.

Amaranthe dropped her forearms on the edge and watched him. Despite the chilly environs, he wore no shirt. Since his usual black shirts were fitted, the sculptors-would-pay-me-to-model physique wasn't a surprise, but it was...eye-catching. The way his relaxed body flowed like water curling along its course before it contracted into steel for a strike was mesmerizing. He went into a series of open-handed blocks, each a demonstration in economy of motion, each followed by what she imagined were joint locks. With those shoulders, he would have no trouble twisting someone's arm off.

After a long moment, she snapped herself out of her gawk with a shake of the head and a self-mocking snort. *All right, girl, we are not going to be attracted to the amoral assassin.*

Amaranthe moved away from the window and noticed a newspaper on the desk. The front-page headline gave her a start. *Rogue Bear Kills Two More on Wharf Street.*

"Bear?" she muttered. "Did a *sober* journalist write that?"

Paper in hand, she slumped down on the hard chair. Stumps was surrounded by hundreds of miles of farmlands and orchards. One rarely saw a raccoon in the city, and she couldn't remember ever hearing of a bear sighting. A bear killing people sounded even more unlikely.

The Wharf Street part stood out for a different reason. She glanced toward the window and the frozen stacks beyond. All the ice houses in the city were near the docks, which meant this building was close to—maybe right on—Wharf Street. Something new to worry about. Wonderful.

Reading the story wasn't enlightening, and she couldn't help but think back to Hollowcrest's admission that the papers didn't always print the truth.

After finishing, she grimaced at the date. Assuming it was today's paper, she had lost four days between the dungeon and the sickness. Only two and a half weeks remained until the emperor's birthday celebration. What could she possibly do to stop Hollowcrest and Forge in so little time?

She had no money, no weapons, no idea who comprised Forge, nothing. She needed an ally, but now that she was on the less desirable side of the law, she could hardly go to her enforcer friends for help. The only one she could ask was someone already marked as a criminal....

Amaranthe laid the paper on the desk, edges lined up with the corner, and walked back to the window. Now Sicarius was sprinting through some sort of twisty footwork course he had constructed. If she didn't say something, he'd be down there all day.

The next time he finished a lap, she cleared her throat nosily. Sicarius looked up at her.

"Just wondering why I'm alive," Amaranthe called down. "And why we're camped in an icehouse."

Sicarius acknowledged her with a twitch of his hand, but continued his exercises.

She returned to the cot. Just walking around the tiny room left her depressingly weak. And cold. She nudged the cot closer to the stove and pulled the blanket more tightly around her. It smelled of sawdust and more pungent sickbed odors.

A few minutes later, Sicarius entered, fully clothed again.

"The icehouse happened to be near where you collapsed on the trail," Sicarius said. "There was a limit to how far I could carry you through the city without drawing attention. It is also fully stocked, so the workers have moved on to filling another warehouse down the block. Disturbances have been infrequent."

"Thank you," Amaranthe murmured. "How did you, ah...I wasn't expecting... They told me the disease was always fatal."

"Yes, unless healed by someone who understands the mental sciences. I recognized the symptoms of Hysintunga and found a shaman."

The mental sciences? A strange synonym for magic.

"A shaman in the empire?" she asked. "In Stumps? You can be hanged for *reading* about magic. I can't believe anyone would risk practicing it here."

Or that it existed. Even when the surgeon had casually discussed magic in the dungeon, it had failed to penetrate her long-held beliefs. Or disbeliefs rather. Amaranthe prodded her arm where the bug had bitten her. Nothing remained of the wound. Perhaps it was time to question those beliefs.

"Most people in the empire either do not believe in the mental sciences or would not recognize them being practiced regardless," Sicarius said. "Though this is not an easy place for foreigners to live, sometimes

it is safer than what they leave behind, especially if they are hunted by fellow practitioners."

Fugitive magic users? In her city? Amaranthe rubbed her face.

"He must not have been too bad of a fellow if he was willing to help me," she reasoned.

"He was paid well."

"Oh." Amaranthe swallowed. She had only meant to seek Sicarius in order to relay information to him. She had not thought he would be able to save her, or that he would bother even if he could. "Thank you," she said again, the words inadequate. "I owe you—"

"An explanation." Sicarius regarded her intently. "Clarify the situation with the emperor. I could not understand the incoherent jumble you spit out before falling unconscious."

So, he had helped her because he wanted her information, not out of kindness. That was not surprising, but it reminded her how much talking she was going to have to do to convince him to become her ally.

Amaranthe gave a detailed description of the conversations she had shared with Hollowcrest. She recited the words on the letter verbatim. Those experiences, when she had thought she was dying, were indelibly imprinted in her mind.

Sicarius's face remained unreadable throughout her narrative. At the end, he gave her that cool stare he did so well.

"Hollowcrest gave his reasons for wanting you killed, described the tea he's using to drug Sespian, and explained why he feels the need to manipulate the emperor in the first place." He folded his arms and leaned against the wall. "To you."

His tone didn't change to suggest it was a question, and it wasn't until he tacked on the last two words that Amaranthe realized it was a statement of disbelief.

It hadn't occurred to her that he might think she was lying. Before, when she *had been* lying to him, he had sensed it. She stared back at him and willed him to sense she was telling the truth now.

"Yes, he did," she said.

"Hollowcrest had no reason to tell you anything, and he doesn't explain himself, or justify his actions, before killing people."

"Honestly, I was surprised myself, especially when he came to chat in the dungeon," Amaranthe said. "Do you suppose... Could he have

thought I'd escape—or that you'd come get me and help me—and that this was a message meant for you?" She looked up at him, again trying to read his face, but it was still expressionless. "You're obviously connected with him somehow. Based on the fact that Hollowcrest and Sespian both recognize your dagger, I'm guessing you were the court assassin or something of that nature, although assassination isn't supposed to be the Turgonian way. Still, I think Hollowcrest is a sneaky old sod, and he wouldn't have minded having someone like you around. From what I remember of Emperor Raumesys, they were similar types. Your enforcer record—your list of *public* assassinations—started up, what, five years ago? That was the same time as Raumesys died. Maybe Sespian, being a rather *good* human being, didn't want an assassin on the payroll, and gave you the boot, so you had to go out and find other work. Of course, that doesn't explain why..."

A warning instinct lifted the hairs on the back of her neck. She had been looking at Sicarius while she spoke but, in her musings, had stopped *seeing* him. Now, her focus sharpened.

His expression had not changed, but he was very, very still, and his dark eyes were colder than ice shards. Amaranthe chomped down on her flapping lip and dropped her gaze to the floorboards. He hadn't said a word, but she could feel the threat hanging between them. She might need *his* help, but with her information delivered, he didn't need anything else from *her*. Probing into his past was not a good idea.

"No," Sicarius said after a long, uncomfortable silence. "Hollowcrest would not send me a message."

"Good," Amaranthe said, trying for a bright tone and not quite achieving it. "Glad we've eliminated that possibility. Maybe he's just getting old and feeling guilty over some of the choices he's made of late. Or maybe he's tired of his usual flunkies and wanted someone new to talk to. Or *maybe*," she said with a self-deprecating eye roll, "it's my friendly personality that got him chatting."

"Huh," he said. It was ambiguous, but at least his tone was a little lighter. Less dangerous.

Still, it wasn't until he clasped his hands behind his back and turned toward the window that she dared look at him again. Despite his recent workout, his black shirt was tucked in, his pants free of wrinkles, and his low boots brushed clean of dust. No hint of beard stubble softened

the hard angles of his jaw. Even his fingernails were trimmed and free of dirt. Only that uncontrolled nest of blond hair did not match his fastidious appearance. At the moment, she could hardly judge cleanliness, though, not when she could smell the stale sickness clinging to her body.

She needed a bath and a change of clothing. But she still had to win him to her side. Delving into his history was apparently not the way to do it. She decided to go back to what had inveigled his assistance before.

"I mean to save the emperor," Amaranthe said. "Not just that. I want to stop Hollowcrest from drugging him and protect him from Forge's assassins. I can't do it alone."

"A monumental task." At least he didn't say, "What makes you think you can do it at all?"

"With my plan, we can do it."

Sicarius faced her again. "What plan?"

If this was to be played at all, it had to be played fearlessly. She took a deep breath. "One that requires me not smelling like a ten-day-old corpse. If you can get me a bath and a couple of changes of clothing, I'll tell you everything."

His dark eyes narrowed, and once again Amaranthe remembered his knack for sensing deception. A long moment passed before he spoke, and it was only to say, "Agreed," before he left the room.

She sagged against the wall with relief. That conversation had drained her more than running the whole lake once had. She wondered how long it would take him to arrange a bath. Or more precisely, she wondered how long she had to come up with a plan. She laid on her back, intending to think of something brilliant. Instead, she fell asleep.

A clank woke her. Amaranthe sat up, cursing the disease that left her so weak. Sicarius had produced a metal laundry bin. Inside, water shimmered yellow with the reflection of lamplight. He had even scrounged a towel and a bar of soap. She beamed with heartfelt pleasure for the first time in days. Sicarius dropped a nondescript set of utility clothing on her cot.

Still clutching the blanket around herself, Amaranthe shuffled over to the tub and dipped a toe in. She withdrew it with a startled squawk. "This is ice water!"

"Naturally." Sicarius tilted his head toward the wall dividing the room from thousands of tons of ice.

Amaranthe bent over the tub and picked out the remains of a block that had not melted completely. Her shoulders slumped. It was not that she had never taken a cold bath—the single room she had shared with her father as a girl had not had plumbing much less hot water. It was just that... She sighed. It had been a rough week, and she wanted a relaxing soak.

She forced herself to thank Sicarius since he had, after all, dragged blocks of ice up there and melted them. Her expression of gratitude was somewhat muffled by the noise she made shoving the tub across the room until it was so close to the stove she would be hard-pressed to get in without searing something important.

"Are you going to watch?" Amaranthe asked when Sicarius did not leave.

"Your plan," Sicarius said, implying he was waiting to hear it.

You too, huh?

"Well, I need to be clean before I can discuss anything of this magnitude."

His flat stare said he knew she was stalling. He probably knew she had nothing. Nonetheless, he was still waiting. Maybe he had faith she could come up with something. Or maybe he could not think of a plan either and was desperate enough to listen to a foolish woman who had almost gotten herself killed twice in the same week.

"Fine," Amaranthe said. "Stay and watch if you want."

She shucked the blanket and grabbed the soap. After stepping in, she scrubbed—and thought—furiously. The emperor was threatened from two fronts: Hollowcrest, and all those who were loyal to him, and Forge, who was nameless and faceless for the time. The organization had to consist of business people and was an entity large enough to present a threat to the emperor. That implied wealth and power. Both her adversaries had power. She had none. She had...desperation. And maybe the help of a trained assassin, if she could woo him with her plan.

She shook her head. She needed to adjust her thinking. No general ever won a victory by pitting his weaknesses against the enemy's strengths. It had to be the other way around. What were her strengths? Since she would soon be labeled a criminal, she supposed there was no need to be constrained by the law. She found that thought unsettling, but it inspired creativity. Criminals did all sorts of unorthodox things to

get what they wanted from each other. What could she do? Use force? Steal? Blackmail?

Amaranthe realized she had been lathering the same shoulder with the bar of soap for some time. She switched to a leg.

Force was out. If she couldn't bring herself to assassinate a murdering assassin, she doubted she could kill anybody else in cold blood either. Nor would stealing get her anywhere. Blackmail? What could she hold over both parties? Economic trouble? That would be a disaster for government and business alike, but she could hardly start a recession by willing one into existence. Not unless she could magically decrease the value of money. She supposed printing counterfeits would achieve that. The addition of fake paper money that was not backed by the gold in the Imperial Treasury could devalue all the real money out there, plus it would undermine people's confidence in the ranmya. The threat alone might be enough to coerce Hollowcrest and Forge into dealing.

Amaranthe let the soap fall from her fingers and leaned on the edge of the tub. You're not actually considering this, are you?

Deliberately sabotaging the economy. Her mind shied away from the potential for widespread devastation, the utter vileness of the idea. Of course, she would be operating on a bluff, with no intention of actually circulating the money. Forge and Hollowcrest would not know that. It would represent a tangible threat to them. In a period of hyperinflation, Forge's fortunes would become meaningless. Hollowcrest would have to deal with the repercussions of millions of citizens terrified their savings would evaporate. Yes, she decided, it might just worry both parties enough to negotiate with her.

She looked at Sicarius. He seemed lost in thought again and was not facing her direction. She experienced a surge of indignity that he did not find her interesting enough to peep at in the bath but forced herself back to more important issues.

"I have finalized the details of my plan," she announced.

"Really," he said dryly.

"We're going to produce counterfeit money." She went on to explain her reasoning and emphasized several times her intent to bluff rather than unleash the fake bills. "We'll have to make enough, however, to lend a sense of verisimilitude to our operation."

Sicarius did not speak for a time after she finished. Amaranthe waited apprehensively, afraid he would reject her plan, point out a dozen reasons it was ludicrous, or simply walk out without saying anything.

"I would not have expected such an idea from an enforcer," he said.

"But do you think it could *work*?"

Sicarius made a noncommittal gesture with his hand. "Theoretically, it's possible. To set everything up in two weeks is improbable."

"I could get some more men to help," she said.

"You have underworld connections? Money to pay people?"

"No, but anyone can run a printing press once it's set up. I'm sure I can explain the situation to a couple of folks and enlist their help." Of course, she would have to *get* a press and find someone to engrave ranmya plates, but she would worry about that later.

Sicarius's blond eyebrows twitched upward. From him, it seemed a riot of emotion. Unfortunately, the emotion was skepticism.

"If I can get a couple men to help with printing, and maybe someone who could assist with researching Forge, would you agree to stick with me for the duration? If Sespian's birthday approaches, and it's obvious this won't work, I won't begrudge you for leaving. If you have a better idea, right now, I won't begrudge you for leaving. I suppose you could assassinate Hollowcrest and the Forge people, if you can figure out who they are, and then you wouldn't need me and my crazy plan. As much as I'd love to clear my name by being the one to rescue the emperor, what really matters is saving him, period."

"I've never heard of Forge before," Sicarius admitted. "With time, I could identify the leaders, but someone who could more easily move about the business world might make a less obtrusive and more efficient researcher."

Amaranthe bit back a smile. In other words he needed a girl, ideally one who had gone to business school before becoming an enforcer. At last she had something to offer him as an ally.

"I'm sure someone from my old school could suggest a starting point," was all she said.

"I know someone who could be a feasible research assistant."

"Oh? A friend of yours?" Amaranthe tried not to grimace. One assassin was all she could imagine working with at a time.

"No."

"But he'd help us?"

"I'd have to threaten him to get him to work for me," Sicarius said. "Perhaps you can recruit him by other means."

"I can. It won't be a problem." She was overselling herself, but for some strange reason she felt more exhilarated than terrified.

"If you can get a team together, I'll work with you."

Amaranthe just managed to curtail a triumphant fist pump. "That'll be acceptable. Any other concerns? Any questions?"

"One," he said. "During what phase of this plan will you start wearing clothes?"

She looked down. It wasn't exactly that she had forgotten she was standing in icy water, stark naked; she'd just forgotten to care. Reminded of her state, she blushed and grabbed the towel.

"Truly, Sicarius, if it weren't for your sinister reputation, I'd suspect you of a sense of humor."

"Huh," was all he said as he walked out the door.

CHAPTER 8

A LOCOMOTIVE ROARED THROUGH TOWN, RAT-
tling barred windows, and kicking up a newspaper that
skidded across the icy street to smack Amaranthe's calf. She
shook it off with a sheepish glance at Sicarius. Dressed all in black—
again—he waited at the base of steps leading up to the Brookstar Tenements. Only his panoply of daggers and throwing knives broke the
monochromatic look of his attire. Fate, she supposed, would never be
so blasphemous as to pelt him with trash.

She adjusted the tight collar of her business suit. Where he had
found the outfit, she did not know, but everything from the boots to
gloves to the parka and fur cap fit reasonably well. And there were no
grizzly bloodstains to suggest he had killed someone to get it. That was
something, at least.

"I'm ready," Amaranthe called over the chugging wheels of the
locomotive.

Sicarius led the way up the cracked concrete steps. Black, textured
mats covered the ice but did little to enhance the decor of the old brick
building. At the door, Amaranthe paused to straighten a sign that promised the availability of rooms for monthly, weekly, nightly, or hourly
usage.

Inside, they stopped before a desk manned by a plump grandmotherly woman. Forehead furrowed, she did not look up. An abacus rested
on the desk, and she alternately flicked its wooden beads and scribbled
figures in a ledger.

"Is Marl Mugdildor here?" Sicarius asked.

"No."

"He may go by Books."

The landlady regarded them for the first time. "Yes, are you relatives? Are you here to pay his bill?"

Amaranthe sighed. Sicarius's acquaintance did not sound particularly reputable.

"No," she said. "We have some business with him. Can you direct us to his room?"

The landlady eyed Sicarius with apprehension. "Books, he's not a bad fellow, just had a rough time this past year. He doesn't really deserve..." She cleared her throat and turned beseeching eyes toward Amaranthe, probably thinking they had come to collect on a loan.

Sicarius did have the icy demeanor of a debt collector. If only he were that benign, Amaranthe thought dryly.

"We aren't going to hurt him," she promised.

"He's usually in the common room on the third floor." The landlady scooted around the desk. "I'll show you up."

"Thank you," Amaranthe said.

A threadbare carpet led them up two flights of stairs permeated with the scent of lye, which did not quite overpower the underlying urine stench. At the end of the hall, the landlady stopped before a door and held up a finger.

"Let me just straighten him, er, the room up." She shuffled inside, shutting the door part way behind her.

For a moment, Amaranthe thought the lady meant to warn Books that someone was looking for him and that he should run, but exasperated words soon tumbled out, eliminating the concern.

"Books? Wake up, there's a pretty young lady here to see you. Are you drunk already? Here, comb your fingers through that, that, why can't you find someone to give you a haircut? And a shave? And, gah, why don't you use the baths? Give me that bottle. It's too early to be drinking. By the emperor's teeth, why don't you do something with yourself? You owe me three months back rent. Straighten up. You're slouching like a—"

"Leave me be, you meddling shrew!" The male speaker, voice raspy from disuse, sounded hung over.

Amaranthe put her hand over her face and shook her head. She looked at Sicarius through her fingers. As usual, his expression was unreadable.

Maybe this was a test. If she couldn't get this Books to help them, Sicarius would know she wouldn't be able to deliver on her other promises either. If that was true, she had better win this fellow to their cause.

She lifted her chin and pushed the door open, entering even as the landlady was on the way out. Arms laden with wine bottles, crusty food plates, and newspapers, she wore a harassed expression but struggled to smile for Amaranthe.

"All yours," the landlady said, as if she had done some great favor in "straightening" Books for his guest. If anything, the man would be harder than ever to talk to after that nagging session.

"Thank you," Amaranthe said anyway and plucked a half-full bottle off the top of the passing stack.

Inside a spacious common room, three men sat near a clean but cracked window, chortling in the aftermath of the landlady's ire. A game of green Strat Tiles sprawled over their table like creeping ivy. A young fellow with the mien of a university student sat reading near another window. When Amaranthe saw the textbooks on mathematics and engineering stacked next to him, she sighed wistfully. Why couldn't this have been Sicarius's acquaintance?

In the darkest corner of the room, in a faded floral chair, sat an unkempt man with gray peppering his bushy beard and scraggily black hair. He glared at Amaranthe, or maybe just at the door in general. Wine stained his shirt in multiple places.

When Sicarius glided in, the man's brown eyes bulged.

"Dark Vengeful Emperor!"

"That's not the name he gave me," Amaranthe said with a smile, "but details aren't important."

The man hunkered deeper in the chair.

Sicarius cleared his throat. The gamers and the student looked at him.

"Leave us," he said.

Amaranthe was glad the cold voice was not directed at her. The four men considered him, and the small armory he wore, for only a second before obeying.

Making no effort to greet—or even acknowledge—Books, Sicarius walked over to a window overlooking the street. It seemed Amaranthe was on her own.

She strolled closer to Books, forcing herself to keep the smile, despite the miasma of alcohol and unwashed armpits clinging to him. His gaze latched onto the bottle she had purloined from the landlady.

"I'm Amaranthe," she said. "Do you have a few minutes? I could use your advice."

His mouth sagged open. He made a show of sticking his finger in his ear, cleaning it out, and turning it toward her. "You're a woman, and you want *my* advice? You don't want to *give* me advice?"

She wondered how many tirades he had suffered from the landlady and felt a sympathetic twinge. "What would I advise you on? I'm sure you can handle your own problems."

"Then by all means, join me."

"Marl Mugdildor, right?" She deposited the wine bottle in his lap, dragged over a lumpy chair, and placed it closer to him than her nose suggested wise. "Or do you prefer Books?"

He seemed surprised to have his bottle returned. "I prefer Marl, but precaution necessitated the assumption of that dubious sobriquet." He took a swig of wine.

Given his sobriety level, Amaranthe was surprised he had made it through that tangle of words without stumbling. She supposed with a nickname like 'Books,' he must be a librarian or a teacher.

"Not that it matters. I don't care if they find me or not anymore." He held out the bottle, offering her a drink.

"You're being chased too?" She accepted the bottle and, doubting he would be impressed if she went and found glasses, took a sip. The wine was as mellow as a steam hammer, but she held back her grimace. She caught Sicarius glancing her way and felt a self-conscious stab. Yes, I'm sharing a drink with someone in the middle of the morning. Go back to watching out the window for enforcers.

"Probably not any more. I don't know." Books's bleary eyes focused on her. "Too?"

Amaranthe debated what to tell him. If enforcers were chasing him, he might not appreciate her occupation—former occupation—but if he found something similar in their stories, it could only help establish a

rapport. "I'm not actually sure anyone is chasing me yet. If I'm lucky, they think I'm dead. But somehow I doubt Commander of the Armies Hollowcrest—"

"Hollowcrest!" Books sat up straight. "That murdering bastard!"

"Er, yes," Amaranthe said, "that was his intent for me. He tried to kill you?" What could an academic have done to earn Hollowcrest's ire? She almost snorted. What had *she* done?

Books slumped back in the chair, accepting the bottle when she passed it to him. "He had enforcers kill my son."

"What? Enforcers wouldn't kill a boy. They—"

"I'm not lying!" He clenched the chair arms, knuckles white. Almost immediately the anger turned to anguish and his face contorted with grief. "Why would anyone lie about...?"

For a moment, Amaranthe was too dumbfounded to respond. Enforcers had murdered a child? Even under Hollowcrest's orders, they should never have done something so horrible. Some orders could not be followed.

No? Maybe they were hoping for promotions.

Amaranthe snapped at her too-frank conscience. She was different. I'm different. Still, the comparison was unsettling.

"I'm sorry," she said. "I can see you're telling the truth."

Books didn't relax, but his voice returned to a less agitated register. "The enforcers do whatever Hollowcrest wants. My son, Enis, was only fourteen. He was so excited to earn a summer job working at the newspaper. He wanted to prove he could do more than run the presses. He set out to find stories, but he was...a little too good at investigating." Books sighed and looked over her head, eyes distant. "He saw Hollowcrest and his flunkies murder a Nurian diplomat. He ran back to me at work, but they'd seen him, and I didn't get him to safety in time. It's all my fault. If I'd believed him right away..." Books drained the rest of the bottle. "The enforcers cut him down in the courtyard below my office window. I screamed, and they saw me. I should have just stayed there, let them finish me. What was left after that? My wife left years ago." He picked at a thread on the chair arm. "But, coward that I am, I ran."

Amaranthe wondered how many times Books had sat here reliving those moments. Maybe the alcohol let him forget sometimes.

"Six enforcers chased me out of the city and into the Emperor's Preserve. They were younger, faster, and they were about to catch me when I ran into..." Books looked at Sicarius, who had moved to another window, checking a different street, and did not look back.

Amaranthe shifted in her chair. This story sounded familiar. Last summer, she remembered hearing about a squad of enforcers who had been found murdered outside the city. The killer had not been identified.

"We'd met the day before, you see," Books continued. "When everything was still normal in my life. He was in the library researching some artifact I later found out he'd been hired to retrieve. I walked up to see if I could help him, told him I was a history professor, and—" Books glanced at Sicarius again and lowered his voice, "—he just stared at me, and I swear he was thinking about killing me just for daring talk to him."

Sicarius, whether curious about something he had seen outside or just aware he was crimping story hour, chose that moment to walk out of the room.

Books lunged forward and startled Amaranthe by grabbing her arm. "What are you *doing* with him? Do you have a death wish?"

The concern on the older man's face surprised her, and she kept herself from pulling away.

"We have an agreement," she said. "He's helping me to protect the emperor and maybe get Hollowcrest out of power."

"He is *not* helping you. If he hasn't killed you yet, it's because you're helping him."

"What happened in the preserve?"

"He was camped there and saw me run in. Apparently, he had a use for a history professor in his research after all. He decided to haul me all over the satrapy to help with his assignment."

"What happened to the enforcers?" She shouldn't ask. It would be better not to know for sure, but she supposed she already did.

"Oh, he killed them. Six men in about six seconds. Maybe ten because the last one had time to get down on his knees and beg for his life, which earned him a dagger in the eye."

"I see." Amaranthe sat back in her own chair, and Books released her arm. She clasped her hands in her lap as she struggled for detachment. It's not as if you didn't know what he is.

"He says he never leaves enemies behind, and I got to see more evidence of that on our little adventure."

"He did save your life," Amaranthe said. "And he let you live afterward."

"Because I was useful to him, and I wasn't a threat. Don't think we walked away friends. I was trying to mourn the loss of my son—actually I was thinking about killing myself—and he didn't care, not one iota. In the end... Never mind. Just, listen to me on this: don't *ever* let him think you're a threat."

"I understand. Thank you." Amaranthe drew in a deep breath. She had meant to get Books sympathizing with her, not the other way around.

"What advice did you want?" he asked.

She shared the last week's events, glossing over Sicarius's role and her suppositions about him. She finished by explaining her counterfeiting scheme.

Books stared at her a while before speaking. Remembering Sicarius's similar pregnant pause, she wondered if she should be worried that her plans stunned men to silence.

"While I suspect a female enforcer is indeed the perfect person to research an underground business coalition, I don't see how you can possibly start a counterfeiting operation in two weeks. It's not something you saw done in your years as an enforcer, is it?"

Sicarius returned to the room and his self-appointed observation post at the window.

"No," Amaranthe said. "I thought there might be a historical precedent you'd know about."

"It has been attempted numerous times in the empire and even more often in the desert city-states. Elsewhere, gold and silver coinage is preferred over paper money, which is more susceptible to clipping than forgery. In any instance, counterfeiting is a huge liability for all governments, and they squash startups quickly. It has, however, been successful in the short term for various criminals seeking to enrich themselves and for governments seeking to undermine enemy nations. It's not so much that your plan doesn't have merit; it's that it would take months to set up. The paper ranmyas are printed on is a proprietary blend of hemp and pulp, and it's not something you can buy. And let's talk about crafting the plates themselves. Do you know a crooked engraver who will help?"

"See—" Amaranthe was more delighted than chagrinned at his logic, "—I knew you could help. You've already thought of more than I had. You're perfect."

Books snorted, but a smile peeked through that overgrown beard, and something more.... Pleasure at being needed again? Maybe that was it.

"Your points are valid," she said, "but, remember, we don't have to successfully print billions of ranmyas and pass them to all the storekeepers of the city. We just have to make some convincing-on-the-surface copies, enough to concern Hollowcrest and Forge and bring them together to deal."

"We?" Books rubbed his lips. "Are you here for my advice or to enlist my aid?"

She smiled. "Yes."

"I see. Well, this is the least tedious chat I've had in a long time, and I could use a distraction." His eyes flickered toward the bottle. "It's clear you desperately need my help."

"Desperately," Amaranthe agreed. "And then there's that landlady who's on the verge of kicking you out."

"Indeed. I suppose payment will be in counterfeits?"

She coughed. "Well, I wasn't planning to circulate any of the bills. I do have a few scruples left."

"So, no payment at all?"

"I can promise you a place to sleep and food to eat." Actually, she couldn't yet, but she would figure out a way to make it happen. "Think about it." She stood and dragged the chair back to its original location, identifiable by the lighter, stain-free square of carpet. "If you decide to come, you can find us at the icehouse on Fourth and Wharf Street in the morning."

"Wharf Street? Didn't something just happen down there?" Books peered about. "Drat, that nag took my papers."

"Nothing to do with our mission." She hoped.

After a farewell wave, she trailed Sicarius into the hallway. Outside the building, gray clouds had thickened, blanketing the city. The breeze smelled of snow, and Amaranthe pulled her parka tight.

She glanced at Sicarius. "What do you think? Any chance he'll come?"

"Perhaps. You found his vulnerabilities and exploited them."

Amaranthe winced. Was that what it seemed like to him? How could she relate to someone who saw everything as a battlefield?

An intrepid bicycle delivery boy skidded out from a narrow street, tires rasping on sanded concrete. He cut across their path, daring icy roads for his employer. A tower of crates strapped down with cords tottered behind him. Amaranthe wished she had a bicycle so she could move around the city without having to walk. She had not fully recovered from her illness and likely would not for several days.

"I'm going to look for more recruits," she said. "Could you find us a place to set up our operation? We'll need more room than the packed icehouse provides, and I'm not convinced someone won't walk in to check on the stores before we finish. Also—" she fished out a scrap of paper she had written on that morning, "—this is my address. For obvious reasons, I'd be stupid to show up there, but perhaps you could slip in undetected at some point. There's a box under a loose floorboard between the bed and the wall. There's about a thousand ranmyas in it." Along with some sentimental mementos she hoped Sicarius wouldn't poke through. "I'm hoping it'll be enough to buy a used press, paper, and ink." She supposed stealing paper and ink would be possible but a printing press?

Sicarius accepted the address and left without a word.

Amaranthe waited until he disappeared around a corner, then she leaned against the nearest wall. She had only been awake a couple of hours, but exhaustion dragged at her. The only thing worse than being weak was being seen being weak. She wanted Sicarius to have confidence in her, not worry about her collapsing.

After resting for a few moments, she headed for the business district. Unemployed men and women often loitered outside shops, hoping to win a day's work. Such folks might be converted to her cause.

A few blocks in, she turned a corner and almost collided with a pair of enforcers on patrol. Her heart lurching, she tried to keep the concern off her face. She nodded greetings to them and continued past. A few steps later, she glanced in a storefront window, pretending interest in a strop-and-razor kit. The enforcers had stopped and were staring at her. Did Hollowcrest already have the word out about her? Had he guessed Sicarius would find someone to heal her?

One man pointed at her. Great.

When she resumed walking, Amaranthe kept her pace normal. This wasn't her old district, and the enforcers did not know her. They must only suspect her of matching a certain description, or they would have already arrested her.

She turned into an alley at the next corner. When she reached the other end, she turned again, glancing back the way she had come without moving her head. The two enforcers were entering the alley. Definitely following her.

Telling herself to stay calm, she eyed the passing storefronts, businesses, and eating houses. Due to gathering storm clouds, or just bad luck, little foot traffic harried the street. No chance of losing the enforcers in a crowd. If she ducked into a building and slipped out the back door, maybe she could elude them. She crossed the street and turned again at the next intersection.

A sign caught her eye: MALE ESCORTS.

Amaranthe darted into the establishment, suspecting her male followers would prove reluctant to step inside. With luck, they would search every other building on the street first.

Inside, a tall ceiling rose two stories and disappeared over the railing of a loft on the second floor. Several fine couches and overstuffed chairs welcomed visitors. Amaranthe, who was no more likely to visit such an establishment than the enforcers outside, half-expected men draped across the furniture. Only one person occupied the room, however, a handsome, impeccably dressed woman.

"Greetings, do you have an upcoming event that you require an escort for?"

Did blackmailing the most powerful man in the empire count as an event? Amaranthe resisted the urge to ignore the woman and hunt for a backdoor. If she plowed through, the proprietor would be suspicious, and likely volunteer information to the enforcers when they came in. If Amaranthe was a potential customer, though, the woman might be less inclined to point her out.

"Possibly," Amaranthe said. "Do you have..." A list? A pamphlet? A room full of naked men lined up like pastries on the shelf at Curi's Bakery? "How does it work?"

"Why don't you tell me what you're planning and I can suggest someone?" the woman said. "We have a wide variety of men available. Their fees vary depending on their popularity and skills. Some are just pretty faces, while others are experts in manners and etiquette appropriate for any occasion. If you need not only an escort but a bodyguard, we have several former military men available."

As if waiting off-stage for this introduction, the most handsome man Amaranthe had ever seen strolled into the room. He was a foot taller than her, a couple of years older, broad of shoulder, and nicely muscular, as revealed by the lone piece of clothing he wore: a—was that fur?—loincloth. To fight reddening cheeks, she forced her attention to his face. Curly brown hair hung tied back from his neck, leaving a few wisps to frame prominent cheek bones and clean jaw. His warm brown eyes glinted with good humor.

After a flustered moment during which she could not remember her name or why she was there, Amaranthe's mind shifted to calculation. She imagined the ink-and-paper purchasing trip she must soon go on. With her buying, the merchant would say, "Yes, that will be full price plus tax and a shelving fee." With him buying, it would be, "Oh, no, I couldn't possibly charge you for these supplies, and are you available for dinner tonight, my treat?" That was probably an exaggeration, but with most of the business in the city handled by women, surely he could arrange hefty discounts simply by smiling.

"Costasce," the man said to the proprietor, "you told me Lady Ludwist was a sophisticated woman from a warrior-caste family. You didn't say she was five hundred years old."

"Nonetheless, I notice you're not returning from your evening's duties until—" Costasce pulled out a pocket watch, "—10:30 the next morning. It couldn't have been that unpleasant."

The man appeared scandalized. He shuddered. "That old crone hung on to me like a starving titmouse grasping for the last piece of corn before winter, but I assure you there were no extra services performed. Not that she didn't try to inveigle them out of me. After the harrowing experience, I chose to spend the night drinking myself into a state of amnesia."

"Maldynado, go sit down. Can't you see I'm doing business?"

"Sure, boss. I just thought you might like to show off some of the wares."

With no sense of humility or embarrassment, Maldynado stuck a thumb in his loincloth and struck a pose that displayed...a lot. An easy-going smile and amused gleam in his eyes suggested he neither took himself seriously nor expected anyone else to.

"Oh, sit down," the proprietor said, tone somewhere between exasperation and affection.

Maldynado offered the sort of sweeping bow the warrior caste had spent generations perfecting, then ambled across the room and flopped onto a sofa.

"What's his story?" Amaranthe glanced toward the door as she spoke, torn between wanting to flee and wanting to recruit this Maldynado.

"Hm, eighth son in an old warrior caste family. Apparently, he refused to go to officer candidate school and join the military. He's been loafing around on the family estate since. His parents disowned him, and he showed up here a few months ago. Despite being lazy, his looks have made him profitable." The woman's face took on a speculative cast as she studied Amaranthe. "He can put on good manners if the situation demands it, and he's one of the top-ranked duelists in the city, if you have need for protection."

"A fencing expert?" Amaranthe knew little about the sport dueling the warrior caste practiced, except that enlisted soldiers had little respect for it. A gentleman's game or not, it was still an art that required years to master. Hardly the pedigree of a lazy man. "May I speak with him?"

"Of course." The proprietor withdrew to give them privacy.

Amaranthe paused at a window to peer both directions down the street. She was just in time to see the two enforcers entering an alley that advertised several shops and cafes. Good, she had a few minutes.

She sat next to Maldynado. "I hear you're a highly ranked swordsman."

He smirked. "In more ways than one."

Amaranthe resisted the urge to roll her eyes. With his looks, anything less than a gargantuan ego would have been shocking.

"Are you a gambling man, Lord Maldynado?" Amaranthe asked.

"Just Maldynado. I've been disowned, you know. What kind of gambling?"

"I have a comrade who is something of a fighter. What would you say to a contest?"

Maldynado's eyes narrowed. "It's not Jano or Kasowits, is it?"

"No."

He relaxed and threw his arm over the back of the sofa. "Your friend prefer saber or rapier?"

"I'm not sure. I've actually never seen him fight." Unless the time Sicarius had almost killed her counted.

"Ah." The confident smirk twitched across Maldynado's face again. "What did you want to wager on the outcome?"

"If my man wins, you will work for me for two weeks without pay, though I will see to it that you are fed and have a place to stay."

"What kind of work?"

He was smarter than she had first guessed. Confident or not, he wanted the details before he committed himself. She leaned forward conspiratorially and lowered her voice.

"I confess, it's slightly illegal, but you shouldn't be in any danger. I just need help setting things up."

Maldynado appeared more intrigued than appalled. But then, the warrior caste tended to think itself above the law. Besides, he was probably bored after spending the last couple months chaperoning old ladies around.

"Danger doesn't scare me," he said.

"I mean to help the emperor. I've recently found out he's in trouble from his trusted advisors."

Maldynado lifted his shoulder, apparently less interested by this addendum. "So, what do I get if I win?" A suggestive leer accompanied the question, but his innuendo failed to obtain a sinister note. The amused warmth never left his eyes.

"What do you want?"

"How about the same deal?" he suggested. "Your buddy loses, and you work for me for two weeks. Doing anything I say."

"Agreed. Though my period of indenture could not begin until I finish my current work. After the emperor's birthday."

"What happens if you get caught?"

"That is a risk," she said. More of one than she cared to admit.

"I want three weeks then."

"Fair."

"Dusk at the Scarbay Gymnasium," Maldynado said. "I'll arrange a judge. You and your pal just show up."

"Agreed." Amaranthe stood. "Oh, uhm, if any enforcers wander in, I wasn't here."

"Of course not." Maldynado winked.

With his help, Amaranthe found a back exit out of the establishment. She eased through the alley, watching for enforcers. Though she did not see any, she decided a quick trolley ride out of the neighborhood was in order.

Her car rumbled beneath a clock tower as it tolled eleven. She had plenty of time to return and talk Sicarius into his evening bout. Since Books was no guarantee, she felt obligated to search for another worker.

She dared not return to the business district, so she let the car speed her toward the factories and warehouses along the waterfront. Before she reached the industrial area, she spotted a crowd gathered in a square near one of the stops. Raucous shouts and curses rose above the churning wheels of the trolley. Curious, she disembarked.

In the center of the throng, a young man stood locked into a pillory, wrists and neck bound by heavy timbers. Expletives flew through the air along with rotten apples. The freezing temperatures gave the fruit the authority of stones, as evinced by a number of bruises swelling on the man's face. Hardly a man. Dressed in oversized clothing, he appeared no more than sixteen or seventeen. On one hand, he bore the circle-and-arrow brand of the Black Arrows. The last time she had seen the mark had been on one of the infected men in the dungeon. They could only be dead now, she thought darkly. Across the back of the prisoner's shirt, someone had chalked WIZARD. That accounted for the flying fruit.

The gang brand on the young man's hand almost made Amaranthe reject him without further consideration, but the clouds started unloading snow, and the crowd thinned in response. She edged closer.

"What's the matter, lady?" His teeth chattered. Fat snowflakes fell and landed on his bare hands and unprotected head. "You forget your apple?"

"I'm not a lady," she said, sympathetic to his shivers. "My name is Amaranthe."

"Like I care."

She withdrew her sympathy. If Maldynado had been charming, this boy was his utter opposite.

"Are you really a wizard?" She doubted it but wondered how he had been insinuated. She was surprised none of his underworld brethren had come to help him escape, or at least ward off the fruit throwers. Shattered apples lay on the ground at his feet, the scent of their rotten insides overpowering the crisp smell of snow.

"You stupid or something?" he asked. "No one in the empire would be crazy enough to practice the mental sciences. They hang you for that."

Amaranthe's head jerked up. He had not replied with the familiar Turgonian mantra: magic does not exist. Even more interesting, he had used the term 'mental sciences,' like Sicarius did when referring to magic.

"Then why are you locked up?" she asked.

"Accusations, that's all."

"Who did the accusing?"

A surge of hurt and anger flashed across his face before he turned it into a snarl. "Doesn't matter. Leave me alone, lady."

"Amaranthe," she corrected. "Amaranthe Lokdon."

"Still don't care."

Oh yes, this one would be a pleasure to work with. "Would you care if I could get you out of that contraption?"

"Don't need your help."

"No? Those contusions on your face suggest otherwise. I've seen relief maps of mountain ranges with fewer bumps."

He snorted. "Once it gets dark and people haul out of this square, I can get out on my own. I don't need your help." His gaze slid to the gang mark on his hand. "I don't need anyone's help."

Ah, betrayed by his comrades, was it? That would make one bitter.

"Planning to use magic to get free?" she asked.

"I told you, no one uses magic in the empire. Cowards here are all scared of it, and there ain't no one you can trust to watch your back if you wanted to learn."

"I see. And it's important to have someone at your back?"

"Unless you're powerful good and can conjure up a bodyguard. The mental sciences take fierce concentration, and that makes you vulnerable to enemies while you're working your art."

A couple bundled against the snow shuffled through the edge of the square, and Amaranthe lowered her voice. If she was not careful, she might find herself strung up next to this fellow for reasons that had nothing to do with her past actions. "Why do you call it science instead of magic?'

"That's what it is: mastery of the mind. Using your brain to move and create things. It's not about praying to gods or chanting no stupid rituals like ign'ant folks think. That's just a show."

"What if I could offer you protection?" she said.

"You? Some businesswoman who doesn't even carry a knife?"

"I have a comrade who is gifted with weapons." Amaranthe wondered how Sicarius would feel about her using him to sway people to her cause. Unfortunately, he was her only asset. "If you would be willing to work for me, I'll see to it that you have food, a place to sleep, and someone to watch over you while you practice your 'science.'"

"Like I said, I'm not a wizard. And I'm not in a hurry to trust anyone like that. Trust is for fools who don't know any better."

"My comrade would probably agree with you. But consider this: while you may not be able to trust people to do what's in *your* best interest, you can always trust them to do what's in *their* best interest. I need a couple of men to work for me, so I can reach my goals. That means I'm going to do everything I can to take care of them, because without them, I fail. I'm giving you a chance to use me, and the comrade I can supply, to reach your own goals. We both win in this situation. No unwarranted trust required."

"Lady, you keep talking like I care."

Amaranthe shrugged and turned away. If nothing else, she had learned something about these mental sciences everyone seemed to know more about than she.

"Who's your friend?"

"What?" She turned back.

"The one you keep talking about. How am I supposed to know if he's good enough to be some wizard's bodyguard?"

"You tell me your name, and I'll tell you his."

"Akstyr."

Amaranthe glanced left and right, then stepped closer to him. "Have you heard the name Sicarius?"

He tried to throw back his head and laugh, but the pillory restricted the movement. "Yes, and if you think I believe he'd be working with a nosey businesswoman, you're dumber than the drooling lawmen who locked me up."

She wondered if there had been a long line of Black Arrows fighting for the pleasure of turning Akstyr over to the enforcers. "The icehouse on Fourth and Wharf Street. Meet us there in the morning, and you can see if I'm lying."

"Whatever."

Akstyr turned his face away and stared resolutely into the falling snow. Conversation over, his set jaw declared. Amaranthe hesitated, then took off her gloves and stuffed them over his hands. She put her fur cap on his head. Even if he could free himself after nightfall, that was hours away and he was not dressed for the cold. The youth gave no indication he appreciated the gesture.

She left, wondering if she had succeeded in winning anyone's aid or simply wasted one of the precious few days she had. At least Maldynado would help, assuming she won her bet. Her weariness and the heavy snowfall precluded further adventures, so she headed back, wondering how to convince Sicarius to take on a dueling match.

CHAPTER 9

WHEN AMARANTHE RETURNED TO THE ICE-house, she did not see Sicarius, but the mountains of frozen blocks hid a lot. Grinding machinery and yelling workers from neighboring buildings penetrated the walls. Inside, nothing stirred.

She padded around the perimeter of the building, her boots scattering sawdust. If Sicarius was sleeping down here, she saw no indication of it.

Her boots clanged on metal. She knelt to push aside sawdust, and the scent of cedar grew stronger. Beneath the wood chips, steel grates covered much of the floor. Many of them had hinges and handles. She unfastened one that was not barred with ice and peered inside the dark well. More ice. Ladders led down another fifteen feet to a massive chamber, where a single narrow corridor allowed access to the blocks. Packed with more insulation than the stacks above, the underground ice would probably last through the heat of the next summer.

She dropped the grate, turned around, and almost bumped into Sicarius.

He held out a familiar box. "Your flat is empty, and two enforcers are watching the building. This was still under the floorboards."

They had taken all her belongings? Her furniture, her weapons, her books, all her treasures and mementos?

Amaranthe sighed and accepted the age-worn alder box. She traced the faded yellow canary painted on the lid. Her mother, whom she barely remembered, had made it for her father when he first started working in the mines. *This is all that's left of my parents and my past.*

"Thank you," she murmured.

Amaranthe turned and took a few steps from Sicarius before lifting the lid. Her savings were still there, nestled next to an old but well-kept knife that had belonged to her grandfather. She removed both. She had never been able to wear the blade at work, since it was not enforcer-issue, but no one was around to set rules now. After a look at drawings of her parents and grandparents, she folded them and laid them to rest amongst running medals from the Junior Games, a marksmanship pin from the Academy, and silly treasures from her childhood.

"I located a fish cannery that's not used in the winter." Sicarius had moved to the stairs and laid out his weapons for cleaning. The tang of blade oil mingled with the aromatic cedar. "It has the prerequisite floor space, and there is little traffic on the street outside. We should not have to worry about someone hearing the creaking of the printing press."

"It'll have to wait for morning." Amaranthe took a deep breath and faced him. "You have a duel this evening."

"A what?"

"A duel. The recruit of one gentleman—" remembering the loin-cloth, Amaranthe almost choked over that title, "—is contingent on your besting him in a sword duel. I apologize for committing you without asking, but our time is limited."

"I don't duel."

Amaranthe had expected refusal or reluctance but not that statement. She surveyed the array of weapons in front of him. Garrote. Dagger. Throwing Knives. Dagger. Utility knife. Serrated jackknife. No swords. A flash of panic clutched at her chest. What if he had never used one? Maldynado, her only near-sure thing, might poke a thousand holes into her assassin, and where would her mission be then?

"Surely," Amaranthe said weakly, "you've some familiarity with swords."

Sicarius finished sharpening a dagger. "I can use a sword. I do not know the rules of sport dueling or much about it."

Great, neither did she. All she knew was that young members of the warrior caste found it fashionable as a means to acquire a scar or two before heading off to officer candidacy school.

"Who's my opponent?" Sicarius asked.

"His name's Maldynado. According to his current, ah, employer, he's highly ranked amongst the city's duelists. You say you've never dueled?"

"Never."

"This should be interesting then."

"I imagine so," Sicarius said.

* * * * *

Darkness was gathering in the streets when Amaranthe and Sicarius arrived at the gymnasium. The sprawling complex covered a city block and included a running track buried under a white field of snow, steam rooms, heated baths, and the area they approached: the rings.

"Remember," Amaranthe said, "the goal is to recruit this fellow to work for us. We don't want him killed or maimed."

Sicarius slanted her a cool look.

"Of course, you know this already. I'm just concerned that your—" she groped to express her concern diplomatically, "—admirably honed assassin's instincts might forget."

Silence was her answer.

She tried not to feel nervous. It didn't work.

They stepped inside a massive chamber open to the night on three sides. Intermittent columns offered the only barrier to the wind. Icicles like spears hung from the roof, which kept out the snow but little else. Bare-chested men, bodies too warm to notice the cold, sparred in circles chalked on the black clay floor. Spectators, and those waiting their turns, crowded the edges of the rings.

With a chill wind skidding fresh powder into the building, Amaranthe did not feel conspicuous keeping her hood pulled low over her eyes, the fur trim nuzzling her cheeks. Though they were in the upscale Mokath Ridge neighborhood, where low-paid enforcers would not make up any of the clientele, running into army officers was possible. Her encounter that morning left her inclined to keep her face hidden. Sicarius, striding along at her side, did not share her inclination. At least he was not wearing his knives and daggers openly tonight.

They passed small rings used for boxing and wrestling and weaved toward the larger circles. Amaranthe craned her neck, searching for

Maldynado. Despite night's approach, the area was well-lit by gas jets burning on the wall and braziers positioned between the circles.

A servant meandered through, offering water, towels, or bandages as needed. A musician wandered from fight to fight, beating an invigorating pattern on a hand drum. He held out his fur cap for donations between bouts.

"There he is," Amaranthe said.

She pointed out Maldynado, who stood near the wall, behind rings full of men sparring with rapiers and sabers. Since their last meeting, he had changed clothes—or at least added a few. Clad in a velvety exercise outfit that probably cost a week's enforcer salary, he was chatting with a balding man.

When they stepped within Maldynado's line of sight, he nodded toward Amaranthe and took in Sicarius with an unconcerned boot-to-head survey. His gaze lingered above Sicarius's eyebrows. Maldynado lifted a finger, walked over to a bag of gear, retrieved a card, and returned. He extended his arm toward Sicarius.

"My barber. He's excellent." Maldynado flicked his fingers at Sicarius's tousled hair. "He can fix that rat's nest."

Sicarius did not accept the card. He gave Maldynado that flat, cold stare he did exceedingly well. Though Maldynado was broader and half a head taller, he was the one who shifted uncomfortably. After a moment of silence, he cleared his throat and pocketed the card.

"Shall we begin then? Ado here will judge. First to five points wins." Maldynado winked at Amaranthe. "And collects the reward."

"A point is what?" Sicarius asked.

"Uhm, are you joking?"

"No."

"Ah," Maldynado said. "We use blunted swords and wear padded vests and helmets. Anything above the waist is a point. Anything below the waist is, well, no man should attack another man down there, eh? It's off target, no point. You have to stay in the ring or it's a penalty. Three penalties and you start losing points. Follow me. I'll show you the communal gear."

Amaranthe tagged along. Maldynado led them to an equipment chest jammed with bent and rusty blades. Another chest held equally dilapidated armor. Apparently, the serious folks had their own gear.

Maldynado set down his saber and shrugged into a pristine padded vest and grabbed a monogrammed helmet. With a wave, he indicated Sicarius should select from the chests and arm himself. Amaranthe crinkled her nose. She could smell the stale sweat from several feet away. Yellow stains marked the armpits of the vests and several sported dried blood spatters.

Sicarius selected a saber for his left hand and eschewed the armor. Amaranthe would have done the same, even if it meant death by impalement. So armed, he walked over to one side of a large circle and waited.

Maldynado nodded to Amaranthe. "What's his problem? He trying to get hurt? I thought you were bringing a serious contender."

"Oh, he's serious."

As she watched Sicarius waiting, dark eyes cold, face a mask, Amaranthe felt new twinges of uncertainty about engineering the match.

Maldynado shrugged. He ambled into the circle opposite Sicarius. He lifted his saber in a salute to his opponent and to the judge, then plopped the helmet over his curls. Sicarius did not return the salute. Amaranthe had heard of wine-stompers displaying more courtesy to the grapes in their vats.

She walked to the side where the judge stood. It might not hurt to get on friendly terms with him. "Good evening. Have you known Maldynado long?"

"Yes."

"Is he as good as he claims?"

"He has a lot of talent, but he doesn't train enough. Everything's a game to him."

As opposed to Sicarius, who had probably never played a game in his life. *I think I made a mistake.* She nibbled on a fingernail.

Maldynado assumed a ready position, elbow bent, weapon raised, side facing his opponent. Sicarius stood casually, sword lowered. Wind gusted through the columns and stirred his short blond hair.

"Ready?" the judge asked the combatants.

Maldynado bounced on his toes. "Ready!"

Sicarius gave a single nod.

The judge clapped his hands. "Begin!"

Sicarius charged like a locomotive, crossing the ring in less than a heartbeat. Maldynado side-stepped and stuck out his sword so his at-

tacker would run into it. Sicarius anticipated the move and blurred past the weapon. He darted to the outside, coming up behind Maldynado. Sicarius grabbed Maldynado's far shoulder, snaked his foot between the bigger man's legs, and thrust up with his hips even as he pulled down with his hand.

Maldynado toppled backward, accelerating to the ground. When he hit, his breath whooshed out, and his helmet spun into the air.

Sicarius went down with Maldynado, albeit in a more controlled manner. Sicarius pinned his opponent and jammed the blunt blade against Maldynado's throat.

Both combatants froze in tableau. Maldynado's helmet hit the ground, clattering as it bounced several feet.

Blunt weapon or not, Sicarius could have killed his opponent easily. Amaranthe read the fear in Maldynado's eyes, a reflection of what she had felt in nearly the same position.

The judge choked out a series of protests. "Warning for illegal use of the feet, body, hands. Out of bounds. No point!"

Sicarius rose lithely and returned to his side of the ring. The judge launched into a lecture on the rules while Maldynado groped for his helmet with a shaking hand. Sicarius listened without expression.

Amaranthe rubbed her face. What *was* he doing?

Maldynado pushed himself to his feet. He plopped the helmet back on his head. It obscured his features, but Amaranthe could read the reluctance in his sagging posture as he stepped back into the ring.

Perhaps sensing more than a practice bout, other men drifted over. Amaranthe resumed nibbling on her fingernail and watched the crowd. This was far too public. She should not have let Maldynado choose the meeting area.

Two of the onlookers whispered and pointed at Sicarius. Making bets or discussing the number of wanted posters they had seen him on?

"Point," the judge called.

Amaranthe started. She had missed the resumption of the match. She glanced at the judge in time to see him stab a finger at Sicarius.

"Begin," the judge said after the two fighters returned to their sides.

This time Amaranthe watched. Sicarius charged across the ring again. Maldynado skittered aside, but not before Sicarius tapped him on the ribs with his saber. Maldynado's attempt to parry came too late.

He was rattled. Sicarius's opening strategy became clear. What man could concentrate on a game when he was afraid his opponent would kill him?

Maldynado charged the next time. That did not keep Sicarius from doing the same. They met in the middle. Maldynado feinted and lunged only to find Sicarius's blade pressed against his chest, his own uselessly wide.

"Three to zero," the judge said.

Shaking his head, Maldynado returned to his side. The onlookers nodded their admiration for Sicarius's speed and accuracy.

"Watch his footwork," someone said.

"It's amazing."

On the next round, Sicarius feinted to the head before gliding under Maldynado's raised guard to prod him in the side. Unlike Maldynado, Sicarius never seemed to lunge. He was just there. Amaranthe had seen men with lightning-fast hands before. She had never seen anyone's feet move so quickly. The last point came when Sicarius side-stepped Maldynado's vain charge and jabbed him in the kidney.

Maldynado, blade drooping, stared at Sicarius's feet as he walked away. Maldynado saw it too. But too late to figure out a way to compensate. If he could.

"Match over," the judge said. "Winner." He pointed to Sicarius, though he grumbled to himself.

"Not a typical bout?" Amaranthe asked.

"It got off to an appalling beginning. Your comrade has poor sportsmanship."

"Yes, I don't think he's really into sports."

"Maldynado should have recovered better though. He wasn't fighting his best."

One hand braced against his back, Maldynado hobbled to the wall and removed his gear. He waited—at some distance—while Sicarius returned his blade. Maldynado's gaze never left Sicarius. To his credit, it was not a glower of hatred, but one of wariness. At least he did not seem to be entertaining notions of vengeance. Amaranthe knew many men would be if they perceived their pride damaged.

"My...comrade rattles everyone," she said to the judge. "It's not Maldynado's fault."

"I wish I could have awarded Maldynado a few points, at least," the judge said. "He has superior style and technique."

"If he hadn't been shaken in the beginning, do you think he would have won?"

"No, your man is too fast. It might have been a more interesting match, but..." The judge massaged his bald pate. "Technically speaking, Maldynado is the better fencer. Your man is the better killer."

Amaranthe nodded. The accolade certainly did not surprise.

Maldynado approached her as the judge departed. Sweat dampened the strands of curly brown hair that hung in his eyes. Sicarius came, too, and Maldynado sidled away, giving him more wary glances.

Amaranthe waved Sicarius back. "Can you give us a moment, please?"

Sicarius went outside with spectators moving far aside to let him pass.

"Two weeks starting tomorrow at dawn." Amaranthe gave Maldynado the address to the icehouse. "Agreed?"

He sighed. "I'll be there. Will *he* be there?"

"Yes, but he won't bother you if you don't bother him. We're all working toward the same goal."

Maldynado rubbed the back of his head. "I'm going to be reliving those opening two seconds over and over for a long time, trying to figure out what I should have done there." He met her eyes. "I don't want you to think I'm...I mean, I know how to fight. I've been in real brawls, not just dueling matches. He...caught me by surprise."

"I know. He did the same thing to me. Had me within a half-inch of breaking my neck before we reached an agreement."

"Huh. And you trust him now?" Maldynado asked.

"As long as we're angling toward the same ends and can benefit from each others' skills, I believe we can work together."

"So, the answer is no."

Amaranthe smiled faintly and shrugged.

"What happens after you two don't have a common goal anymore? He whacks you and moves on? Some trust."

"It's enough for now," Amaranthe said. "Just as I trust you to show up tomorrow and work for me for two weeks."

Maldynado blinked. "You do? Why?"

"I believe you're an honorable man."

Another blink. Several actually. Amaranthe only meant it to inspire him to come in the morning, but he straightened and nodded, as if the comment meant something.

"Yes," he said. "Right. I'll see you tomorrow."

* * * * *

Sespian looked up from a report when the door opened and Jeddah walked into the suite. Trog sauntered into the servant's path, but Jeddah managed to maintain his poise—and hold onto the tray with Sespian's tea—without tripping when the cat rubbed against his shin. His lips flattened, but he was too professional to scowl at the creature leaving hairs on his uniform.

"Thank you, Jeddah," Sespian said when the man set the tray down. Steam rolled off the freshly poured cup of tea. "Is Hollowcrest in his suite?"

Sespian kept hoping for a chance to snoop in Hollowcrest's office, but the honor guard that trailed him everywhere made it impossible to ensure his movements would not be reported. As a boy, he had crawled through the old hypocaust ducts in the walls and under the floors, and he was thinking of taking up the hobby again.

"Yes, Sire," Jeddah said. "I believe he has a guest."

Sespian glanced at the grandfather clock ticking against one wall. "It's late for entertaining."

"Yes, Sire."

"Do you know who it is?"

"I don't know the gentleman's name."

"Has he been here before?" Sespian asked.

"I have served him a few times, Sire."

"Thank you."

After Jeddah left, Sespian stared thoughtfully at the door. Maybe he should take more of an interest in what went on in Hollowcrest's private meetings.

He pushed himself to his feet, only to double over with a hiss. Stabs of pain ricocheted through his head. The problem was getting worse every day.

Sespian sucked in a few deep breaths. The stabs subsided into a more manageable ache.

His guards came to attention when he exited the suite.

"Just going across the hall," he said.

Three steps took him to Hollowcrest's door. He lifted a hand to knock but paused midair. He always knocked before entering. Emperor or not, he felt it the polite thing to do. Yet he could do as he wished, right? Maybe he should surprise Hollowcrest.

His hand lowered to the knob. He twisted it and stalked inside.

Hollowcrest and a brown-clad man Sespian had never seen before stood in front of a desk. Surprise blossomed across Hollowcrest's face, but he quickly recovered. The other man looked...guilty. What were they discussing in here so late at night?

"What can I do for you, Sire?" Hollowcrest asked.

Got to be faster, Sespian. You should have spoken first. "Who's this?"

"This is Malford, the assistant to the Chief of Finance in the Urkart Satrapy," Hollowcrest said. "He's here on business."

Mud and some sort of damp green gunk adorned the stranger's boots. A worn leather jacket hung nearly to his knees with something that might have been a pistol bulging at his side. Neither the scarred cheek nor shaven head suggested finance expert. In addition, a hint of the sewers clung to the man.

"One wonders what route he took to arrive here," Sespian said.

"What can I do for you, Sire?" Hollowcrest repeated.

Sespian could challenge him then and there, demand to know who the man really was. But if Hollowcrest continued to lie, what could Sespian do?

"My birthday celebration is coming up," he said, "a huge holiday for everyone, and there'll be the gala here at the Barracks, of course. I'd like to invite all the foreign diplomats in the city. It's time to build real relations instead of simply humoring them."

"Of course, Sire, I'll take care of it personally."

Uh huh, sure you will.

"Anything else, Sire?"

"No. Nothing at all."

As soon as Sespian returned to his suite, he shoved aside an antique armoire. He grabbed a nail file from a drawer and unfastened a grate at the base of the wall.

He squirmed into the dark and narrow duct. It barely provided enough room to wriggle through on his belly. He had grown in the ten years since he used it last—the age he had decided it was unseemly for the future emperor to crawl through the ducts, spying on people. Perhaps he never should have stopped.

Dust blanketed the inside, and cobwebs wrapped around his face. Drafts of warm air stirred his hair. When he reached a T-section, he folded himself in half to turn right. Before he reached the blob of light that represented the grate to Hollowcrest's room, he heard voices.

"From your promises, I was expecting a drooling simpleton." It was not Hollowcrest's voice—it had to be the supposed finance assistant.

"For a man of average intellect, that would be the result," Hollowcrest said. "The boy's naïve but bright. I have everything under control though. The poison has dulled his faculties and is on its way to rendering him bedridden."

In the stillness of the duct, Sespian's quickened breaths stirred the cobwebs. His head throbbed dully. Not a tumor. Poison. It was hard to feel relief, since the latter was just as bad as the former. Although poison he might be able to do something about.

"I don't think he believed your finance chief cover."

"If you'd avoid mucking around in the sewers, your true occupation wouldn't be so obvious," Hollowcrest muttered.

"My work takes me to fabulous and varied places." The man laughed and something sinister in it chilled Sespian further.

Hollowcrest sighed. "Sicarius never smelled of his work."

Sespian's stomach lurched at the assassin's name, old fear rearing to the front of his mind.

"Sicarius, Sicarius, Sicarius," the other man snarled. "The way you always talk about him, you'd think you were lovers."

"He was efficient. Very efficient. A man in my position values that."

"I hear he's in the city. Maybe you two should kiss and make up. Unless you're afraid you're his next mark. Or perhaps the boy is." That sinister laugh again. "Many would benefit from the emperor's death and

the succession confusion it would bring. I'm sure there's a lot of money in that job." He sounded wistful.

"Let's focus on why you're here," Hollowcrest said. "What have you found out about Forge?"

"I can't get into the lead lady's place. I ran up against a bunch of magical protection, and I was almost discovered by some scarred-up security guard."

The men moved to another room in the suite where Sespian could not hear them. That was fine. He had heard enough. He backed through the duct until he reached his room. When he tried to screw the grate back in place, his hands shook too much for the job.

Hollowcrest was poisoning him.

Sespian stalked the room, mind whirring. How was the old curmudgeon doing it? Putting it in his food? Was the kitchen staff a part of it? Was Jeddah?

His peregrinations halted in front of the tray with the cup of tea on it. He sank to the floor before the steeping liquid. Not his food. His tea. The one thing that most reminded him of his mother. Sespian clenched his jaw. That bastard had ruined it.

He picked up the cup, crossed to the water closet, and poured it down the wash-out. A part of him wanted to stalk across the hall and hurl the empty cup at Hollowcrest—a big part of him. But that would do no good. It would only tip Hollowcrest to what Sespian now knew.

Sespian stared into the empty cup. What was he going to do?

* * * * *

At the icehouse, Amaranthe woke in the middle of the night with her heart slamming against her ribs. Fleeting memories of a nightmare dissipated like plumes of smoke from a steam engine. All she remembered was something dark chasing her, emitting a horrible, unearthly screech.

The sound came again. She frowned with confusion as dream and reality mixed. Had the screech been real or was she still sleeping?

She sat up on the cot. The wool blanket pooled around her waist. Darkness blanketed the room, though she could feel heat radiating from the nearby stove. She sat motionless and listened.

At first, she heard nothing. Deep in the industrial district, the ice-house neighborhood saw little traffic at night, and silence stretched through the streets like death. Then another screech shattered the quiet. Amaranthe cringed involuntarily; it jarred her nerves like metal gouging metal. An eerily supernatural quality promised it was nothing so innocuous. And it originated nearby, within a block or two.

Thinking of the bear-mauling story in the paper, Amaranthe slid off the cot, reluctant to make any noise. She managed to thump her knee against the desk. So much for not making noise. She groped for the lantern and turned up the flame. The light revealed her neat pile of boots, business clothing, knife, and the box containing her savings. She tugged on the footwear, then grabbed the weapon and lantern. When she opened the door, it creaked. Loudly. She hissed at it in frustration.

On the landing, she glanced around, hoping Sicarius would step out of the shadows. The vastness of the dark warehouse mocked her tiny light. The floor was not visible from the landing. When Amaranthe leaned over the railing, her light reflected off exposed ice, mimicking dozens of yellow eyes staring at her.

Another inhuman screech cut through the walls of the icehouse. It echoed through the streets and alleys outside, surrounding and encompassing. In the distance, dogs barked. The hair on her arms leapt to attention. She shivered and clenched the handle of the lantern more tightly.

"Help!" came a male voice from outside. "Anyone!"

The nearby cry startled Amaranthe. It sounded like the speaker was directly in front of the icehouse.

She crossed the landing, her boots ringing on the metal. A pounding erupted at the double doors below.

"Is someone there?" the voice called.

"On my way!" Amaranthe hustled down the stairs.

He had to be trying to escape whatever was hunting the streets. The doors rattled on their hinges.

"It's coming!" he shouted.

Amaranthe took the last stairs three at a time. She slid on sawdust when she landed at the bottom, recovered, and ran to the doors. She reached for the heavy wooden bar securing them.

A deafening screech sounded right outside. Amaranthe jerked back.

On the other side of the door, the man shrieked with pain. She wanted to help, to lift the bar, but fear stilled her hand. Armed only with a knife, what could she do?

Coward, you have to try.

She yanked her knife from its sheath. Outside, the cries broke off with a crunch. She reached for the bar again.

"Stop."

She froze at the authoritative tone of Sicarius's voice.

"Someone's dying out there," she said, more out of a sense of obligation than a genuine desire to open the door.

Sicarius walked out of the darkness beneath the stairs. If he had been sleeping, it was not evident. He was fully dressed and armed.

"He's already dead," Sicarius said.

Amaranthe forced her breathing to slow and listened for activity. She had a feeling Sicarius was right.

Footsteps crunched on the snow outside, but they did not sound human. They were too heavy. The crunching stopped, and snuffling replaced it. The door shuddered as something bumped it. Amaranthe backed away. The snuffling came again, louder and more insistent.

She continued backing up until she stood beside Sicarius.

"Are we safe in here?" she whispered.

"No."

"Oh." *Better to know now than later, I suppose.*

The door shuddered again, louder this time.

"It's coming in, isn't it?" she asked.

"So it seems."

Amaranthe searched for escape routes. If she ran up the stairs and climbed onto the railing, she might be able to pull herself up into the rafters. From there, she could crawl along the network of steel beams and supports to the high windows. If she performed an amazing acrobatic feat, she might be able to kick out the glass, then swing out and climb onto the roof. *Good, Amaranthe, that works for Sicarius. Now how are you going to get out?*

She remembered the grates and the stacks of ice stored beneath the floor. She shoved aside sawdust and found an entrance. The inset handle required a twist and pull that only someone with thumbs could open. She hoped that thing out there had nothing of the sort.

"You coming?" she asked over her shoulder.

"It's cramped down there; a poor place to make a stand." Sicarius's gaze drifted toward her, then toward the windows and up the stairs, as if he sought an alternative.

The creature slammed against the door. A hinge popped off. Wood splintered. Only the bar kept the door standing. And that would not hold long.

"Fine," Amaranthe said. "Let me know how it goes up here."

She grabbed the lantern and climbed down the ladder. She paused to close the grate. Sicarius appeared and caught it before it fell. He waved for her to continue down, then slipped in and secured the grate behind him.

"I thought you might change your mind," she said.

A crash came from above—the sound of the bar shattering and the door collapsing. Feet or paws or something like padded through the sawdust.

Amaranthe wished she knew what the creature looked like, specifically if it had digits that would allow it to turn the handle to their hideout. Or if its strength might let it rip the grates open without bothering with a handle. She shivered. Maybe she should have tried the window route.

There was not much room between the stacks of ice and the wall. A block pressed against her shoulder and numbed her arm. She wished she had grabbed her parka.

The footsteps altered pitch as the creature moved from solid floor to the grate. Tiny flecks of sawdust sifted through. With the darkness above, Amaranthe could not see anything through the tiny gaps in the metal. She could only hear the creature. Sniffing.

Sicarius faced the entrance, his back to her and the lantern. Neither of them spoke, though there was little point in silence. It knew where they were.

The scrape of claws on metal replaced the sniffing. Slow and experimental at first, the noise then grew faster, like a dog digging under a fence.

When claws slipped between the gaps in the grate, she sucked in a breath. It was the span between them that unsettled her. No animal she had ever seen had paws that large.

She lowered her eyes and stared at Sicarius's back, the steady expansion and contraction of his rib cage. The air felt tight and constricting, and her own breaths were shallow and fast. She tried to emulate his calm. After all, he had not drawn a weapon. Maybe he knew they were safe. Or maybe he knew fighting the creature was pointless.

Above, the clawing stopped. Nothing moved.

A soft splatter to Amaranthe's right made her jump. At first she thought it had come from the ice above, a drop melting. But it steamed when it hit a block. Another drop struck the back of her hand. As hot as candle wax, it stung like salt in a cut. Not melted ice, she realized. Saliva.

Slowly, she looked up. More drops filtered down. Puffs of steam whispered through the grate—the creature's breath, visible in the chill air. Two yellow dots burned on the other side of that fog. Eyes reflecting the flame of her lantern.

Amaranthe sank into a crouch and buried her face in her knees. She closed her eyes, willing the thing to go away. A drop of hot saliva hit the back of her neck.

Time seeped by like molasses. The footsteps finally started up again. They padded away and moved beyond the range of her ears.

For several long moments, she and Sicarius hunkered there, between the wall and the ice. The cold bit through Amaranthe's night clothes. Her teeth chattered and she shivered. She held her hands close to the lantern, but it gave off little heat.

"Is it gone?" she asked.

"Impossible to tell," he said.

"Well, I'm freezing. Either one of us is going to have to check or we'll have to start cuddling."

Sicarius climbed the ladder. He opened the grate, peered out, then disappeared over the edge.

"There's something wrong with a man who chooses to face death over cuddling with a woman." Amaranthe grabbed the lantern and followed him out. "Of course, there may be something equally wrong with a woman who goes after him instead of waiting in safety."

Once up top, she left the grate open in case they needed to jump back down in a hurry. She looked for Sicarius, but her light did not illuminate much of the icehouse. Snow falling outside the broken-down

door caught her eye. The body had been dragged to the side, and only an arm remained in view. Amaranthe swallowed.

"It's not inside," Sicarius said.

He stepped out from behind the ice stacks carrying a couple of boards. He resealed the door as much as the warped hinges would allow. The splintered wood did not make a reassuring barrier. Sicarius threw the old bar—now snapped in half—to the side and replaced it with the boards.

"Maybe we should go out and check on that man. See if..." He's dead Amaranthe. You were too late to help.

"I wouldn't," Sicarius said.

He was as cool and emotionless as ever, but his unwillingness to leave the building concerned her. If, with all his skill, he did not want to confront whatever stalked the streets, who else could?

CHAPTER 10

AMARANTHE WOKE TO SICARIUS SAYING, "Lokdon," from the doorway of the tiny icehouse office.

She dropped her legs over the edge of the cot, feeling the chill of the floor even through socks. "We've been drooled on by a horrible man-slaying beast together. I think you can call me by my first name."

The coals had burned low in the stove, and it gave off little warmth or light. She groped for her boots.

"Your team is here," Sicarius said, a hint of bemusement edging his voice.

Either I'm getting better at reading him or he's starting to emote. "You sound surprised."

"Aren't you?"

Yes. "Of course not."

"Huh."

Sicarius left before Amaranthe could inquire who or how many had come. She dressed and left the office. At the bottom of the stairs, Akstyr and Books waited. Books yawned and rubbed red eyes. The bulge of a bottle sagged outward from his jacket pocket, and the sword attached to his belt looked like it hadn't been used since his boyhood weapons classes. Akstyr slouched against the wall, his baggy clothes rumpled, his hands jammed in his pockets. Bruises and lumps splotched his face.

The men stood taller when they saw her, though the effect was not particularly inspiring. At least they had come.

As Amaranthe descended the stairs, Maldynado strolled through the broken door. He wore a jaunty sword belt with a sheathed saber hanging

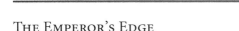

from his left hip. An obnoxious amount of gold gilded the hilt and scabbard. Akstyr's gaze lingered on the valuable weapon.

When Maldynado came even with Books and Akstyr, his upper lip wrinkled. "Which one of you boys fell in a vat of cheap wine on the way over here?"

Akstyr sneered. Books glared. Unperturbed, Maldynado surveyed them further, then pulled out a case and extricated two cards.

"Your barber?" Amaranthe asked.

"Tailor. I've never seen two people in such need of sartorial attention."

"Considering you were wearing a furry loincloth when we met, I'm not sure you should be offering fashion advice."

"Ah, but it was a stylish loincloth that showed off—" Maldynado winked, "—everything."

She could not argue.

He raised a finger. "Say, did you know there's a half-eaten body in the street out there?"

"Yes." Since she did not want to alarm her troops this early into the mission, lest they decide to leave, she decided on nonchalance. "It's not the best neighborhood."

"On that we can agree," Books said.

Maldynado waved a hand in front of his face. "Is your breath always that rank?"

"If I offend you, you have my permission to move to the other side of the room." Books lowered his voice. "Or the empire."

"Since you're the offensive one, maybe you should do the moving so the rest of us can breathe. There's a dumpster down the block where you might feel at home." Maldynado turned to Akstyr. "Do you believe this fellow?"

"Who cares?" That surly curl to Akstyr's lip seemed permanent.

Amaranthe realized getting these men to come had been the easy part. Getting them to work together without blood, and business cards, flying would be the true test.

"You said you'd have food. And a place to sleep." Akstyr eyed the towers of ice. "Figured it'd be warmer inside than outside."

"We won't be staying here," she said. "As soon as Sicarius returns, he'll show us to the place we're going to set up. We'll buy food then."

"That was him, wasn't it?" Akstyr's tone changed for the first time. He sounded reverent. "The one who let us in? Is it true he's a Hunter?"

A what?

"I'm not sure," Amaranthe said. "You can ask him."

Akstyr prodded the sawdust with his toe. "I wouldn't want to annoy him."

"I'll ask him for you," she said.

"Who asked you to?"

So much for the reverence.

"I'll let you know what I find," Amaranthe said dryly.

"Whatever."

"Wait," Maldynado said. "Are we talking about the same fellow who trounced me last night?"

"Yes," she said.

"That was Sicarius? *The* Sicarius? The assassin?"

Surprised someone from the upper echelons of Turgonia's social hierarchy had heard of him, she only said, "Yes."

"I wish you had told me that last night before the fight. When he slaughtered me, I wouldn't have felt so..." Maldynado's mittened fingers flexed in the air as he groped for the word.

"Inept?" Books suggested. "Inadequate? Unmanned?"

Maldynado scowled at him. "I'm *manned* just fine, thank you." He turned back to Amaranthe. "I figured he was just some random thug you picked up at the docks."

"Not a random one," she said.

"Is Sicarius working for you?" Akstyr asked dubiously. "Or are you working for him?"

Amaranthe hesitated. Her "team," especially Akstyr, might be more inclined to obey her if they believed she commanded Sicarius, but his cooperation was just that, cooperation.

"It's my plan," she said. "He's going along with it for now."

"But you're giving him orders?" Akstyr asked.

"I'd call them suggestions."

Sicarius chose that moment to return from wherever he had been skulking. She wondered how much he had heard.

"We should go," he said. "That body is likely to draw enforcers."

"Lead the way," Amaranthe said.

Several more inches of snow had dropped during the night, obliterating the creature's footprints. Sicarius stepped around the corpse, which dogs had partially uncovered. Amaranthe could not keep herself from looking and remembering. If she had been faster, if she had not hesitated, she might have saved the man's life.

Under the surface gnawing, longer and deeper wounds ravaged the chest. Wind gusted, and a few snowflakes flitted off the corpse's frozen hand, revealing a Panthers' mark. Amaranthe never thought she would feel sympathy for gang members, but it seemed these folks were being preyed on from every front.

Her group traveled along the bottom of the hill fronting the lake. Despite the fresh snow, a handful of young athletes jogged past on their way to the lake trail. It was months until the summer Games, but the dedicated souls trained all year around.

A wagon loaded with ice rumbled through a cross street, and the driver whistled at Amaranthe. Maldynado snickered, and she quirked an eyebrow at him.

"Sorry," he said. "Am I supposed to defend your honor when they do that? I'm a little unclear on the boundaries of our agreement."

"No, I was just wondering why it was funny."

"Because he was eyeing you like he thought you'd be a good time, and you're...ah..."

"Reserved?" Books suggested. "Dignified?"

"No," Maldynado said. "Do you think you're a dictionary or something?"

"A thesaurus perhaps," Books said.

"Proper?" Akstyr asked. "She's kind of proper."

"No," Maldynado said. "It's more..."

"Focused," Sicarius said.

The others considered, then nodded and grunted agreement of this pinpoint description. Amaranthe smirked; at least dissecting her character together kept them from snapping at each other. She might be able to create a cohesive unit after all.

"Yes, exactly," Maldynado said. "You didn't notice any of the men at the gym last night, I guess because you're busy with your emperor scheme. You didn't even look at me when you first saw me, and I was very look-at-able at the time."

Amaranthe blushed. She *had* looked.

"Praise her good taste," Books muttered, stepping into the street to avoid a lamppost—or perhaps Maldynado's glare.

"Old man," Maldynado said, "you are crippling my serenity. If you keep insulting me, I might have to come over there and—"

"Gentlemen," Amaranthe said. "I believe we're almost there."

She decided to forgo her ambitions of creating a cohesive unit. An occasionally functional one with tendencies toward violence seemed more within reach.

They passed the last of the city's industrial buildings and crossed the railroad tracks skirting the lake. Along the waterfront, fisheries, warehouses, and boatyards reigned, their long docks stretching into the frozen water. In spring and summer, the area would bustle with activity. For now, it lay sedately under its snowy blanket.

"This is it." Sicarius stopped before a tottering wooden structure on a dilapidated dock.

The building hunched over the lake like an old soldier, arthritic from a lifetime's worth of battle wounds. Icicles hung from the eaves, and frost edged the panes of broken windows. Age-yellowed buoys and frayed nets dangled from the walls, someone's idea of decorating. Amaranthe touched a splintered piece of cedar siding. It fell off. The odds of this building keeping that creature out were not good.

She leaned over the edge of the dock. A few feet below, ice and snow gathered around the pylons.

Akstyr peered in a window. "A fish cannery?"

"There are bunks inside, and it has a large work space," Sicarius said. "It's winter. Nobody human will bother us."

And the inhuman? Amaranthe would wait until she had him alone to ask.

She withdrew a ten-ranmya bill and handed it to Maldynado. "Will you find the nearest market and buy as much food as you can, please?"

"Will do." Maldynado trotted up a street running perpendicular to the waterfront.

"You're sending him to purchase supplies?" Books asked. "That overgrown fop from the warmonger caste has probably never shopped in his life."

"He'll get a good deal," Amaranthe said.

A sizable lock on the front door of the cannery precluded a direct entrance.

"I bet I can get in." Akstyr produced a large clip with at least three dozen keys of various shapes and sophistication dangling from it. "I've got a couple of skeleton keys that—"

"Unnecessary," Sicarius said.

He led them to the lake side of the building. The lock in the back also remained in place; however, the door had been removed and was leaning against the wall.

When Amaranthe stepped inside, glass crunched beneath her boots. Weak light filtering through grimy windows, revealing rows of long counters littered with salt, dented cans, and torn labels. Rotting wooden bunk beds lined one wall. Here and there, rats scurried beneath the fish-gut-spattered sawdust spread across the floor. Only the cold kept the smell tolerable. Sort of.

"Lovely place," Books murmured.

"At least it comes without a meddling landlady," Amaranthe said.

"This is true."

"Pick out a bunk and settle in," she said. "As soon as Maldynado gets back, we'll get started. Sicarius, a word?"

He stepped over to a corner counter with her as Akstyr and Books explored their new home.

Amaranthe stacked a few of the scattered cans into a neat pile. "You went shopping for this building before we knew there was a man-slaying creature roaming the streets. Do you still think it's a suitable hideout."

Sicarius lifted his gaze toward the rafters. Some thirty feet up, solid beams ran from wall to wall below the peaked ceiling. If one could clamber up there, one might be safe. As long as that creature couldn't jump that high.

"I don't see a ladder," she said.

"You can climb the support posts," Sicarius said.

Amaranthe eyed the dented and scarred wood of the nearest post. "*You* can do that, I'm sure. The rest of us might find that feat challenging, especially with a monster crashing through the door."

"Hang rope."

"I guess that works." The last of the rusted cans went into her organized pile. One counter down, thirty to go. "I'm going to send Books and Akstyr to get a press. I'll take Maldynado ink and paper shopping. I want to start researching the Forge people, but that'll probably have to wait until tomorrow. We need to get the press set up, and we need to get money plates made. I don't suppose you know an engraver and can get that done?"

"Easy," Sicarius said.

"Really?" She had expected this to be a sticking point. Maybe she ought to just let him go and do it, but... "Easy because you know a criminal engraver who owes you a favor, or easy because you'll pick someone with the skill set, force him to do it, and kill him afterwards?"

"The latter."

"Oh."

"Asking someone to help you commit a crime and then leaving him alive to point you out to the enforcers is foolish."

"Well, we've got three people already who are going to be privy to our plans. Perhaps adding another wouldn't ma..." A chilling thought whispered into her mind. She glanced at Books, sitting on a bunk, and Akstyr, poking around in discarded debris. "Please tell me your logic doesn't require killing everyone we work with over the next couple weeks."

"You can't trust random people acquired from the street. Don't get attached."

"Sicarius." She gripped his arm, distantly aware that she had never dared touch him before. "I did not talk these folks into helping just to have you kill them at the end."

"Once our need for them is done, they're disposable."

"And does that go for me too?" As soon as she asked the question, she regretted it. If the answer was yes, what would she do?

"You're not disposable," he said. She almost had time to wonder if he might actually care, but then he added, "It's your plan."

"Lucky me. Well, here's an addendum to my plan: it will not involve killing the men we've coerced into helping us, nor will engravers be found in bed with their throats cut."

"Propose an alternative."

Amaranthe rubbed her chin and gazed thoughtfully about the building. Akstyr was stretched out under a table, digging through dirty sawdust. He came up with a copper coin and grinned.

"Akstyr," she called.

He stuffed the coin in his pocket and threw her a suspicious look. Nonetheless, he slouched over.

"What?"

"Where'd you get all those keys?" She jerked her chin at the ring on his belt.

"Made 'em."

"Are they copies? Or originals?"

"Copies."

"Am I correct in assuming you're not a trained locksmith?"

"Yup. It's pretty easy to make copies of keys, using..." he shrugged, "ways."

Amaranthe took that to mean magic. "So, using these *ways*, you can carve things out of metal. Could you engrave something?"

"Oh, sure. I used to leave my gang sign all over the city that way. This one time, a man was in the water closet at the baths, and I—"

Amaranthe lifted a hand. "Sufficient details, thank you." The width of his grin convinced her she was right in cutting off the story. She fished out a ten-ranmya bill. "Think you could copy this into metal?"

"Sure, using the Sci—er, my way is even easier than tracing. It's like burning a brand with your mind. As long as I'm just making an exact copy and not getting artistic."

He reached for the bill, but Sicarius plucked it out of the air first.

"Copying this won't get us anywhere," Sicarius said. "It needs to be in reverse."

"Like a stamp, of course." Amaranthe sighed. "Too bad the Imperial Mint is in Sunders City, otherwise we could just steal plates. Though that would—"

"I'll make it," Sicarius said.

Amaranthe and Akstyr stared at him.

"Make what?" she asked. "The reverse drawing?"

"Yes. I'll need good paper and a fine pen. I hear Maldynado on the dock. Go get the supplies."

She wanted to question him further—why would an assassin know how to draw?—but Maldynado staggered inside with arms full of bags, wrapped meat, a jug, and a crate with...

"Are those air holes?" Books asked.

Amaranthe hastened over to help Maldynado unload. The crate squawked.

"Chickens?" she asked.

"You could have sent someone to help me carry things," Maldynado said.

"You bought all that for ten ranmyas?" Books asked.

"Actually, I got it for free," Maldynado said smugly. After setting the crate down, he fished out Amaranthe's bill and returned it. "I was just going to buy some cans of corned meat, but I started talking with the shopkeeper, and she told me about this problem she was having. Apparently, some farmer rode his dogsled—" Maldynado rolled his eyes at this notion of antiquity, "—out of the fields and across the lake to barter for supplies. He brought lots of fresh farm things to trade."

"Like chickens?" Akstyr peered into the crate and licked his lips.

"Indeed so," Maldynado said. "Anyway, this shopkeeper had all these chickens in the back making noise, needing to be fed, doing what chickens do after they're fed. Apparently, one escaped and pecked a customer yesterday. The shopkeeper sent a message to the closest butcher, but he wanted to charge her to take away the chickens. So I smiled and said, 'Why don't I take those chickens for free?' She was so relieved that she gave me a bunch of the other food the farmer had brought in. We have fresh bacon, goat cheese, dried apples, cider, and tomorrow, we'll have eggs."

"Nice," Akstyr purred.

"Good work," Amaranthe said. "Let's have something to eat, then we'll get busy. Maldynado you're the official shopper for the group now."

"Wise choice," Sicarius murmured.

"Shopping?" Maldynado's smugness melted away, replaced with a chagrinned slump.

"Yes, in fact, we're going paper shopping right now," she continued over Maldynado's groan. "Books, we need a printing press. Akstyr, can you help him find one and bring it back here?"

"I don't want to go on some stupid errand," Akstyr said.

Amaranthe rummaged through her mind for something she could offer to make the task appealing to him. Of the three men she had recruited, Akstyr was the most likely to be a problem. She doubted Mal-

dynado or Books would turn her into the enforcers, but if Akstyr saw a better opportunity than the one she offered...

Sicarius had the knack of moving without anyone noticing him move, so when he appeared at Akstyr's side, the younger man jumped several inches. Sicarius rested his hand at the base of Akstyr's neck. Though the touch was light, the meaning was unmistakable. Akstyr stood utterly still, not even breathing.

In the silence that descended, Amaranthe heard the breeze bumping the buoys hanging on the outside walls.

"Follow her orders," Sicarius said softly.

Akstyr closed his eyes and gulped. "Y-yes, sir."

Sicarius lowered his hand. His gaze flicked to Maldynado.

"Oh, I like her orders," Maldynado said. "Official shopper, excellent. No strenuous labor for me."

"Yes, I have no issues either," Books said, almost as pale as Akstyr.

Amaranthe's lips stretched, though she did not know if in a grimace or a smile. As handy as having some muscle to back up her wishes was, she detested the idea of winning people's cooperation that way.

Books opened his mouth, hesitated, glanced at Sicarius, and then raised a finger as if he were a student asking a question in class.

"Yes?" Amaranthe asked.

"I'm not complaining about this task—" he shot another glance at Sicarius, "—but how do you propose I find a printing press? I assume you're not providing funds for its purchase. And supposing I do acquire one, how should I get it back here?"

"I can allocate up to five hundred ranmyas if you find something."

"That won't buy the handle."

"We don't need a steam-powered press. Just find something old and rusty we can fix up."

"I don't think—"

"I came looking for *you* specifically," Amaranthe said, rushing to speak before Sicarius could make any more sinister innuendoes, "a highly educated and experienced professor, because I knew *you* would be able to come up with solutions that I, a lowly ex-enforcer, could not. I know you can do this, Books."

The narrowed eyes and head tilt Books gave her said he saw through her manipulation, but his expression suddenly grew thoughtful, and he tugged his beard. "Hm."

"What?" she asked.

"I have an idea."

* * * * *

Ink Alley, a frequent stop for business supply shoppers, meandered through four city blocks. Shops advertised stationery, accounting books, wax and seals, ink, and paper of various weights and sizes. Despite being a well-known destination, the ancient street was narrow, and Amaranthe had to dodge bundle-laden shoppers. Maldynado, who walked at her side, made no apologies for his broad shoulders and let others do the dodging. He did offer a smile if the person happened to be young and female.

"I gave Books a large portion of my funds," Amaranthe told him, "so I need you to get me a good deal on paper and ink."

"Your big plan involves blackmail and counterfeiting," Maldynado said. "Why don't we just *steal* your printing supplies?"

"And damage the livelihood of some poor businesswoman trying to make a living? I couldn't do that."

"You need to work on this criminal stuff."

"I'll keep that in mind. Anyway, we don't need to leave a trail of burglaries that would tell some enforcer investigator what we're up to."

Etchings in the window panes of a shop portrayed old-fashioned ink pots, quills, and scrolls of parchment. Bins of pencils and pens and myriad types of paper lay behind the glass.

"How about this place?" she asked.

"Sure. I'll probably have greater success if you wait outside."

"Why?"

"Because if you come in hanging on my arm, it'll look like I'm not available. Charming women works best if they think they have a chance."

Amaranthe hesitated, not sure whether to trust him to get the right items. But, if it meant getting a better deal... "Very well. I'll write our needs down for you."

"I don't need a shopping list. I've got a great memory."

"We'll need rag paper, not pulp-based. And pay attention to the weight. We won't find an exact match, but we want the closest we can find. Make sure to get printing press ink. Books says it's made from soot and turpentine and nut oil. Anything else will smear. We'll need a paper cutter too. And plates, but I'll select those from an engraving shop."

"Rags and what oil?" Maldynado asked.

"I'll write it down."

"Good idea."

After he went inside, Amaranthe continued down the street. Newspaper articles plastered a brick wall near a window, and she stopped, wondering if any mentioned the "bear" slayings. The yellowed clippings only highlighted old stories featuring Ink Alley.

About to move on, she paused at a reflection in the window. A boy of ten or twelve watched her from across the alley.

Ensconced in numerous layers of raggedy clothing, he slouched against a wall. When she turned, he yawned and looked away.

Amaranthe wandered farther down the street. A low rail paralleling a wall offered a place to park bicycles and street skis. She propped her foot on it and peeked under her arm while pretending to adjust the fit of her boot.

The boy lurched to a stop, hunkered over a trash can, and rummaged through it.

Great, who set this child to following me? Enforcers used youngsters as informants, since adults tended to ignore them, but she could not assume he was one of theirs. Other people employed youths for similar reasons. Businesses used them to spy on other businesses. Gangs gathered intelligence on rival gangs. Even lovers sent children to watch partners suspected of cheating. Given how long it had been since Amaranthe's last romantic relationship, she easily eliminated the last possibility.

A few stores down, she found a shop that sold engraving tools. She stepped inside and browsed the display case nearest the window. The boy appeared again, whistling as he strolled past the shop. He sat against a wall a dozen paces down, took off his fur cap, and begged for coins.

Definitely watching me.

"Help you, ma'am?" a clerk asked.

"I need a couple of metal plates about so big." Amaranthe outlined the rectangles with her hands. "Better make it four of them." Akstyr might need to practice first.

While the clerk wrapped the plates, Amaranthe glanced out the window again. The boy had not moved.

"Mind if I cut through the back?" she asked after she paid.

The clerk pointed to the rear exit. Amaranthe entered an 'alley' as wide as the front street, though it smelled less pleasant. Discarded food wrappers frozen to the icy cobblestones crinkled beneath her boots. Streaks of yellow decorated the dirty snow piled against the walls.

Amaranthe knocked on the back door of the ink and paper shop. Nobody answered, so she tried the knob. Unlocked.

Inside, Maldynado was...posing? Amidst the shelves and cases of paper, he stood with one leg propped on a chair. One of his hands rested on his raised knee, the other on his waist. His jaw jutted toward the ceiling. A seated woman wearing a blouse and a long felt skirt hunched over a sketch pad in her lap, drawing him.

Amaranthe cleared her throat. "I thought you were—"

"Yes, yes," Maldynado said without breaking his pose. "It's all over there."

Three boxes and several wrapped bundles waited on a counter next to a paper cutter. On the way across the room, Amaranthe shot Maldynado a what-are-you-doing look that he ignored. She peered under the lid of the topmost box to make sure he had purchased rag paper. She picked up a sheet and rubbed it between her fingers. It didn't feel exactly like ranmya paper, but the heft was right. It would have to do.

"Maldynado, what are you doing?" she asked.

"Posing."

"Why?"

The woman with the sketch pad frowned over her shoulder at Amaranthe. "Who's she?" she asked Maldynado.

"Uhm."

"I hope you're being paid," Amaranthe told him.

"What?" he asked.

The woman's frown deepened.

"I suspect she's going to use your likeness in her advertising literature. Your handsome face will be a marketing gimmick to sell more

paper to her predominantly female clientele. That means she'll make money, so you should too."

Maldynado's chin dropped, and he addressed the artist. "Is that true?"

The woman shrugged.

"You said you wanted to immortalize my face in your memory."

"And on her promotional pamphlets." Amaranthe tugged the paper cutter and one of the boxes into her arms, leaving the rest for Maldynado. "Finish up. I'll wait outside."

Before leaving, Amaranthe checked the front window to make sure the boy was not standing out there with his face pressed to the panes. In the alley, she tapped her foot until Maldynado came out the back door with the rest of the supplies.

"Is there a reason we're taking the alley?" he asked. "The air is a tad ripe out here."

"Unfriendly eyes out front."

"Enforcers?"

"A ten-year-old boy."

"Oh, yes. Terrifying."

"He's someone's spy," she said.

"I could go thump him around a bit, find out whose."

"Let's try to avoid child-thumping for now."

They walked to the trolley stop, and at every intersection, Amaranthe glanced left and right for the boy. She did not see him again but did not relax until she and Maldynado boarded. He set down the packages, dug out a wad of bills, peeled a couple off the top, and handed them to Amaranthe.

"Your split." He winked.

With a team to feed, she saw no reason to reject it. "You seemed surprised that was what she wanted. I would have thought you'd have run into that kind of situation before. Were you really taken in by her flattery?"

"We had servants who did the shopping. Never had much reason to interact with those kinds of people."

Amaranthe wondered what kind of people he considered her.

"That was good of you back there," he added. "To catch that. Maybe after you're done with your current scheme, we could work together. You can get me posing gigs. I'll be pretty and you can be..."

"Your agent?"

"Precisely."

"Assuming I survive this, I haven't thought too closely about what my next career should be." She had never wanted a 'next career.' "I'll remember your offer though."

"Excellent, boss."

Amaranthe smiled. Maldynado seemed to be loose with who he called boss, and she doubted it came with any heartfelt feeling of indenture—he had left his previous employer quickly enough—but the title warmed her nonetheless. Maybe she had earned a modicum of his respect.

None of the others were there when Amaranthe and Maldynado returned to the cannery, though two knotted ropes hung from the rafters, their tufted ends dangling a foot from the floor.

Thank you, Sicarius.

"What are those for?" Maldynado asked.

"Calisthenics."

Afternoon light flowed through the cracked and missing windows, and dust motes floated in the air. Dust floated everywhere, Amaranthe corrected. And coated everything. How could she possibly plot a government coup in a filthy base reeking of fish guts?

After some searching, she found a closet with cleaning supplies cowering under grime dating back to the Bronze Era. She strode triumphantly out with mop in one hand and broom in the other. Maldynado had dumped the ink and boxes on a counter. He leaned against it and watched her warily.

"How about I sweep and you mop?" Amaranthe asked.

He eyed the cleaning implements with the enthusiasm of a child debating a plate of spinach and liver. "My father used to warn me that gambling would land me in jail or the poorhouse. He neglected to mention indentured cleaning."

"I could mop and you could sweep."

"Oh, gee. Much better." Sighing, Maldynado accepted the broom.

Hours later, Amaranthe surveyed the cannery with satisfaction. Despite Maldynado's propensity for using the broom to spar with imaginary foes instead of sweeping, the hardwood floors gleamed. The now-pristine counters would allow them to work without worrying about sawdust or fish guts sticking to their bills.

She wondered where Sicarius had gone. Even his daily training ought not take all afternoon.

Akstyr returned before any of the others.

"I need Maldynado," he blurted as soon as he entered.

If he noticed, or cared about, the new cleanliness of the cannery, he did not show it.

"Why?" Amaranthe asked.

"To help with the press."

"You found one? Good. Is somebody going to deliver it with a steam wagon?"

"Not exactly."

"Then how—"

"Don't worry. Books has a plan. But we need Maldynado."

"Even he isn't big enough to port a printing press on his back."

"Don't worry, it'll be fine."

"You're not going to steal a wagon, are you?"

"No, no. Maldynado, you coming?"

Maldynado shrugged and shuffled over to join Akstyr at the door.

Amaranthe leaned on one of the counters and frowned at Akstyr. "Why can't you tell me what you're doing?"

"Because it's Books's plan."

"Yes, you said that. I notice he's not here, however."

"I know." Akstyr grinned. "He didn't want to explain it."

"Maybe I should come with you."

"No, no. We don't need you. Why don't you make dinner? It'll be fine. Don't worry." Akstyr dragged Maldynado outside.

"Telling someone not to worry three times is not the way to ensure it doesn't happen," she muttered.

Through a window, she watched the two men trot up the hill. She lifted her index finger to her lips, found the nail already chewed to the quick, and started in on her thumb.

After chewing and pacing for a while, she decided to follow Akstyr's suggestion. A master chef she was not, but they were working for her—for free—so she could certainly prepare some food.

Before dusk settled, she dragged in metal barrels from a neighboring dock and started a couple fires for light and warmth. For dinner, she laid out ham slices, flat bread, carrots, and dried apples on 'plates' pilfered from the building's siding. Just as she set out a jug of cider, shouts came from outside.

Amaranthe ran out the back of the cannery, skidding on the snowy dock. After Akstyr's admonitions, she expected the worst. She slid around the edge of the building in time to see a large makeshift sled barreling down the snowy hill. A bulky canvas-wrapped object rode on it. The press?

Maldynado perched atop it like a lizard rider from the desert. He leaned left and right in a semblance of steering. Shouting with glee, or maybe terror, he weaved and wobbled down the slick street with Books and Akstyr pounding after him. Runners scraped on sand and ice. The press slid from side to side, barely restrained by the flimsy rope tying it to the sled.

Amaranthe glanced up and down the waterfront, afraid someone would see the strange scene. Counterfeiters were supposed to be inconspicuous. Maldynado whooped, voice ringing from the buildings. Amaranthe shook her head. This was not inconspicuous. Fortunately, twilight had brought the end of the work day, and no one remained on the streets to witness this un-clandestine delivery method.

Through some feat of agility or raw strength, Maldynado and his cargo stopped in front of the cannery instead of skidding out onto the lake. Books and Akstyr came slipping after, shouting and laughing at their success.

"That was fun," Maldynado said, eyes bright, lips peeled back in a toothy grin.

"I want a turn," Akstyr said.

Only Books had the sense to peer uncertainly at Amaranthe.

"Whose idea was this?" She struggled to keep her voice even.

Akstyr and Maldynado pointed at Books in unison.

"We found it in the back room of a bookseller who's closing her business," Books said. "She was willing to sell it cheaply. It's an archaic

model, maybe the first one ever made if the rust is any indication, but I'm certain I can get it working. As for our arrival..." He cleared his throat. "It occurred to me that the bookshop, though many blocks away, is almost in a straight line from our current location and, uhm, at a rather higher elevation."

"I see. Well, this was..." Something that could have attracted attention. Something that could have gotten one of them injured or killed. An insane idea that could have seen the printing press go careening onto the lake, through the ice, and straight to the bottom. "Inspired. Very clever of you, Books. I'm glad it worked. Thank you all." So, this is command. *If Hollowcrest doesn't kill me, these men surely will.* "Let's get it inside."

It took the group longer to manhandle the press into the cannery than it had to move it several blocks. Amaranthe chose the corner farthest from the street to set up. Through it all, Maldynado sported a grin he would probably wear to bed.

"There's more to be done," Amaranthe said, "but relax and have some dinner first."

The men mauled the neatly spread table like bears crushing a hive to extract honey. She salvaged a hunk of ham and some apple slices for herself. While munching, she examined the press.

Dents gouged the wooden frame, and rust coated the screw and most of the metal joints. She doubted the press was functional at the moment. Remembering some oil and wire dish cloths from the supply closet, she retrieved the implements and set to work on the rust.

Books came over to help. "Have you figured out how to make the plates yet?"

"Yes." She squirted oil between grooves on the giant screw and scrubbed with the wire mesh.

"We better board the windows. You do realize this is treason and death for all of us if we're caught?"

"We're not going to be caught."

"Counterfeiters are *always* caught eventually," Books said. "Debasing the currency is too much of a threat for the government to be anything less than hyper-vigilant."

"People get caught because they try to pass the money. That's not our plan." She wiped a rag over the loosened rust and met Books's eyes.

"If we're discovered, I'll do everything I can to make time for you and the others to escape."

"Sicarius too?" he asked with a hint of amusement.

"If Sicarius is discovered, I'll have to try and make time for the enforcers to escape."

Books snorted but did not disagree.

Sicarius returned late that night. He walked directly to Amaranthe and handed her a folded poster. She opened it and found herself staring at her own likeness. She had expected it. The details, however, surprised her.

Amaranthe Lokdon wanted for attempted sedition and illegal magic use. Do not attempt to apprehend. Kill on sight. By order of Commander of the Armies Hollowcrest.

"Magic use?" she asked. "I didn't even know the stuff existed until last week."

"It doesn't matter," Sicarius said. "Hollowcrest has learned of your survival and fears what you know. You must move around the city with caution."

"Kill on sight," she said.

"You get used to it."

Amaranthe searched his face for humor. There was none.

CHAPTER 11

AMARANTHE WOKE SEVERAL TIMES DURING THE night to pull her blankets tighter and throw more wood into the nearest fire barrel. Drafts like gusts off mountain glaciers whistled through the broken window panes, and what little heat the flames emitted floated to the rafters.

When she noticed someone else awake, she gave up sleep and rolled off the hard bunk. Sicarius sat at a counter, drawing by the light of a fire barrel. The roaring flames looked enticing.

Blanket wrapped about her, Amaranthe shuffled over and perched on the wobbly stool across from him. His hair was damp. Had he already been out running? No hint of dawn brightened the sky beyond the window, but daylight came late this time of year.

A twenty ranmya bill lay on the counter, the imperial army marching across the back. Sicarius's pen moved with sure strokes, drawing a reverse version of the tableau.

Leaving him alone to work would be wise. Curiosity trumped wisdom, though, and she said, "You were gone a long time yesterday. Did you do anything interesting?"

"No."

"Would you tell me if you had?"

Sicarius neither looked up nor answered. The pen continued to scrawl.

"I'm going to my old school today to start researching Forge," she said. "I thought I'd take Books. Do you want to be in charge of getting the press running? We got a good portion of the rust off last night. I can leave Maldynado and Akstyr to help."

Sicarius's fingers moved with precision. "Books will doubtlessly know more about printing presses than I."

"Yes, but we recruited him to be a research assistant." Amaranthe raised her eyebrows. "Unless you want to help me shovel through piles of papers in dusty archive buildings?"

"I will go."

Er. She had not expected him to accept the invitation. It was hard to imagine someone whose daily attire included a dozen knives wandering through shelves, delving into books and ledgers. But then, the same knife-clad man was sitting here, drawing her pictures with—she leaned closer for a good look—amazing accuracy.

"That's unbelievable," she said. "Where did you learn to draw?"

The pen left the completed soldiers to work on the numbers and borders.

"You know," Amaranthe said after a moment of silence, "when someone asks you a question, the socially acceptable thing to do is answer."

Another silent moment passed, broken only by the crackle of the fire. Burning boards shifted in the barrel, and a burst of sparks flew into the air.

Amaranthe tapped her finger on the counter. "If you answer my question, I'll leave you alone."

"For how long?" he promptly asked.

Her shoulders drooped beneath the blanket. She was annoying him.

"Never mind." She slid off the stool and headed toward the food area.

"Lokdon." Sicarius looked up.

She paused. "Yes?"

"I had cartography instruction as a boy."

She bit her lip to hide a smile. A simple answer to a question shouldn't mean so much. "Is that what you were hoping to do before you decided to take up your current, uhm, profession? Or—" a new idea struck her, "—was that a part of your training for your current profession? Like for spying? You could infiltrate an enemy stronghold and map the terrain and layout for your employer. You said you were just a boy though. You haven't been training for this since you were a

child, have you? It's not like someone turns ten and decides they want to be an assassin. Do they?"

"I thought I only had to answer one question."

"Oh. Right." This time she did smile. The other questions lingered in her mind, but she probably *was* walking the line of being annoying, so she merely gave him a wave and left to prepare a meal.

By the time dawn slanted through the boarded windows, Sicarius had finished. He woke Akstyr and gave him the finished drawings. After some bleary eye rubbing, Akstyr took the pictures and the plates into a dark corner. He, apparently, did not need light for his work.

The replicas had looked accurate to her, but it was difficult to tell with them in reverse. She hoped Akstyr would succeed at his portion of the scheme and that they could test the press before the day's end.

"Thank you," Amaranthe told Sicarius.

He merely crossed his arms and waited for her to get ready. They had research to do.

* * * * *

A security guard loomed at the entrance to the Mildawn Business School for Women, a clean, three-story brick building with rows of pristine glass windows. In the eight years since Amaranthe's last class, she had forgotten about the guard. As she and Sicarius approached, she groped for ways to get him—and his knife collection—through the door without starting an incident. Of course, if the guard had browsed the wanted posters lately, Sicarius's weapons might be the least of her problems.

"Hold." The guard held his mittened hand out as they climbed the steps. "Only parents and students are allowed inside."

"Yes, of course," Amaranthe said. "We're thinking of enrolling our daughter. Does Headmistress Dona still give tours to parents of prospective students?"

"On the last day of the month, which is not today."

"I understand, but we're heading to the gulf on a purchasing trip, and we'll be gone for weeks. I so wanted to get an application in before we left, but my husband—" she patted Sicarius's arm, not quite daring to check his face for a reaction, "—doesn't think we should force little

Jaeleka into business. I, of course, told him that an education at Mildawn would be excellent preparation for any career. I attended classes here myself, back when Oskar worked door security."

"Oh! Oskar is my uncle."

A fond expression accompanied the guard's words, so she decided to focus on that instead of her hastily created cover story.

"Is he?" she asked. "He was a fabulous man, always said hello to everyone. Did he retire?"

"Yup, moved down south to escape the winters."

"Understandable." Amaranthe nodded to the inches of fresh snow balanced on the stair railing. "Did he get you this job?"

"Yes, I was a soldier before, and that's a mite more glamorous, but I don't miss those months in the field."

"I'd imagine not. You know, Oskar occasionally broke the rules. He let us keep a stray cat in the basement one winter. He even helped us find fish to feed it."

The guard chuckled. "That was your class? My uncle told me that story. Something about Ms. Maple stomping around the building all winter, wondering what was eating her ferns."

"Little Raggles had a fondness for greens."

Sicarius flicked a glance at Amaranthe, probably wondering why he had to endure story hour.

"Could you possibly make an exception for us?" she asked the guard, who was still smirking.

"I guess you can go up and talk to the headmistress." He waved her through, then frowned at Sicarius. "You're going to have to leave your weapons at my desk inside. When your daughter is enrolled, it'll be different, but we can't let strangers wander the halls armed. You can pick them up on your way out."

For the first time, Amaranthe looked Sicarius in the eye, silently willing him to follow the school policy. After a long stare her direction, he unstrapped and unsheathed.

"Those are beauties." The guard reached for one of the throwing knives.

Sicarius caught the man's wrist. "Touch nothing."

"No, sir, of course, not."

"Now, now, dear. Let's be cordial." Amaranthe pulled Sicarius's arm back. "We want to make a good impression. This is a prestigious institution, and we don't want to ruin Jaeleka's chances of acceptance."

When Sicarius released his wrist, the guard gave her a relieved nod.

"Jaeleka?" Sicarius murmured, when they passed into the halls. His soft boots made not a whisper on the polished hardwood floors.

"You don't approve?" she asked.

"It wouldn't be my first choice."

"Perhaps you could make a list of acceptable baby names for next time."

Since classes were in session, the halls were still, except for an occasional student ambling to the water closet. Familiar names on doors and the sweet scent of freshly applied beeswax floor polish stirred nostalgic twinges. Was Lady Arranton still a bigger gossip than any of her students? Was Lord Colonel Maxcrest still the only male teacher—and still the hero in all the girls' soldier fantasies? Were students still stealing Widow Tern's hardboiled eggs and hiding them in various places around the school?

When they entered an empty staircase, Amaranthe asked, "How was my lying back there? Is it getting any better?" She was still wondering how Sicarius had seen through her prevarications the first time they met.

"I wasn't watching your eyes."

"My eyes?" she asked. "Is that how you can tell?"

"You look up and to the left when you're getting creative."

"Really? Does everyone?"

"It's not a science," he said, "but many right-handed people look right when they're accessing actual memories and left for imagined."

"Huh. And the opposite for lefties?" Amaranthe led him into the third-floor hallway and headed for the administration offices at the end.

"Yes."

She would have to conduct some experiments; that information might help her someday. They passed the headmistress's domain and tapped on a door labeled Scholarship Office.

"Come!"

Inside, a gray-haired lady peered at them through spectacles with lenses the size of magnifying glasses. A closed door behind her read, "Files." She sat at a simple desk adorned with a potted fern. Amaranthe

stifled a delighted snort when she spotted a hardboiled egg nestled beneath the fronds.

"Amaranthe Lokdon!" Despite a diminutive stature, and a fondness for calling everyone "dear," the woman had the assertiveness of a drill sergeant.

"Yes, Ms. Maple, I'm flattered you remember me."

"Of course, dear. And who's this?" When she stood up, she almost reached Sicarius's chest.

"My husband," Amaranthe said.

"Really! I would have guessed bodyguard."

Yes, even without visible weapons, he had that aura.

"No, no, we're going to launch a business together. I remember you talking to our class about grants for students needing startup funds." She hoped Ms. Maple wouldn't remember that Amaranthe hadn't actually graduated.

"Yes, there are many, depending on the type of business you're looking to start."

Amaranthe took a breath. Time to make a guess she hoped proved right. "A lady I met at the library said an outfit named Forge offers nice grants."

Ms. Maple frowned. "Nice, yes...but really dear, you're not thinking of getting into gambling and gaming, are you?"

So relieved that her guess had been right, Amaranthe almost missed the rest of the question. "Er, no, well." She needed whatever Forge information Maple had on file, so she thought fast, rearranging her story. "You see, your guess was actually correct. Hansor, here, isn't *my* bodyguard, but he does have professional experience in the field, and we're going to start a business training bouncers and bodyguards. It seems like gambling and gaming establishments would want to hire our students, so, ah..." She was botching it. Her eyes were probably shooting sideways in her head.

"That's not exactly the type of business I imagined you starting, dear." Ms. Maple glowered up at Sicarius, as if suspecting him of being a bad influence. She was the first person Amaranthe had met who showed him no fear.

"It's not finalized," Amaranthe said, assuring herself Sicarius would not maul an old schoolteacher just to prove how dangerous he was. "If

we could see some of the Forge grant offerings, and any other ones you think might be applicable, we'd be grateful."

"Very well, dear."

Ms. Maple grabbed a lamp and disappeared into the file room behind her desk.

Sicarius leaned against the wall, positioned so he could see both doors, and folded his arms over his chest. "Hansor?"

"Not your first pick?" she asked.

"No."

"You're a tad finicky, aren't you?"

A hint of eyebrow movement was his only response.

"At the least, we'll get an address associated with Forge," Amaranthe said. "The applications have to be turned in somewhere."

"Indeed. How did you know about the grants?"

"It was a guess. If the Forge people are vying for more power in the government, then it makes sense for them to fund more startups. Then they can place people out there in the business world who will grow in power and wealth and later be loyal to the ones who granted them their opportunity."

"Huh."

Ms. Maple returned to the room. "Here are a few you can apply for, dear. Larocka brought that top one by personally just a couple weeks ago."

Amaranthe accepted the small stack. "Larocka?"

"Larocka Myll, yes. The founder and chairwoman of Forge. I assumed you knew."

Amaranthe couldn't stop herself from throwing a wide-eyed significant look at Sicarius, who—standing statue still—looked right back at her with equal understanding.

"I only knew of the organization," Amaranthe said, painting a neutral expression on her face before Ms. Maple could think her odd, "not the leader. I don't imagine she handles the grant awards personally, though, so it probably doesn't matter."

"No, I understand she's very busy."

Threatening to kill the emperor, yes. Amaranthe barely kept the edge out of her smile as she thanked Ms. Maple for her help.

* * * * *

The Imperial Real Estate Library was located in a bland concrete building. Above the double doors, an engraved timeline marked the significant dates in the seven hundred years of imperial expansion. What more could one need in the way of adornment?

"Are you sure you don't want to go back and send Books out here?" Amaranthe asked at the base of the stairs. "The next step is to find out where this Larocka Myll lives. This will involve long, tedious research." As soon as she said it, she winced. That sounded condescending. As if she didn't think he was capable of doing it. "I'm sure you'd have no problem with it, but I don't want to bore you." Was that any better? Maybe she ought to just stop talking.

"You'd rather bore Books?" Sicarius asked.

"He used to grade papers for a living. He's probably used to it."

"I can do tedious research. Let's go."

He must want Larocka's address badly. Maybe he thought he could get it by this evening and stick a dagger in her back that night.

"As you wish," Amaranthe said.

She led Sicarius past a young desk clerk who did not look up from his book when they passed. The cavernous interior had one main floor, surrounded by four tiers of balconies. Tall rolling ladders allowed access to the wall-to-wall shelves, which rose from floor to eighty-foot ceiling. They were crammed with books on property taxes, real estate law, underwriting, and other scintillating topics. Tall windows let in light, and gas lamps shed bubbles of illumination, but even in the afternoon it felt like twilight inside the building.

"The residential plat maps are in the back." Amaranthe weaved through a maze of standing bookcases, filing cabinets, and dusty tables. They only passed one other person, who was on the way out. "Industrial and business are in the basement." She pointed to a couple places where narrow stairs led down.

"With Larocka's name, we can look up where she lives?" Sicarius asked.

His eyes probed the shadows, out of habit, she supposed. Somehow she doubted many bounty hunters lurked at the Real Estate Library.

"Unfortunately, it's not that easy," she said. "If you know an address, or lot number, it's a simple matter to find out who owns the property, what they paid for it and when, who owned it before, and all sorts of semi-interesting stuff. But, you can't just look up names and find people's addresses."

"We have to look at maps of all the houses in the city and hope to find her name? Lokdon, there are a million people in Stumps."

"Regretting your quickness to volunteer for this?" She slid him a smile over her shoulder. "Don't worry. First off, only about ten percent of the people in the city own property. Second, the new rich gravitate toward the Ridge, where the houses—and the parcels—are big, so it'll be easy to skim through the names on the plat map. I'd bet two weeks of pay she lives up there. Well, I would if anyone was paying me anymore."

They spent the afternoon hunkered over maps in the back corner of the building. The daylight filtering through the windows waned, and the property lines grew squiggly before Amaranthe's eyes. It was a good thing Sicarius had not taken her up on that bet.

"That's it. We've looked at every house on the Ridge." Yawning, she leaned back, tipping the front two legs of her chair off the ground. Maps scattered the table with books keeping the edges from rolling up. "I was sure she'd live there. It's a status symbol. Every business man or woman who makes it buys a house up there."

"She could be married with the house in her husband's name," Sicarius said.

"Not unless she bought it more than twenty years ago. Today's law says both names go on the property. I suppose she could be that old, but..."

"Can a house be purchased under a business name?"

Amaranthe's chair slammed down. "Of course! Sicarius, you're brilliant. I should have thought of that." She shoved the chair back and bounced to her feet. "I can look up all her businesses with just her name. In fact, the building is just down the street. Oh, but it'll close soon. I've got to hurry. Be back in a half hour. Why don't you..." She looked around. There wasn't anything for him to do until she had the information. "Why don't you go back and make sure our team isn't burning down the cannery? You've been a lot of help already. I can finish here."

Before he could answer, she skipped into the nearest aisle and raced to the front of the building.

It took forty-five minutes, and some negotiating with the clerk to stay past closing, but she came out with a list of businesses. Larocka was involved in everything from smelters and canning to tourism and gambling.

When Amaranthe returned to the Real Estate Library, the clerk had disappeared. She glanced at the hours posted on the desk. Though darkness had descended outside, the building was supposed to be open another two hours. She hoped Sicarius hadn't had some altercation with the man that required...removing him.

Telling herself it was unlikely, she headed for the back corner.

Sicarius was gone. Even though she had told him to go, she found herself wishing he had stayed. He was a quick study, and she doubted Books could have done anything Sicarius hadn't.

The plat maps still sprawled across the table. Looking now for companies on the list instead of Larocka's name, Amaranthe leaned down, prepared to go over them again.

Almost immediately, an uneasy feeling made her straighten. Had she heard something? She wasn't sure.

She peered down the aisles of bookshelves behind her. The lamps on the outside walls barely illuminated the rows, but nothing moved amongst the deep shadows. None of the tables within sight were occupied, nor had she seen or heard anyone else since entering. Still, she sensed eyes upon her.

Slowly, Amaranthe tilted her head back.

A man stood on the balcony above, his arms draped across the railing. It was not Sicarius.

Dressed all in brown, including a long leather jacket, he wore a pistol and almost as many daggers as Sicarius. Thick shadows played across his bald head, scarred face, and beard stubble. He folded a piece of paper and slipped it into a pocket.

"You're not what I was expecting." His dark eyes ran up and down her body, lingering on her breasts.

She touched a bulge in her parka, reassuring herself she had her knife.

In one liquid motion, the man vaulted over the rail, dropped fifteen feet and landed on the table in an easy crouch. She skittered back, bumping against the end of a bookcase. His soft boots hadn't even rustled the papers.

Fear shot through Amaranthe's limbs. This was not some random molester. That paper he'd pocketed—it must have been one of her wanted posters.

"Can I assist you? What are you looking for?"

The man—bounty hunter?—fingered the paper she had set down, the list of Larocka Myll's business entities. "Indeed you can. You can *assist* me all night long." His leer had none of the charm of one of Maldynado's. "As much trouble as you've given Hollowcrest, I figured you'd be some giant beefy woman with arms like cannon barrels. Not a perky little kitten. Yes, you'll have to assist me quite a bit before I hack off your head for Hollowcrest."

"You've been following me for him?" She eased to the side so the bookcase did not block retreat, though she doubted she could outrun him. Who would she run to anyway? Night had fallen, and the streets were empty. The image of the vacant clerk desk flashed through her mind. Was there even now a body stuffed behind it, out of sight?

He only smiled, his eyes chilling and invasive. "Not at all. This was the purest stroke of luck. Hollowcrest has me researching Myll, too, you see. Maybe you can share your findings with me before..."

"I'll have more information if you leave me alone to work a while." She backed into the aisle. Nothing but books stood within reach; she doubted throwing a book at someone who moved like Sicarius would help. "Why don't you come back tomorrow?"

"I don't think so." He leaped off the table.

Amaranthe whirled, using the movement to hide the drawing of her knife. She sprinted down the aisle. At the end of the row, she darted behind the bookcase and dropped into a crouch. With luck, he would expect a standing target when he lunged around the corner. She might have a fraction of a heartbeat to surprise him.

But many heartbeats skipped by, and he didn't round the corner. She dared a glance down the aisle. It was empty. She looked down the one on the other side of the bookcase. Empty too.

He's toying with me.

She looked up. Too late.

The dark form dropped from the top of the bookcase. She leaped to the side, slashing at the inside of his ankle.

Too fast to see, he kicked the blade from her hand. By the time it thudded onto the carpet, he was on her, his hand around her neck. He tore her parka from her shoulders.

She tried to jerk her knee into his groin, but he blocked and pressed her into the end of the bookcase.

He loomed broader and a foot taller than her. He pinned her with his body, trapping her arms. A sewer odor rolled off him and assaulted her nose. He shoved his hand into her blouse and mashed her breast.

She'd escaped from groping men before, but he was too big, too strong, and he didn't give her any space to gather any leverage.

If she could get his pistol, or one of his knives...

She needed to free her hand first. She twisted, and her knuckle bumped against a knife hilt.

His hand tightened on her neck, a vise on her windpipe.

"More fun if you're alive," he rasped, hot breath flooding over her, "but not a requirement."

Tears pricked her eyes. She wasn't going to be able to get away from him. "Thought you...wanted...information."

His fingers denied her air, but she couldn't give up. She dropped her chin, thinking she might bite his wrist, but he knew what he was doing.

"Later," he panted.

He yanked her skirt down and his maw lunged in close. She bit his lip. She tasted blood, but he laughed. He drew back his arm to punch her. The movement gave her just enough space to grab for the knife. The angle was awkward, but she yanked it out, twisted her wrist, and jabbed it into his chest...

...only to have the blade deflected by his ribs. Cursed ancestors! He'd kill her for sure now.

But a spasm jerked through him, and his eyes bulged wide.

Quick to take advantage, Amaranthe shoved him, preparing for another stab. But he stumbled away. Shock plastered his face as he grabbed at his back and staggered around.

A knife hilt protruded from between his shoulder blades. He wobbled, pitched forward, and collapsed on the carpet.

Twenty feet away, Sicarius stood, rolled plat maps in one hand and a second throwing knife ready in the other.

"Thank the emperor." Amaranthe sucked in deep breaths, dropping her hands to her knees for support.

"You should have screamed," Sicarius said blandly. "I was in the basement."

"I thought you'd left."

"Work's not done."

She tried to pull her clothes into a semblance of order, but her hands wouldn't stop shaking, and the buttons thwarted her. She grabbed her parka, slid down the bookcase, and pulled her knees up to her chin. Feeling vulnerable, she watched Sicarius with more wariness than he deserved.

After scanning the shadows and listening for a moment, he searched the dead man's clothing. An inner pocket offered up a wad of money and a small notepad. He flipped through the latter, then held it and the cash out, silently asking if Amaranthe wanted them.

She did not yet trust her hands. "Yes. Just...in a minute. You can..." Go? Stay? She wasn't sure what she wanted.

For a moment, he simply stood, gazing down at her, and Amaranthe felt a stab of bleak amusement. *He doesn't know what to do.*

She was about to tell him to get started on the business names and that she'd be fine—he'd arrived in time, after all—but he stepped around the body, and sat beside her, not quite touching.

Sitting in the shadows, with a killer, in an empty building, gazing at the corpse of another killer. When had her life grown so strange?

"Anyone you know?" Chin on her knees, she pointed her nose toward the body.

"An assassin. I've met him before."

"Then I appreciate your willingness to stab an acquaintance in the back on my behalf." Talking felt inane, but she did not want to dwell on what had almost been.

"Any assassin who allows himself to be distracted by his work deserves a knife in the back. It's not professional."

Amaranthe almost laughed, imagining some handout in Assassinry 101, where rules of etiquette were passed out with Sicarius's wisdom at the top of the page. She doubted he had intended the statement to do so, but it lightened her mood. "I guess I'm lucky to have recruited a professional assassin."

"Yes."

Modest, he wasn't, but compared to the dead man on the floor, he was a gentleman. Remembering the way he had not looked at her while she bathed, she wondered if his apparent lack of interest was an actual lack or self-imposed detachment. Might it be a "professional" choice to define her as "work" and stay focused on his goals? It was probably better not to ask. If he just wasn't interested, did she really want to know? And if he were, what would she do with the knowledge anyway? Ask him out on a date in between the blackmailing, counterfeiting, and assassination attempts? Still, curiosity got the best of her tongue.

"Am I work?"

The sideways look he gave her was the closest thing to humor she had seen from him. "You're a *lot* of work."

"I meant, uhm, never mind."

His eyes glinted, and he held out the notepad, already open to a specific page.

"Right." Amaranthe accepted it this time and gawked when she read it. "Larocka's address!"

"If his notes are correct, yes."

"This is all we need, then. We can—wait." She tapped the notepad on her knee a couple times. "He was here looking for more information on Larocka for Hollowcrest. I assume that means Hollow wants the Forge leader assassinated—he wouldn't want someone killing the emperor he's drugging into submission, now would he? But the home address wasn't enough for some reason. Why wouldn't an assassin be able to get in and kill her at home?"

"Wards?"

"What?"

"Barriers or alarms made using the mental sciences," Sicarius said.

"A Turgonian businesswoman who knows magic?" she asked skeptically.

Sicarius held up the thick rolls of paper. "These are the plat maps for the industrial and business sections. If you have the name of her business—"

"Businesses. She owns more than a dozen in her name, and there are numerous partnerships as well."

"Let's find all her properties then," Sicarius said.

Amaranthe nodded. "I bet that's what Hollowcrest's assassin was looking for. If you can't kill them at home, kill 'em at work."

"A valid strategy."

CHAPTER 12

FEVER FLUSHED SESPIAN'S FACE, TREMORS coursed through his body, and nausea writhed in his stomach. At least he could think straight—when he wasn't hunched over in the water closet. Fortunately, the doctor had declared his illness the flu, rather than guessing drug withdrawal, and that was the diagnosis Sespian gave to the parade of faces passing through to check on him, each offering condolences, sincerity levels varying. Not sure who he could trust, he viewed everyone with suspicion.

As night darkened the windows, the most suspicious of them all strolled in with a tray. Hollowcrest held a single cup of apple herb tea.

Fear replaced the nausea in Sespian's belly, even as saliva filled his mouth. Steam wafted from the cup, carrying the scent of cloves and cinnamon. Feeling betrayed that his body should want the drugged tea, he struggled to mask his expression.

Had Hollowcrest simply come to ensure Sespian received his nightly dose? Or did the old curmudgeon suspect what was really behind this "flu?"

Hollowcrest pulled a chair to the bedside and perched his lean frame on the edge. Hawk eyes peered from behind those glasses.

"How are you feeling, Sire?" He held out the cup.

"Horrible." Sespian accepted it and set it on the table next to the bed.

"It's a good idea to drink your liquids when you're ill."

"I know. I will."

Hollowcrest's eyes narrowed. Yes, that was suspicion. Sespian picked the cup up with a weak smile. He drew his knees up and held it

in his lap. Hollowcrest watched him intently. Sespian pretended to take a sip.

Hollowcrest relaxed an iota, but he made no move to leave. Worse, he settled back in the chair. "You've missed a couple days of meetings. Let me apprise you of the latest imperial news."

As he launched into a monotonous spiel, Sespian slumped against the pillows. He's going to stay until I've finished *the cup.*

What could Sespian do? If he drank it and his symptoms suddenly disappeared, Hollowcrest would know Sespian knew about the drug. If he did not drink it, Hollowcrest would also know.

Minutes ticked past. Hollowcrest droned on. Sespian pretended to take another sip.

He drew his knees up further, blocking the view of his lap from Hollowcrest. With one hand, he edged the blankets up. Careful to hide his movements, he slid the cup under the sheets and poured it onto the mattress. Moisture dampened his pajamas, but he kept his face blank. The staff would think him incontinent, but as long as it fooled Hollowcrest....

He feigned several more sips, then set the empty cup on the table. Hollowcrest's eyes tracked the motion. His update of imperial affairs soon ended.

Hollowcrest stood and leaned over the cup. Once he saw it was empty, he plucked it up and smiled. "Good night, Sire."

Sespian glared after the old man, waiting until the door snicked shut to move to the dry side of the bed. He slipped a folder out from under the pillows, ensuring it had not been damaged. He flipped open the roster of men working downstairs in Imperial Intelligence. It was time to find some allies and get rid of Hollowcrest.

* * * * *

The final rasp of the paper cutter sent a nervous quiver through Amaranthe's stomach. She and Books stared down at the culmination of their work. Elsewhere in the cannery, Akstyr was hanging paper on lines. Outside, Maldynado stood watch. Newly nailed boards across the broken windows shut out the night's chill and, more importantly, denied prying eyes.

Amaranthe pushed a kerosene lamp closer, and Books inspected both sides of their first completed twenty ranmya bill. A legitimate bill rested beside it for comparison.

"It looks real," she breathed.

"An accurate facsimile." Books held the fake bill up to the light. "The image is perfect. The paper is...well, we can wash the bills and crinkle them up. I think they'll pass all but a thorough inspection."

Though this had been Amaranthe's plan all along, and their success should have elated her, misgivings tangled her mind. Even if she meant her scheme to save the emperor, counterfeiting was high treason—punishable by death—whether she intended to circulate the bills or not. Nobody had been hurt yet, but how long could her luck hold? Did she have the right to risk these men's lives? Even if their sacrifices might save Sespian? And if luck favored her, and the counterfeiting succeeded, could she actually bluff Hollowcrest and Larocka Myll into succumbing to her demands with these bills?

Yes, the answer had to be yes, or she might as well give up now. But she could not do that. Sespian deserved a chance to rule as he envisioned, and after seven hundred years of war and conquering, the empire needed someone who'd rather wield a pen than a blade. And, philosophical factors aside, she needed her name cleared. Sicarius might be able to walk the streets with a million ranmya bounty on his head, but she wasn't the fighter he was, and she wouldn't live long with people hunting her.

"I am uncomfortable with this." Books set down the counterfeit and reached for a pungent bottle of apple brandy.

"As am I, but what choice do we have?"

"The choice to do nothing and let events unfold as they will."

"That's unacceptable," Amaranthe said.

Books considered the two inches of liquid left, removed and replaced the cork a couple times, but ultimately set the bottle back down without taking a swig.

"Saving the rest for later?" she asked.

"I haven't had a drink today. I was thinking of quitting."

"Oh?" Normally, Amaranthe would applaud the resolution, but having one of her few resources incapacitated for days with the shakes would not be convenient. Still, she could hardly encourage him to drink. "An admirable goal."

Books shrugged and looked away. "How do you know your boy emperor will be any better than Hollowcrest or whatever lackey Forge would put forth?"

"He's better. I've met him. He's a good man." She tried to forget she was basing her beliefs on a couple of three minute conversations.

"I hope you're right."

Akstyr sauntered over. Paperclips hung from his ear lobes, his nostrils, and the hem of a threadbare shirt several sizes too big for him. "Is that a finished one?"

"Indeed," Books said.

"Let me see." Akstyr reached for it.

Books jerked the bill away. "Careful, you'll damage it."

"I'm not a three year old."

"No, you only dress like one."

"Gentlemen." Amaranthe plucked the bill from Books's grip and handed it to Akstyr. "I'm sure there will be no damage done, but if there were, we do have plenty more."

After a quick sneer at Books, Akstyr surveyed both sides. "Want me to try spending it?"

"No," Amaranthe said and Books shouted.

If not for the gust of cold air blowing snow through the back door, Amaranthe would not have noticed Sicarius's entrance. He glided to their counter, white flakes dusting his hair and shoulders. They had finished researching Larocka's long list of properties that morning. She did not know where he had been since then.

Books returned to the press to prepare the next batch.

Wordlessly, Amaranthe gestured for Akstyr to let Sicarius see the bill.

Sicarius studied it briefly. "Sufficient."

"Ready for a mission?" Amaranthe asked him. "You too, Akstyr."

"Huh?" Akstyr glanced at Sicarius. "With him?"

"You wanted someone who could watch your back while you worked your science, didn't you?" She smiled, willing Akstyr to forget that Sicarius had threatened to break his neck a couple days earlier. "There isn't anyone better."

"Uhm." Akstyr didn't look sold.

"What mission?" Sicarius asked.

"I would like a chance to observe Larocka Myll. We've got a long list of businesses and properties she owns, but if we have to visit each personally, hoping to catch her there...it'll be fool's luck if we run into her before the emperor's birthday. Someone with as many apple tarts in the oven as she has won't be personally overseeing any of her businesses. Our best bet will be to catch her at home."

"Which is likely warded," Sicarius said.

Akstyr's eyes twitched; he recognized the term. Good. While she doubted someone so young would have much of a magic arsenal, if he could identify it being used, that alone would be worth a lot.

"Maybe," Amaranthe said. "That's what we need to verify. We can't assume that just because Hollowcrest's assassin had trouble getting in means there isn't a way. That fellow didn't have Akstyr's help investigating. And he was an unprofessional lout."

"So, we scout the house." Sicarius nodded.

"And if there is a way in—"

"I'll kill her tonight," Sicarius said bluntly.

"Er, yes, that would preclude the need for me to observe her." Amaranthe would have preferred a solution that did not include killing people, but she doubted Sicarius would agree and did not want to argue with him in front of the others. "Just make sure she doesn't have accomplices with orders to carry her work on. Forge could be a large coalition."

"I know how to question someone," Sicarius said.

"Of course." She lifted an apologetic hand.

Though his expressionless facade remained in place, he seemed testier than usual tonight. Did he simply taste the chance to rid the emperor of his biggest threat? Or was something else going on? Where did he go when he wasn't with them at the cannery?

"Boy, come." Sicarius gestured for Akstyr to lead the way out the door.

Akstyr gulped and glanced at Amaranthe before scurrying for the exit. Remembering Sicarius's earlier admission that all these men were disposable, she hoped she wasn't endangering Akstyr's life. But surely Sicarius would recognize the advantage of keeping a fledgling wizard around in a city where magic was believed the stuff of myth.

"You look concerned." Books turned the wheel to screw down the press.

"It's my new normative state," Amaranthe said. "Are you up to helping me with some research tomorrow? If they don't succeed in killing anyone tonight?"

"What do you need?"

"I want more information on Larocka and her businesses. I have names for all of them, but some aren't illuminating. Right now, we know where she lives and where her properties are located. That's a good start, but it'd be useful to know more about her history and her connections. Maybe they could lead us to other members of the Forge group. Also, if her home is magically protected, how did that come to be? Has she traveled out of the country? Does she bring back wizards like others bring back souvenirs?"

"You suggest a trip to the library?" Books said. "Some time spent perusing the newspapers and industry publications?"

"I think it'd be an enlightening experience."

"Enlightening enough to keep me from having to stand outside tonight, pretending I know how to pull watch duty?"

Amaranthe smiled. "Perhaps."

* * * * *

When Amaranthe stepped outside after midnight, she caught Maldynado peeing his name in the snow. The bright, starry sky revealed a little too much and she cleared her throat as she approached.

"So much for keeping our hideout inconspicuous," she said.

"Standing out here is about as exciting as watching cherries ripen." Without a glimmer of embarrassment, Maldynado buttoned his pants. "I've got to keep myself amused and awake somehow."

"Anything happen while you were out here?"

"Not really. A grizzled old veteran using a musket for a cane took up residence in the warehouse on the next dock, but I think he's just squatting for the night. He built a fire and went to sleep."

"All right, thanks," she said. "You can go to sleep now."

He started past her, but paused and frowned down. "Have you had any? That press was in there creaking longer and louder than...my bed most nights."

"I'm fine." Amaranthe stretched and jumped to ward off the chill. When he hesitated, she added, "You're welcome to stay out here and regale me with tales of your bedroom exploits, but I assume you want some sleep."

"Depends on whether Books is snoring again," Maldynado muttered, but he lifted a gloved hand in parting and tramped indoors.

Amaranthe paced the perimeter of the cannery to stay warm. She alternated between yawning and shivering. If not for her mittens, she would have added fingernail nibbling into the rotation. Hours passed, and Sicarius and Akstyr did not return.

What if Sicarius had found a breach in Myll's house defenses and gone inside? What if he had been caught? What if, even now, under the influence of some magical torture, Akstyr and Sicarius were spilling kegs full of information on the emperor's drugged state and Amaranthe's plans? What if—

A screech tore through the air.

Amaranthe jumped. Before her heels hit the ground, she ripped her knife out of its sheath. She knew that screech. And she knew it wasn't far away either. A block, maybe two?

The inhuman scream had caught her on the far side of her circuit, and the cannery blocked her view of the street. She could run inside and shimmy up one of those ropes. Or she could sneak out front for a look.

"It was a couple blocks away," she breathed. "I ought to be..." She didn't say safe. To investigate could be stupid, and she knew it. And yet...

The wind shifted, blowing from the north instead of in across the lake. A hint of something meaty tinged the air. Blood?

You're imagining things, girl. You're not a scent hound....

She had to look. Stepping toe first, as lightly as she could, she eased around the corner of the building and crept along the dock toward the street. Something crunched on the snow in front of the building. Amaranthe froze, knife ready, though she doubted her insignificant blade could do anything against that creature.

Akstyr and Sicarius trotted around the corner.

Before she could sag in relief, Sicarius said, "Inside."

"We just passed a big bloody body in the street," Akstyr blurted. "It was still gushing!"

"Inside is good." Amaranthe meant to jog before them at a calm and confident pace. Nerves nipped at her heels though, and she sprinted down the side of the building and through the door.

Sicarius and Akstyr followed right behind. Sicarius shut the door.

"Think we need to be in the rafters?" Amaranthe pointed at the ropes and wondered if she should yell to wake Maldynado and Books. If that creature was nearby, yelling might attract attention.

"Perhaps not," Sicarius said. "It's near dawn."

"You think the creature is nocturnal?" she asked.

"It's been hunting at night thus far."

"Because that's its natural time, or because it's trying to remain unseen?" She eyed her two male companions, wondering if she was being silly for ascribing intelligence to this creature. "Either of you have any idea what we're dealing with?"

"I'd be guessing at this point," Sicarius said.

"That's allowed," she said.

He did not extrapolate.

The screech sounded again.

"That's it," Amaranthe said. "Up to the beams." She ran to the bunks and shook Maldynado and Books.

Maldynado groaned and stuffed his head under his arm. "What time is it?"

Books sat up, his beard sticking out in all directions.

"Early," Amaranthe said. "We need to make a short trip."

A scuffle sounded from above as a climbing Akstyr reached the top and threw himself over the beam. Books mumbled under his breath but grabbed his boots and headed for the swaying rope, apparently accepting the need to do so without a big explanation.

"Up there?" Maldynado, less accepting, stared. "Is there a reason you're encouraging pre-dawn climbing calisthenics?"

"What's that!" shouted a muffled male voice from the warehouse on the nearby dock.

A musket fired, and for a moment all grew still. Then a scream of pain sent a chill hurtling down Amaranthe's spine. The sound broke off with a crunch.

"There's a reason," she answered Maldynado grimly.

"Uh huh, got that." He scrambled out of his bunk, shoved Books aside, and flew up one of the ropes.

Amaranthe skimmed up after them, fear lending power to her arms and legs. In a couple heartbeats, she straddled the beam between Maldynado and Books.

Silence had returned to the waterfront, and the men's heavy breathing mingled with her own. One of the fire barrels still burned below, casting shadows. Smoke gathered in the rafters, obscuring Sicarius, who crouched on the beam closest to the door, ten feet away.

"What are we hiding from?" Books whispered. "Nobody ever explained the ropes."

"Remember that dead man you saw outside of the icehouse?" Amaranthe asked.

"Yes."

"We're hiding from the thing that killed him."

"The bear the papers mentioned?" Books asked. "The one that's been mauling people?"

"The papers mentioned it," she said, "but it's not a bear."

"It sounds like the veteran next door shot it," Maldynado said. "Or shot at it."

"If it's wizard-made, no sword or pistol ball is going to stop it," Akstyr said.

"Wait," Amaranthe said. "Akstyr, do you know what it is?"

He shrugged. "Haven't seen it."

"If you saw it, could you identify it?"

"If I say yes, are you going to push me off the beam and make me go look?"

"I won't," she said.

"I might." Maldynado, who perched nearest Akstyr, patted him on the shoulder.

Akstyr slid out of reach. "I've read about creatures wizards can create. If I saw it, or you described it to me, then maybe I could say what it is."

"Great," Maldynado said. "Let's invite it in for breakfast. Who wants to volunteer to be the meal?"

"You're beefiest," Books said. "And most expendable."

"There are no free meals here," Amaranthe said before Maldynado could return the insult. She eyed the ceiling, wondering if any panels led to the roof. If she could figure out a way to get up there, maybe she could see the creature without endangering herself. Unfortunately, the dim light did not highlight any access panels, nor were the boarded windows high enough to provide a gateway to the roof.

"I believe it's gone," Sicarius said.

"I believe I'll wait a little longer to hop down and find out," Maldynado said. "Whose idea was it to set up shop in the middle of this critter's hunting grounds, anyway?"

Amaranthe looked at Sicarius, who remained motionless, ear cocked in the direction of the last outside noise.

"An unfortunate coincidence," she said.

"Are you sure it's a coincidence?" Books asked.

She adjusted her weight on the narrow perch. A sliver of wood broke away and spiraled to the floor. "If it was looking for us specifically, I think it'd take a more direct route."

"Perhaps," Books said, "but isn't this the second time it's killed someone within meters of your location?"

Yes, and she could not dismiss the possibility that her research was making her a target. Could Larocka Myll somehow know about her already? The wanted posters implied Hollowcrest knew Amaranthe was still alive, but he would not have access to magical creatures, would he?

"What did you two find at Larocka's house?" she asked. Better to spend this time working on a problem she could control.

"It's blocked to outsiders," Akstyr said. "The wards are invisible until you smack into them like a concrete wall. Someone powerful made them." Excitement tinged his voice. Either the spy mission had agreed with his sense of adventure, or perhaps the proximity to real magic stirred his passion. "There were lots of folks coming and going, though. Rich street eaters with their own steam carriages and drivers."

"And they walked through these wards?" Amaranthe rubbed her eyes. The smoke from the barrel was making them water. Several mo-

ments had passed without a sound from outside, but Sicarius had not yet climbed down.

"Sure did," Akstyr said. "It looked like they had invitations."

"They did," Sicarius said. "I listened in on several conversations in the street."

Without anyone ever knowing, Amaranthe wagered.

"Larocka and a male business partner named Arbitan Losk host events for the influential among the warrior caste and the business elite," Sicarius said.

"Events?" she asked.

"Social balls, dinner parties. Tomorrow night's event..." Sicarius glanced toward the hint of light seeping through the boarded windows and corrected himself. "Tonight's event is pit fighting. It sounded like a weekly venture with high-stakes gambling over outcomes."

"Dog or cock fights?"

"People," Sicarius said. "Slaves chosen to fight to the death."

Books shifted on the beam. "That's outrageous!"

"And against the law," Amaranthe said. Slavery hadn't been allowed since the Revolt of 654 had threatened the imperium from within. And human pit fighting had been illegal in the capital even longer.

"An easy change once Forge puts their own puppet on the throne," Sicarius said.

"Do you think they have that much power?" she asked. "The note I read mentioned civil war, but numerous forces would come into play if that happened."

"We've reached a point where businesses may command more funds than the government or even the old warrior caste families," Books said. "In such a war, an entity like Forge may very well come out on top."

"That's not going to happen," Amaranthe vowed. "I need to get in, observe Larocka, and figure out how many people are a part of the kill-the-emperor scheme. Is it just her, or does she speak for all Forge members?" She tapped on the wood beam. "Since sneaking in won't work, the logical route is to get an invitation. Maldynado, this is your circle. Do you know anyone who could get us in?"

Maldynado stretched and cracked his spine. "I know a man who could probably get you invitations to any event in the city. His family

has been powerful since the first days of the empire, and they know *everyone* who's important."

"Can you talk to him today?"

"I can take *you* to talk to him. He won't give me anything."

Amaranthe had planned to help Books research. If she was visiting Larocka's home that night, there was more urgency than ever to learn everything possible about the Forge leader. "Are you positive you can't do it alone? You could be underestimating your charm."

"Trust me, I never underestimate my charm or any of my other magnificent attributes. They work great on women. Alas, men tend to see me as an unwelcome rival. You, he might listen to. You're good at talking people into things."

"What makes you say that?"

"Because I'm perched in the rafters of a cannery, at risk from a man-slaying magical creature, and spending time with a drunk, a gangster, and an assassin at...what time *is* it?"

* * * * *

Amaranthe tugged at the collar of her blouse. The businesswoman's outfit Sicarius had purloined for her was dressier than any of the clothes she had in her own closet—back when she had a closet—but she still felt grossly underdressed. She and Maldynado stood before the Onyx Lodge on a street lined with steam carriages. Chauffeurs chatted between the massive vehicles while their employers loitered inside. Replete with marble steps, gold-gilded trim, and ornate columns, the exclusive club had doubtlessly never invited an enforcer in without warrant-waving beforehand.

"Quit fidgeting," Maldynado said.

"I'm not fidgeting; I'm adjusting." Amaranthe *adjusted* the constricting collar again.

"You look fine. If you didn't, I wouldn't be seen with you."

Maldynado had spent the morning arranging the meeting. Sometime during the hours he had been gone, he had also arranged attire fitting a scion of the warrior caste. Beneath his greatcoat, he wore an exquisitely-tailored black suit with a flamboyant red silk waistcoat. The cut of the clothes accentuated his broad shoulders, narrow hips, flat stomach, and all other physical characteristics men coveted and women drooled over.

"Thanks," she said dryly. "What's the name of the fellow we're meeting?"

"Avery Mithsaranu Exaltuscrest the Fourth."

"Is he as pretentious as the name makes him sound?"

"More," Maldynado said.

Inside, a butler in clothing almost as fine as Maldynado's took their coats. He led them to a parlor where low tables, leather sofas, and indolence-inspiring armchairs awaited. Dividers and indoor foliage made each seating area private.

They stopped at a table near a floor-to-ceiling window overlooking a courtyard where bare-chested men boxed and wrestled in rings. Though the warrior caste might appreciate the luxuries their wealth bought, few forgot their roots.

Dressed in a suit accented with leopard furs, the man waiting at the table sneered at Maldynado and did not seem to notice Amaranthe. He might have been Maldynado's age, but the thin hair swept over his head in an attempt to camouflage a balding pate made him look older.

"Maldynado," Avery said. "Surprised to receive your message. Last I heard you were whoring yourself out to old hags."

Amaranthe gaped. Those were not exactly the dulcet word choices one expected from a gentleman.

"Ave, always a pleasure to hear your genteel tones," Maldynado said. "Though I'm sure you only agreed to meet so you could get the latest gossip on my life and update all your lowly cronies."

"Lowly? You dare call anyone lowly when you're the one who avoided military service because you were afraid some enemy might come along and break your pretty nose?"

"As opposed to the nine months you served in that tropical resort on the gulf—that is until your medical discharge. Ankles still swollen?"

"A congenital weakness, alas."

The two men flashed edged smiles at each other, reminding Amaranthe of circling wolves, albeit extremely well-dressed wolves. It was a bad start to the meeting. She needed to jump in.

"Introduce me," she mouthed as Maldynado pulled out her seat.

"Ave, this is my friend, Amaranthe," Maldynado said.

"A businesswoman, how pedestrian."

She forced a smile. "It's good to meet you, Lord Exaltuscrest."

"I know. For business peons like you, it usually is."

And I thought Maldynado had an ego. As if he heard her thoughts, a snicker escaped under Maldynado's breath.

"Do you have an aversion to businesses?" Amaranthe asked.

"No," Avery said. "Just the greedy money-mongers who run them. It's disgusting the way people fawn over their coin nowadays, as if that meant more than blood."

"I can see how that would be frustrating to you." Amaranthe tapped a spoon and tried to think of a tactic to win over this man. Plates, tea cups, and more silverware than she knew what to do with lay before her. She nudged a slightly crooked fork into alignment with the neighboring utensils. "Maldynado tells me your family goes back hundreds of years."

"We were on the boats that came over from Nuria. We built this empire. That's why it's irritating to see mixed-blood peasants, most of them descendants of people we conquered, stumbling their way into positions of power."

A servant brought a platter of pastries. He set it on the table, then passed around mugs of steaming cider. Amaranthe debated on whether to take one of the sweets. She had not run since before her sickness. Maldynado grabbed a fat one and demolished half of it with a single bite. A smudge of creamy frosting stuck to his lip. He licked it with relish.

She grabbed a pastry. I'll run tomorrow.

"So," she said, meeting Avery's eyes, "your family must have fought at some of the greatest battles in history. Frontier Hill, the Aquifer Wars, the Southern Railroad Scandals?"

"Yes, of course. There was a General Exaltuscrest at Frontier Hill who went on to become the first Commander of the Armies."

"Truly? I confess, I know little of the origins of that title."

Avery leaned forward. "It's quite fascinating actually. The emperor used to personally lead troops into every battle, but as the empire increased in size, we often faced enemies on multiple fronts. The position of Commander of the Armies was created so someone with imperial authority could lead the troops when the emperor was elsewhere. Turgonia was glorious back then. We were a nation run by true warriors, not administrators. Lord General Exaltuscrest, now he was a warrior. He..."

Amaranthe was not sure she found the information as fascinating as Avery did, but at least he had an interest in the topic. She nodded and offered encouraging comments between bites of her pastry. Apple, cinnamon, and frosting danced on her taste buds. It was the best thing she had eaten in days, maybe weeks. Maldynado devoured two more.

Avery's lecture transitioned from military heroes to stories highlighting the dangers of the early frontier days. Any time he slowed, Amaranthe prompted him with questions. The man had at least one relative in every major event in imperial history. She could only trace her lineage as far back as a grandfather who had died in a logging accident when she was three, the same year the Southern Blood Fever had taken her mother. She wondered what it would be like to have a claim to all that history. Easy to get lost in it, she guessed, watching her host.

As Avery's stories spun into a second hour, Maldynado's expression vacillated between boredom and bemusement—but mostly boredom.

Avery drained his third cup of cider and checked his watch. "I need to go soon. I forgot, was there something you needed?"

"I'm hoping to find a pair of invitations to Larocka Myll's pit fights tonight," Amaranthe said. "I hear those are good events for burgeoning businesswomen to make useful contacts. Maldynado said you were the one to see since you have connections with everyone in the city."

"Quite, quite, the old boy actually got something right." Avery assumed the edged smile again, this time only directed at Maldynado.

Maldynado sneered back.

"I'll arrange the invitations," Avery told Amaranthe. "Be careful on the Ridge at night though. There's something hunting the streets."

A boy with a bin came in and cleared their plates.

"Yes," Amaranthe said, "I've read about it in the newspapers, but I didn't think this neighborhood had seen any deaths."

"It hasn't," Avery said, "but yesterday before dawn, Sassy Inkwatercrest said she saw a giant brown creature run across her yard and leap the ten-foot fence as if it were a street curb. Others on the Ridge have made similar claims over the last couple weeks."

Amaranthe leaned forward. "Anyone able to identify it? Say for sure what it is?"

"Nobody knows. It's nothing that's been seen in the city before."

Avery insisted on paying for the cider and pastries. Amaranthe thanked him and signaled to Maldynado it was time to go. She almost tripped over the dish boy as she left. She frowned at him, finding it strange he had lurked and listened to their conversation. After starting guiltily, he scampered into the kitchen.

CHAPTER 13

AS THE WAN WINTER SUN DROPPED BELOW THE horizon, Amaranthe and Maldynado hopped off a trolley on Mokath Ridge. Mansions dotted the plowed streets, each on a park-sized lot with a view of the lake. On the sloping lawns, children skied, sledded, and hurled snowballs. A lovely neighborhood on the surface, but Amaranthe did not expect Larocka's house to be so idyllic.

They strolled along the sidewalk checking addresses. Squirrels chattered in maple branches overhead, and one darting critter dislodged a clump of snow. It smacked Amaranthe's cheek and slid down the front of her blouse. With an amused Maldynado watching, she wriggled and untucked to free herself of the icy intrusion.

"I hope that isn't some indication of how the night's going to go," she muttered, smoothing her clothing.

"Oh, I don't know." Maldynado offered a lazy wink as he pointed out an errant button. "I rather enjoyed the show."

After a brief glower, she checked to make sure she still had not dislodged the small pad of paper tucked inside her parka. If she had the chance to take illuminating notes tonight, she would not be unprepared. Her knuckles brushed against her grandfather's knife—also tucked inside her parka. Note-taking could be dangerous.

"I wish we had Sicarius along," she said.

"Why?" Maldynado tapped the emerald-jeweled hilt of his saber, a different weapon than he had worn to the Onyx Lodge—he probably had a sword to match every outfit. "I'm not big and intimidating enough?"

"You're...big, and you do tower over people nicely. It'd just be reassuring to have Sicarius watching our backs. I didn't realize the invita-

tions would have our names on them." She had almost handed Sicarius the second invite anyway, but Akstyr had implied the house's guardian wards would detect name swaps.

"We'll be fine," Maldynado said. "These aren't the kinds of people who loiter at Enforcer Headquarters, eyeballing the wanted posters."

"I'm more concerned about the Forge folks than enforcers," Amaranthe said.

"We have invitations. And we're just going to their party to watch the fun. What could happen?"

"I'm not going for fun; I'm going to snoop."

"Snoop? This morning you said you were going to *observe*."

"Maybe it's the enforcer in me, but I've always thought the terms have a great deal of overlap." Amaranthe veered to avoid branches with more frolicking squirrels. They were fat. Someone in the neighborhood must run a nut buffet.

"Well, I don't think Sicarius would fit in up here. These sorts of events have dress requirements."

"Perhaps with the right costume," she said.

"Not unless you could separate him from his knives. He sleeps with them, you know."

"Does he?" Amaranthe asked. "I've yet to see him sleep."

"I've yet to see *you* sleep."

Amaranthe yawned. Too true. When she returned that night, she hoped to succumb to a twelve-hour slumber. The others could handle the press and watch shifts while she did.

"There it is." Maldynado pointed to a mansion.

Like something from ancient history, the five-story structure boasted stone walls, arrow slits, turrets, and even a crenellated rooftop. Modern additions such as picture windows, glass doors, and new wings crafted from brick and timber suggested the building had seen numerous renovations over the years. They did little to dilute the impression that Amaranthe and Maldynado were visiting a fortress.

They headed up a long walkway with gas lamps burning at intervals. Flagstone steps led to a vast porch swept clean of snow. Waterfalls on either side of the entrance emptied into steaming pools, and the smell of lilacs wafted from them. Amaranthe rolled her eyes at the ostentatious display. If the house was any indication, Larocka was not in need of extra funds. *Then why is Forge blackmailing Hollowcrest for tax breaks?*

Before Maldynado could knock, the door opened. A majordomo dressed in a crisp red uniform held out his hand. His thick arms and the pair of long knives at his waist suggested he was as much security guard as greeter.

"Invitation, please," he said.

Maldynado offered the envelope Avery had supplied. The majordomo opened it and inspected it as if forgeries were common.

No, we don't counterfeit invitations. Only money.

"Very good, Lord, ma'am. The other guests are downstairs."

A grand foyer opened before them, but the majordomo directed them to stairs directly to the right of the door. There was no chance for snooping around the mansion or even the main floor. They went down a long flight and turned a corner to travel another batch of stairs before reaching the bottom.

The cavernous basement reminded Amaranthe more of a construction zone than a chic entertaining venue. Pallets of bricks, slabs of limestone, a steam-powered cement mixer, and other lesser tools and materials cluttered the floor along the walls. Massive posts and reinforced steel beams supported the high ceiling. Vehicle doors almost as high stretched along the back wall.

More than a hundred people milled, gravitating toward a central pit with wooden bleachers on two opposing sides. Like Maldynado, many of the men bore swords, gold- or silver-gilded affairs they wore as a woman might jewelry. Women modeled flowing dresses draped with exotic furs such as grimbal, tiger, and black leopard.

On the way to join the crowd, Amaranthe and Maldynado skirted a second pit, a recent excavation with a mound of dirt piled next to it.

"Not done with your renovations yet, Larocka?" someone called.

Recognizing the name, Amaranthe searched for the speaker, or more specifically to whom he spoke.

"Not yet," came the response, a female voice, "but before long, this place will be ready for two fights at a time and it'll hold five times as many spectators."

"We've been busy planning a big celebration for the emperor's birthday," a male voice added.

Amaranthe located the speakers, a couple with linked arms, just in time to see the man give the woman a knowing look. A big celebration indeed. The innuendo screamed at Amaranthe. He had to be in on the assassination threat. What had Sicarius called the business partner? Arbitan Losk, that was it.

Larocka and Arbitan were in their forties or early fifties. Though not beautiful, Larocka Myll oozed warmth and good cheer. Arbitan had a handsome face that drew smiles from the women, though his lifted chin gave him an unattainable feel.

"That's who we're here to observe," Amaranthe murmured to Maldynado. "Let's get closer."

Before she could walk far, a bare-armed, bald man stepped in front of her. Scars crisscrossed his pale-skinned face and head like brambles in a blackberry patch. Though he lacked the height of a Turgonian man—his blue eyes were level with hers—the powerful muscles revealed by his red, sleeveless shirt made him intimidating. His slitted eyes locked onto her accusingly, as if he could guess her thoughts.

She decided to try a smile. "Hello, I'm Amaranthe. Who are you?"

The scarred man's eyes widened, but he quickly resumed his suspicious mien. *What do I say to get rid of this fellow?*

"Security?" Maldynado drawled. "Run along, chap. You're blocking the view."

Apparently, Maldynado's condescending tone was the expected address, for the man inclined his head and strode off. He wore a utility belt bristling with daggers.

"Looks like we found a playmate for Sicarius," Amaranthe murmured.

"Yup. Those were knife scars. I bet he's a former pit fighter who won his way into a security gig."

Larocka stepped onto a bench, so her head and shoulders rose above the crowd. "Thank you all for coming tonight. The first two fighters will be out shortly so you can assess them before making your wagers." She waved toward a bettors' cage carved into one wall. "You know the rules; all bets go through the house. Odds are provided. Take advantage of the complementary drinks and enjoy yourselves."

She stepped down into Arbitan's arms and took a glass from a passing servant. The couple's closeness suggested more than a mere business partnership.

A grinding noise reverberated through the floor. The crowd jostled into place around the pit. Some sat in the bleachers, while others leaned over the edge. With Maldynado's brawn, he and Amaranthe pushed their way into good seats.

Unlike the newly dug hole on the other side of the basement, the main pit had fifteen-foot brick walls with a tunnel leading into it. A steel portcullis was disappearing into the ceiling of the passage.

Four men marched into the pit: two nude fighters and two handlers carrying whips and wearing short swords. Chain leashes and collars secured the necks of the slaves, who trundled forward with slumped shoulders and downcast eyes. On the pit walls, sconces held torches rather than lamps, lending a primeval feel to the arena. Mirrors hanging from the ceiling ensured a good view for all.

While the crowd appraised the fighters and made their bets, Amaranthe watched Larocka and Arbitan. The shaven-headed security man never strayed far from the couple. If he was a bodyguard, he would likely show up at any meeting Amaranthe arranged to present her deal. *Blackmail, call it what it is, girl.*

When the bets had been made, the two handlers unleashed their charges and retreated to the tunnel. One pulled a lever and the portcullis clanged into place.

Larocka held out her hand and waved for the security man with the other. Almost like one of the dejected slaves in the pit, his chest narrowed, and his shoulders sagged. He gave her two identical daggers from his collection, weapons for the fighters apparently. When Larocka held the security man's eyes, he straightened and resumed his stern mien.

"Let the fight begin!" Larocka dropped the daggers into the pit.

The blades pierced the sand floor, hilts quivering. The fighters surged forward, each grabbing a weapon. They did not attack immediately though. They circled each other, hands guarding their knives. Neither growled, snarled, or shouted. They appeared not like riled wolves ready to rip each other's throats out but like friends forced to fight. A few threats from the guards invigorated them.

When the battle engaged in earnest, Amaranthe felt like a twig in an avalanche of craziness: shouting, screaming, and cursing echoed from the ceiling beams. People stamped and jumped, and the wooden bleachers trembled beneath her feet. She would have thought the women in the audience would prove less bloodthirsty, but one rail-thin, gray-haired lady next to her chanted, "Kill him, kill him!" with alarming vigor. Though Amaranthe had ordered Maldynado not make any wagers, that did not keep him from choosing someone to root for.

She glanced over her shoulder toward the stairs. It seemed like all the guests had arrived. She wondered if the majordomo had left his post upstairs. With the majority of the household in the basement, exploration of the upper floors might be possible.

In the pit, a dagger found a chest, and the crowd cheered.

The victor dropped to his knees, hands over his face. His handlers came out and chained him. One hoisted the corpse over his shoulder and carried it out as if it were a grain sack. Two more grim-faced combatants waited in the tunnel.

During the next battle, Amaranthe paid more attention to the hosts. As engrossed in the entertainment as her guests, Larocka cheered, fist pumping. Her partner wore a different expression. Arbitan viewed the fights with detached boredom. More often he surveyed the crowd, but even then he appeared bored, yawning and picking at his fingernails. If he was hosting the fights for profit, Amaranthe would have expected enthusiasm for the success of the event or at least calculation as he contemplated the money his guests were spending. She knew Larocka's list of businesses; maybe it was time to find out Arbitan's interests.

His cool gaze shifted, and he caught her staring.

She looked away, feigning interest in the combatants. In her peripheral vision, she could see him watching her. She swallowed. He couldn't possibly know her thoughts. Could he?

Even when he resumed his scan of the crowd, her discomfort did not wane. Arbitan's aloof detachment reminded her of Sicarius, and she had already seen how dangerous *he* was. She suddenly felt her grand plan terribly juvenile and doomed to failure. She needed more of an edge than some counterfeit bills. And this might be her best chance to find it.

She waited for two more fights to pass, so Arbitan would forget about her, and then tugged on Maldynado's arm. He leaned closer without taking his eyes off the blood-spattered men in the pit below.

"I'm going to look around," she said.

"Now?" Maldynado shouted to be heard. "This is a great fight! You won't see who wins."

"Darn."

She ducked and twisted past gesticulating people and hopped off the bleachers. Someone's elbow clipped her shoulder as the man pumped his fist and shouted. She slid free of the last audience member only to run into several servants with empty trays heading for the stairs. She turned back toward the fights and waited for them to leave.

Then, using the backs of the bleachers for cover, she headed up the stairs. She had not noticed a water closet in the subterranean arena and figured searching for one would make a plausible excuse should someone question her. At least it would if she was accosted early on. It would be a less persuasive story should someone find her on the fifth floor rummaging through the owner's desk drawers.

When she entered the foyer, she saw no sign of the majordomo.

Plush carpeting swallowed her footfalls as she headed for the nearest hallway. Dishes clanked in a kitchen somewhere in the back of the house. Candles and gas lamps burned sporadically, but did little to stave off the depths of the winter night. Intermittent roars and applause floated up from the floor below.

The water closet was behind the first door she checked. As soon as she passed it—and her excuse for wandering—she grew more cautious. She clung to the shadows along the walls and paused to listen every few steps.

Just as she was coming to a staircase, a door creaked open and kitchen noises grew louder for a moment. Amaranthe darted into a closet. She left the door cracked to watch the hallway. A train of servants glided past, trays full of brandy glasses and chilled cider mugs.

Time to get off that floor. She assumed the bedrooms would be upstairs anyway.

She spent the next half hour winding through the numerous floors of the mansion, checking doors, and dodging servants and security guards. Just as she was cursing the house for not having a directory, Amaranthe

spied a single door by itself at the end of a hallway. A golden, ornate LM marked it.

"Finally," she whispered.

The door was unlocked, but she paused before stepping into the short, wide hallway that led into the first room. If magical wards protected the grounds, might not something protect Larocka's suite?

Unfortunately, she had no idea what such wards might look like, if there were physical clues at all. She was about to chance walking in when she noticed a pair of lizard medallions on the walls behind potted rubber trees. The leaves almost hid the medallions. Set a couple feet above the floor, they were identical and level with each other. The intricate metalwork had more flair than most imperial art.

Amaranthe plucked a brown leaf off a plant and dropped it so it would fall through the space between the statues. An orange ray shot from each lizard's eyes, met in the middle, and incinerated the leaf. Tiny ashes wafted to the carpet.

"Magical protection," she murmured. "Check."

She crawled under the lizards and watched for more traps as she moved into the suite. The collection of spacious rooms took up hundreds of square feet. There was a private water closet, an elegant bath, a sitting room, and a book-filled office with two desks. Someone had started fires in each of the three hearths in preparation for the couple's return—someone who might come in at any time to stir the logs.

Amaranthe veered toward the office, avoiding suspicious variations in the carpet and wall ornamentations on the way. She assumed the pink stationery identified Larocka's desk and checked that one first. A drawer held correspondences, but none mentioned anything except legitimate business matters. She found no papers that demonstrated a tie to the Forge organization and certainly nothing as incriminating as a to-do list with "assassinate emperor" at the top.

The handwriting of those notes and letters did look familiar though. Amaranthe gripped the edge of the desk as her mind caught up to her instincts and she identified it. It was the handwriting from the Forge note she had seen in Hollowcrest's office. Larocka had penned that message.

Amaranthe chewed on her lip and released her grip. While it was good to know she was on the right track, she hadn't actually learned anything new. She grabbed one of Larocka's discards from the waste bin

and pocketed it; later, she might need to emulate that writing to send a note to Hollowcrest.

A couple steps took her to Arbitan's workspace. The desk was immaculate. No loose papers littered the top, a wood caddy restrained pens, and, when she peered in a drawer, rows of alphabetized files peered back. She sifted through a couple folders, enough to learn Arbitan was a Turgonian entrepreneur who owned hundreds of acres of orchards around the capital, but she did not have time to poke into every file in every drawer. She feared she had already been gone too long.

Amaranthe glowered. As if the couple had anticipated a search, they had left nothing suspicious anywhere. She drummed her fingers on Arbitan's desk. Criminals always made mistakes. There had to be something. She moved to the built-in bookcases. Maybe a secret compartment hid behind the tomes on business and economics. She prodded and pulled at various books. The titles of some were in languages she did not recognize. At least one of the two had an ecumenical education.

After poking at most of the books, she gave up. Reluctant to return with nothing, she went back to Arbitan's desk and pulled open the drawers and read the file labels more closely. One near the back of the bottom drawer snagged her attention.

Newspaper Clippings.

She stuck her finger in the folder to mark the place and withdrew an article trimmed from the Gazette. *Bear Slays Homeless Man in SoDoc.*

It was the paper's first story about the deadly mystery creature.

Amaranthe poked through the rest of the clippings. They all contained stories about the murders, all in sequential order by date. None were missing. There were even a few from a smaller newspaper that usually focused on business.

She returned the articles to their positions in the folder. Why was Arbitan keeping the clippings? For a moment, she wondered if he might be the wizard who warded the house—and created deadly magical creatures—but she snorted in dismissal. Surely becoming a powerful wizard was a full-time, lifelong pursuit, not something one did between pruning, harvesting, and selling apples. Running orchards wasn't even the type of business that would take one out of the empire where one could stumble across foreign instructors. She closed the drawer. Maybe Arbitan was just interested in mysteries.

A clock on a shelf chimed. Amaranthe cursed. She had been gone over an hour.

Avoiding the known and suspected traps, she hustled out of the room. She forced herself not to leap down the flights of stairs in her rush to return to the anonymity of the fights. She crossed no servants this time and had almost made it to the foyer when footsteps sounded on the stairs leading from the basement.

Amaranthe darted into the water closet and pressed her ear to the door. Muffled voices started up in the foyer, both male and female, though she could not understand the words. She waited for the speakers to wander out of range, but they stopped moving. The voices continued.

Back against the door, Amaranthe stared around the small room, seeking inspiration. A single candle burned on top of the cistern on the opposite wall. A few feet below it, the wash-out squatted, its ceramic bowl embossed with flowers. The room was a perfectly functional place to pee and a perfectly useless place for plotting an escape.

At least she was in a less condemning place than she had been for the last hour. With no better alternative, Amaranthe pushed open the door and stepped out, abandoning her attempts at stealth.

"...don't know," came Maldynado's voice, now distinguishable. "She said the blood was making her sick."

Emperor's warts, he was trying to explain her absence. She shut the water closet door loudly, to ensure it would be heard. Going along with his story, she dropped a hand onto her stomach and hunched over. She shuffled forward, sculpting her face into an expression of discomfort.

"A shame," responded a cool masculine voice. "One expects a stronger stomach from an imperial woman. We are a nation born of warriors after all."

Amaranthe recognized the voice at the same time as she entered the foyer. Arbitan and Larocka were facing Maldynado at the top of the basement stairs. The scarred security man also stood in the room, muscled arms folded across his chest. Though pale beneath the light of the chandelier, Maldynado portrayed little of the nervousness that had to lurk in his thoughts.

Amaranthe wiped the alarm off her face as the Forge folks turned toward her.

"Now, now," Larocka said, "there's no need to be snide, dear. Some women are more interested in numbers than war." She smiled at Amaranthe, who could not tell if genuine warmth backed the gesture. Doubtful.

"I'm sorry to have been gone so long," Amaranthe said in a raspy voice she hoped connoted illness.

"Apology accepted, my dear." The pleasure Maldynado exuded at her approach seemed unfeigned.

That security man regarded her with narrowed-eyed suspicion again. Maybe that was his usual expression. Either way, it did not inspire one to linger. A wild part of Amaranthe wanted to stay and stir up a conversation with the couple, see what she could learn about them, but she had already drawn far more attention than was safe. Also, she suspected Arbitan might learn more about her than she did about him.

"We must be going, dear," she said to Maldynado.

"I was saying just the same thing," he said, "a half hour ago. Women—what they do in the water closet for so long is beyond me." He tossed an aggrieved brotherhood-of-men look at Arbitan, who did not acknowledge it with anything more than a chilly stare.

Amaranthe stepped on Maldynado's foot as she sidled out the door. He winced but managed a goodnight for the hosts as he backed out.

"Do come again," Larocka said.

The door thudded shut. Outside, the lanterns burning along the walkway allowed Amaranthe to read the incredulous expression Maldynado fixed on her as they walked.

"Where were you for that long?" he asked.

"Exploring," Amaranthe said. "You could have left without me."

"Hah! You need a keeper to watch over you." He paused, face twisting with displeasure. "I sound like my mother."

"Careful, you may turn into a responsible fellow."

"Never!" His ferocity startled her. He cleared his throat. "No responsibility for old Maldynado," he added in a lighter tone.

They turned off the walkway and onto the wide street. Stars glittered in the clear night sky, and their breaths fogged the air. Infrequent streetlights burned, more like beacons to guide one from point to point than lamps illuminating the darkness. Hedges, thick and dense despite a lack of leaves, lined one side of the street.

"I can see working for you is going to be an adventure," Maldynado said.

Movement stirred branches ahead of them.

"Looks like we're in for one now," Amaranthe said.

When the figures stepped out of the shadows of the hedges—in front of and behind them—it was too late to avoid being surrounded. An icy gust hustled down the street, swirling powdery snow about eight sets of enforcer boots.

Maldynado drew his sword. Amaranthe, though she feared the effort futile, held her arms up, palms out. She did *not* want a fight with enforcers.

One of the figures turned up a lantern. The light glinted off brass buttons and insignia, revealing the face of the bearer.

"Wholt," Amaranthe blurted.

Sergeant's rank pins shone at his collar. His face was grim, but an inkling of hope entered Amaranthe's mind. This was his squad, his command. If she could convince him Hollowcrest's charges were false, perhaps she and Maldynado could leave without a fight.

"I knew you weren't happy about being passed over for promotion, Lokdon, but I didn't think you'd turn criminal."

"I didn't. Listen, Wholt. I stumbled onto a plot against the emperor. It's Hollowcrest. He's the one—"

"Don't listen to her, Sarge," the enforcer at Wholt's side barked. "Remember what the report said? Kill on sight. She's a witch! She'll turn our blood to stone!"

The annoying upstart rattled the others. The seven men lifted their sword arms, blades reflecting the flame of the lantern. A single word from their commander would send them charging.

"You *know* me, Wholt," Amaranthe said, still not reaching for her knife. "We worked together for six months. If I knew anything about magic, you'd have seen proof surely. Besides, you *have* to know I wouldn't betray the empire."

"Also," Maldynado said, "just to be clear before this all starts, no one has a poster out accusing *me* of magic use, so that kill on sight thing need not apply here."

"Have your man drop his weapon, Lokdon," Wholt said. "We'll make your death quick."

"No, thanks." Maldynado sketched a fencer's salute and dropped into a ready stance. He was probably a better swordsman than any of the enforcers, but they would not attack one at a time in a sporting manner.

"This isn't your fight," Amaranthe whispered to Maldynado. "If you drop your sword, they probably won't hurt you."

"No talking!" Wholt barked, his gaze shooting back and forth between them.

"My two weeks isn't up, boss," Maldynado said. "What's the plan?"

Good question. Amaranthe searched her old partner's face.

"You don't have to do this, Wholt," she said.

"I have my orders, Amaranthe," he said. "I have to..."

Wholt didn't want to do it. If there weren't seven men standing behind him, he would have turned his back and let her walk away. She was sure of it. But if he let her go in front of them, his career would be destroyed. Wind gusted, tugging at her hair as Amaranthe sought a solution.

"Kill them, Sarge?" the most vocal enforcer asked.

"Why not just capture us and take us in?" Amaranthe ignored the others and kept her eyes locked on Wholt. "Let the chief put us to death if that's the order." And, with luck, she would have time to think of something else before that happened. "No innocent blood on your hands."

"Kill on sight, Sarge! We shouldn't be yapping."

"Bet she's weaving magic right now with her words," another muttered.

"Witch," someone behind Amaranthe whispered.

Boots shifted nervously and the circle tightened. The sword tips behind Amaranthe and Maldynado loomed closer. Another moment and whatever order Wholt might say would be lost in yells and clashes as fearful men attacked without waiting.

"Wholt," she whispered. "Give the order. We'll surrender if you agree to take us in. None of your men get hurt. You're still doing your job."

Wholt opened his mouth to speak.

A dark shape loomed behind him, and a dagger appeared at his throat.

"No!" Amaranthe shouted.

Too late. Blood gushed from severed arteries.

The lantern clattered to the ground.

A fast-moving head of short blond hair identified the newcomer. Amaranthe had already known.

"Back to back," she barked to Maldynado. There was no way out of a fight now.

Chaos erupted, and swords slashed in multiple directions.

"Get the witch!"

"Watch out for—"

"Over there!"

Metal screeched behind her as Maldynado engaged someone. Amaranthe held her knife before her, but she only parried when a blade streaked at her chest.

How could she attack enforcers? They were on the same side as her!

Her opponent lunged again, slashing at her face. She ducked the blade and angled into his body. With her knife in hand, she could have finished the fight with a stab to his chest, but she struck with her free hand. She hammered a palm strike into his solar plexus and drove her knee into his groin.

His breath whooshed out, and he bent double. He reflexively brought his elbow down, clipping her shoulder. Wincing, she rammed the heel of her hand into his nose. This time, he pitched backward, hitting the street and curling onto his side.

All around her, deafening screeches of metal tore through the night. Darkness hid the details, and she struggled to tell friend from foe.

"Try not to kill them!" she called, wondering if Sicarius or Maldynado would hear.

An enforcer stepped out of the shadows of the hedge. "Witch." It was the one who had egged Wholt on. "You die!"

He lunged and attacked, not with an efficient fencer's stab but like a logger hacking at a tree. She leaped backward, then jumped in again while the enforcer was trapped by the momentum of his great swing. When he tried to recover, he bumped the foot of the man she had downed earlier.

His attention flickered to the ground, and she kicked his sword hand. The blade flew into the hedge. Branches rattled and snow flew.

"We're not enemies!" she yelled. "Let me explain."

He reached for the utility knife at his belt, but she darted around him. She pressed her blade to his throat, keeping her body beside and behind his, so he couldn't easily kick or punch. She need not have bothered, for he froze at the first touch of cold steel.

"Witch," he breathed.

Not sure what she could possibly say to sway him, she opened her mouth to try anyway. A throwing knife thudded into his chest.

Stunned, she could only gape as he went limp in her arms.

Sicarius appeared to retrieve the weapon before the enforcer hit the ground.

Amaranthe stammered a moment before finding words, and even then they weren't elegant. "What did you...why... He couldn't do anything!"

"Any you leave alive today will be after you tomorrow." Sicarius wiped his blade on the enforcer's uniform and sheathed it with his others.

She could only stare.

He reached out a hand. "Are you injured?"

"No, curse your ancestors, I was never—damn it, you can't try to save the emperor on one hand and kill his civil servants on the other. It doesn't work that way, you—"

She cut off further expletives. Her voice rang, far too loud on the suddenly silent street. Besides, this wasn't his fault. It was hers.

All the enforcers lay sprawled all on the ground, dead or dying. Only a blurry Maldynado stood, sword drooping, chest heaving, as he watched her uncertainly. Everything was blurry. Amaranthe cursed and wiped tears from her eyes.

How had this gone so wrong so quickly?

Legs so numb she could hardly move, she stumbled to Wholt's prone form. With a trembling hand, she turned up the lantern light. There was no use checking for a pulse. He had been dead before he hit the ground. She brushed his eyelids down, closing the accusing gaze.

"I'm sorry, Wholt," she whispered.

CHAPTER 14

THE MOON HAD COME UP, AND SILVERY LIGHT IL-luminated the canneries, warehouses, and docks crowding the waterfront. Amaranthe stared across the frozen lake without seeing any of it. Footsteps crunched on the snowy dock behind her. She winced and rubbed away tears, her wool mittens scratchy against puffy eyes. At least the noise meant it wasn't Sicarius.

Books cleared his throat. "Maldynado told us about the fight."

"Massacre," she muttered.

"And that you...bellowed at Sicarius and cursed his ancestors."

"He killed them all without a thought. He killed my *partner*, Books. Someone I worked with, someone I knew."

"Someone who was about to kill you?" he asked.

"No. That's just it. I was talking to him. I think he was listening. I think he was going to take us to headquarters instead of attacking, and then...well, there would have been a chance to escape. I don't think it had to end this way. People didn't have to die."

"What if you *thought* incorrectly?" Books asked.

"He could have waited to see. He just slithered in and started—" Amaranthe swallowed and sank into a crouch, head buried in her hands as the experience flashed through her mind again. Wholt's slashed jugular.... The shocked expression on his face.... She grabbed a fistful of snow and hurled it off the dock. "We just had to escape. There was no *need* to kill everyone for that to happen."

"And then they would have come after you again."

"You sound just like *him*." For the first time, Amaranthe peered over her shoulder at Books. "Are you actually condoning the murder of those enforcers? Wholt was just doing his duty—something I told him to take more seriously. He didn't deserve to die for following orders."

"That was his decision. When he put on that uniform, he agreed to risk his life for the city, for something he believed in. A lot of men die for nothing at all."

"Books!" She stood and slashed her hand in exasperation. "You were married; don't you know how this is supposed to go? The woman doesn't want you to argue or try to solve the problem with logic. The woman wants you to commiserate with her. You don't have to *fix* anything. Just stand there and nod and say 'uh huh' and 'I understand.' That's all you're supposed to do."

She dropped her gaze and brought her clenched fist to her lips. Get a hold of yourself, girl. You're going to drive them all away. She opened her mouth to tell him she appreciated him coming out, but he spoke first.

"Is that really what women...?" He prodded thoughtfully at his beard. "Hm, maybe that's why my wife left. I always thought I was helping, but she never appreciated it. I never understood why."

At least someone was having useful revelations tonight. She managed a faint smile for him. "Do they not teach these things at professor school?"

"A deficiency in the curriculum, it seems."

She gripped his parka sleeve. "Thank you for coming out here. I'm sorry I snapped at you. You're not the one I'm mad at."

And it wasn't Sicarius either. Amaranthe sighed. She knew who and what he was, and she had cajoled him into helping anyway. Sure, it had been out of desperation, but she could hardly start carrying a sword and then later be surprised it could cut someone. It was her own stupid choice she was angry about. How had she ever thought becoming a criminal to stop criminals would do anything except add horror to the world?

"Yes," Books said, "about that... I don't mean to, ah, try to fix anything, but you may want to apologize to him."

It took her a moment to wrench her mind back to the conversation. "Sicarius?"

"He's not a man you want to turn against you."

"I don't think that's going to happen."

"He has no morality, no conscience. I've seen him kill enforcers too. It's not as if this is a new hobby for him. He's utterly heartless. I'm not sure what hold you have over him..."

The emperor.

"But if I were you," Books continued, "I wouldn't presume it to be absolute. Be careful. You trust too easily. The first day we met, you told me you were wanted by the enforcers. What if I had turned you in?"

"I knew you wouldn't."

"How could you possibly know that?" he asked.

"You weren't sober enough to find Enforcer Headquarters."

Books snorted. "You see people the way you want to see them, not the way they are. You think Maldynado is a gentleman, for spit's sake."

"What do you think he is?"

"A worthless scoundrel who's never worked in his life. And Akstyr— I'm shocked he hasn't murdered us all in our sleep. You're going to get surprised someday. I...don't want to see that. Please be careful. Sicarius isn't someone you can trust. Don't push him too far."

"All right, Books. I'll consider your advice."

"Good." His tone lightened. "I came out here for another reason. I did some research for you today."

"Oh?"

Paper rustled. He held something up, though darkness obscured the details. "It's your list of Larocka's business names. You had question marks by a few of them."

"Yes, it wasn't clear from the names what the businesses did."

"That's what I assumed, so I looked into them. Interden builds steam carts for farm use and the annual Plains Races. Yestfer is a local smeltery, the first in the empire to use raw anthracite coal in the blast furnace. And Tar-Mech creates steam vehicles for military use."

Amaranthe frowned. "Vehicles for the military? One wonders if that might somehow come into play if she carries through her assassination attempt."

"Probably not, unless she intends to run Sespian over with a steam tramper. Though being a supplier to the military might give her some privileged insights into imperial affairs." Books rustled another paper. "I also created a diagram for you. It has Larocka at the center and shows all the people she's been mentioned in concert with in newspapers and

publications. And it shows which of those people are connected with each other. It's all supposition at this point, but some of the names that link most heavily amongst each other could indicate key players in the Forge organization."

"Excellent work, Books." She couldn't stomach the idea of perusing it that night, but perhaps by morning, she would have her resolve—her focus—back. "Are you sure I trust people too easily? I seem to have made the right choice with you."

He lifted a mittened finger. "Yes, but..."

Amaranthe waited.

"Well, I'm obviously more reputable than someone like Maldynado or Akstyr, and...I..."

"Of course," she said. Best to let him off the hook. "Did your research uncover the name Arbitan Losk at all?"

"He's on the diagram, connected to a lot of people," Books said. "It was interesting though, as he doesn't appear to have been anyone worthy of a mention in the papers until the last year."

"According to his desk files, he's an orchard owner. Not as big time in the business world as someone like Larocka. Perhaps a year ago is when they first hooked up, and through her influence he's become someone notable who..."

"What?" Books asked.

"I don't know. Maybe he's using her for something."

"Sleeping his way to prominence and power?"

"You never know," Amaranthe said.

"Well, this is all I have. I'll leave the papers for you to look over in the morning."

"Thank you."

Before he left, he put a hand on her shoulder and said, "Think about what I said regarding Sicarius, please. For all our sakes."

* * * * *

When Amaranthe woke, early morning light slipped between the boards across the windows, streaking the maze of hanging papers with slashes. She could have slept longer, much longer, and quickly identified the sound that had roused her.

Maldynado was chasing a chicken around the building. Shrill squawks bounced from the walls.

"Isabel," he called. "Come back here, girl."

Isabel? Amaranthe rubbed crud out of her eyes. He had named the chickens?

Books, manning the press, said, "Apparently you're not as smooth with the women as you claim."

"Oh, be quiet. You could help. Isabel, stop running!"

"I have *real* work to do." Books had shaved his matted, unkempt beard, and would have looked good, except for his red-rimmed eyes and snow-pale face.

An alarmed curse brought her attention back to the chicken chase. After ramming his hip on a counter, Maldynado fell behind. Isabel rounded a corner and sprinted for the exit, her tiny claws clacking on the floorboards.

Sicarius appeared in the doorway. The chicken squawked and tried to dart past him. He bent and deftly plucked it from its escape route.

Maldynado skidded to a stop, arms flailing to keep from crashing into Sicarius. A stricken expression twisted his face as he looked back and forth from bird to man, as if he feared Sicarius would snap Isabel's neck. Surprisingly, the agitated chicken calmed in his grip. Though his slitted gaze was cool, he extended his arms so Maldynado could take her.

Shaking her head, Amaranthe swung her legs over the edge of the bunk. Sicarius might be pragmatic to the point of deserving Books's 'utterly heartless' tag, but he was not sadistic.

Maldynado accepted the chicken and headed back to the makeshift pen he had constructed. Isabel promptly began fussing in his tight grip. Amaranthe almost smiled, imagining Maldynado as an overprotective father, until Sicarius strode her way. Wholt's slashed throat invaded her mind again. She closed her eyes against the vision.

When she opened them, Sicarius stood before her. He held out a sealed envelope. "A boy came to the dock with a message for you."

Ugh, she wasn't supposed to be getting mail here. That meant people knew where she was and possibly what she was doing.

"What is it?" she asked.

"I would not presume to read your private correspondences." His tone was as warm as the ice under the dock.

Maybe Books was right. Maybe she should apologize. It wouldn't hurt her, though it seemed a betrayal to Wholt's spirit. Would it even mean anything to Sicarius? He never said "please" or "thank you" or seemed to have any use for social rituals.

She fiddled with the envelope. "Did you question the boy?" Perhaps it was one of the children she had seen spying on her.

"No."

Amaranthe frowned up at him. "Why not?"

"If you would curse me for defending you from enforcers, I suspect you'd want me to interrogate a child even less."

"I said question, not interrogate."

"I don't differentiate," he said bluntly.

Jaw slack, she stared as he walked across the room and out the door. No, she did not need the image of a broken and battered child joining Wholt's dead body in her mind. Emperor's teeth, she would have to be careful what she asked Sicarius to do in the future.

Maybe you shouldn't be working with him at all.

She broke the seal on the note and read: *Time to redeem your favor. Mitsy.*

"Feh." Amaranthe glared at Maldynado and Isabel, wishing neither had conspired to wake her.

* * * * *

By day, the towering building that housed the Maze loomed silent and lifeless. Amaranthe tightened her parka against a breeze that whipped at the fur edging her hood. A twinge of trepidation stirred in her belly. What could Mitsy want?

"Thanks for inviting me to come," Books said as they navigated an icy sidewalk toward the steel double doors. "I needed a distraction."

"How long since your last drink?" Amaranthe asked.

"A couple—three days maybe." Sweat gleamed on his forehead. "It's been hard to sleep, and I can't stop thinking about it. I hope I can be of use to you today."

"Me too. I don't trust Mitsy. I wouldn't be here if I didn't owe her a favor. And, now that I know the Forge folks have their fingers in the gambling arena, I wonder if she may be a member of the coalition." Still, Mitsy deserved to know Hollowcrest's men were rounding up her gang members for medical experiments in the Imperial Barracks' dungeon. Maybe sharing the information could help turn her into an ally.

"What's her full name?" Books asked.

"Mitsy Masters."

"I didn't come across it in my research."

"She leads the Panthers gang. I'm not sure she'd be quick to volunteer her life's details to journalists."

Amaranthe tapped on the steel double doors. They swung inward with a hiss of escaping steam. No one waited on the other side.

She and Books walked into the empty building. Before, the crowded arena had instilled claustrophobia, but the absence of people made the place feel eerie, like a long-abandoned ruin. Not a single janitor, bouncer, or maintenance man moved through the descending rows of benches. Nothing moved behind the dark window of Mitsy's office in the rafters. In the corridors of the Maze, the ambulatory walls stood immobile, and no treasure sat on the dais.

"Maybe we've arrived prematurely," Books said.

A hiss of steam came from behind. Amaranthe turned in time to see the big doors swing shut. The clang echoed through the building. She ran to them, grabbed a handle, and yanked. The door did not open.

"Oh, I think we're perfectly mature," she said.

Two internal doors on opposite walls flew open. Five bouncers marched out of each, veering straight for Amaranthe and Books. Their heavy footfalls echoed from the walls and rafters. The bouncers bore a mix of muskets and repeating crossbows, all loaded and aimed toward Amaranthe.

Books tried the door, as if he might have better luck opening it. "This is more of a distraction than I had in mind," he said, fear creeping into his voice.

"Stay calm," she murmured, as much for herself as for him.

The men fanned out and surrounded Amaranthe and Books. Mitsy entered from the door behind the bettors' cage.

"You didn't need to send out quite so many men, Mitsy," Amaranthe said. "I'm just an average fighter without any special training in dodging crossbow quarrels and musket balls."

Mitsy stalked across the aisles. Her frosty eyes felt more dangerous than the weapons. "I thought you would bring Sicarius. I hear you two are close now."

"Not exactly."

Mitsy stopped at the edge of the semi-circle of bouncers. Her flamboyant "my dears" and superior smile had vanished. Pink swam in the whites of her eyes, as if she had been crying.

"I came to redeem my favor," Amaranthe said quietly.

"You came to die, bitch."

The words stunned Amaranthe to silence.

"Don't look at me like you don't know," Mitsy said. "You people have been stealing our brothers and sisters from the streets for months. They disappear mysteriously until we find them dead in a canal, their bodies mutilated. And if that wasn't appalling enough, now you've thrown this...*creature* into the streets to hunt us down. The other deaths were hard enough, but Ragos..."

Amaranthe remembered Ragos, the friendly bouncer who had showed her to Mitsy's office. He was dead now? Surely, he had not deserved such a fate.

"I know of the creature," Amaranthe said, "and the medical experiments in the Imperial Barracks may be responsible for the earlier deaths, but I don't believe they're connected. I don't know why you—"

"You lied! You're a govie, not some businesswoman. You've been an enforcer for years—did you think I wouldn't find out?"

"I'm not anymore," Amaranthe said. "Now I'm—"

"Working with Sicarius. That's even worse. He's Hollowcrest's man, everybody knows that."

Books sucked in a startled breath. Amaranthe was less surprised by the statement, since she had already guessed Sicarius had been associated with Hollowcrest and old Emperor Raumesys at some point.

"My boys have seen you," Mitsy whispered, voice low and hoarse. "All over the city with some warrior caste dandy and Sicarius—Hollowcrest's every-whim-doer. Don't pretend you're not working for the

government. They've probably got you finding targets for whatever it is they're doing to my people."

Mitsy's boys? Amaranthe remembered the child who had followed her through Ink Alley. So, he had not been an enforcer informant but one of Mitsy's. And the dish boy in the Onyx Lodge—had he been one of hers too?

"I'm trying to help the emperor." Amaranthe spread her arms in a conciliatory gesture. "I don't have anything to do with Hollowcrest or that creature."

"If you're working with the emperor, you're a murdering govie."

"I haven't murdered..." Amaranthe could not get out the "anyone." Thoughts of Wholt and his dead men reared in her mind. She may not have personally killed the enforcers, but that did not make her any less responsible.

Mitsy sneered. She wanted Amaranthe to argue, wanted a fight.

Amaranthe eyed the bouncers and the weapons trained on her. She needed to try something else if she and Books were going to get out of here alive.

"I'm sorry," Amaranthe said, meeting the other woman's eyes.

Surprise stole the sneer from Mitsy's face.

"I met Ragos when I came to see you last time," Amaranthe said. "It must have been devastating to lose him."

"He didn't deserve to die like that," Mitsy said. "I should have been able to..."

"I know. When I lost my father, I was powerless to save him. It's frustrating. You feel you have to hurt somebody. But if you can't hurt the ones who were actually responsible, what's the point? It's not your fault, Mitsy. It's not mine either. I don't work for Hollowcrest. I want to put an end to that man's machinations. If we work together, we'll be strong enough to do it, to keep more of your people from being killed."

For a moment, Mitsy was nodding and listening, but then her eyes narrowed and she snorted.

"You almost had me, Amaranthe, but I remember you from school. You could always win over the teachers with that tongue, but not me."

"Mitsy—"

"Silence!"

Even the bouncers jumped.

"No more speaking for you, my dear," Mitsy said. "It's my turn to leave mutilated bodies in the streets." She waved to the bouncers.

Two of the brawny men headed for Amaranthe, two for Books. The rest kept their weapons trained. There was no chance of escape.

"Wait," Books said, shying away from the approaching men. "You need to listen to her. She's—"

The bouncers grabbed him beneath the armpits, lifting him from his feet, despite his height. Books lost his composure. He kicked and thrashed, trying to claw and bite his captors.

Two men grabbed Amaranthe in the same manner and dragged her down the steps between the rows of benches and to the railing. Below, a corridor ran parallel to the outside wall. Twenty feet down, the Maze's brick floor promised a hard landing.

"Mitsy, this won't change anything." Amaranthe doubted her words would sway anyone at this point, but she had to try.

"It's not about change, my dear. It's about avenging the family." Mitsy nodded to her men. "Throw them in."

"Release me!" Books yelled.

The bouncers hoisted him up first. He grabbed the rail on his way over, so he hung over the side, legs dangling into the pit.

When Amaranthe realized her destination inevitable, she slithered over on her own, the better to take the fall without hurting herself. She landed with a roll. The floor pounded the breath from her body, but no excruciating stabs of pain announced broken bones.

The bouncers laughed as they peeled back Books's fingers. When he would not let go, one man lifted his leg, boot aimed at the tenacious digits.

"Let go!" Amaranthe called.

Whether out of obedience or because he could not hold himself up any longer, Books released the rail. He dropped, hitting first with his heels and collapsing onto his back. He cried out. Face contorted with pain, he curled onto his side and made no move to rise.

Amaranthe knelt beside him and put a hand on his shoulder. "Did you break anything?"

He panted, tears filming his eyes, and did not answer. Amaranthe glared up at Mitsy, who stood at the railing with one of her bouncers.

"Turn on the Maze and set the clacker to kill," Mitsy said. "Then you men go outside and make sure Sicarius isn't hiding somewhere. There'll be no rescue attempts."

As the bouncers withdrew from the rail, Books clambered to his feet. He gritted his teeth against the pain from whatever injuries he had received.

"Mitsy," Amaranthe said, "you're making a mistake."

"It won't be my first."

"I can help you!"

"Save your words for the clacker. A machine would be more likely to listen." Mitsy moved out of view.

"Fiends." Books turned one way, glanced down the corridor, then spun the other way and did the same. "She'll have all the exits secured. A clacker. The army uses those on the front lines, doesn't it? They're automated to fillet people like fish. We're doomed."

"Books," Amaranthe said.

A low rumble pulsed through the earth. Next came a cacophonous screech. The walls started their peregrinations, leaving slots, grinding along tracks, and clicking into new slots. In the distance, a clang sounded—a cage door going up.

Books's head spun toward the noise, face stricken. "That's it, isn't it? It's out. There's no hope. We're dead."

"Books." Amaranthe grabbed his arm. "We're going to escape."

His gaze latched onto her. "How?"

How indeed. As Books had said, Mitsy would not have left a gate unlocked. Amaranthe craned her neck back. The only way out was up.

She touched the cold, copper-plated wall. No handholds or crevices marred the surface. The exterior walls were too high to reach even if she stood on Books's shoulders. The interior maze walls were a few feet lower. Maybe they could reach the top of them.

"Clackers run on treads; they're not built for jumping," Amaranthe said, "and these walls are too smooth for them to climb."

"Yes, we share that problem."

"Get on my shoulders."

Amaranthe placed her palms against an inner wall and leaned toward it, feet planted. She bent her legs, so he could use her thigh as a step.

"You should go first," Books said.

"I want you on top."

"I don't think I can—"

"Books, go!"

He approached her uncertainly. "You're too small. I could hurt you. This is a bad idea."

A clank echoed through the Maze. The clacker was near, no more than a couple corridors away.

"Good idea," Books muttered. "This is a good idea."

He stepped on her thigh, put a hand on her head, and pushed himself up. Amaranthe grunted as he clambered onto her shoulders. His boots ground into her muscles like a pestle working the bottom of a mortar. Once he was standing, she pushed her heels into the ground and, back rigid, inched up.

Heat rushed to her face, and her legs trembled. Sweat sprang from her skin.

"I can almost reach it," he whispered.

A piece of wall detached to Amaranthe's left. It pulled away from the main section and followed the tracks in the floor, eventually disappearing around a corner. Through the vacant orifice came an ominous rumble and the soft clacking of metal on metal.

Amaranthe pushed up to the balls of her feet.

"I think I can..." Books jumped off Amaranthe's shoulders.

The force drove her to her knees, but Books grabbed the top of the wall first. Legs scrabbling against the smooth surface, he inched himself higher until he hooked his armpits over the edge. He swung his leg up and straddled the wall. Once he found his balance, he flattened onto his stomach and reached down to her.

"Hurry," he whispered. "It just turned into the corridor over here. It seems to be finding us awfully quickly for some machine running on a random loop. "

A flaw in her plan presented itself. Books's hand hung too far above to reach. Amaranthe tried to jump for it anyway—and missed by three feet.

Books's eyes widened with distress. "That's never going to work. You need to, ah, to..."

"Yes, professor?"

He pounded his fist against the wall. "I'm good in a classroom, I swear."

"Don't panic," Amaranthe said. "I'll think of something." *Yes, Amaranthe. Think of something.* "What's it doing?"

"It's looking at me. Technically, I know it's just a machine taking directions from a punchcard brain automated for a simple task. But I swear it's looking at me. And it's rubbing a pair of razor-edged pinchers together. Actually it's clacking them. I suppose that's where it derives its name."

Brilliant analysis. Amaranthe kept the thought to herself. She was just as guilty of nervous rambling at times. She could not do so now though. One of them had to think of something. She looked around, seeking a tool to use, anything.

"Uh oh," Books said.

"What now?"

"It says Tar-Mech on the back."

"Larocka's company?" Amaranthe asked.

"I think it heard you—it's heading toward that gap in the wall."

"It can't hear me, Books. Let's be logical here."

"Maybe Mitsy bought an upgraded version with special *features*."

Amaranthe froze, hands on the wall. "Like magic?" If Larocka could protect her home with it, what else might she be able to do?

"I don't know, but it's coming your way. You'll be dead soon."

"Thanks for the optimism." Amaranthe looked down at her boots and her clothes. "Parka, of course." She tore off the garment. "Catch the end."

She swung it up. Books grabbed the hood and let the rest dangle.

"Brace yourself." Amaranthe jumped and caught the bottom. The thick material supported her weight.

A huge blocky form rolled through the opening in the wall. Reminiscent of a giant beetle on treads, the metal creature had no head, but the back of its carapace reached seven feet. Two sets of arms extended from the front. The bottom ones were hooked, for grabbing. Above them, pinchers with three-foot blades snapped at the air. The clacker paused in the opening, like a wolf sniffing for a scent.

Hand over hand, Amaranthe pulled herself up the parka with new urgency. The smooth wall offered no purchase for her feet. Her arms and shoulders shuddered with the effort.

The clacker rolled toward her. Ten feet away. Five.

She reached for Books's hand. Their section of the wall lurched into motion. It jarred her and she missed her target. Her knuckles cracked against metal.

The clacker's pinchers extended toward her.

Books wriggled lower and grabbed Amaranthe's wrist. He yanked her up.

His efforts tipped him off balance. Amaranthe hooked her arm over the top, and she in turn grabbed him to keep him from pitching backward.

The clacker rammed into the wall. Amaranthe hung on tightly. Metal shuddered, but the wall continued its ponderous route along the track.

She pulled herself the rest of the way up. Books righted himself, and they faced each other, straddling the six-inch wide perch. Amaranthe wiped her damp forehead with the back of her wrist.

The clacker rolled back and forth below, hissing steam and snapping its pinchers. It did seem rather peeved for a simple machine.

Books had managed to retain hold of Amaranthe's parka, and he handed it to her. Out of immediate danger, he was noticeably calmer. "Now, I see why you had me go first. You wouldn't have been able to pull me up."

"I'd like to pretend my plan was that premeditated." Amaranthe looked for Mitsy, but no one sat on the benches. She must be in her office. "I just wanted you off the ground because you seemed..."

"Distressed? Frantic?" Books grimaced. "Useless?"

Amaranthe hesitated, searching for something more tactful. He seemed to read the answer in her expression though.

"I'm sorry," he said. "I'm not good in stressful circumstances. It was the same way when the enforcers came after me. A bunch of brutes with less intelligence than that thing—" he stabbed a finger toward the clacker, "—and all I could think to do was run. Pathetic."

Amaranthe held back a comment about enforcer entrance exams ensuring there were no dumb brutes on the force and only said, "Composure during life-threatening situations takes practice."

"Somehow, I suspect you were born with it." Books studied his hands. Even now they gripped the wall with enough force to whiten his knuckles. "If the others ask about this, can we pretend it was the alcohol withdrawal that made me nervous?"

"I don't see how our errand is any of their business."

The creases at the corners of his eyes deepened as he smiled. "Indeed. Thank you."

Their section of the wall clanked into a new home. Amaranthe repositioned her legs to turn around. Ahead of her, the route zigzagged but eventually met up with an exterior wall.

"Time to get out of here," she said.

She and Books wiggled their way across the tops of the walls. The clacker trailed after them, like a dog still hoping for a treat.

The exterior wall rose only a couple feet taller than the interior corridors, and Amaranthe pulled herself over it without trouble. With his long, gangly limbs, Books made it look difficult. She decided to leave him out of tasks that might require athletic prowess in the future. He was definitely not a field man.

"What are the odds of locating an unlocked door before your chum's goons find us?" Books asked.

"I don't know, but I need to talk to her before we try to escape."

"That didn't go well last time."

"She thinks I'm collaborating with Hollowcrest to murder people," Amaranthe said.

"And does her opinion of you ultimately matter?"

Amaranthe climbed the stairs to the main walkway. "She has a lot of connections in the city. She knows where our hideout is, as evinced by the delivery of the note. If she wants to give us trouble, she could sabotage our cause, maybe end it altogether."

"You're not going to emulate Sicarius, are you?"

"Assassinate her?" Amaranthe shuddered. "No."

From the walkway, she squinted up at Mitsy's office. Darkness behind the window obscured all interior details. She could not tell if anyone had observed the escape.

"You don't need to come with me," she said.

"Someone has to trail after you and pull you up to safety when needed."

Amaranthe gave him a bemused smile. "Thank you."

The door behind the bettors' cage was not locked. Amaranthe paused with her hand on the knob. The last time she entered, Ragos had let her through. She had only known him for a few minutes, but he had seemed a decent fellow. Nice smile. Had the beast killed him or had it been Hollowcrest's medical zealots from the dungeon? And why did Mitsy think they came from the same source? Amaranthe felt certain Hollowcrest was a traditionalist, not someone who would flirt with the unnatural, and Akstyr believed that creature of magical origins. She shook her head. Only one person could answer her questions.

She pushed the door open. Empty stairs rose to the catwalk. Amaranthe and Books climbed them and crossed to Mitsy's office. Books leaned heavily on the railing, limping now that his blood had cooled. The rumbling of machinery thrummed through the empty building. Below, pieces of the maze glided about the corridors, making and breaking routes.

At the office door, Amaranthe pressed her ear to the cold metal. Though she heard nothing, her nose caught an earthy scent like decomposing leaves.

Books crinkled his nose. "What is it?"

"Caymay," she said.

"Which is?"

Mildly surprised he had not explored the city's drug offerings during his months of depression, she said, "A mood-altering mixture concocted by one of Stumps's turn-of-the-century gangs. Taken orally, the substance is deadly, but you can burn it to inhale the fumes. It dulls pain, but it tends to leave one volatile."

"As opposed to the paragon of serenity she was before?"

Again, the door was not locked. Amaranthe opened it slowly. No lamps burned in the office, and only ambient light from below filtered through the window. A haze blurred the air, and the earthy smell intensified.

Amaranthe lifted a hand to stay Books. "Stand watch in case any of the bouncers are still around." She stepped inside and walked around a couple boxes but did not see anyone. "Mitsy?"

The clutter in the room had not changed, though two open bottles of wine on the desk had been added, both liberally sampled. In a bronze bowl, a stick of compressed caymay burned like incense.

"I'm not working for Hollowcrest," Amaranthe said. "Yes, I lied to you last time, and I'm sorry. I didn't think I could trust you. But we have a common enemy. We could work together to end the threat to your gang. Mitsy, are you in here?"

A rustle came from beneath the desk. Amaranthe tensed. Mitsy's head rose over the edge, hair disheveled, eyes swollen.

"You killed him." Mitsy hiccupped. "You."

"No." Amaranthe spread her arms to show she had no weapon. "Let's talk. I'm not armed."

"I am."

Mitsy lifted a loaded pistol clear of the desk and leveled the weapon at Amaranthe. Mitsy's finger flexed on the trigger.

Amaranthe dropped in anticipation. The pistol fired. The ball zipped over her head and pierced the window with a loud crack, leaving a web of splintered glass. The pungent scent of black powder smoke mixed with the caymay.

With a knife in hand, Mitsy clambered over the desk and launched herself. Amaranthe slid to the side. More agile than expected, Mitsy threw out an arm and hooked Amaranthe around the neck. They went down in a tangle.

Amaranthe slammed an elbow into Mitsy's ribs and scrambled to her feet first. Once up, she hesitated. She didn't want to kill Mitsy, just subdue and question her. But how could one reason with a drugged-up crime boss?

Her hesitation gave Mitsy time to find her feet. She crouched and charged, knife leading. Amaranthe should have evaded the attack easily, but her heel caught on something. She landed on her back on a pile of folders and papers. Stacks of boxes loomed, blocking escape routes. The knife flashed.

"Look out!" Books yelled.

Mitsy raised her arm over her head. Amaranthe kicked her in the stomach. At the same time, Books rammed into Mitsy's back. His weight sent her tumbling over Amaranthe's head. Folders rained down from the pile.

Amaranthe rolled to her feet and turned, fists up in anticipation of another attack.

Mitsy did not rise. Face down on the heap of clutter, she did not move at all. Blood pooled beneath her, soaking scattered papers.

"Mitsy?" Amaranthe asked, a sick feeling creeping into her belly.

She edged forward and turned Mitsy over. The knife protruded from her chest, and she was not breathing.

Books hissed. "I didn't mean to..."

Amaranthe kneeled back, shaking her head slowly. "Not again," she whispered.

First the enforcers, now a woman she had gone to school with. How many people were going to die on her quest to help the emperor? Maybe she was the wrong person for this mission. She rubbed her face and sighed. Though she had chosen the task for herself, she could not bring herself to walk away from it. It was her only chance for...

What, Amaranthe? What do you hope to gain from this? A pardon? A reward? Recognition? She stood up without answering her mind's nagging questions. If her motivations were that selfish, she did not want to admit it, even to herself.

She stared at the body. I'm sorry, Mitsy. We were never friends, but I didn't want this.

Amaranthe set her jaw. She still owed Mitsy a favor.

I'll find the creature that killed Ragos, and I'll get rid of it. I swear it.

CHAPTER 15

BEFORE DAWN, ON THE ICY DOCK OUTSIDE OF THE cannery, Amaranthe tightened her boot laces. Despite chilled fingers, she took the time to ensure each loop was the same size and tails of identical length hung free from each knot. She wished Hollowcrest's minions hadn't taken her spiked leather training shoes—and everything else she owned.

She grabbed her mittens, stood, and jumped in surprise when Sicarius coalesced out of the darkness. No hint of pink brightened the sky over the distant mountains, so she could not see his face, but then it rarely expressed much anyway.

"Where are you going?" he asked.

Was his voice less cool than it had been the day before? She wished she had offered that apology, but bringing it up now would feel awkward.

"To run the lake trail," Amaranthe said.

"It's too early. The creature could still be hunting."

Which was the point. She needed a good look so she could describe this deadly mystery beast to Akstyr. If he could identify it, maybe he could also suggest how to kill it. She planned to run along the waterfront and out toward Fort Urgot, where copious mature trees lined the trail. If it did show up, she hoped to have time to climb out of reach.

All she said to Sicarius was, "You're out here training every morning before dawn."

"Very well. Let's go."

She blinked. Was that an invitation to join him?

Before she could ask for clarification, he trotted up the dock toward the street. A backward glance suggested he meant for her to follow.

She subdued a grimace and jogged after him, snow and ice crunching beneath her boots. A witness for her first day back, wouldn't that be lovely?

They turned onto the street and headed for the trail.

"I'm usually a decent runner, but I'm sure I won't be able to keep up with you today." Amaranthe hated the idea of wheezing at a mediocre pace in front of him. "Not after being sick and missing so many days of exercise."

When he did not respond, she forced herself not to utter more preemptive excuses. Why did it matter what he thought anyway?

They passed the first mile in silence, and the docks and warehouses of the waterfront dropped behind. Bare-limbed trees, evergreen shrubbery, and snowy hills marched past. No doubt Sicarius's gaze absorbed it all. Amaranthe tended to use her running time for inward thoughts, but this morning her eyes probed the shadowy terrain as well.

"May I ask a question?" she asked when minutes drifted past with nothing jumping out at them. Since he was letting her set the pace, her words came out conversationally rather than in spurts and puffs.

A glance her direction was his only response. Not exactly a yes but close enough.

"What's a Hunter?" She had not forgotten Akstyr's question from that first morning at the ice house.

"Do you refer to the Nurian word, *istapa*?" Sicarius asked. "Wizard Hunter?"

"Uh, maybe."

"How much do you know about Nuria's history?" he asked.

"About what your average former-business-student-turned-enforcer knows."

"Little, then."

"Exactly." Amaranthe jogged around a large broken branch stretched across the trail.

Sicarius glided over it without breaking stride. "Where we have a warrior caste, Nuria is ruled by a wizard caste. Those who cannot access the mental sciences—the majority of the population—are laborers and slaves. As with our system, there is friction between those with power and those without. Hundreds of years ago, an anti-wizard organization developed with the intention of usurping the government. They believed

people could develop an immunity to the mental sciences, especially invasive telepathy, by conditioning the mind." He spoke as easily as if he were sitting at a table rather than running, but then this pace could hardly challenge him.

"Is that possible?" Sweat dampened Amaranthe's shirt and stung her eyes. She removed her mittens.

"To some degree. With decades of mental training, you can learn to defend against mind-control techniques. It does no good against indirect attacks, however. A wizard could still levitate a rock and hurl it at you. Nonetheless, the idea of creating a man who could resist mental torture and whose thoughts could not be read by telepaths appealed to many. The cerebral training was combined with combat training, and the organization called their warriors Wizard Hunters, which is often shortened to Hunters."

"I assume they didn't succeed in overthrowing the government."

"No, the time and dedication needed to complete the training meant few finished it. Though Hunters have become legendary in Nuria—and feared by wizards—the organization never developed enough clout to threaten the status quo."

Time to ask what she was really wondering: "Are you one of these Hunters?"

"No."

"Akstyr heard it somewhere."

"There are many rumors about me."

"No kidding." Amaranthe wasn't yet panting, but carrying on a conversation was growing more challenging. Another mile and she would turn back. "One does wonder where Akstyr would have gotten that idea."

He did not respond. Only the scrape of her boots on the sanded trail broke the silence. As usual, Sicarius whispered soundlessly over the earth, like a spirit. She couldn't even hear him breathing, and only small puffs of fog appeared in the air before his face.

"Did you have any training for it?" Amaranthe asked. "I apologize for prying...but I'm curious because...if you have any special skills...that would help fight this creature...it'd be good to know."

"I do not," Sicarius said. "If that creature is some wizard's spawn, it would be made from the mental sciences—probably crafted to be impervious to weapons—but it could not access them itself. A full Hunter may be able to harm the maker, but would be ineffective against the beast."

Full Hunter? Did that imply he was a partial one? Maybe he had had some training—the same way he had had cartography training—but not as much as one needed to qualify for the title. Or maybe she was imagining hints that weren't there. Still, he did seem to have a better idea what the creature was than he was admitting.

"Regardless, there are no Hunters in Stumps," Sicarius said.

"Too bad."

Before she could pepper him with further questions, a pair of soldiers clomped into sight on the trail ahead. With their black fatigues and training rucksacks, their occupation was unmistakable even in the dark.

Amaranthe's breath caught. Wholt's death reared in her mind again. Sicarius wouldn't attack them, would he? Surely, he didn't kill every enforcer or soldier he passed. Maybe he would veer into the trees to avoid them.

Sicarius's gait didn't falter, nor did he leave the trail, though he did speed up and move in front of Amaranthe. The soldiers passed on the left without a word, and she blew out a relieved breath. Several times, she glanced back, but in the darkness, they appeared not to have recognized either of them. The men soon disappeared around a curve in the lake.

Lights appeared on a distant hilltop, outlining the walls of the fort.

"This is far enough for me for the first day." Amaranthe slowed and then stopped to grab a handful of snow. "We haven't seen any sign of the creature, so there's no reason for you to run back with me. I'm sure you'll want to do some real training." She chomped on the snow, rolling it around in her mouth to melt it. The water sent a chill down her gullet, but it felt good.

Sicarius looked farther down the trail. He probably ran twice as fast and four times as far on his own.

"Very well," he said.

"Before you go, uhm. About the other night." Amaranthe thumbed the clump of snow, sending powder to the ground. Why was it so hard to apologize for this? Because she wasn't really sorry? Because Wholt had been her partner? "When I yelled at you, I didn't mean... I mean, I

did sort of, but you thought you were helping. You *were* helping, and—"
Just spit it out, girl. "—I'm sorry." *There.*

He said nothing.

She sighed, not really expecting anything else. Still, she had said it.
Maybe it would matter to him in some small way.

Amaranthe turned back toward the city. Time to get moving again.

"Lokdon," Sicarius said.

She looked over her shoulder, hoping for...she wasn't sure exactly.
"Yes?"

"Stay alert."

Her lip twitched up and she gave him a soldier's salute. It was a
start.

She headed back.

In his absence, the predawn darkness felt lonely and oppressive. Few
sounds disturbed the lakeside. No animals skittered across the trail; no
birds chirped from the trees. A breeze stirred the bare branches, rattling
them like bones. She regretted urging Sicarius to leave.

A scream sounded beyond a bend in the trail. She skidded to a stop,
then darted for the closest tree before her mind caught up with her re-
flexes. That had been a human scream, not the unearthly screech of the
creature. Still, humans rarely screamed on dark trails for good reasons,
and a moment passed before she coerced her legs into moving forward
again.

Hand on her knife, ears cocked, she eased around the bend. Beneath
the waning starlight, two bodies sprawled on the trail, limbs twisted
at unnatural angles. Rucksacks, black fatigues... The soldiers. Neither
figure moved.

Her foot bumped something on the edge of the trail. It rolled away
from her. The object lacked the heft of a rock, but in the weak light, she
could not make out details. Amaranthe reached down to investigate, and
her fingers brushed against human hair.

She jerked her arm back, and her heart leapt into double time. She
took a steadying breath, forcing reason into her mind. However distress-
ing, a severed head was not a mystifying find next to a couple of bodies.

She examined it more closely. The head had been torn off.

The creature.

Light blue had crept into the eastern sky, but trees and bushes created shadows and offered dozens of hiding spots on either side of the trail. Ears straining, she listened for footfalls or breathing. This had just happened, so the creature could not have gone far.

Amaranthe skirted the head and approached the bodies. The gouges tearing flesh and bone apart appeared the same as those she had seen on the dead man outside the icehouse.

A familiar screech tore through the foothills. Even though she expected it, Amaranthe flinched.

At least the creature was not right on the trail beside her. It had headed inland.

Several moments of squinting into the gloom let her find tracks trampling the snow beside the trail. She knelt and probed the cold craters. The size of the prints dwarfed her hand, but it was the shape that drew her interest. They were asymmetrical, even lopsided, with five clawed digits on one paw and four on the other, none of them balanced. She had long suspected the creature was nothing natural, but a thrum of excitement went through her. Perhaps she finally had some proof. No one could look at the prints and think bear or panther. Amaranthe glanced at the sky, noting the lack of clouds. With no snow heading in, the tracks would remain for searchers to discover.

"Once the soldiers see this, they'll know there's magic about," she muttered.

"Perhaps."

Maybe she was growing accustomed to Sicarius's stealthy approaches, because she did not jump this time. She could have hugged him though. Being out here alone was about as appealing as roaming an old battlefield during a full Spirit Moon.

"I doubt their upbringing will allow them to see the truth," Sicarius said.

"Some of the soldiers who have been stationed on the borders must know these mental sciences exist."

"Some." As he spoke, Sicarius circled the area, head up, eyes scanning. "It's been almost twenty years since the last war with Nuria though. Of late, the empire has used more subtle tactics to keep neighboring nations off-balance."

More subtle, huh? Like sending in assassins? She recalled he spoke at least one foreign language, enough to chat with the shaman who healed her anyway.

"This creature is likely the work of a Nurian wizard," Sicarius continued.

"And what would the Nurians have to gain by mauling random people in our capital? An invasion I could see—they'd love all our ore and natural resources, but simple mayhem?"

He did not answer.

Amaranthe stepped off the trail. "We have to get a look at it to tell Akstyr, see if he knows more. It left tracks, so we can follow it."

"The creature has nothing to do with our goal," Sicarius said.

"Someone has to stop it or it'll go on killing people."

"So?"

She scowled at him. "So, the emperor wouldn't want his citizens being mutilated by some bloodthirsty monster."

Since she had stopped running, her body had cooled. Cold air licked through her damp clothes, and she shivered. "Let's go."

Amaranthe started up the hill, following the tracks. She had only taken a few steps when Sicarius's voice halted her.

"No."

She turned. "No?"

"We cannot fight it."

"I'm not planning to fight it. We just need to find out what it is we're dealing with."

Sicarius pointed at the shredded corpses. "*They* found out. It killed them. It will not let us walk up, shake its hand, and walk away. If we get close, it'll kill us too."

"You're afraid," Amaranthe blurted.

As soon as she voiced the words, she regretted it. She had uttered them as a revelation, but they sounded like an accusation. Or a challenge.

Sicarius did not respond, though he stood still, face like stone.

While she could not retract her words, maybe she could soften them. "I do not judge you for it. I merely wonder why, when you seem to fear no one."

"I have no fear of men. They are soft and easily dispatched. Their creations are more powerful and less predictable. It's likely our weapons won't work against it."

"I understand. And I'm scared too," Amaranthe said. At least he did not sound angry. She had never seen him lose his temper and never wanted to. "But I think this *is* tied to our goal. Arbitan Losk had newspapers clippings of every story that's been printed about this creature, and there's magic guarding that house, when magic is forbidden in the empire. You and Akstyr both tell me this creature was made with the mental sciences. I don't think it's a coincidence."

"You said nothing to me of the newspaper clippings."

"No, because you were displaying...snippiness yesterday."

"Snippiness?" he asked.

"It's a word."

"I think not."

"I'll ask Books when we get back." Amaranthe smiled and held out her hand toward the tracks.

"Very well." Sicarius led the way inland.

As they climbed the incline, the trees near the lake dwindled, replaced by cleared fields around the garrison. The ground leveled to an oft-traversed area used by the soldiers for parades and training, with a pavilion and bleachers in the distance. A nervous twinge ran through Amaranthe. The emperor's birthday celebration was usually hosted out here. Was it possible the creature was scouting the area?

Hundreds of footprints tamped the snow, and she kept losing the creature's trail. It took enormous bounds that left wide gaps between the tracks, and its path was not entirely linear. Sicarius followed the intermittent traces with some sense she did not possess.

To the distant left, a road wound up to the front gates of the garrison. Voices counting in unison drifted out—soldiers doing warm-up exercises before their company runs. Across the parade field and up a hill, a water tower rose, its bulk dark and distinct against the brightening sky. The creature's tracks steered away from the garrison and headed toward the tower.

"Maybe it's thirsty after all that killing," Amaranthe said with grim humor. "Though I suppose it could be passing through."

"No," Sicarius said. "That is its destination."

Amaranthe eyed the tracks, wondering at his certainty. "Why a water tower?"

"It's strategically important."

"And this would be relevant to the creature because..."

"The tower is always guarded by a couple of men," Sicarius said.

"Oh," Amaranthe said. And then, "*Oh*," as the true meaning poured over her. "Two targets with no one else around."

"Precisely."

A crumbling wall and scattered chunks of brick and concrete littered the hilltop, remains of the original water tower, Amaranthe guessed, likely built before the Turgonians mastered steel production. Four metal columns and a central stem supported the new structure, a gleaming cylindrical tank more than fifty feet high at the top. A squat, windowless hut sat beside it. Smoke billowed from the chimney, and the rumbling of a steam pump reverberated from the walls.

A throwing knife in hand, Sicarius stayed low as he advanced, hugging the ruins. Amaranthe tried not to make noise as she trailed him. If the soldiers on guard were still alive, she did not want to draw their attention. If they were dead and the creature lurked, she did not want to draw its attention either.

Her foot snapped something brittle beneath the snow. Sicarius looked at her.

"Sorry," she mouthed.

After that, she went her own way. He would not appreciate her giving away his position.

She skirted the other side of the ruins. Prints tracked through the snow—first only boots, but soon familiar massive paw marks trod across them.

The only thing we're going to find up here is more dead soldiers.

The wall ended in a crumbled heap. When Amaranthe moved around the end, she almost stepped on a mauled body. Before stopping to.inspect, she glanced around, searching for the killer. The still, white landscape showed her nothing.

This body was worse than the others. An arm and leg had been ripped off, and the face was shredded beyond recognition. Brain matter spilled from the shattered skull and steamed in the chill air. Several yards away, a musket stuck out of a drift, its barrel warped and the stock missing. A dusting of black powder scattered the snow.

"This just happened," Amaranthe called, struggling for detachment.

"Another body over here," Sicarius said from the other side of the ruins. "Still twitching. We should leave before—"

The primal screech clutched Amaranthe's heart like a vise. She whirled toward the source. Down the hill, across the field, at the edge of a copse of alders, two eyes reflected the pink rays of dawn. They were looking straight at her.

In the next heartbeat, the creature charged out of the trees. Though panther-shaped, it reminded her of the blocky vagueness of a clay statue sculpted by a child. But there was nothing childlike in the way it moved. Power surged beneath those muscles. It soared toward them, covering twenty yards with every bound.

"The shed." She ran to the building. A lock hung from the door, barring entry. "Need the key. Search the bodies."

"There's no time," Sicarius said. "Climb!"

He leapt onto the nearest column and scaled it like a squirrel running up an oak. Amaranthe searched for a ladder. There was not one.

She grabbed the icy steel with both hands. The edges cut into her hands, and her boots slipped off the smooth metal rivets. Her progress was slow. Too slow.

The unearthly shriek came again, much closer. The beast surged over the crown of the hill, snow churning beneath its paws.

Amaranthe was less than half way to the bottom of the tank. Surely the creature would leap and tear her from her perch. She would probably be dead before she landed.

Stop thinking. Climb!

Fingers scrabbling for grips, she tried to pull herself up faster. The beast bunched its muscles to jump. Amaranthe braced herself.

A flash of silver spun down from above. The throwing knife struck the creature in one yellow eye. The weapon bounced off as if it had hit steel. It landed in the snow, blade glittering uselessly.

Fortunately, the attack distracted the beast. Instead of leaping, it bounded past Amaranthe's pole.

She renewed her climb. Ten feet to go. A growl from below drew her gaze.

The creature jumped straight up. A claw slashed at Amaranthe. She jerked her leg up. The wind of the miss rustled her pants.

The beast backed up to get a running start. Without stopping, Amaranthe looked up. Five feet. Almost there. Sicarius had long since made the narrow access ledge surrounding the base of the tank. Doggedly, she kept going.

The creature leapt.

Time slowed. The beast arced toward Amaranthe. Its open maw grew level with her knees. The misshapen head was bigger than her torso. She lifted a foot, ready to kick at it, knowing it would prove futile.

Sicarius's hand wrapped around her wrist. He yanked her up. The creature soared past the spot she had occupied. A frustrated howl tore from its throat as it descended.

On the ledge, Amaranthe collapsed next to Sicarius. She tucked her legs into a ball, ensuring no limbs hung over the edge.

"Was that a close enough look for you?" Sicarius asked dryly.

He was not even sweating. Bastard.

Amaranthe pushed hair out of her eyes with a shaking hand. It was a moment before she caught her breath and could answer. "I can describe it well for Akstyr now, so, yes. Do you know any more now that you've seen it?"

Sicarius watched the beast pacing below. Yellow eyes glared up at them from above a thick snout fenced with four-inch fangs.

"It's Nurian."

"Careful," Amaranthe said, "you'll overwhelm me with the details."

The creature rammed into one of the support columns. A tremor pulsed through the structure. The columns were set in concrete. The beast could not possibly have the mass needed to knock the tower over. She hoped.

"It looks like it's made out of clay, though obviously it's stronger than your average ceramic..." She trailed off, remembering.

"What?" Sicarius asked.

For the first time, Amaranthe described to him the fire, the murders, and the shards scattered about the giant kiln she had been investigating the day she first came to Hollowcrest's attention. "Would a magic creature like this be crafted from mundane materials? And would people need to die for the spell, ritual, or whatever to be completed?"

Sicarius looked at her sharply. "If it's a soul construct, yes."

"What's the purpose of a soul construct, besides—"

The creature rammed the column again before turning its head and gnawing at the steel.

"—killing people and chasing us up water towers?" Amaranthe finished.

"Guarding its maker," Sicarius said.

"And would that maker be nearby?"

"Perhaps not near the creature's kills. These appear random, as if it's simply replenishing itself with people's souls, choosing victims unlikely to be missed—though the soldiers could have been a mistake. It is likely the maker is in the city."

Amaranthe remembered Avery's gossip about a creature seen leaping fences in the Ridge neighborhoods. "I have a hunch it's Arbitan Losk."

"Based on newspaper clippings in his desk?"

Before she could defend her hunch further, Sicarius pointed. A line of twenty armed soldiers marched toward the tower.

"At least they'll see what they're up against," Amaranthe said, struggling for a positive tone. She wanted the soldiers to see the creature but feared it would attack them, leaving more dead scattered on the cold snow.

Sicarius rose to a crouch. "We can't be captured."

Amaranthe grimaced. If they were, it would be her fault, just as their current situation was.

The soldiers reached the base of the hill. Several bore repeating crossbows or muskets. They all wore swords. One man pointed at Sicarius and Amaranthe. From the bottom of the hill, they could see the top of the water tower, though not its base yet. They didn't know about the creature.

The soldiers began climbing. Their voices ascended ahead of them.

The creature cocked its head. After a frozen moment, it ran. It veered not toward the soldiers but away, down the back side of the hill. Amaranthe's shoulders sagged. The soldiers would never see it.

"Now," Sicarius urged.

He swung over the lip of the ledge and grabbed the column. He half-slid, half-dropped to the ground. As the lead soldier crested the hill,

Sicarius landed with a roll and came up running. He dodged through the columns and took off in the same direction as the beast.

"Murderer!" the lead soldier shouted. "Alpha Squad, get him."

Eleven men chased after Sicarius. That left a mere nine staring up at Amaranthe. Knowing she could not duplicate Sicarius's descent without breaking bones, she did not try.

"Hello," she called down to the soldiers.

"Come down," the leader said, "or we'll shoot."

"I've done nothing," Amaranthe said. "I was only trying to escape from the monster that killed your men."

A couple soldiers shifted uneasily at the word "monster."

"Save it for my C.O.," the leader said.

Amaranthe slid over the ledge and navigated a cautious descent. At the bottom, soldiers surrounded her. One man searched her and took her knife.

"Tomsol is dead too," a soldier said from the ruins where Amaranthe had discovered the first corpse. "Body torn up, limbs missing."

The corporal in charge—she could see his rank now—glared at her as if she was responsible.

She spread her arms, palms up. "I've done nothing. I was just out for a run and followed the tracks up from the lake."

A soldier plucked Sicarius's throwing knife from the snow. "Just out for a run, huh?"

"The lake's not as safe as it used to be."

"Take her back to the fort," the corporal said. "The C.O. will want to question her."

Four men detached from the squad. Two clamped their hands around Amaranthe's biceps, grips strong. The other two followed them, muskets aimed at her back. They left the corporal kneeling over one of the bodies, fist pressed to his lips.

On the way to the garrison, the efficient soldiers gave Amaranthe no opportunity to escape. The sun peeked over the city. Its rays landed on her back but warmed her little. With dawn's arrival, people moved about outside the fort, heading toward a fenced compound where steam vehicles were being fired up. A gate stood open, and an armored artillery truck trundled out for practice maneuvers, its steel frame bristling with cannons.

Everyone they passed wore army uniforms with the exception of a couple dozen civilians, mostly women. They were opening a variety of kiosks outside the front gate. Signs advertised boot polishing, fresh-baked pastries, and other goods and services. The scent of warm flat-bread wafted through the crisp air, and Amaranthe's stomach rumbled.

Though the front gate was open, two soldiers guarded it. When Amaranthe passed through, she might as well have entered a steel cage. With so many soldiers crossing the brick square inside, she did not see how she could escape.

She should have taken the route Sicarius had and risked the broken bones. Now it was too late.

* * * * *

Sespian strode down a windowless passage in the back of the Imperial Barracks. His six guards clanked and clattered behind him. Long periods of shadow lay between the unadorned gas jets; their pipes ran along the outside of the old stone walls. No one else walked the hallway. Few knew of its existence.

He clutched birthday invitations for diplomats of eight nations. Should Hollowcrest learn of this jaunt, Sespian hoped the invites would provide a plausible cover for his sudden interest in visiting the head-quarters of the Imperial Intelligence Network.

At the end of the hall, he opened a door and entered a windowless room ordered with numerous tidy desks and tables. Wooden file cabinets lined three of the four walls, while shelves full of books and maps rose along the last. A couple doors led to tiny interrogation cubicles.

Eight men worked in the office, though Sespian knew they represented only a portion of the intelligence network. Some wore army uniforms and others bland civilian attire, though all were soldiers.

"Room, attention!" someone barked upon spying Sespian.

Each man dropped his paperwork, stood, and thumped a palm to his chest in salute.

"At ease," Sespian said, feeling silly as soon as the army lingo came out of his mouth. These men knew he had never commanded a squad at physical training much less led soldiers into battle. Given their intelligence-gathering manifesto, they probably also knew each and

every excuse a younger Sespian had used to escape Weaponsmaster Orik's lessons. Still, he figured they'd be more likely to listen to a confident, commanding emperor, not the inexperienced idealist Hollowcrest claimed Sespian was. "Colonel Backcrest, see me, please."

The keen-eyed head of the intelligence office hustled forward, snapping his heels as he assumed a rigid attention stance. His black uniform included polished boots, gleaming brass buttons, and creases so perky one wondered if he ironed with a steam roller.

"Colonel, I'd like you to check up on these diplomats." Sespian handed over the invitations. "Make sure they're not a likely threat, and, if they pass muster, deliver these messages before my birthday celebration."

"Of course, Sire. Can we be of any other assistance? Would you like to see our most recent reports?" Backcrest asked, eyebrows rising hopefully.

Sespian guessed officers cloistered back here rarely received the recognition of field soldiers, men constantly tried in battle and drills that let them shine in front of their comrades and commanders. These men were probably all hungering for praise. Maybe Sespian didn't need to act like an experienced commander after all; maybe he just needed to give them attention.

"Not just now," he said, "but I'd appreciate it if you'd start sending weekly updates to my office."

The colonel brightened.

"Hollowcrest only takes bimonthly reports," a voice in the back murmured, not with displeasure but with excitement.

Sespian felt a guilty twinge. He should have been back here previously, talking to these people, learning from them. His father had demanded Sespian go over imperial reports with him, but when Hollowcrest took over... Hollowcrest had always given the impression he preferred it when Sespian took no interest whatsoever.

"I'll have the first copy on your desk by dawn," the colonel said. "Anything else, Sire?"

"Actually, I was wondering if you might spare somebody for a couple weeks for a special assignment." Since Sespian knew Hollowcrest also talked to these men, he made his request vague.

"Of course, Sire. Anyone in the office would be honored to serve you personally." The colonel extended an arm to encompass his men, who straightened further under Sespian's gaze. "Choose any you please."

Sespian knew from their files they were all competent—they had to be to work in the Imperial Barracks—but he needed more than competence. He needed someone unlikely to have developed an allegiance to Hollowcrest. A younger man seemed best, and it would be good to have peers his own age with whom to work. Sespian hoped he was not making his choice based on personal feelings instead of logic.

"Lieutenant Dunn," Sespian said.

"Sire?" Bright, hopeful eyes met his. The twenty-two-year-old officer was less than six months out of the academy, his record said, where he graduated at the top of his class. Though not of the warrior caste, he had already impressed his superiors and earned numerous accolades.

"Care to work with me for a couple of weeks?"

"Absolutely, Sire."

"Let's talk."

Sespian pointed to one of the cubicles. They went inside, closed the door, and sat across the table from each other.

Dunn fidgeted in his chair. Sespian felt nervous too. Had he chosen the right man?

"You'll report only to me," he said. "If your superiors ask you for details, tell them you're under secret orders."

"I understand, Sire."

"You usually focus your efforts on the empire's borders and beyond, so this will be a different type of task for you. I need you to investigate every soldier working in the Barracks."

Dunn tilted his head. "Sire?"

"Hollowcrest has been poisoning me for the last year. I'm sure he's had help." Sespian watched Dunn's face intently.

The shock that widened the lieutenant's eyes seemed genuine. "Why?" he asked. "Why would he dare?"

"To keep me and my ideas out of his way. He grew comfortable as regent, and he didn't want to give up that power."

"Despicable," Dunn whispered.

"Quite." Sespian held Dunn's eyes. "That's why I need your help. I think you're a man I can trust."

"Of course! What can I do, Sire?"

"Find out who's with me and who's loyal to Hollowcrest. I wish I could lead the investigation myself, but people have a tendency to be on their best behavior when I'm about." When they're not trying to drug me....

"Quite." Dunn smiled as he echoed Sespian's earlier comment. "On the other hand, who would notice a young lieutenant in one of the ubiquitous soldier uniforms around this place?"

"We're thinking alike already. Your skills will serve you well in this. One other thing..." Sespian cleared his throat. "Find out everything you can about a female enforcer named Amaranthe Lokdon. In particular, I want to know if she's dead or alive. Hollowcrest says dead, but I've decided it'll be best for my health to question everything he's ever told me."

"Yes, Sire," Dunn said.

"That's all. Report to me daily before breakfast."

"Yes, Sire."

Sespian sat in the cubicle for a few minutes after Dunn left, wondering if he could trust the man. Even if he could, this was only a start. He would have to round up Hollowcrest's minions and do something with them—all before Hollowcrest figured out Sespian was off the drug. He hoped he had enough time, but feared he did not.

CHAPTER 16

"**Y**OUR NAME?" THE SERGEANT ASKED.
            Perched on an uncomfortable wooden chair, Amaranthe flirted with making up an identity, but with her wanted posters plastering the city, the soldiers would figure it out sooner or later. Besides, her interrogator would probably see through her lies.

Hard, experienced eyes studied her from beneath graying eyebrows. A scar ran down his cheek, tugging his lip into a sneer that made it look as if he had eaten something unpleasant for breakfast. His last prisoner perhaps.

"Amaranthe Lokdon," she said.

No one sat at the lone desk, but two armed guards stood by the office's only door. It was open, and a man wearing captain's pins leaned against the frame and further blocked the route. At least the soldiers were questioning her here instead of some dank interrogation chamber, though the vertical iron bars securing the sole window offered little hope of escape. No one had bound her hands, but with so many soldiers around, she failed to see how it mattered.

"Occupation?" the sergeant asked.

Counterfeiter of money, plotter against business coalitions, and all-around hindrance to Commander of the Armies Hollowcrest. "Enforcer."

"What district?"

"Commercial."

The sergeant strolled around the room, hands clasped behind his back. His boots alternately clacked or thudded as he crossed back and forth over a thin rug. It did little to cover the web of cracks marring the concrete floor, evidence of the building's age.

"A female enforcer," he said. "There can't be many. It'll be easy enough to check your story."

"I imagine so."

"Women warriors. Ridiculous notion. You can't beat a man in a fight."

"Depends on the man," she said. "Why don't we leave the fort, just you and me, and we can test your theory?"

The sergeant steered a frosty look her direction. "Who's your friend that ran?"

Amaranthe hesitated. In the doorway, the captain's eyes narrowed. She shifted on the hard chair. The sergeant dropped his fists on the desk, leaned on them, and glared at her.

"My partner," she said.

The sergeant snorted. "That man is no enforcer. He evaded our soldiers slicker than a greased fish."

"Did he kill anyone?" Amaranthe asked. *Please, no more deaths on my hands.*

"It depends on how much you two had to do with the men who were murdered by the lake and under the water tower."

"We had nothing to do with that," Amaranthe said. "We were only following the trail to see what *did* kill them." She leaned forward and gripped the edge of the desk. "And we did. We saw it, and we fled from it. Your men need to be very careful. It's not a bear or panther, like the papers said. It's much worse."

"Oh?"

Amaranthe frowned. The sergeant sounded more skeptical than interested. Was he not concerned about his lost men?

"Yes, *oh*," she said.

"What did you see?"

"It was like a cougar but much bigger. It was strong, but it wasn't graceful. It was ugly and blocky—like something molded out of clay. It's not of natural origins."

The sergeant exchanged significant glances with the captain, who was apparently content to let his man do the questioning while he observed. A part of her wanted to tell them about everything: Forge's assassination threats, Hollowcrest's drugging of the emperor, and her suspicions about the creature. But they would never believe her. Still, if there was a chance she could get them in on the monster hunt, she had to try. After seeing Sicarius's knife clank uselessly off the beast's eye, she knew killing it was beyond her team.

"What do you mean not of 'natural origins?'" the sergeant asked.

Amaranthe leaned back and felt the hard edge of the chair against her shoulder blades. She considered her next words. If she simply said the beast was a magical Nurian creation—something imperial subjects were supposed to know nothing about—she would find herself thrown in a cell as a conspirator. She had to lead them to make their own conclusions.

"I don't know," she said. "I've never heard of anything like that monster. My comrade threw a knife at its eye, and the blade didn't penetrate."

"The weapon must have spun and hit with the hilt," the sergeant said.

Amaranthe shook her head. "The point struck true. Right in the eye. It clanged off as if it had hit steel."

"Impossible. You saw wrong."

Believe me, curse you. "I'm just an enforcer, and I don't know too much about politics, but isn't it possible that some—I don't know— enemy of the empire sent the creature over here to make trouble? Especially now, with the emperor's birthday celebration only days away? Foreign diplomats and hundreds of important officials from all across the empire will be in town. Don't you think it's a bad time for soldiers to start showing up dead?"

"It's never a good time for soldiers to show up dead." The sergeant dropped his chin to his chest. "It is kind of suspicious though. The timing and all. I suppose..."

In the doorway, the captain cleared his throat. The sergeant glared at Amaranthe.

"I'm asking questions," he said. "For all I know, you're trying to distract me from your involvement in the deaths of our men."

"Did you *see* the bodies?" she asked. "They were mutilated. By something with fangs and claws. How could I possibly have done that?"

"Human beings are vile and resourceful creatures. I've seen 'em do wicked things to each other."

"Yes, I had retractable six-inch claws installed beneath my finger-nails to do this job." Amaranthe thrust her hand out. There was not even room to hide a speck of dirt under the chewed nubs at the ends of her fingers. "Besides, you saw the tracks. You know something inhuman is about."

"What are you suggesting? That this is some sort of magical beast planted by enemies of the empire?"

Yes! "Magic? I thought it didn't exist."

The sergeant rapped his knuckles on the edge of the desk. "That's exactly what you should think."

. "But if it did exist..." Amaranthe furrowed her brow thoughtfully, silently urging him to make the connection.

He stared blankly at her.

Exasperation welled in her. "If it did exist, we could all be in danger. If someone using the mental sciences shows up at the emperor's birthday—"

The captain and sergeant's heads snapped up like bloodhounds that had caught a scent. *Idiot, wrong word!*

The captain jerked his chin toward the hallway, and the sergeant followed him outside. The two statuesque soldiers who had guarded the exit followed. The door thudded shut. A lock clanked.

Amaranthe went to the door and pressed her ear against it.

"...worse than murder... Nurian collaborator."

"...said science, not magic... dangerous."

"...jail?"

"...influence prisoners. Leave her... general will want..."

The voices moved out of range. The cool wood of the door felt deceptively calming against Amaranthe's cheek. *What are they going to do with me?*

She sank to the floor, back against the door. The concrete radiated warmth beneath her palms. No fireplace or stove burned in the room, but the air was comfortable. A lot of large buildings in the city were heated by hypocausts. If this one was, that would mean flues in the walls and crawl spaces beneath the floor where hot air flowed.

Her fingers drifted toward one of the many cracks. It meandered into a corner by the window wall. Might the building be dilapidated enough that she could escape through the floor?

On hands and knees, Amaranthe crossed the room, probing at promising rifts. After pushing aside the rug, she found an area where multiple cracks intersected, creating a diamond-shaped island in the middle.

She dug her fingers into the wider crevices and wiggled the piece. It shifted slightly, but she could not lift it free.

Amaranthe stood and investigated the desk. A smooth stone being used as a paperweight caught her interest. She grabbed it, then rummaged through the drawers. A stash of wrapped flatcakes occupied one. Apparently, the captain had a sweet tooth, or maybe he bribed his men with rewards. She dumped them on top of the desk. Maybe she could use them if she escaped the building.

The letter opener stashed behind a collection of writing supplies had a more immediate use. Though too blunt to make much of a weapon, it had sufficient heft for an impromptu chisel.

She grabbed a scarf from a peg near the door and used it to muffle her work. The tap of the paperweight against the end of the letter opener still sounded too loud in her ears. Fortunately, the remaining threads of mortar shattered easily. Amaranthe lifted the one-inch-thick slab free. Beneath the top layer rested two foot square tiles. Though not surprised, she groaned at the additional barrier. Her captors would not leave her alone indefinitely.

Only one tile was fully visible and it held no cracks or signs of weakness. Nonetheless, she would have to work with that one or try to pull up more of the floor, which would take too long.

Amaranthe placed her hand on the tile. Warmth seeped through the ceramic. She tapped on it with the paper weight, and the hollow thuds gave her reason to continue. It sounded as if a duct or crawl space ran underneath. She grabbed the letter opener again and chipped at the worn mortar around the edge of the tile.

Time bled past. Whenever voices or footsteps sounded outside, she glanced at the door, letter opener clenched in her fist.

Finally, she wiggled the tile free. A black opening yawned beneath it, and warm air wafted from the gap. Pillars supported each corner where the square had laid, and darkness lurked all around them. Amaranthe reached down to measure the space to the bottom. Moist grime and mold cloaked the rough concrete beneath. She shuddered and wiped

her fingers on the rug. *What were you expecting? A freshly scrubbed crawl space?*

She estimated a depth of two feet to squirm through. Good enough.

Amaranthe grabbed the wrapped cakes and stuffed them into her shirt. Feet first, she squeezed into the hole. Hunkered on her knees, she dragged the rug back into place behind her. Her escape route would not remain a mystery for long, but she need not be obvious about it.

Darkness swallowed her, stealing sight. She inhaled deeply and forced herself to remain calm in the tight space. Hot smoky air, heavy with the scent of burning coal, irritated her nostrils and throat.

She groped around, skinning her knuckles against a pillar. The heat seemed to originate from her left, so she belly-crawled that direction. Mold squished beneath her fingers. Sweat soon bathed her body. Grit and dust stuck to her palms. Something furry brushed her wrist and scurried away. She jerked her hand up. Though she doubted she had anything to fear from rats, she couldn't keep from imagining hordes of the little beasts swarming over her and gnawing at her flesh.

Amaranthe sighed with relief when she made it to a shaft slanting down. She climbed in and wriggled through it. As she descended, the smoke grew more concentrated and the heat intensified. Stifling coughs, she turned a corner and a square of light appeared below her. When she reached the end of the shaft, she swung out, scattering the burning embers of a fire. She banged her head as she hustled through the flames. Once free, she stomped her feet and swatted her clothes to make sure nothing was burning.

Two sooty, bare-chested men gaped at her. Both held shovels heaped with coal. Aside from the glow of the fire, a single lantern provided light. Stairs rose behind the workers.

Amaranthe pulled two mashed flatcakes from her shirt and handed one to each man. "You fellows are doing excellent work. You never saw me, right?"

They jabbered in a foreign language. Perhaps Arbitan and Larocka were not the only ones exploiting illegal slaves. Fortunately, the men showed more interest in the cakes than her.

Amaranthe slid past them and climbed the stairs. She cracked open the door at the top. A few feet away, a brick wall loomed. She was behind the building near the edge of the compound. A guard clanked past on a walkway above. No going over the wall, but the smooth brick defied scaling anyway.

She brushed dust, mold, and other dubious smudges from her clothing. Then she arranged her remaining flatcakes in one arm and stepped into the sunlight. An ice-and-gravel path took her along the wall, then veered through an alley between buildings.

The gate came into sight, but the busy square stretched before it. Dozens of soldiers streamed here and there. Two more men guarded the exit, but at least it was a different pair than at dawn.

Amaranthe lifted one of the cakes with her free arm and walked into the square.

"Fresh flatcakes! One for two ranmyas, two for three." She waved the sweet and meandered toward the gate. "Get your flatcakes right here! No need to wait until chow call for a tasty snack. You, sir. You look hungry. Just two ranmyas for a sumptuous sweet."

A soldier brushed past her but did not look up. Excitement thrummed through her limbs. Maybe this would work. The men barely noticed her. Soldiers who would have pounced on a fleeing prisoner avoided eye contact with a pushy vendor.

She was halfway to the gate and congratulating herself when a hand clamped onto her shoulder. Amaranthe turned, locking the expression of an eager merchant onto her face.

"Sir," she said to the corporal who restrained her. "I can see you're a man who appreciates the delicious taste of a fresh flatcake. My sweets use superior ingredients and—"

The corporal growled and jerked her around. He propelled her, not toward a jail cell, but toward the gate.

"How did you get in here? How many times have I told you people the fort is off limits to civilians? Sell your junk *outside* the walls if you must."

"Sir, I protest," Amaranthe said, as the corporal manhandled her through the gate. The two soldiers avoided glares the corporal sent them, no doubt wondering how they had let her pass. "How is a good businesswoman—and a loyal citizen, I assure you—supposed to make a living with such stringent rules? I have children in need of new parkas."

"Not my problem." The corporal released her with a shove.

"I'm going to complain to the emperor!"

"You do that."

Thrusting her chin in the air, Amaranthe marched down the road away from the fort. She bit her lip to keep from grinning. There were still soldiers to avoid. Numerous men strode the snowy paths beyond the walls on some errand or another. If one of the soldiers who had captured her was about, it would mean trouble.

She had to reach the curve in the road ahead. Trees there obscured the view and would provide cover for her to run down to the lake. Only then would she relax.

Pounding boots thundered down the snow-cleared road behind her. Amaranthe winced. So close.

She turned, and a soldier bigger than Maldynado stopped before her. He was armed but by himself. Maybe she could...

"Two, please," he said.

"What?" Amaranthe asked.

The soldier pulled out three bills. Relief made her smile genuine. She handed him two flatcakes. He gave her the money, a curt wave, and ran off, fingers peeling away the wrappers.

Amaranthe hurried down the road, certain she had surpassed her luck quota for the week. When she turned into the trees, she almost tripped over Sicarius. He was crouching on the balls of his feet, watching her approach.

"They let you go?" His gaze fell on the cakes and ranmyas clutched in her hands.

"Not intentionally." An alarm bell clanged at the fort, and Amaranthe winced. "In fact, we should leave. Now."

They ran down the slope and onto the lake trail.

"What were you doing?" she asked.

"Waiting for nightfall so I could retrieve you."

"Really? Like a rescue operation?" Touched, she smiled at him. "Is it possible the stodgy, emotionless assassin has perhaps grown to care about me?"

"You are needed to implement the final phase of the plan."

Her smiled deepened. "Don't worry. You don't have to say it."

"What?"

"You like me."

"Since it's your plan we're following, it is logical to make a priority of your safety until Forge is thwarted."

"Easy, Sicarius. If you're not careful with all these affirmations of affection, I might assume you want to be friends."

He gave her a sidelong look with the faintest hint of amusement seeping through his stony façade. "Did you warn the soldiers about the creature's origins?"

"I tried. My new knowledge of magic only drew their suspicion."

"We must focus on the emperor," Sicarius said. "There's nothing else you can do about this creature."

"We'll see."

* * * * *

"Where's Akstyr?" Amaranthe asked when she and Sicarius returned to the cannery.

She wanted to know if Akstyr knew anything about soul constructs, such as how to kill them. She peered past counters and drying bills but did not see him.

"Dunno." Maldynado dropped the handle of the paper cutter to slice a new counterfeit twenty into existence.

"Nor do I." Books was applying ink to the press. "I thought he was on watch."

"No one's on watch." Amaranthe looked at Sicarius. "Can you check outside and see if there was a scuffle?"

Sicarius inclined his head and left.

"It's not my fault," Maldynado said.

Amaranthe joined them. "I didn't say it was."

"No, but women like to blame things on me, so I figured I'd announce my innocence preemptively."

"What type of *things*?" Books asked. "Their unwanted pregnancies?"

"Of course not. To bear my offspring would be an honor. They know that."

After trading eye rolls with Books, Amaranthe grabbed a pen and several sheets of paper. With stacks of counterfeit bills ready, it was time to see if her bluff would work.

She sat at a counter and penned a note:

Have a compromise that will benefit both our interests. Imperative we meet before the emperor's birthday. Midnight three days prior in the scrapyard outside the Oak Iron Smelter.

Sicarius entered the cannery, and Amaranthe waved him over.

"Akstyr walked away of his own volition," he said.

"Thank you for checking." She pushed the note across the counter to him. "I'm in need of your artistic abilities."

Silently, he sat across from her and read the note.

Amaranthe spread the crumpled reject she had removed from Larocka's waste bin. "Could you make a copy of my note in her handwriting? And I need an identical note in Hollowcrest's handwriting."

She folded her hands on the counter and watched his face, half expecting Sicarius to deny knowing what Hollowcrest's handwriting looked like, half expecting him to say nothing and simply stare at her.

He did give her a bland gaze, but picked up the pen and started writing. Both notes.

"The Oak Iron Smelter isn't one of Larocka's, correct?" His work complete, he set down the pen.

"No," Amaranthe said. "A warrior caste family has owned it for generations; it should be neutral territory for all parties."

Sicarius stood, but seemed to recall something. He withdrew a folded piece of paper and handed it to Amaranthe. Remembering her wanted poster, she winced. What now?

She stared at the drawing and wasn't sure whether to be amused or chagrined by the familiar image. "Maldynado, this one's for you."

"Eh?" Maldynado left the paper cutter and ambled over. "What do you—ho, I recognize that gorgeous fellow."

"I imagine so," Amaranthe said.

The wanted poster featured the picture the woman in the ink shop had sketched of him. This version came with a few words at the bottom: *Maldynado Monticzhelo, Wanted Dead or Alive: 250 ranmyas.*

"*Two hundred fifty* ranmyas? That can't be right." Maldynado raked his fingers through his soft brown curls. "My last hair cut cost more than that!"

"I see you're regarding this with the utmost seriousness," Amaranthe said.

"It must be a misprint. Don't you think it's a misprint?" Maldynado gave Sicarius a pleading look.

Sicarius stared back without comment.

"Two-fifty." Maldynado's gaze shifted to Amaranthe. "Yours is for ten thousand! And Sicarius, they're offering a million for him."

"Surely you don't put yourself in Sicarius's league," Amaranthe said, amused at Maldynado's whining, despite regrets that she had somehow gotten him noticed by the law.

"No," Maldynado admitted, "but you're just a girl. How can yours be for..." He stuck out his fingers and started figuring under his breath.

"Forty times more, you dolt," Books said, eyes glinting with apparent appreciation for the poster.

"Forty times?" Maldynado clasped his forehead. "That's insulting. I'm much more, er... I'm... Look!" He stood sideways, thrust out his chest, and flexed his biceps.

"Indeed," Amaranthe said, struggling not to laugh.

"Two-fifty." His head dropped, and his hair flopped about his angular cheekbones as he slunk back to the paper cutter. "Bounty hunters won't even bother to get up from the table when they see me in an eating house. Why risk a muscle pull drawing a sword for such a measly reward? I'll be lucky if they throw a fork."

A moment later, Akstyr sauntered through the doorway. Amaranthe stared at a frosting-drenched pastry hanging from his mouth. He clutched a greasy sack that read Curi's Bakery.

Apparently forgetting his disgruntlement, Maldynado sidled up and smiled at the sack. Akstyr graciously offered him a pastry, which Maldynado stuffed in his mouth.

"I thought you didn't have any money," Maldynado said.

"Don't." Akstyr grinned at Amaranthe. "Your fake money works real good."

She almost fell off her stool. "You used the counterfeits?"

"Uh huh."

"How could you? You've put us all in danger. That merchant is going to realize it's not genuine eventually, if she hasn't already. If it gets traced back to us..." Amaranthe resisted the urge to run to the front of the building and peer through the boarded windows facing the street.

It was probably too soon for a squad of enforcers to tramp down the dock to their door.

"Imbecile," Books said to Akstyr. "How could you be so thoughtless? To jeopardize everything for a sweet."

"I didn't know it'd be a problem."

"How could you not know? What you mean is you didn't think."

Akstyr threw the sack on the table. "This chews rat balls."

"What a colorful colloquialism," Books said. "Clearly your gang years educated you well."

Akstyr's hands clenched into fists. "I've been working night and day, and I'm getting nothing out of this. If you're going to treat me like an idiot, I'm leaving."

Amaranthe frowned, tempted to let him go. If he was going to be more of a liability than a help, why keep him? But, no, she needed all the man power possible to finish printing bills and stage the meeting with Forge and Hollowcrest.

"It'll be fine," she soothed. "Just don't spend anymore. And you make a good point. We've all been working hard. From now on, we'll only have two people working the press and one standing watch. The other two can relax." She opened her hand, palm up to Akstyr. "Or study."

"Whatever." Akstyr grabbed his sack and headed for a corner.

Maybe involving him more in the plotting and planning would engage his interest, or at least keep him focused and loyal.

"Akstyr," she said, "can you arrange a meeting between me and your old gang boss?"

"Whatever."

"Is that a yes?" she asked.

A silent glare answered her. Lovely. A Sicarius in training.

Amaranthe joined Books at the press. Eyes wide with concern, he shook his head. She shared the feeling.

"Let's start packing the dry bills in Maldynado's chicken crate," she said. "Just in case we have to leave in a hurry."

CHAPTER 17

COLONEL BACKCREST'S FIRST INTELLIGENCE report arrived well before dawn, and Sespian shuffled to his desk to read it. Still wearing slippers and pajamas, he slid into the icy wooden chair without bothering to shovel coal into the stove. Someone would figure out he was awake and come in to feed the fire shortly. The staff always wrung their hands in respectful distress when he did that sort of thing himself.

According to the report, the borders were oddly untroubled and no one had seen a Nurian warship in months. Perhaps that signified a lessened interest in hostilities, but more likely it represented a pause for plotting and planning. An unidentified creature murdering citizens on the waterfront struck him as a more immediate concern. He scribbled a note for Backcrest that requested more information.

When Sespian set the report aside, he glimpsed the sketches he had made a few weeks earlier for a new art wing at the university. Pretty but not structurally stable. His mind had truly been affected by that drug. Poor Amaranthe Lokdon—harassed by a simpleton.

His frown deepened as he again considered that evening she had leaped from Hollowcrest's window. Why had she even been in the Barracks? She must have been returning from Hollowcrest's special mission, a mission Sespian still knew nothing about. Maybe Dunn would find out more. Why would Hollowcrest have chosen her for secret work? He was barely cognizant of the city's enforcers—why would he have brought one to the Barracks?

Because of me. Fool. With his love-struck babbling, he had brought Amaranthe to Hollowcrest's attention. Dully, he realized whatever

trouble she had found since was very likely his fault. But how had she ended up with Sicarius's knife? Surely Hollowcrest had been lying; she couldn't possibly be working with that monster.

A tentative knock sounded on the door.

"Come in, Lieutenant," Sespian guessed. Hollowcrest never knocked tentatively or showed up that early.

Papers in hand, Dunn entered the office. Despite the early hour, his uniform was pressed, his hair combed, his beard shaved, and his boots polished. Wondering whether he should feel pleased at the dedication or embarrassed of his own pajama-clad state, Sespian waved the lieutenant to a seat opposite the desk.

"I've identified some of Hollowcrest's cronies, Sire," Dunn said. "It's going to take time to complete a thorough list without drawing attention, but I've started with the higher ups. They'd have more power to influence subordinates, I imagine."

Sespian nodded and leaned forward to examine three papers Dunn laid out.

"Those are men loyal to you." Dunn pointed to each list as he spoke of it. "Those are Hollowcrest's men, and these are the indifferent ones who said they're just here to work and don't care who's in charge."

"Those men don't worry me." Sespian's chin drooped as he read the long list of names under Hollowcrest. "The Commander Lord General for *every* satrapy?"

"Regrettably, yes, Sire."

Don't panic, Sespian. It was alarming, but those men were hundreds or thousands of miles away and a less immediate threat than the traitors in and near the Imperial Barracks. "General Lakecrest," he named the base commander for Fort Urgot, outside of Stumps. "That's a problem."

"Yes, Sire."

"I see you've placed yourself on my list," Sespian said. "Right at the top too." He smiled.

"Of course, Sire."

"We're outnumbered. Sure you don't want to change sides?"

Dunn's nostrils flared with indignation. "I would never back someone who would drug his emperor. Hollowcrest has no honor."

"Indeed not." Sespian slid the papers into a stack and cleared his throat. He strove for the appearance of no-more-than-casual interest on

his next question. "I'm sure this kept you very busy, but did you happen to find out anything about Corporal Lokdon?"

A guarded expression came over Dunn, and Sespian braced himself for bad news.

"She's still alive, Sire."

"Oh?" Excitement fluttered in Sespian's belly, but Dunn's grim expression stole his pleasure. "But?"

"Yesterday morning, she escaped from Fort Urgot, where she was being held for questioning about some dead bodies. It's believed she has something to do with the creature that's been murdering people around the waterfront."

"Yes, I read about the creature," Sespian said, though he did not see how Amaranthe could be related to it.

"Also, there was a man with her who escaped," Dunn said. "He was later identified as the criminal Sicarius."

Sespian sank low in his chair. "Maybe it just looked like... Maybe she's not..." No, he couldn't think of a logical reason as to why she'd be with the assassin. "Damn. I wanted..." Aware of Dunn watching, Sespian sat up and shut his mouth. He could mull and moan when he was alone.

"All right," Sespian said. "Just complete these lists for me, please. And if you can, requisition someone to keep an eye on Hollowcrest. Someone on the housecleaning staff perhaps. I want to know if he leaves the Barracks or meets with guests here."

Sespian wasn't going to have time to spend hours lurking in the ductwork to spy on Hollowcrest himself. He had to figure out how to subvert—or was it un-subvert?—General Lakecrest and all the other local men on the list. All soldiers, he noted grimly. All men he had nothing in common with. Nothing to worry about.

* * * * *

"When you asked how to get in touch with my former gang," Akstyr said, "I didn't think you were planning to take me along."

Amaranthe trailed him, her scabbard dragging in the knee-high drifts lining the path. She felt silly wearing a short sword with her business-woman's long skirt and jacket, but in this neighborhood no one worried about fashion. The packed-snow trail parted a narrow street, and spurs

provided access to dilapidated tenements, brothels, and alcohol shops. Behind wrought iron bars, the cracked window of a smoke shop promised illegal drugs in several languages. The bundled men and women they passed bore pitted and rusted swords, long knives, or axes.

"I thought you might want to brag to your old comrades that you escaped and were well," she said.

"And working for a crazy woman for no pay?"

"Careful, you'll make them jealous." Amaranthe stepped over a wad of human excrement mashed into the snow. "Besides, you know these people. I can't think of anyone better to have along when dealing with them."

"Except him." Akstyr jerked his chin to indicate Sicarius, who walked a few steps behind, scanning their surroundings alertly.

"He's just here in case there's trouble," Amaranthe said. "It's your advice I'll need."

"Whatever. I don't see why you can't use official couriers to deliver your messages."

"Because..." I'm trying to involve you with our mission and get you to care so you don't turn us in for our bounties. "The Courier Network requires too much personal information about the sender. I can lie, but if someone comes back later asking about me, they'll answer. We need people we can count on for discretion."

"And murdering gang members came to mind?" Akstyr asked.

"Surprisingly, yes. Can you imagine them answering honestly if Hollowcrest's minions come around asking questions?"

"Probably not," Akstyr said. "They'll charge you more than couriers would though."

"I expected it."

"We are being watched," Sicarius said.

"I expected that too," Amaranthe said.

Her group turned a corner. Beggars, drunks, and drug dealers lined the drifts. Amaranthe guessed most served dual purposes as lookouts and spies.

"The entrance is down there." Akstyr pointed to an alley barely two feet wide.

No obvious doors marked the chipped sides of the brick buildings, though a narrow metal stair on one wall rose in switchbacks to the roof.

"Do we invite ourselves up or wait for a welcoming party?" Amaranthe asked.

"It's already here."

A boy of nine or ten detached from a shady nook and planted himself in front of Akstyr, fists on his hips. "You're s'pose to be dead, you magic-cursed cur."

"We here to see the boss, Pigeon," Akstyr growled. "You can eat street."

"Tuskar don't want to see some pretend wizard," the boy said.

"How about me?" Amaranthe lifted a finger. "Would he consent to seeing me?"

"What you want, woman?" the boy asked.

"I have a job for someone in your gang. Paying job."

The work ethic ran strongly through the empire's citizens, a social construct too embedded to be cast aside as easily as the legal code. Amaranthe hoped even gang members would value the idea of earning their pay.

"That truth?" The boy pointed at Sicarius. "Who's he?"

Amaranthe suspected more ears than this youth's were listening to the conversation. "My secretary."

The boy snorted. "Whatever. Follow me."

Amaranthe led her men into the alley, trailing their new guide.

"Secretary?" Sicarius murmured behind her.

She tossed a smile over her shoulder. "You did write my letters."

The narrow stair rose so steeply, Amaranthe decided to reclassify it as a ladder. Make that a deathtrap. As they ascended, the rickety contraption quaked with such enthusiasm that she pictured falls and broken bones.

Three stories up, the climb ended on top of the building where much more than a roof awaited. A permanent camp consisting of wood and scrap-metal huts sprawled across the footprint-laden snow. The elevated village spanned at least ten adjacent buildings connected by flimsy planks. The roof provided an excellent view of the icy lake, which sparkled white beneath the blue sky.

"Nice location," Amaranthe said.

The boy bowed as if he had orchestrated the construction. He led them past defenders posted at the roof's corners. Crossbows or muskets

leaned against the low walls for easy access. A moment of doubt sank into the pit of Amaranthe's stomach. These were the types of folks who would be up-to-date on the latest wanted posters. Perhaps she should have looked elsewhere for messengers. Still, these men would have underworld connections, too, and could probably deliver her notes without drawing attention.

"Tuskar's office." The boy stopped before one of the larger shacks.

Two meaty brutes stood guard outside. One presented missing front teeth as he leered at Amaranthe.

The boy did not stay to make an introduction. Amaranthe glanced at Akstyr, who merely shrugged. When she reached for the door latch, the guards made no effort to stop her. *Expected, are we?*

The room inside seemed more of a recreational area than an office. Ten or twelve men loitered. Some played Tiles on top of a crate, one gave another a tattoo, and two practiced at knife fighting. At least, Amaranthe thought they were practicing.

Everyone paused and glared when Akstyr entered. At the far end of the room, a rangy man sat behind a desk—if one could call a couple boards propped on concrete blocks a "desk." He lounged in a chair with his muddy boots atop a stack of papers. He, too, affixed Akstyr with a frosty glare and worked a toothpick back and forth with his tongue.

Amaranthe crossed the room and stopped in front of the man. "Greetings." She decided not to mention her name. "Are you the leader? Tuskar? I have a job proposition for you."

Tuskar's eyes never left Akstyr. "How'd you escape from the pillory, boy? 'Round here, magic's forbidden, death penalty."

"I wasn't doing no magic," Akstyr growled. "Though it was real nice of you to turn me in without even asking about it."

"You gotta fit in to be one of us. You never did. Always having airs, pretending you're something better. Truth is you just crawled out of a piss pot, same as the rest of us." Tuskar pointed at Akstyr's hand. "I see you with my brand after today, I'll put my boys on the hunt for your hide."

"What am I supposed to do?" Akstyr asked. "Gnaw my hand off?"

Tuskar surged to his feet and around the desk. "If you can't figure out a way to get it off, I'll do it for you." He slid a dagger out of his belt.

Amaranthe did not notice Sicarius move. Between one eye blink and the next, he was simply there, standing in front of Akstyr, blocking Tuskar's path. Sicarius did not draw a weapon or posture threateningly. He merely offered his cold stare.

The gang leader sheathed his knife and propped his hip against the edge of his desk as if he had never thought to do more.

Akstyr looked at Sicarius with wide-eyed surprise. That turned into a smug smile when he faced Tuskar again.

Behind Amaranthe, men stopped talking and the room grew silent. Her skin crawled under the gazes that had to be focused on the confrontation. She resisted the desire to turn around and look. No doubt by design, Sicarius stood at an oblique angle so everything in the room fit in his peripheral vision. Amaranthe shifted her own stance.

"Perhaps," she said, "if we're done menacing each other, we can talk business."

Tuskar curled his lip at her and sniffed twice. "You smell like an enforcer."

"Is that a guess?" Amaranthe asked. "Or is olfactory career identification your special talent?"

Akstyr snickered. Tuskar glared.

Amaranthe put a hand on Sicarius's shoulder. "Can you smell his occupation?"

"Assassin."

She hid a grimace. Yes, Tuskar knew who they were, and he probably knew how much of a bounty hung over their heads.

"You *are* good," she said. "I bet you're popular at parties."

Tuskar withdrew his toothpick and flicked it into a corner of the room where it landed in a pile of similar discards. He took the stack of papers off his desk, shifted through them, and pulled out two sheets. He slapped down the wanted posters for Amaranthe and Sicarius.

"We like to keep track of criminals with bounties on their heads," Tuskar said. "You never know when we'll chance across one and have the opportunity to collect. Never had someone dumb enough to come to us before. Sure is convenient." Tuskar perused the documents. "Looks like you two are wanted dead. That simples things up. No need to capture you and force march you up to Enforcer Headquarters."

The door creaked open. Two men with muskets stepped in, the barrels trained on Amaranthe and Sicarius.

She lifted her hand to her mouth and yawned widely. Tuskar frowned at her reaction. If only she truly felt that calm.

"May I?" Amaranthe gestured to the posters.

Brow furrowed, Tuskar handed them to her.

"Sicarius," Amaranthe read. "Assassin. Crimes include but are not limited to: murdering Satrap Governor Urgaysan and burning his residence to the ground, stealing priceless documents and blowing up the First Imperial Museum, killing enforcers, sinking a navy ironclad, and slaying a platoon of imperial solders." Amaranthe looked at Sicarius. "A whole platoon?"

"Yes," Sicarius said.

"Was that all at once?"

"One night. In a swamp."

The musket men exchanged worried glances. Others in the room shifted uneasily.

"Reward: one million ranmyas," Amaranthe said. "Impressive. I imagine you get lots of would-be bounty hunters stalking you."

"Yes."

"And yet, you're still alive. Based on what I've learned about you, I'm guessing those hunters are not."

"A correct surmise," Sicarius said.

In the back of the room, one of the knife fighters set his weapon down on a crate. He edged toward the door.

Amaranthe flipped to the second sheet of paper. "Mine isn't so extensive, but this is my favorite part: illegal magic user."

"That true?" one of the musket wielders asked.

Tuskar scowled at the speaker.

"Would Commander of the Armies Hollowcrest print it if it wasn't true?" Amaranthe smiled.

She let Tuskar mull for a moment before speaking again. "My friend, with this many people, you could possibly take us down. But is the reward worth the lives you'll have to sacrifice to get it?"

Tuskar opened his mouth.

"Including yours," Amaranthe said. "Sicarius always goes for the leader first."

"Always," Sicarius said.

Fury leapt into Tuskar's eyes, and his fingers snapped into a fist.

He was going to let them go—Amaranthe saw that—but she did not like what else she saw. The quickest way to humiliate a leader, and make an enemy for life, was to force him to back down in front of his troops. Maybe she could let him save face.

"But," she said, "I'm sure you've found that it's always smart to make powerful friends. Even more, it's smart to have *others* know you've made powerful friends." She arched her eyebrows and looked Sicarius up and down. "Wouldn't you like to brag to your associates about how you sat down and chatted with the infamous assassin, Sicarius, the last time he was in town? Drank some applejack together? Went out hunting for women?"

Akstyr made a choking sound and watched Sicarius as if expecting him to strike her down for her audacity. When she glanced at him, however, Sicarius's expression seemed no fiercer than usual. She even thought she detected a hint of amusement in the glance he flicked her. Her imagination, no doubt.

"And what's it going to hurt," Amaranthe continued to Tuskar, "if you imply you have his ear?"

She watched Tuskar's face for a reaction. His eyes grew speculative, and his fist relaxed.

"I can see how that maybe would be a smart decision." Tuskar plucked another toothpick off his desk and slipped it into his mouth. He eyed the men in the back of the room. A few of them nodded encouragement. "What's the job you want done, girl?"

"Two messages delivered to two different people," Amaranthe said.

"That sounds doable."

They negotiated the details, and the three of them walked away without anyone else pointing weapons at them.

Back in the alley, Akstyr said, "I can't believe they're going to deliver your messages for free."

Amaranthe caught Sicarius's gaze. "I'm sorry about using you that way."

"You are not," he said.

"You're right." She grinned. "You're my biggest asset. I can't imagine not using you."

"They don't do anything for free," Akstyr said, still staring up the ladder.

Amaranthe murmured to Sicarius, "Can you make sure our notes are delivered?"

He nodded and disappeared into the shadows. Amaranthe and Akstyr headed out of the gang's territory, setting as brisk a pace as the snow would allow. With Sicarius gone, she wanted to escape the neighborhood as soon as possible. Too many faces peered at them through broken windows. A fresh blood stain splattered the snow in front of a stoop.

"We're out of Black Arrow territory now," Akstyr said, perhaps sensing her feelings.

"Good, I—"

Two men stepped out of an alley. They carried clubs fashioned from broken boards jutting with nails. Akstyr cursed. Though she had a sword, Amaranthe stopped a generous ten feet from them.

"Is there a reason you gentleman are blocking our way?" she asked.

"Not you." One slapped the wood against his palm and pointed the weapon at Akstyr. "Him."

The two men wore brands on the backs of their hands, human eyes with Xs through them. A rival gang.

"We heard you was using magic," the bigger of the two said. "Magic ain't allowed in the empire, and we sure not gonna stand for you Arrows using none. We gonna smash it outta you like a potato."

"This man is working for me," Amaranthe said. "I need him fully functional, not smashed like sort of food item."

"Who talked to you, woman? You can get gone. We here for *him*." Again the thug pointed at Akstyr with his club.

"I'm not with the Arrows anymore," Akstyr said.

"Sure you ain't," the big man said. "And that's why you're walking outta their territory just now."

"It might be smart to run," Akstyr muttered to Amaranthe.

No doubt, but the men blocked the street. If she and Akstyr ran, it would have to be back into Black Arrow territory. Even if she had parted on good terms with the leader, she had no faith in the safety of the neighborhood.

"Let's be reasonable, gentlemen." She decided not to reach for her sword. It wouldn't deter them and might escalate the violence. "There's nothing to be gained by—"

The attack was not unexpected. The men charged, one at Akstyr, one at Amaranthe.

Inspired by Sicarius's style, Amaranthe also charged. A falter in her opponent's step betrayed his surprise at her choice.

The snow did not give much room to maneuver, but she managed to sidestep the downward arc of the club without leaving the path. She jumped in close behind his swing. The man's attack left him tilted forward, off-balance. She slammed her palm into the side of his jaw. His head snapped to the left, and he grunted in pain.

The blow might have hurt, but it did not incapacitate him. He grabbed Amaranthe's wrist.

Beside her, Akstyr and his man floundered into the drift and started wrestling. Snow flew.

To distract her opponent, Amaranthe kicked him in the shin. She clamped her free hand on top of his, pried his grip loose, and forced his arm into a twisting arc that left his wrist upside down and her elbow on top of his locked arm. She leaned on him, forcing his arm against the joint. The thug folded in half, and something snapped. He yelled and pulled away from her.

She tensed for another attack, but he stumbled back, clutching his arm to his chest. After an incredulous look at her, he staggered away.

In the snow next to the path, Akstyr struggled with his opponent. They writhed, each groping for a devastating hold. She jumped out of the way as the two men thrashed and rolled through the trail and into the snow on the other side. They bounced off a wall, and the gang member came out with the advantage. He straddled Akstyr, hands wrapped around Akstyr's throat.

Amaranthe lunged through the snow, came up behind them, and clapped her palms over the man's ears with all her strength. He yelled, grabbed his head, and rolled away.

Akstyr lunged to his feet and kicked the thug in the stomach. He curled into a ball, but Akstyr kept kicking.

"He's had enough," Amaranthe said.

Akstyr showed no sign of hearing her. His face was contorted in rage that seemed to go beyond the fight.

"Akstyr!" This time, she gripped his shoulder.

Panting, he turned toward her.

"*Now* is the time to run," she said. "They may have friends."

Akstyr stared at the bleeding and battered man for a moment, as if he could not believe he had been responsible. Finally, he managed a curt nod, and when Amaranthe ran from the scene, he followed.

They did not slow until they left the gang-run neighborhoods and reached a trolley stop. Amaranthe kept a nervous lookout until they boarded.

"I didn't think you could fight," Akstyr said.

"I've had the same training all enforcers have," she said. "Those are the kind of brutes we're drilled to subdue. Besides, imperial men tend to underestimate women since most of us don't study combat."

"So, you were sure you could take care of them?"

"Not really, no."

Akstyr grinned. "That's what I thought. I was surprised you..."

"What?"

"Stuck around when they gave you an out. Tuskar wouldn't have, for the same reason he backed down in his office. He doesn't start a fight unless he's sure he can win."

"That's how most people are," Amaranthe said. "It's called a self-preservation instinct."

"Yours broken?"

"I'm beginning to think so."

"Well, uhm," Akstyr said, "thanks. For staying."

It was the first time he had thanked her for anything. She kept her show of pleasure to a simple smile. "You're welcome."

* * * * *

Amaranthe stepped outside of the cannery with an egg-and-flatbread sandwich for Sicarius. It was his turn on watch, and he stood at the base of the dock, talking to a man dressed in bland civilian clothing. Now who had stumbled onto their hideout?

Both men noticed her well before she reached them. Sicarius held out a staying hand, and the stranger turned his back to her to finish the conversation. She stopped. This wasn't some random passerby, but someone Sicarius knew. A folded sheet of paper went from the stranger's hand to Sicarius's and, after a wary glance at Amaranthe, the man walked away.

Sicarius opened the note to read. Curiosity propelled her forward, and she glimpsed a couple lines of pencil before he turned his back to her. *All right, what are we being so secretive about here?*

After reading, Sicarius crumpled the note, turned back, and accepted the sandwich.

"News on the creature?" Amaranthe asked.

"No."

"The emperor? Hollowcrest? Counterfeiting?"

"I need to leave." Sicarius strode down the dock toward the cannery.

"For how long?" She tried not to feel like an attention-seeking puppy bouncing at his heels as she trailed him inside. "Are you coming back tonight?"

Sicarius did not answer. He walked past Books and tossed the crumpled note into a fire barrel. Amaranthe's shoulders slumped. He wasn't going to tell her what it said, and now she had no chance of reading it either.

"You *are* coming back, right?" she asked as he walked out the door.

Without answering, he was gone.

Amaranthe grabbed the burning paper out of the fire. Heat seared her fingers, but she managed to get it to the nearest counter before dropping it. She blew on the flames, but the note had already transformed into a charred ball. When the fire burned out, she could only stare glumly as smoke wafted from the illegible black remains.

Books slid onto a stool on the opposite side of the counter. "Sicarius isn't sharing his secret missives with you?"

"This is the first secret missive that I know about. I'd trade my grandfather's knife to read what it says." She tapped a finger on the lacquered wood of the counter.

Maldynado's snores competed with Akstyr's in the sleeping area; they had both pulled long watch shifts the night before. She supposed she ought to go outside and take over Sicarius's abandoned post.

"Hm." Books lowered his chin to the table and squinted at the charred ball. "I wonder if it was written in pen or pencil."

"It looked like pencil. Secret missives should be erasable, you know."

"Hm."

"You said that already," Amaranthe said. "You don't by chance know some way to read this?"

"I should not like to make promises, but the grease in pencil lead makes it fairly fire retardant. The words are likely still there. It's just a matter of seeing them." Books stood. "Let's take a look in your cleaning supply closet, shall we?"

"Whatever you say, professor." Amaranthe followed him to the cubby.

He pulled open the door and gaped.

"What is it?" she asked. "Did you find what you need?"

"It's spotless in here. You *cleaned* the cleaning supply closet?"

She blushed. "Possibly."

"I assume there's soap in...ah, there. And an atomizer, excellent." Books tossed Amaranthe a bar of soap, then puffed a rubber ball attached to an empty glass bottle. It hissed a few times. "Shave some soap into this and fill it with water. I'll find a couple panes of glass."

Trying not to feel bewildered—and dumb—Amaranthe completed her task and met Books at the counter. He nudged the charred ball onto a dirt-free square of glass and picked up the spray bottle. He shook the soapy water and squirted the ball. Mist dampened the black paper.

Amaranthe leaned forward, not sure what to expect, but barely breathing. Once it was wet, Books eased the crinkled mass apart. Instead of crumbling into ash, the black paper slowly but surely flattened onto the glass.

"The soap makes it stay together?" she asked.

"The glycerol in the soap." Books laid a second pane of glass on top of the first, sandwiching the black paper between them. "Here, hold it up to a light."

Amaranthe lit one of their kerosene lamps. After a glance at the door, she picked up the glass by the corners.

One of Maldynado's chickens squawked. She fumbled and almost dropped the glass.

Books watched her, and she feared a mocking comment about her nerves, but only grimness marked his face. "You realize if he finds out we did this, he'll kill us," he said.

"Maybe it's just a grocery list." Amaranthe tried a smile, but her mouth felt dry and her lips couldn't manage the position.

"You read it. I'll wait outside."

"And leave me holding the condemning evidence?"

"Precisely," Books said. "He likes you more than me."

"Warn me if you see him coming."

Books waved and stepped outside.

Alone except for the snoring men, Amaranthe hesitated. Should she really be spying on Sicarius? If she wanted him to trust her, shouldn't she *be* someone he could trust? But if they were at cross-purposes, ignorance of it could be fatal. She chewed on her lip. The obvious attempt at justifying her actions did not sit well with her conscience. Still, she did not set the note down.

She lifted the glass before the lamp, and the light illuminated the pencil through the black paper.

It was not a grocery list.

The past is forgiven. Your old job awaits. Name your price.

CHAPTER 18

THE INK HAD DRIED ON THE COUNTERFEITING plates, and Amaranthe tucked them into the crate beside the stacks of bills. She, Books, and Maldynado had removed the drying lines and paper cutter. Of course, someone ambling into the fish cannery would find the printing press loitering in the corner a tad odd. Sicarius had not returned since receiving his note the day before, and Amaranthe feared he would not return at all.

Footsteps thundered on the dock. Akstyr grabbed the door frame and swung into the cannery.

"Enforcers!" he blurted. "Coming down the hill."

"Spitted dead ancestors," Books cursed.

"Don't worry." Given the number of people who had delivered messages to their secret counterfeiting hideout, Amaranthe was surprised enforcers hadn't come down their street sooner. The meeting with Forge and Hollowcrest was that night; the cannery had served them long enough. "We're ready. Everyone grab something, and let's go."

Books and Akstyr lifted the crate.

"How many enforcers?" Maldynado belted on his sword.

"It doesn't matter," Amaranthe said. "We're not killing any more of them. Door. Now."

Books and Akstyr hustled onto the wharf. Maldynado sprinted to his chicken pen and threw open the latch. His charges streamed out, squawking uproariously. Amaranthe cringed at the noise. Maldynado tried to usher them to the door.

"Leave them," she hissed.

"Not for some enforcer to throw in a stew."

Amaranthe grabbed Maldynado's arm and dragged him through the doorway. Using the building for cover, she headed for the edge of the dock. She waved for the others to follow and slipped over the edge. When she ducked beneath, the five foot clearance left her hunched, but it was enough. Maldynado followed. Akstyr handed the crate down to him, then came after. Books, the last over, skidded on the ice beneath the snow and landed on his backside.

"I'm too old for this," he muttered as Amaranthe helped him up.

"There's never a good age to fall on your butt," Maldynado said. "That's why the rest of us stayed upright." He grimaced as his head brushed the underside of the wharf. "Mostly upright."

"There're at least ten coming," Akstyr whispered. "Where are we going?"

"Across the lake?" Books suggested.

Chin on the top of the crate, Akstyr said, "I'm not hiking to the other side with this."

"Just be glad we didn't decide to forge coins." Amaranthe pointed to the shoreline beneath the head of the dock. "We'll hide in the shadows until they're in the building."

Before they had gone halfway, synchronized footfalls pounded the boards above them. Snow trickled through the cracks in several places.

They reached the shore as the footfalls faded. Amaranthe peered over the edge of the dock. A single man paced in front of the building. The rest had gone inside. Before long, enforcers would move their investigation outside, looking for trails. Her team had to move now, or chance being found later.

Only a few yards separated their dock from the neighboring one. If they stayed low and did not make any noise, maybe the enforcer guard would not see them.

"Slow and subtle," she whispered, "we're heading over there."

Hugging the shoreline, Amaranthe eased toward the next dock. She resisted the urge to sprint—sudden movement was more likely to draw an unfriendly eye. No shouts arose from the cannery, and she made it to the protective cover of the dock.

She hunkered behind a piling and waited for the others to catch up. Between the ice and the weight of the crate, Books and Akstyr crossed ponderously.

Voices sounded on the street.

"Corporal, take your men and check the warehouses in the nearby docks," someone said.

Amaranthe winced. Back up.

"Hurry," she mouthed. She waved for Maldynado to help with the crate, even as she watched and hoped the enforcers on the street didn't look down to the lake. With luck, the men searching the cannery would be content with the evidence they found and assume the building's occupants had left hours before.

"Find their tracks," an enforcer called from inside the cannery. "The fire barrels are still warm. They haven't been gone long."

So much for luck.

A chicken strutted down the dock alongside the cannery.

"Oh, good," Maldynado said. "Isabel got out."

Amaranthe envisioned the chicken hopping down to squawk cheerfully at them. Did other leaders have these kinds of problems?

"We better put a couple more docks behind us," she whispered.

But, before they reached the far side of their current dock, two pairs of standard enforcer-issue boots skidded down the snowy bank and onto the ice. The owners, two men armed with repeating crossbows and swords, landed on the frozen lake and looked about.

"Uh oh," Akstyr muttered.

Amaranthe inched forward. They ought to be able to subdue two men if they could surprise them.

Before she could close, the nearest enforcer spotted them. "Down here!" he called to the street.

She frowned. If several were up top, waiting to help, subduing these two was less likely.

"Drop your weapons and your...uh...chicken crate," the younger of the two said, "and come out with your hands open, or it'll be crossbow quarrels up the nose."

Amaranthe's eyebrow twitched—that wasn't the line taught at the academy. She glanced back and nodded slightly to her men. She hoped the group had been working with her long enough to recognize it as meaning, "We can't get caught with all these counterfeits so if the odds are in our favor smash these lads into the ice."

"Very well," she told the enforcers and stepped out.

If it had just been the two men, she would have led a charge, but as soon as she came out from under the dock, four enforcers on the street came into view. They also bore crossbows. A couple of familiar faces stared down the shafts—no one she ever worked with but men she had passed in the hallways at headquarters. Footsteps announced the arrival of two more enforcers on the dock above, bringing the total to eight. Eight versus her four. Wonderful.

The enforcers stirred with surprise as several seemed to recognize her. Weren't expecting me, eh? They must have come for the money, probably traced Akstyr's note to the area. Apparently no one had put her together with the counterfeiting scheme. Until now.

"Isn't she the one with the death mark on her head?" someone asked.

The enforcers shifted their crossbows from the vague direction of Amaranthe's party to dead center at her chest.

"Fire!" one of the men on the street shouted.

Amaranthe thought it was the order to shoot. She crouched, ready to throw herself into a defensive roll, but no quarrels launched from the crossbows. Instead, yells erupted from the cannery. Smoke roiled from the broken windows, and screams of pain followed.

"Help!" someone cried.

Four of the enforcers on the street sprinted toward the burning building, leaving only two above and two below to deal with Amaranthe and crew.

It was the best chance they would get.

She charged the distracted enforcers in front of her. Her heel struck ice under the snow, and she lost her footing. The charge turned into an ungraceful dive, and she tumbled lengthwise at the group. She collided with two pairs of legs. An enforcer crashed to the ice. The other flailed and tried to keep his balance, but Books bowled into him. Soon a jumble of thrashing bodies and limbs writhed about on the ice.

In the confused tangle, Amaranthe grabbed someone's crossbow even as a hand latched onto her ankle. She kicked out and clipped an enforcer in the jaw. His head cracked ice, and he stilled.

Crossbow quarrels hammered the frozen lake. Maldynado and Akstyr charged up the snowy slope to get at the bowmen.

With the crossbow in hand, Amaranthe skittered away from the fray and got her feet beneath her.

"Get back, Books," she barked.

He obeyed, and the enforcer saw her crossbow. His hands opened and spread.

On the street above, Maldynado and Akstyr had flattened their opponents.

"Go help your comrades with the fire," Amaranthe told the sole conscious enforcer. She twitched the crossbow for emphasis.

He looked at his inert partner and the two unmoving men on the street, nodded curtly, and scrambled across the ice toward the cannery.

Amaranthe strapped the crossbow to her back. "Books, help Maldynado with the crate. Akstyr, let's grab the other crossbows. We're going back to our first hideout."

So loaded, they hastened inland. They ran between two buildings, through an alley, up the hill, and into the next block before Amaranthe found a vantage point to peer back along their trail. No one was following them. Flames ate at the cannery's walls. A loud snap echoed across the lake, and the building's roof collapsed. More destruction in her wake. She sighed as she led the men away from the scene.

Three blocks farther on, Sicarius fell in beside them.

"You missed the opportunity for daring heroics," Maldynado told him.

Amaranthe knew better. That fire had not started by magic. And she suspected the cries for help that had come from the building had less to do with burning rafters than with a dark figure stalking the shadows.

"How many dead?" she asked grimly.

"Two or three," Sicarius said. "It was meant primarily as a distraction. Most of the men made it out."

He watched her as he spoke, no doubt wondering if she would yell at him again. Amaranthe could not. By now, she understood the ruthlessness of his methods and she was still using him. When people died, she could only blame herself. Besides, she was relieved he had come back at all. After reading that note, she had not been sure.

She wanted to ask him about Hollowcrest, about his 'old job,' why he'd returned to help, and if he was truly on her side or working toward some other agenda. But she could hardly do so, not without confessing her privacy-defying reading habits.

"Glad you came back," was all she said.

* * * * *

Sespian leaned against the wall outside his office, feigning nonchalance as he chatted with Dunn and a couple of soldiers. Sespian kept catching himself tugging at his collar or wiping moist hands on his trousers, so the casual facade probably wasn't fooling anyone.

Inside the office, Lord General Lakecrest waited, as he had for the last twenty minutes. Sespian wanted Hollowcrest's loyal officer to have time to feel nervous. Unfortunately, Sespian probably felt more nervous than the experienced general.

"I suppose it's been long enough." He reached for the doorknob.

"Are you sure you don't want to start with one of the lower ranking traitors, Sire?" Dunn asked.

No, he wasn't sure. Sespian hated the idea of confronting a man thirty years his senior, but he'd make more headway starting at the top. If he could get one of Hollowcrest's generals on his side, maybe he could win over other men from that list. Better a bit of politicking than dozens of hangings.

"I'm sure," Sespian said. "Get your men ready. You'll need to take Lakecrest into custody after this. He can't be allowed to speak with Hollowcrest before we lay our tiles."

"Yes, Sire," Dunn said.

Sespian set his jaw, pushed back his shoulders, and strode into the office.

General Lakecrest rose from a wingback chair beside the low cider table. His concave frown mirrored the curve of his bald head, though the expression looked natural on him, rather than an indicator of nerves or concern. Enough medals and badges armored his uniform jacket to deflect arrows.

Sespian's instinct was to wave the general back into his seat, but he waited for the salute and seated himself first. This man was not a friend, not someone for whom rituals should be relaxed.

"Did you know about the poison?" Sespian asked abruptly, wanting to unsettle his guest.

Lakecrest blanched. His expression, filled not with surprise but dread, answered Sespian's question as surely as words: yes.

"Because," Sespian continued, "if you didn't know, I could forgive your unwavering devotion to Hollowcrest, who is theoretically supposed to be serving me. But if you did know he was drugging me and didn't do anything to warn me—well, that's treason, isn't it? Punishable by death. And of course you'd be stripped of your warrior caste status, title, and holdings. Your family would lose everything. Your daughters, I understand, haven't much of an aptitude for business or snaring husbands. I suppose it would be hard for them to support themselves, and without that warrior caste title, they'd be even less appealing as marriage candidates."

Sespian forced himself to stare into Lakecrest's eyes as he spoke, all the while hating himself for the threats coming out of his mouth. If this was what it took to get his power back from Hollowcrest, he would do it. Later, he could wonder if he had done the right thing.

"I see." Lakecrest leaned back in his chair and considered Sespian through new eyes. "The real question is not of what I know or don't know. It's whether you have the gumption and the wiles to challenge Hollowcrest."

Sespian withdrew a folded paper from his pocket. He opened it and placed it on the table before his guest. Lakecrest leaned forward. It was Dunn's now-complete list of men working in Fort Urgot and the Imperial Barracks who were loyal to Hollowcrest. When Lakecrest's frown gave way to a slack-jawed gape, Sespian felt a thrum of satisfaction in his breast.

"I've discovered that Hollowcrest has an appointment that will take him out of the Barracks tonight." Sespian didn't know where or with whom, but he could find that out later. "While he's gone, I'm having all these men arrested. Without their support, Hollowcrest will be easy to oust." Unless, of course, Hollowcrest already knew what Sespian was doing and had some plan in place to outmaneuver him. The old warthog had seemed distracted the last couple days, but that could be an act. Sespian cleared his throat and forced his mind back to Lakecrest. "If I arrested you, it would leave Urgot without a commander, and it seems a shame to dethrone a man of your experience. If you willingly choose to come to my side, perhaps some of the soldiers in your command could be spared."

"Spared?" Lakecrest's frown deepened. "You're planning on killing the men you arrest?"

Here was where the acting came in. Sespian could not imagine killing anyone in cold blood, whether they were Hollowcrest's lackeys or not, but... "That is the law, is it not? Traitors are always put to death."

Lakecrest slumped in the wingback and massaged his jaw. All the while, he stared at Sespian, who did his best to look determined and righteous.

It either fooled Lakecrest, or he was feeling magnanimous, for he said, "It seems the boy has become a man."

Something that tended to happen naturally when drugs weren't involved. All Sespian said out loud was, "You'll join me, then?"

"I shall not impede your plans."

It was not exactly an endorsement, but it was as much as Sespian had dared hope for.

* * * * *

Drips of melting snow pattered from the eaves of the icehouse. Inside, darkness and layers of sawdust insulated the frozen blocks from a similar demise.

Amaranthe chose to take the warming weather as a positive sign, though that didn't make her any less nervous. Broom in hand, she was cleaning everything in sight as she rehearsed her words for the meeting.

Sicarius took a break from running a new obstacle course he had set up for himself, and Amaranthe waved him over. He grabbed a jug of water and joined her. His hair stuck up more than usual, but he was otherwise neat in his typical black. If they lived through the mission, she decided to buy him an obnoxiously cheerful shirt. Something in sunflower yellow, perhaps.

The other men were swatting at each other with swords near the back wall. Maldynado was supposedly leading a fencing practice, though copious amounts of chatter punctuated the clanks of metal. All that mattered for the moment was that the others were out of earshot.

"Tonight's the night," she told Sicarius. And then winced. Emperor's teeth, could she have uttered anything more inane?

Predictably, he said nothing.

"There's something I need to know." Amaranthe brushed a shred of sawdust off her sleeve. How could she say this without alluding to the note? "Tonight when Hollowcrest shows up..." No, wait, she had to explain why she was doubting him. "Uhm, Mitsy Masters from the Maze said you're still Hollowcrest's man and the bounty is just a cover. I don't believe that, otherwise you wouldn't need me to help the emperor, because you'd be right there in the Barracks, but I *do* believe you worked for Hollowcrest in the past and..." *I spied on you and read the note where he invited you back.* No, couldn't say that. "Anyway..." She should probably be looking in his eyes. She lifted her gaze but only made it as far as his chin. "I certainly owe you a lot—you've saved my life half a dozen times in the last couple weeks—so I'd like to trust you one-hundred percent, but you're always so reticent and I'm never sure..." Amaranthe took a big breath. "What I need to know is if we're all out there tonight, me and Hollowcrest and the Forge people, who are you going to back if there's a physical confrontation?"

Finally, she met his eyes.

If her doubts troubled or insulted him, he did not hint of it. Sicarius returned her gaze without evasion—and without answering.

Swords clashed and laughter sounded on the other side of the ice-house. Between Amaranthe and Sicarius...silence.

Frustrated, she wiggled her fingers in a give-me-something gesture. "Please, Sicarius? I need to know how to plan."

"I'm not backing anyone," he said. "My only concern is protecting the emperor."

"So I should plan this as if you won't be there?" She struggled to keep the disappointment out of her voice. It wasn't as if he had ever implied he was doing things for her. From the beginning it had been the emperor's name that had swayed him to her side. "Very well."

He turned back toward the obstacle course.

"Are you ever going to tell me what he is to you?" she asked.

Sicarius did not answer.

* * * * *

Amaranthe's group arrived at the Oak Iron Smelter a half hour before midnight. The huge plant lay dormant, its massive smokestack black against a starry sky. Carts on railroad tracks walled in one side of a huge scrapyard that stretched for a block around the central building. Mountains of raw ore, scrap metal, and coal created snow-covered hills, and she led Books, Akstyr, and Maldynado into the valleys. All four of them carried swords, and Akstyr and Books toted the repeating crossbows taken from the enforcers. Sicarius had disappeared with the remaining crossbow before they arrived.

Amaranthe had left the majority of the counterfeit bills behind, stored amongst the rafters in the ice house. She carried a knapsack with a sample of their work, enough—she hoped—to give her adversaries cause for alarm.

As they walked, her kerosene lamp created a yellow sphere that wobbled along the ground litter. Silvery splashes of hardened metal glinted on a discarded mold. She stepped over food wrappers, scattered ore, and spilled slag. What snow melted during the day had frozen into ridges of icy slush that made the footing capricious. A cold breeze scraped at her cheeks, and her breath fogged the air.

"Maldynado, you'll come with me to the meeting, where I need you to look big and imposing," Amaranthe said.

"And dangerous?" Maldynado asked. "Like someone deserving a *huge* bounty on his head?"

"Precisely so. Books and Akstyr, I want you on top of the mountains of junk where you can see us and shoot at troublemakers if you need to. I'm hoping this won't devolve into a fight, but if it does, be ready."

"What's Sicarius doing?" Akstyr asked.

"Being independent," she said.

"How new for him." Books lifted a finger. "May I speak with you for a moment, Amaranthe?"

They stepped away from the others and into the shadow of a warped flywheel.

She gave him a frank look. "If you're going to tell me that I'd be better off with Sicarius by my side, I already tried to talk him into that. He has his own reasons for being here, but that's fine. I know what I'm doing." *I think.*

Books held out a fist full of crossbow quarrels. "I merely need to know how to load this contraption."

"Oh."

She plunked the quarrels into the magazine and showed him how use the lever to chamber new bolts. Books thanked her and jogged between two rubble heaps. Before disappearing from sight, he slipped on a frozen puddle and rammed his shoulder against a junk pile. Shards of metal rained down around him. He staggered to his feet, acknowledged his survival with a wave, and continued into the maze.

It'll be a miracle if I walk out *of here tonight without being shot by my own team.*

Akstyr, too, disappeared into the scrapyard. Amaranthe and Maldynado resumed walking.

"If this doesn't work out tonight..." he started.

"I've enjoyed working with you, too, Maldynado. You've been a tremendous help, and it's been an honor knowing you."

"Oh. Thanks."

"Isn't that the sort of thing you were going to say?" she asked.

"I just wanted to ask..." Maldynado cleared his throat. "If I get porcupined full of arrows tonight, could you tell my mother I died a hero?"

"Of course. And if this *does* work out, you never know, you could *be* a hero."

"Like with a statue?"

"Sure, why not? The emperor is an artist. Maybe he'd design it himself."

"That'd be a step up from a wanted poster," Maldynado said. "As long as it isn't a *small* statue."

"Still miffed about the meagerness of your bounty?"

"Two hundred and fifty lousy ranmyas." He kicked a rusted doorknob into a pile of equally rusted scrap metal.

The silver light of a quarter moon easing over the smelter made maneuvering through the metal heaps easier, so Amaranthe dimmed her lantern. They reached the center of the yard, a rubble-free area with a steam shovel quiescent on one side. Against the night sky, its tall silhouette reminded her of a skeleton she had seen in the Stumps Museum as a girl, the bones of a giant carnivorous reptile from a southern rainforest.

She deemed the clearing the most likely meeting place and tugged Maldynado into a shadowy nook where they could observe.

At midnight, voices sounded, accompanied by the clanking of mail armor. Amaranthe tried to count the people based on the sounds of their footfalls, but there were too many. Sicarius would know. He would probably know not only the numbers but the height and weight of each man. She wished she had him at her side, stern and dangerous as he glared at her foes.

Before she could decide whose troops approached, another collection of voices and clanking armor arose from the other side of the yard.

"You weren't supposed to tell them to bring armies," Maldynado whispered in her ear.

"I didn't. Considering they're both committing treason, I didn't think they'd want to involve many people. Seems they're more paranoid of each other than of revealing their secrets."

The two parties entered Amaranthe's vision. They met in the cleared space and faced off, Hollowcrest on one side, Larocka and Arbitan on the other. Fifteen to twenty armed fighters backed each party. They bristled with swords, muskets, and pistols. Apparently, neither side was concerned about the legality of the weapons choices. Several men carried lanterns as well, which illuminated the clearing but left the junk piles in the shadows.

"Sorry, Hollow," Arbitan said with none of the respect the office of Commander of the Armies required. "You weren't willing to put into place any of our reasonable requests, and we've decided the emperor must die. The Strat Tiles have already been laid, so it's too late for whatever scheme you've thought up."

"What are you talking about, you power-hungry commoner?" Hollowcrest glared. "You're the one who wanted a meeting."

The two men fell silent, staring at each other, gazes more frigid than the surrounding air. Larocka, arm-in-arm with Arbitan, whispered something in his ear.

A howl sounded in the distance. Amaranthe recognized it immediately. Arbitan's lips curved into a disconcerting smile.

Amaranthe nudged Maldynado, cleared her throat, and approached the circle of light.

"Good evening, gentlemen." She wanted to surprise no one, especially not the nervous guards with firearms, so she kept her movements slow. "I'm the one who sent the messages, Amaranthe Lokdon. Please forgive my presumptuousness, but I needed to speak with all three of you together."

She paused at the edge of the light, making the third point of a triangle between herself, Hollowcrest, and the Forge duo. Sword drawn, Maldynado guarded her back.

"Aren't you dead yet?" Hollowcrest asked, sounding far more annoyed than intrigued by her declaration.

"Indeed, I thought the enforcers I tipped off had slain you." Arbitan sniffed and added, "What do you want that you didn't find snooping around our house?"

A flicker of surprise crossed Larocka's face at Arbitan's words, but she recovered quickly and joined the two men in glaring at Amaranthe.

"I don't think they like you," Maldynado whispered.

Amaranthe waved him to silence. She had to lay out her proposition quickly, before one of the guards decided to fire a musket ball into her chest.

"I want the emperor to live—free of drugs—and be permitted to do the job the people depend on him to do. In order to ensure my wishes are fulfilled, I've printed five million ranmyas in counterfeit bills." *Closer to two million.* "If you do not cease your manipulations—" she looked at Hollowcrest, "—and drop your assassination plans—" a look at Arbitan and Larocka, "—I will flood Stumps with this fake currency, and I will continue to make more until the entire monetary system of the empire is devalued. Hyperinflation will destroy the economy. If you kill me tonight, it will change nothing. My team will carry on." *Doubtful.* "Even now, men are guarding the money. They will begin distributing it at dawn if I do not return and countermand the order." *And finish with a lie.*

Would any of them believe her?

A furrow between Hollowcrest's lowered eyebrows suggested concern. Larocka wore an open-mouthed, appalled expression. The smug condescending smile on Arbitan's face never wavered.

Amaranthe shrugged her knapsack off her shoulder and tossed it between the two parties. "To prove what I say is true, I've brought a small sample of my work. The paper isn't quite the same, but every time we've used the bills, they've passed easily." *Well, Akstyr managed to buy pastries once.*

Hollowcrest eyed the bag as if it writhed with live snakes. "You crawled out of my dungeon half-dead—no, *dying*—less than two weeks ago. You haven't had time."

"It's amazing what a good team can accomplish," Amaranthe said.

"What team?" Hollowcrest demanded. "You had nothing. I turned the enforcers against you. We confiscated everything in your apartment. You're lying."

Amaranthe extended her hand toward the bag. Any satisfaction she might have felt at Hollowcrest's disbelief was dashed by the amusement on Arbitan's face. Larocka looked alarmed at the prospect of economic upheaval, but Arbitan...pleased. If he was bluffing, he was doing an utterly convincing job. Why do I get the feeling he's not fighting in the same ring as the rest of us?

"Let's see if this young lady is in earnest." Arbitan sauntered forward and plucked up the bag. He shuffled through its contents, withdrew a bill, and examined it near a lantern. "Excellent forgeries. I'd estimate at least thirty thousand ranmyas here."

"We can't let this happen," Larocka said. "My investments—most of them are in Turgonia. Even global commerce would be affected. The imperial ranmya is the world's anchor currency!"

"Nothing's going to happen," Hollowcrest said. "I've read the woman's record; she's not going to do anything illegal." He sounded as if he was trying to convince himself. Good.

"You're wrong, sir," Amaranthe said. "It's true you have forced me to do something I would have once never considered, but I believe in what I'm doing. Illegal or not, I *am* committed."

"How noble for you," Arbitan said.

A faint click sounded on one of the nearby junk heaps. A crossbow quarrel zipped out of the darkness and struck Arbitan's chest.

The air in front of him shimmered, and the bolt bounced off, as if it had hit metal.

Instead of crying out in pain or being thrown back, Arbitan merely smiled.

Hollowcrest's eyes grew round. Amaranthe grimaced; it seemed her suspicions about Arbitan being a wizard were correct. But who had fired the shot? Sicarius?

"Emperor's blood," Maldynado whispered. "How are we supposed to—"

"Basilard!" Arbitan called. "How progresses the hunt?"

Amaranthe glanced around. Hollowcrest, too, searched about, brow furrowed. He waved and his men gathered closer about him.

Soon a reluctant shuffling of footsteps grew audible. Books and Akstyr marched into view, their crossbows and other weapons absent. Behind them came Arbitan's shaven-headed security man and several more guards. Amaranthe spotted the confiscated weapons in their keeping. Apparently, Arbitan's men had not found Sicarius. She did not know how much hope to place in that fact. Her plan had failed. What use did he have for her now?

"Take her." Arbitan jerked his head at Amaranthe.

Guards surged around her.

She tensed, then slumped. Fighting so many would gain her nothing. Except death.

"As you wish," Amaranthe said. "May I remind you, my men who stayed behind have orders to begin releasing the counterfeits in the morning if I don't return. Assassinating the emperor and replacing him with some obedient sycophant will do little good if the empire's economy is suffocating in a sewer. Killing me would be a mistake."

"Don't worry, girl," Arbitan said. "You'll tell me everything you know before I kill you, certainly enough for me to take over control of your little ploy."

She noted the words take over instead of stop.

"Boss?" Body tense, Maldynado stood with his knuckles white on the hilt of his sword as the men approached.

"Do nothing," Amaranthe said.

Arbitan flicked a finger at her, and guards grabbed her. Invasive hands searched for and removed weapons. The guards tied her wrists. The rope bit into her skin, cold and abrasive. She stared at the knots, trying not to see her bindings as the shackles of failure, trying not to feel as if the last two weeks had been for nothing.

Toying with a bit of rope, Arbitan considered Hollowcrest through slitted eyes, as if thinking of taking him prisoner as well. Perhaps Arbitan regarded the odds too even, for he merely said, "I'd get out of the city before the emperor's birthday, Hollow. We've already made arrangements for his capture. You'll just be in the way after the boy's death. And I'm sure you know what happens to people who get in the way."

"Dungeons and death warrants," Amaranthe growled.

Hollowcrest, Arbitan, and Larocka started arguing, but the guards dragged Amaranthe away before she could hear anything vital. *So glad I could set up a meeting for them....*

CHAPTER 19

OUTSIDE THE IMPERIAL BARRACKS, SESPIAN stood before the steps, shivering beneath his parka. To his left stood Lieutenant Dunn, to his right General Lakecrest. With the hour past midnight, night lay thick about the courtyard, and the gas lights lining the walkways did nothing to warm the air. Sespian did not want to appear restless or nervous, so he did not pace or stamp his feet. He merely balled his fists inside his gloves to keep his fingers from going numb.

"I got the signal," Dunn said. "Hollowcrest should be arriving shortly. He left a couple hours ago and took fifteen loyal men with him. I have someone following, but I'm not sure yet where he went."

Arrows of anxiety pierced Sespian's stomach, but he simply said, "Very well."

The gate to the courtyard rattled open. Hollowcrest strode through with his men marching behind him. A scowl rode his face, one that deepened when he spotted Sespian.

For a moment, Hollowcrest looked as if he would stride right past, but he stopped when he spotted his loyal general. "What's going on, Lakecrest? Staff meetings are usually reserved for daylight hours."

"You won't be here after dawn," Sespian said. "In front of these witnesses, I hereby revoke your title of Commander of the Armies and all privileges and rights associated with that rank."

"That's ridiculous," Hollowcrest snapped. "I don't have the patience for this. Do you know what's going on out there?" He pointed behind him in the direction of the city. "Powerful people are plotting to assassinate you, and your enforcer girlfriend is making a mess of the economy."

Sespian stared. Amaranthe? Was that who Hollowcrest had been meeting?

Sespian pushed the thought away. He dared not lose his forward momentum or give Hollowcrest time to think. "You have committed treasonous acts against the throne—specifically drugging me—and your crimes demand death. For your years of loyal service to my father, I've decided not to have you killed, but you will leave the Barracks by dawn and Stumps by nightfall. Failure to obey will result in your prompt and permanent imprisonment in the dungeons."

"I have to collect reinforcements and go deal with Forge." Hollow-crest waved to his closest men. "Take the boy inside. We'll discuss his accusations in the morning."

"I don't think so." Sespian lifted an arm and waved two fingers.

Behind him, the front doors opened. Forty armed soldiers jogged out and lined up before Sespian.

"Lakecrest?" Hollowcrest asked.

The old general avoided his eyes.

The sound of footsteps marching over packed snow came from around the side of the building. Hollowcrest looked that direction. Sespian did not. He knew who was coming.

Soldiers, marching in a column two wide, tromped into view, shackles binding their wrists. Men from the loyal-to-the-emperor list led them. They parked the column of prisoners next to the front gate.

Sespian dug in his pocket and withdrew a key ring. He threw it toward Hollowcrest, who caught it and stared at it, eyebrows drawn down.

"The keys to their chains," Sespian explained. "You can release your men once you're on the other side of the gate."

"How did you—" Hollowcrest started but slammed his mouth shut and scowled instead.

Sespian exchanged a triumphant look with Dunn. Without the lieutenant's help, he never could have arranged this. Knowing he had chosen the right man for the duty thrilled Sespian.

"You'll regret this," Hollowcrest said. "By dawn."

"Is it necessary to be so melodramatic?" Sespian asked. "Whatever business deal you've ensconced yourself in, I care not."

"Fool," Hollowcrest growled. "If I fail tonight, you're a dead man, and the empire will be in chaos."

"We'll handle it." Sespian hated to ask Hollowcrest for anything, but curiosity drove him to voice the next question. "How is Amaranthe involved?"

"Since you're so clever these days, figure it out yourself."

Hollowcrest strode out of the courtyard, taking his long string of men with him. Guards slammed the wrought iron gate behind them.

General Lakecrest almost looked like he wanted to follow, but after a cool look at Sespian and Dunn, he stomped inside the building.

"That was well played, Sire," Dunn said. "I wish..."

Sespian looked at the lieutenant and raised his eyebrows. "What?"

"Nothing." Dunn's face grew masked. "It's late, Sire. Perhaps you should rest. I can alert you if Hollowcrest makes more trouble."

After a moment of hesitation, Sespian nodded. "Very well."

* * * * *

The pair of steam carriages waiting down the block from the scrap-yard featured modifications Amaranthe had never seen: massive cater-pillar treads instead of wheels. The vehicles stretched longer than usual with room to seat more than a dozen men.

Accompanied by two guards and a driver, Arbitan and Larocka took one steam carriage. The other fifteen guards clambered into the second, forcing Amaranthe and her men to join them. The closed passenger area had a single barred window in the door. Getting in was like crawling into a cave. Or a dungeon cell.

Once her captors shoved her into a seat, Amaranthe found herself facing the scarred security leader. Basilard, Arbitan had called him.

The modified machine easily climbed the steep, icy hills out of the industrial neighborhood. Nobody spoke. The rumble and hiss of the vehicle reverberated through the carriage. Despite the large interior, the number of broad, muscled people made scratching one's nose difficult. Escape seemed even more unlikely. Amaranthe avoided looking at her men. She felt too ashamed. She had failed them. She had failed the emperor. And she had failed herself.

Stop it. We're not giving up yet. She had not given up when she was dying in the Imperial Barracks' dungeon, and she would not give up now.

Amaranthe lifted her chin and met Basilard's eyes. A few guards held lanterns, and their light bounced off the wood-paneled walls, providing enough illumination to see his face. His cool blue eyes studied her in turn. Occasionally imperial citizens possessed light-colored eyes, but the paleness of his skin promised no conquering Turgonians had waltzed through his bloodline. An imported slave. Was he one still, or had Arbitan granted him his freedom?

"Were you a pit fighter, Basilard?" she asked.

He nodded once after apparently deciding the question posed no security risk.

"How does that system work? Do you all train together until it's time to entertain the wealthy gamblers? Then you're dumped into a situation where you have to kill the other fellow?" She remembered the reluctance of the fighters she had seen in the pit. Also, she remembered Basilard's chagrin at being the one who provided knives to arm them.

He nodded again.

"Ever have to kill someone who was a friend?" she asked. "Or who could have been, if things had been different?"

He looked at the floor. Yes.

Maldynado nudged her. "What are you talking to him for? Look at his neck. It's all scarred up. I bet he can't even talk back."

Basilard shot an icy glare at him. Amaranthe gave Maldynado a briefer stop-talking look.

"I've recently had something like that happen myself," Amaranthe said to Basilard, drawing his gaze back to her. She tried to ignore the large, muscled audience looking on. "A friend died because of a choice I made. Just because someone else manipulated the encounter doesn't take away my responsibility for that person's death, a person who didn't deserve it. I might as well have killed him myself." Thinking of Wholt, she did not have to feign the thick emotion in her voice. "It was the same with you, wasn't it? Because of a natural instinct for self-preservation, you made the decision to take another's life so that you could live. Probably more than once." She eyed his scars. "A lot more than once. That kind of guilt is hard to carry. The only thing you can do now is make

sure you do something worthwhile with your days, make a difference, justify your survival."

One of the guards snorted. "Want me to shut her up, boss?"

Basilard made a few gestures with his hands. Amaranthe could not tell if it represented a language or simply some code he had worked out with his men. Either way, the guard shrugged and sat back.

The steam carriage trundled to a stop before Amaranthe could finish her attempts to sway Basilard. Two guards grabbed her arms and shoved her into the night. Manhandled in a similar manner, her comrades followed.

The back of the Forge mansion loomed, the crenellated roof dark against the starry sky. Icicles hung from the gutters like daggers. Piles of snow framed a driveway, and gravel crunched as they walked toward the house.

The guards hustled Amaranthe and her men through drab utility hallways, down stairs, and into an unfamiliar part of the mansion. She watched for escape possibilities, but Arbitan must have ordered the entire contingent of men to accompany them. Even if her hands had been unbound and her team armed, the odds would have made a confrontation suicidal. Force would not free them.

Amaranthe maneuvered herself close to Basilard as they descended another staircase into a windowless hallway with a concrete floor.

"Emperor Sespian is a good man," she said. "You would be able to see that if Hollowcrest wasn't keeping him drugged. He wants to help people—workers, not wealthy business elitists. If he knew about the pit fights, he would put a stop to them."

Basilard halted. Amaranthe watched him hopefully, but he merely pushed open a heavy oak door. A black cell gaped before her. He gave a curt gesture, the meaning clear.

Amaranthe entered but turned to face the hallway as soon as she passed the threshold. While Maldynado and the others slouched in, she tried one last time.

"If you don't do anything to stop Arbitan, you'll be as guilty as he is for killing the first Turgonian leader to care about strengthening relations with other nations instead of destroying them. Arbitan, Larocka, and their figurehead of an emperor will bring dark and corrupt times. Can you live with yourself, knowing you'll be a part of that?"

The door closed in her face, plunging the cell into blackness.

"Apparently you can," Amaranthe muttered.

"I think you were closer in the carriage," Books said. "You sounded less...desperate."

"Thanks for the critique."

"This chews rat balls," Akstyr announced.

"I concur," Books said.

"Sorry, fellows," Amaranthe said. "My plan was...fanciful at best, it seems."

"I believe Hollowcrest was ready to negotiate," Books said. "Larocka, too, appeared worried. Arbitan was the one who was less concerned than he should have been at the prospect of losing his fortune."

"I know." She shuffled around the cell and located—by thumping her knee painfully into it—a bench set into the wall opposite the door. "I thought maybe Arbitan was a Turgonian who had studied the mental sciences on trips to Nuria, but I had it backwards. He's got to be a cursed Nurian wizard posing as an imperial businessman. That's why he wouldn't care about the money; devaluing our currency would only help Nuria. He must have infiltrated the business class and wooed Larocka into giving him a voice with Forge. He's probably been spying for his government for the last year, maybe more." Amaranthe stared into the darkness in the general direction of the floor. "What if he wants to kill the emperor and put a figurehead on the throne, not because he wants a leader who's sympathetic to capitalist interests but because his government wants someone who can be manipulated into working for them, maybe even helping to set up an invasion? The Nurians might not hate us as much as the Kendorians or other nations we've conquered, but they would certainly gain a lot from our fall. Imagine their magic combined with our technology. They could control the world."

"That's all supposition," Books said. "Just because that crossbow quarrel didn't strike him down doesn't prove he's a wizard with magical powers."

"Sure, it does," Akstyr said. "That's why I shot him."

Amaranthe shifted on the cold bench, turning toward his voice. "You fired the bolt?"

"I thought it might catch him with his guard down, but even if it didn't, it'd show everyone he was a wizard."

"A daring effort," she said, surprised at his initiative.

"Besides, Scar Head and his goons had me surrounded and were about to pounce on me," Akstyr added.

"Ah." Amaranthe leaned back. She could feel the iciness of the brick wall through her hair. "How do you kill a wizard, Akstyr? If he can deflect crossbow quarrels without even lifting a hand..."

"Aside from creatures and tools you can make with the mental sciences, actual spells only last so long as you can keep thinking about them. Break his concentration and you can break his armor. Of course, he'll feel pretty safe and free to concentrate so long as his soul construct is around, so you better plan on killing that first."

"And how does one kill a soul construct?" Books asked.

"I dunno. I don't think you do."

"Akstyr, you can't suggest a plan of action that's impossible to implement," Amaranthe said.

"I can't? I didn't know that was a rule."

"Women like to make up rules to befuddle you," Maldynado said. "It's part of living in their world. Get used to it."

"Give me some ideas, Akstyr," Amaranthe said, ignoring Maldynado.

"Well, you could probably kill it with powerful magic," Akstyr said. "Once created, they're very strong though. Even their makers can barely control them."

"Why would a wizard make something he couldn't control?" Amaranthe asked.

"The wizards can control them. Sort of. Soul constructs obey basic commands like 'go kill that man' or 'watch my back while I work,' but they're made from the owner's mind. Well, his soul, if you believe in that. They end up with the same temperaments as their creators, only they don't know about laws and stuff. They're just..."

"Creatures possessing all the evil of man without any of the restraints society places on us?" Books suggested.

"I guess," Akstyr said. "They'll obey their creator's orders, but they'll do it their own way."

"Sounds like Sicarius," Books said.

"Sounds much worse," Amaranthe said. "Sicarius may have been trained to put pragmatism ahead of feelings, but I think he's fairly innocuous as long as you don't get in his way. To be honest, he seems kind of mellow to me."

Maldynado snorted.

Akstyr snorted.

Books had the audacity to say, "For the first time, I think you're letting your feminine side blind you. You're romanticizing him."

Amaranthe blushed. "Fine." How had they gotten on this subject? "You don't have to agree with me on that. I'm more concerned about Arbitan and this creature at the moment."

"Maybe you could sway Larocka to help us," Books said. "If she knew what Arbitan was, would she still support him? If she's a native-born Turgonian, you'd think she would feel more loyalty to the empire."

"I don't know." Amaranthe shrugged. "Arbitan is a handsome man, and they seem...close."

"How could she fall for a slimy Nurian wizard?" Maldynado asked.

"Even an intelligent woman can be taken in by a pretty smile," Amaranthe said.

"Really?" Maldynado asked. "Because every time I try my pretty smile on you, you put me on watch or give me work."

"Not now, Maldynado," she said. "Let's focus."

"Been wondering if I should be looking for a girl for you," Maldynado grumbled.

Akstyr snickered.

"Perhaps her interests are simply elsewhere," Books said. "Remember, she thinks Sicarius is *mellow*."

"Mellow," Maldynado said. "Oh, sure. Throw a girl in his bed, and he'd probably start doing push-ups on her breasts."

The snickers intensified to guffaws, and not just from Akstyr.

"I'm glad everyone's enjoying this dungeon bonding time," Amaranthe said, "since we're probably going to be tortured to death in a few hours."

That stilled their guffaws. Silence descended on the cell. Amaranthe was glad for the darkness, since her cheeks felt a tad warm again.

"Think there's any chance of Sicarius coming to break us out?" Akstyr asked.

Amaranthe felt a similar hope, but... "Now that we've executed the plan and failed, he has no reason to risk himself for us. It would be more

logical for him to try something on his own, and he is nothing if not logical."

Maldynado snorted. "Why don't you just say we're of no more use to him, so he's leaving us to be tortured?"

"I think I did say that. Regardless, we're going to have to get out of here ourselves." Amaranthe stood up and groped around. If she could find a puddle of water or something slippery, maybe she could loosen her bonds. "Anyone have any ideas?" She bumped into somebody's head.

"Certainly," Maldynado said from beneath her. "Come sit on my lap and we'll discuss them."

She paused thoughtfully.

"Amaranthe." Books sounded scandalized at her silence. "Please assure me you're not considering succumbing to this troglodyte's advances."

"Well," she said, "I was debating the merits of certain fluids as a means of loosening ropes, but let's, ah, explore other possibilities first."

Footsteps sounded beyond the door. Frowning, Amaranthe turned. She had hoped they would have longer.

The lock *thunked* as a key turned in it. She shuffled forward, tensing to spring if an opportunity arose.

The door swung open. Basilard stood in the hallway. Alone.

Amaranthe held her breath, barely daring to hope. She studied his face, searched the eyes behind all those scars.

Basilard pulled a knife from one of numerous sheaths. Maldynado jumped in front of her, lowered into a defensive crouch.

Never breaking gazes with Basilard, Amaranthe stepped to the side and extended her arms. He carefully sliced through the ropes and waved her into the hallway. After an indecisive pause, he cut Maldynado's bonds as well. Books and Akstyr lined up for the same treatment. As soon as they were free, the men charged for the stairs. Amaranthe hesitated.

Basilard lowered his knife and stared forlornly at the shreds of rope on the floor. Surely, his choice tonight had condemned him. Originally, Amaranthe had only hoped to talk him into freeing them. After his act of kindness, she felt compelled to see him to safety. But then, she was not going anywhere safe.

"Do you want to come with us?" she asked.

He rotated his head, turning sad blue eyes on her. He shrugged ambivalently but followed when she headed for the door.

They caught up to the others on the floor above where the stairs bisected a hallway. Books and Maldynado had stopped to argue.

"The exit is this way." Maldynado pointed one direction.

"We can't just leave; we have to do something." Books pointed the other way.

"I am doing something," Maldynado said. "I'm leaving."

Amaranthe pushed past them and into the hall leading deeper into the house. She was surprised when all of the men followed.

"Do you know where we can find Larocka?" she whispered to Basilard. "I just want to talk to her, see if she'll reveal what's been set into place as far as the emperor's assassination."

Basilard lifted a shoulder but took the lead.

The group climbed a dark staircase and entered a short hallway. At one end, black night pressed against a frost-rimmed window. They had reached the ground level. A door marked the other end of the hall. The sound of voices and a staccato of footfalls came from behind it.

Surely, their escape couldn't have been detected already.

"Do you know what's going on?" Amaranthe whispered to Basilard. He shook his head.

She eased the door open and peered into a vast, dimly lit kitchen. When she spotted no one, she led the men inside. They passed multiple fireplaces and stoves. Storage bins, mixing bowls, and giant cauldrons cluttered rows of tile counter tops. On the other side of the kitchen, light leaked under a second door. The voices grew more pronounced as Amaranthe neared it. Though she could not make out words, a definite urgency edged them. Different speakers seemed to be moving in and out of the area.

When she hesitated, Basilard moved past her and slipped through the swinging door. She hoped that meant he was bringing back information. In the meantime, she considered looking for another staircase leading up, since the one she had used on her previous visit was in the midst of the commotion. Although, if something important was happening on the ground floor, Arbitan and Larocka would likely be the middle of it.

Amaranthe cracked the door and peered through. Someone blurred past her narrow angle of vision.

A loud crunch came from behind and she jumped. The door swung closed and almost smacked her on the nose. She turned to find Maldynado eating, practically in her ear.

She glared at him.

"What?" Maldynado stuck a hand out, displaying a row of crackers. "You want one?"

Books grabbed the crackers out of Maldynado's hand. "This is *not* the time for snacking."

"This could be my last meal," Maldynado said.

"And you chose crackers?" Akstyr said around a full mouth.

They turned to find him noshing on a piece of frosting-drenched cake.

"Oh, excellent," Maldynado said. "Is there more?"

Amaranthe leaned her forehead against the cool wood of the door jamb. Maybe she should have asked Basilard to leave them in the cell.

Basilard reentered, clutching a pen and paper. He scrawled a note:

Hollowcrest brought a shaman to break through the wards and has surrounded the house with a company of soldiers. He is waiting to negotiate with Arbitan in the Upstairs Parlor.

"What about Larocka?" Amaranthe asked.

More scrawling. *No one knows.*

"We could escape in the chaos," Books pointed out.

"Probably, but where does that leave us?" Amaranthe asked.

"It leaves us escaped," Akstyr muttered.

"And the emperor still in danger." She turned back to Basilard. "Would it be possible to spy on the meeting in the parlor without being seen?"

Basilard's hand rocked in a 'maybe' motion.

"Let's try."

Basilard found a lantern, led them back to the hall behind the kitchen, and eventually to a spiral staircase. Two floors up, they entered a series of attached rooms and a closet that turned out to be a secret entrance to a narrow passage. Dust-cloaked and cobweb-draped, it twisted through the house like an abandoned mine shaft. Amaranthe pinched her nose to stave off sneezes.

Basilard stopped at a wall comprised of wide wood panels. He put a finger to his lips for silence. He slipped a knife into a seam in the wall, then turned down the lantern. Blackness swallowed the passage, but the seam soon expanded as he eased the panels apart a couple inches.

Amaranthe pressed her face to the gap.

Hollowcrest stood by a large window, looking out at something—his troops perhaps. Gaming tables, sofas, and club chairs stood between him and the secret entrance. Kerosene lamps illuminated his side of the room, but no lights brightened the back half, and Amaranthe hoped she could observe without drawing attention.

No one else occupied the parlor yet, and only the crackle of a wood fire in a hearth on the far wall broke the silence.

Amaranthe chewed on her lip. Maybe she should talk to him, see if she could turn him into a temporary ally. He had men, a magic user, and every reason to want to stop Arbitan and Larocka.

A dark figure stepped out of the shadows behind the main door. Sicarius.

Amaranthe twitched with surprise. Hollowcrest, still facing the window, did not notice the movement. Sicarius glided around the furniture and stopped on a shaggy rug in front of the fire. His reflection appeared against the dark window. Hollowcrest's startled jump was impressively high considering his advanced years.

"Sicarius," he blurted.

Hands clasped behind his back, Sicarius regarded him without expression. Back to the fireplace, he had positioned himself so he faced Hollowcrest, yet kept the other door within view.

"Where have you been?" Hollowcrest said. "Didn't you get my message? Did you know what that enforcer girl was doing? Why didn't you kill her when I sent her to you? Never mind. That's not important now. It's good that you're here. Forge must be eliminated. I want the whole insidious group terminated, Arbitan in particular."

Amaranthe felt hope that Sicarius had not run straight to Hollowcrest after receiving that letter. Whatever the exact nature of their estrangement was, it seemed Hollowcrest's promise of forgiveness had not alleviated it. She wondered who had originally broken whose trust.

"I do not work for you anymore," Sicarius said.

Good.

Hollowcrest patted the air. "Just because we had a...disagreement a few years ago doesn't mean we don't still need you. I'll drop the charges Sespian placed on your head, remove the bounty. The boy won't be a problem."

"Yes," Sicarius said softly. "I understand you've been drugging him."

"All we need you to do is help with Forge," Hollowcrest said. "And then it'll be as it once was. Simple, efficient times where the—"

Footsteps sounded in the hallway. Sicarius vaulted over a sofa, landed without a sound, and blended into the shadows behind the door again. When Arbitan entered, he gave no indication of realizing Sicarius was in the room.

"Hollow." Arbitan poured a glass of brandy from a decanter. "I thought I told you to get out of the city."

"I don't take orders from common-born sewer rats."

"Common. I assure you, I am anything but—where I come from." Arbitan sniffed the brandy, took a sip, and swished it around in his mouth before swallowing. He did not offer Hollowcrest a glass. "You've brought quite a few soldiers with you, I see. Wherever did you find a shaman gifted enough to slip your men past my wards?"

"You forced this on yourself," Hollowcrest said. "Did you really think I would stand aside and let you replace my emperor and dictate policy for Turgonia?"

"Did *you* think I wouldn't plan for your every contingency?" Arbitan smiled, a frigid smile that sent a chill through Amaranthe even though she was not the recipient. "This house is protected by more than wards."

The creature.

"Your shaman is insignificant, and your army will not survive the night," Arbitan said.

Hollowcrest snorted. "You're bluffing. There's no—"

Outside, someone screamed.

"Run!" multiple voices cried.

The smiling, superior expression that branded Arbitan's face left little doubt to who was responsible.

Hollowcrest turned back to the window. His fingers came up and pressed against the glass, and his jaw dropped. More screams pierced the walls of the house, cries of pain and terror. Amaranthe's stomach sank. Without looking, she knew what carnage Hollowcrest witnessed.

Curses in a foreign language rose over the din. The voice switched to screams, which broke off abruptly.

"Oops, was that your shaman?" Arbitan asked.

"What is that...*thing*?" Hollowcrest demanded.

"A pet." Arbitan sipped from his glass. "I instructed it to eat your shaman first, but it'll chase down and slay all your men shortly."

Amaranthe wondered if this might be the best time to make a move. The creature was distracted, and Arbitan might not be prepared for an assault. Too bad the guards had taken her team's weapons.

She scanned the room, searching for inspiration. Her gaze landed on the shadows by the door. Maybe if she charged out of the hidden passage, it would distract Arbitan—break the concentration he needed to weave his defenses—and Sicarius could sink a knife into his back. Of course, it might also see her incinerated by wizard fire or whatever magic Arbitan could throw.

She had to take the risk.

Only Sicarius's eyes moved, watching the interplay between the two men. She willed him to look her direction, but as Arbitan lifted his glass again, seemingly oblivious to any threat, Sicarius blurred into motion.

One of his throwing knives whirled toward Arbitan's back, and a second weapon appeared in his hand instantly. He raised his arm, poised to strike again.

Arbitan was not as defenseless as he appeared. Like the crossbow quarrel, the knife stopped before it sank into his torso.

It bounced away as if it had struck a stone wall and landed on the plush carpet with a soft thump. Amaranthe sagged against the panel. She, too, had hoped he wouldn't have his defenses up here, in his sanctuary.

Sicarius's arm drooped. He did not throw the second knife.

"Your pet is not as effective as mine, Hollow," Arbitan purred. He glanced over his shoulder. "Come out of the shadows, assassin." Arbitan turned his head to look at Amaranthe. "And the escaped prisoners lurking in the passage may as well come out too. Along with my treasonous Basilard."

Scuffles of surprise sounded behind Amaranthe. After recovering from the shock of being discovered, she considered fleeing instead of

obeying, but Arbitan's sure gaze conveyed the futility of such an action. She pushed the panels farther apart and stepped into the parlor. Her team slunk after her. Basilard hung his head like a beaten hound.

Arbitan pointed for the group to join Sicarius.

Amaranthe ended up in front of the fireplace, its burning logs warming her back. Hollowcrest stared out the window doing nothing useful. She felt a stirring of disgust; he could at least try to barter for the lives of his men.

And what am I doing that's so helpful?

She eyed a set of fireplace tools next to the hearth. Maybe she could still provide the distraction that would lower Arbitan's defenses. Her hand drifted toward the poker.

"Well, my dear." Arbitan's gaze pinned her and she froze. "The counterfeit money would have been fun to play with, but you're too troublesome to keep around." His eyes flickered toward Basilard and back to her. "You'd probably subvert the torturer I sent to interrogate you."

Amaranthe swallowed. She recognized a death sentence by now. Time to take a chance.

She grabbed the poker and leapt for the wizard.

And was flattened to the floor. The rug mashed her cheek. It felt as if the ceiling had fallen on her, compressing her torso, her head, and every limb. She could scarcely breathe.

The poker pulled free from her hand and returned to its place amongst the tool set.

Out of the bottom of her eye, she saw her comrades similarly flattened. All except Sicarius. He was on one knee, knuckles pressed against the floor.

Fight it! Amaranthe wished she could. She exerted every muscle, trying to press her chest up from the floor. She couldn't budge.

Sicarius managed to rise from his knees, though his back bowed from the effort. Jaw clenched, face reddened, he glared at Arbitan and inched higher.

She needed to help him. Somehow.

Amaranthe stopped struggling. It was getting her nowhere, and if Sicarius were rising on muscle strength alone, Maldynado, with his powerful bulk, should have been able to force himself up as well. This was a mental battle, she realized, remembering Sicarius's history lesson on the Hunters. Too bad she had no such training to call upon. Suspecting the effort in vain, she tried to will herself up.

Sicarius staggered forward a step. Amaranthe sensed the wave of force lessening around her as Arbitan shifted more of his focus toward Sicarius. She wished she could see the wizard's face. Was he tiring? At least sweating a bit?

She closed her eyes and imagined herself swimming in the lake during the summer. She slipped under the surface and stroked to the depths, cutting through the water's resistance with ease. Her head inched off the carpet. Her shoulders and neck trembled under the weight. In her mind, she skimmed along the lake bottom, algae-slick pebbles passing beneath her. Then she angled for the surface, and the buoyant water carried her toward the sunlight. She wedged one elbow under her chest to prop her torso up, and then, with a gargantuan effort, lunged to the side and grabbed a burning brand from the fireplace.

Embers seared her flesh. The pain gave her a jolt of energy, and she used it to hurl the log.

It sailed at Arbitan's head. He threw his arm up reflexively, and in that instant his magic dissipated.

Amaranthe surged to her feet in time to see Sicarius ram a dagger into Arbitan's chest. It glided between the ribs and pierced vital organs. Shock widened Arbitan's eyes and stole the arrogant smile from his face. He crumpled to the ground, fingers clutching uselessly at the dagger hilt.

Amaranthe slumped against the fireplace mantel. Sicarius looked at her.

"Good to see you," she said.

His mask had returned, but he inclined his head. "I believe he is an undercover Nurian wizard, sent by their government to create chaos and plant a compliant heir on the throne."

"Amaranthe figured that out in the dungeon." Maldynado sent a smug look at Books.

"Really." Sicarius regarded Amaranthe with...respect?

She bit her lip to hide her smile.

"Excellent work, Sicarius," Hollowcrest crooned. "As expected. You were always invaluable. Good to have you back. Arbitan was the most dangerous, but I'll need someone to remove the remnants of Forge. That Larocka woman is a pest as well."

Amaranthe frowned at the old man. Did he think Sicarius had killed Arbitan for *him*?

"Sicarius, you can't help Hollowcrest," Books said. "He's the one who had my son killed. Amaranthe says—"

"Amaranthe says?" Hollowcrest snorted. "Sicarius doesn't take orders from street trollops. He's always worked for the throne—" Hollowcrest nodded at Sicarius, "—and he will again."

"Perhaps so," Sicarius said, inscrutable.

His agreement gave Amaranthe a horrified start, until she realized "the throne" meant Sespian these days.

"The first thing I'll need you to do is eliminate these witnesses," Hollowcrest said. "We don't want the papers sensationalizing this debacle." He prodded Arbitan, who still twitched on the floor.

Despite the mortal wound, Arbitan was slow dying. His mouth kept opening and closing, as if he was trying to utter one last snide comment. Amaranthe hoped he could not use his power to somehow heal himself. Surely, all that pain provided the ultimate distraction.

Nobody else paid Arbitan any heed. Books watched the two men, teeth clamped on his lower lip. Maldynado and Akstyr, too, seemed worried that Sicarius would take up with Hollowcrest. Their concern, etched so clearly on their faces, made Amaranthe doubt her own certainty.

Am I wrong?

Sicarius crossed the room and stopped an arm's-length away from Hollowcrest. His face offered no hint of malice. He reached for no weapons.

"Excellent. Now..." Hollowcrest waved at Amaranthe and the others. "Kill this riffraff."

"I knew it," Maldynado muttered.

Akstyr backed toward the door. Books's shoulders slumped, as if the battle was already lost.

"You're drugging Sespian," Sicarius said, eyes locked on Hollowcrest.

Hollowcrest waved a placating hand. "Only to make him compliant to the empire's needs. Besides, it shouldn't matter to you. You always worked through me more than Emperor Raumesys. Nothing's changed."

"Sicarius," Amaranthe said, "ask him the name of the drug. Is it something that causes long-term consequences?"

He did not look at her. His stony gaze remained fixed on Hollowcrest, who frowned as he watched Sicarius. For the first time, uncertainty took the edge off his haughty expression. Hollowcrest tried to take a step back but bumped into the windowsill.

"What drug are you using on him?" Sicarius stepped forward. He stood nose-to-nose with Hollowcrest. "Zawyat?"

"You're not going to take orders from her, are you?" Hollowcrest squeaked.

Sicarius glanced briefly her direction. "They're more like suggestions."

Amaranthe might have smiled, remembering the time she had explained it the same way, but the tension between the two men stole her mirth.

"*What* drug?" Sicarius asked.

"Iklya Bark," Hollowcrest whispered, his back pressed against the window.

"Why—why would you use something so potent?" Sicarius asked, his mask slipping briefly, his dark eyes stunned. "That would *kill* him eventually."

Amaranthe felt sick. How long had Sespian been on the drug? Had years already been stolen from his life?

"I tried Zawyat, but the boy resisted it," Hollowcrest said. "His lifespan doesn't matter. Sespian isn't suited to rule a nation. He'll live long enough to produce an heir."

"He'll live longer than you."

True to his nature, Sicarius made the kill swiftly, but he seemed to take more satisfaction in it than usual. The snap of Hollowcrest's breaking neck echoed through the room, lingering along with the savage fury in Sicarius's eyes. Amaranthe shivered. She was relieved when a twitch from the still-dying wizard distracted her.

Arbitan's lips were moving, repeating something. Amaranthe edged closer and knelt to listen before he finally stopped breathing.

"What does *armon atask ku* mean?" she asked.

"Return to me," Books and Sicarius said together.

Akstyr cursed. "The soul construct. He called it back. It's going to—"

A familiar shrieking howl came from the street. Amaranthe's stomach descended into her boots. She had assumed killing the wizard would destroy the creature as well.

"Avenge its master's death," Akstyr finished.

Amaranthe looked at each of her men, who in turn stared back at her, as if brilliant solutions would soon flow from her lips. Only Sicarius's gaze rested elsewhere. His expressionless mask back in place, he stared at the door, calm, accepting.

He's already given up. She clenched her jaw. Well, I'm not going to. "How do we kill it?" Amaranthe demanded.

"Impossible," Sicarius said. "They're impervious to blades and firearms. My old dagger might have cut it." He opened his hand, palm up.

The dagger she lost. Of course.

"Go," Sicarius said. "It'll be after me, not you."

"Bye." Maldynado headed for the door.

"Stop," Amaranthe said.

He surprised her by obeying.

She stepped over the fallen wizard and grabbed Sicarius's arm. "You're coming with us."

"I cannot. It will know whose hand slew its master. It will follow me. There's no escape." He retracted his arm. "Go."

Maldynado, Akstyr, Basilard, and Books looked askance at Amaranthe. She could not tell them to sacrifice themselves to a hopeless fate. Besides, their mission was not over yet. Arbitan said the emperor's assassination had already been arranged, and Larocka was still alive somewhere.

Amaranthe turned back to Sicarius. "What happens after it kills you?"

"It continues doing what its master created it for," he said.

The howl came again, this time from the yard directly below. She looked outside and reeled back at the blood, dismembered bodies, and entrails spattering the snow.

"Terrorizing the empire?" she asked.

"Apparently."

"Unacceptable," Amaranthe said. "We have to stop it."

"We can't," Sicarius said quietly.

A loud splintering echoed through the house. The front door being broken down, Amaranthe guessed. Feminine shrieks traveled through the intervening floors. Apparently the servants were not exempt from the monster's attentions.

"Amaranthe," Books said, "we *have* to go."

"No. Akstyr, there's got to be a way to kill it. And don't tell me about powerful magic being required, because we don't have any!"

"Uh." Akstyr shrugged helplessly.

"Maybe..." Books started.

Amaranthe whirled on him. "What?"

"It's a physical creature living in our physical world, so even if it's magic, surely it must obey laws of physics, right? Like if you dropped it to the bottom of the ocean or collapsed a mountain on it, the pressure would have to crush it, wouldn't it?"

"Drop a mountain, brilliant." Maldynado kicked the door to the hallway shut. "Why don't we do that right now? Oh, wait—no mountains in the parlor. Drat!"

Claws scrabbled on the hardwood floor of the hallway. The door to the parlor shattered inward and threw Maldynado against a table. The soul construct loomed, its bulky dun-colored body crusted with snow and gore.

The beast blazed into the room, straight at Sicarius.

He shoved Amaranthe out of the way. The construct leapt at him. He ducked and rolled to the side, and it crashed through the glass window.

Startled, Amaranthe jumped to her feet and stuck her head out. The three-story fall did not faze the creature. It hit the snow on its feet and twisted back toward the front door, running through the torn bodies of soldiers it had slain.

"It'll never stop," Sicarius said.

"At least we know it's not smart," Amaranthe said.

And with that, an idea came. She grabbed Sicarius again.

"Distract it for fifteen minutes," she said. "Lead it on a chase. Then bring it to the basement."

"Lokdon..."

"Do it! That's not a suggestion." She released him and waved to the others. "Follow!"

Amaranthe grabbed a lamp from a table and dodged around the sofas to return to the secret passage.

"To do what?" Akstyr asked, but thankfully he and the others chased after her.

"Make a mountain fall."

CHAPTER 20

THE BASEMENT HAD CHANGED LITTLE SINCE AMA-ranthe's first visit. She had feared the remodeling project might be completed as she raced down flights of stairs, her men thundering behind. Thus she was relieved to see the mess: the freshly-dug pit, a tarp-draped pallet of bricks next to it, coils of rope, and, yes, the concrete mixer was still parked against the wall. The four-wheeled machine with its vertical boiler, cylindrical mixer, and driver's cab looked to be operable—all she needed was time to start it up.

Amaranthe ran through the arena, lighting lanterns and barking orders. "Books, figure out a way to drop that pallet in the pit on command."

Books gawked at the bricks. "They must weigh a ton. There's no time."

"You've got ten minutes. Akstyr and Basilard will help you. Maldynado, we need to get this engine started."

She checked the level in the boiler, then added water from barrels standing by for that purpose. She threw open the grate to the engine's firebox and shoveled coal in. The wood handle rubbed against her palm, which was raw from grabbing the burning brand, but she gritted her teeth against the pain.

"Uhm," Maldynado said, "I think you need to start with kindling before—"

"Just jump into the cab and figure out how to drive this thing."

Amaranthe lit a piece of cloth with her lamp, then shattered the kerosene oil cache on the coals. She dropped the burning cloth on top. Flames surged to life.

She bounced from foot to foot and watched the others while waiting for the fire to grow and produce enough heat to power the engine. Books and Akstyr took the tarp from the top of the stack of bricks and wrapped it around the side facing the pit. Basilard tied ropes from the corners to the overhead beam. Books found a jack and wedged it under the far side of the pallet after reinforcing the bottom with a sheet of metal. Laboriously, he cranked the lever up and down. Amaranthe ran over to help.

Despite the leverage the jack provided, sweat soon ran down both their faces. As one side of the pallet lifted higher than the other, the bricks shifted toward the pit. A few fell in, but the makeshift sling held the rest back. Basilard sat astride the beam, knife drawn, ready to cut the ropes restraining the bricks.

Amaranthe threw another rope up to him. "For Sicarius."

Basilard tied one end around the beam and let the other dangle into the pit.

"I think it's ready," Maldynado called, voice vibrating along with the machine.

The mixer quivered under the pressure of pent up steam. Amaranthe called Books and Akstyr over to help. They lifted barrels containing dry aggregates and dumped them into the churning cylinder. A trough of water followed. With little construction experience, she could only guess at the ratio. There was no time to experiment.

With Amaranthe guiding him, Maldynado backed the concrete mixer to the pit opposite the bricks.

And then they waited.

The mixer rumbled, its cylinder spinning. Maldynado sat with his hand on the lever that would pour the wet concrete. Above, Basilard waited on the beam. The others stood on the far side of the pit, gazes transfixed on the stairs. Amaranthe chewed on her pinky nail—the only finger with more than a nub available.

"This is too obvious," she said. "It's not going to work."

"The beast threw itself out a window," Books said. "It's not bright."

"I've thrown myself out a window recently," Amaranthe said, remembering her fall from Hollowcrest's office.

"Oh."

"It's been more than fifteen minutes, hasn't it?" she asked.

"I believe so, yes," Books said.

"If he doesn't make it, one of us will have to find the creature and try to lure it back," she said.

Akstyr snorted. "If Sicarius can't stay ahead of it, none of us can."

Amaranthe was dwelling on that unpleasant reality when a familiar voice shouted, "Incoming!" from the top of the stairs.

Sicarius raced down the steps five at a time, the beast riding his heels. Without slowing, he took in the scenario, sprinted through the basement, and leapt for the rope dangling over the pit.

The soul construct jumped after him. Sicarius caught and scrambled up the rope.

The beast twisted in midair to rake a massive paw across his back. Claws glinted. Sicarius kicked it in the face. Gravity caught up with the creature, and it plummeted into the pit.

"Now!" Amaranthe shouted.

Basilard cut the rope, and the bricks crashed in.

In the cab, Maldynado yanked the lever. The concrete came slower, and Amaranthe held her breath as it oozed into the pit. Below, bricks shuddered and shifted. When the mixer had dumped its load, only half the pit was filled.

The moist pile trembled. The creature was still alive...and trying to escape.

"Back the truck in too!" Amaranthe shouted.

Maldynado jammed it into reverse and jumped out of the cab. Rear first, the mixer crashed onto the top of the pile, sinking partway into the soft concrete.

Amaranthe held her breath as she watched the pit for movement. Her heartbeats felt thunderous in the sudden silence. Nothing moved.

Finally, Sicarius swung from the rope and landed in a crouch beside her, fingers pressed against the floor. Blood saturated his ravaged shirt. Three slashes across his lower back laid open the material, along with the skin and muscle beneath it.

"Watch the pit," Amaranthe told Akstyr.

She knelt by Sicarius. "Are you...?"

"Fine."

Despite the declaration, he did not rush to stand up. His breathing had already returned to normal, but sweat bathed his skin and drenched his hair and clothing. Blood dripped onto the floor.

"Take off your shirt," Amaranthe told him.

"How come you never say that to me?" Maldynado asked.

"Because seeing you topless would confirm our suspicions that you're related to yetis," Books said.

"Actually," Amaranthe said, as Sicarius pulled off his shirt and handed it to her, "I'll watch the pit. Why don't you gentlemen go look for Larocka?" She wadded up the shirt and pressed it to the wounds to stop the blood flow.

"She was standing in the doorway when we killed the wizard," Akstyr said.

Her breath caught, and Amaranthe stared at him for a stunned moment before speaking. "How much did she see?"

"I don't know. She ran away when I looked at her."

"Why didn't you say anything?"

"Sicarius was doing his big showdown with Hollowcrest." Akstyr shrugged. "I got distracted."

"Just go find her," Amaranthe said.

The men trooped off, and silence returned to the basement.

"I'm sorry," she told Sicarius.

"For what?" he asked.

"Getting you mauled."

"This is a far better outcome than I would have guessed possible a few minutes ago." Sicarius turned his head to regard her, a faint frown tugging at his lips. Perhaps his injuries were too distracting for him to maintain the usual façade.

"What?" she asked.

"Barring tonight, I've lived as long as I have because I've never underestimated my enemies. You keep...exceeding my expectations."

"Thank you," she said, more pleased than she would admit, "but not everyone is your enemy."

"Whether realized or not," he said, "everyone you talk to is trying to use you to further his own interests. You must always be ready to protect yourself."

"There are such things as friends," Amaranthe said.

"That does not negate my statement. Friendship is as selfish as any other relationship, perhaps more so because it masquerades as something noble. I am more comfortable with those who approach me with blades drawn."

"I suppose this will disappoint you," Amaranthe said, "but I'd rather be your friend than your enemy. I'll try not to make you suffer too much from the association."

He looked away. "I am not...disappointed."

She put her free hand on his shoulder. "You've exceeded my expectations too."

Amaranthe lightened her pressure on the wounds and peeled back a corner of the shirt. Most of the bleeding had stopped, but the gashes needed to be stitched.

"Sit down on the bleachers," she said. "I'll hunt for suturing supplies."

Given the nature of the entertainment here, well-stocked medical kits seemed likely.

"Sicarius?" Amaranthe asked as she poked through desk drawers in the bettors' cage. "You don't owe me any answers or explanations, but there's one thing I've been wondering since the day we met—well, since the day you didn't kill me when you should have. Why do you care about the emperor? What are you to him?"

"An enemy."

She frowned, considered her words, and rearranged them. "What is the emperor to you?"

Those lips stayed shut. At least he wasn't glaring threateningly at her as he had the last time she pried into his past.

As she checked cabinets, Amaranthe mulled over Hollowcrest's words in the parlor. Almost until the end, he had believed Sicarius would return to his side. Like a father speaking to a son he thought he knew— or perhaps an old general addressing a soldier he had supervised from the earliest days. Just how long had Sicarius worked for Hollowcrest? How long had he had access to the Imperial Barracks? Maybe Sicarius had been around when Sespian was growing up. Maybe Sicarius had developed an affection for him. Only one problem. Sicarius was about as affectionate as a freshly blooded dagger. As practical as he was, she could not imagine him forming an emotional attachment to someone just because they had passed in the halls for a few years. Look at what he had done to Hollowcrest. There had to be a greater bond.

She found bandages, suturing thread, and scissors, and returned to the bleachers. A new thought came to her, and she hesitated.

"Are you related?"

There was not an obvious resemblance, but they did have the same dark eyes. Sicarius could even draw, if dispassionately compared to the emperor.

"Brothers?" she went on. "One trained to rule the empire, one to defend it?"

Sicarius snorted.

"No," Amaranthe said. "If that were true, you would have been the heir. You're at least ten years older." She studied his face. It was unlined and he had the speed and strength of youth, but he was too experienced at too many things to be mistaken for a young man. "Maybe fifteen or more," she said slowly, her mind edging toward an idea that was nothing short of blasphemous. She tried to squash it and look for other—less seditious—possibilities, but once acknowledged, the thought grew like a plant steeped in sun and fertilizer.

Sicarius, watching her face even as she watched his, sighed and looked away. *When did we get to know each other so well that he can see my thoughts?*

"Sespian is your son," Amaranthe said.

For the first time, his silence was readable. Yes.

Amaranthe stared at the floor, almost wishing she hadn't asked. This meant Raumesys had left no true heir. Sespian's claim to rule was only through his mother and therefore no better than a dozen others. If anyone found out, nothing short of civil war would follow. Bloody years of infighting in which the empire's copious enemies could strike while the soldiers were distracted choosing sides and fighting each other. In the end, some jaded old general, some vague relation of Raumesys's, would end up in power. Little chance of the next emperor having any of Sespian's tolerance or progressive passion. She imagined some contemporary of Hollowcrest's on the throne and felt sick. Though it might make her a traitor to the empire, she would take this secret to her funeral pyre.

She turned her attention to Sicarius, feeling a guilty twinge that her first thoughts had been political. "Hollowcrest obviously didn't know. Sespian doesn't either, does he?"

A minute shake of the head confirmed this.

"If you told him, he'd probably abdicate the throne," Amaranthe said, sure the emperor's conscience would trouble him into that route. "But perhaps you two would have a chance for...something, a relationship. From my brief meetings with him, I got the feeling Sespian has led a lonely life."

"He has. Thrusting this knowledge into it would not improve matters. He has read my records. He knows everyone I tortured and killed for Raumesys and Hollowcrest. And since. He's the one who put the bounty on my head. I am likely the only person in the world he truly wants dead."

"You might..."

Might what, Amaranthe? What are you going to suggest he do? Change? Repent his cold-hearted assassin ways? Mourn for those he's killed? Become someone Sespian might admire? Be a good person? Sicarius might not scoff out loud, but surely that would be his mental reaction. He was too pragmatic to give up his system, however callous, for something less effective. That he cared for his son did not mean he felt any concern for people in general. Asking him to change would accomplish nothing.

"You might find it easier to protect Sespian if you were at his side," was all she said.

"That was my plan once. But I underestimated his...idealism. He would not employ a killer, even to his benefit. I should have foreseen that."

Amaranthe smiled gently. "It is difficult to understand those who are least like ourselves."

Sicarius twitched an eyebrow. "You understand me."

"Hm."

She laid out the medical supplies on the bench, filled a bucket with clean water, and sat behind him. The wounds must have stung, but Sicarius did not flinch when she washed them. She picked up the needle and considered the task before her. It would be better to find a surgeon to sew up the gashes, but she did not know where to look in this neighborhood at this time of night. Anyway, a part of her liked the idea of being the one to help him. He had saved her life a number of times over the last two weeks, and now she could do something for him.

She slid her hand across his back. Surprisingly, no other scars marred his flesh. Even relaxed, his muscles were like steel, each distinct and delineated beneath warm skin. Sicarius looked over his shoulder, eyebrows raised. She blushed and bent to thread the needle. Medics probably weren't supposed to ogle their patients.

"I'm afraid you're going to have some wicked scars," Amaranthe said.

"I'll survive," he said.

"A little soon to say that. You haven't felt the prod of my inexperienced needle yet."

"Surely as an enforcer, you've had combat medic training."

"Training, yes. Real-world experience, no. Unless you count the times I did this on dolls."

"Dolls?"

"Memela, the woman who watched me while my father worked, gave me the dolls her children had played with growing up. They were a little battered from use, so I frequently had to put the stuffing back in and sew the rips."

"It's the same principle," Sicarius said.

He looked over his shoulder again.

"What?" she asked.

"Dolls." His eyes crinkled.

Amused, was he?

"What's wrong with dolls? I am a girl, you know."

Sicarius turned his head back forward. Amaranthe was about to start on the first wound when he spoke again.

"I'll wager you lined them up and ordered them around like a general commanding his troops."

She smiled. "Maybe."

She had finished stitching Sicarius's back when footsteps sounded on the stairs. Amaranthe expected one of her men, but it was a servant in the crimson house uniform. Sicarius stood. The servant approached them slowly, eyeing the bare-chested Sicarius. He looked even more intimating without a shirt on.

"I mean you no trouble. Please don't hurt me." The servant's voice squeaked. He fingered a sealed envelope. "My mistress bade me deliver this message to you." He crept toward Sicarius, the hand with the envelope trembling.

"Your mistress is Larocka?" Amaranthe asked.

"Yes, ma'am."

"Is she in the house?"

"I really can't say, ma'am."

As soon as Sicarius took the envelope, the servant darted away. Amaranthe worried Sicarius would follow, perhaps torture the man for information, but the message arrested his attention. He broke the seal on the envelope, slid out a folded sheet of stationery, and read.

Only one line marked the paper. Nonetheless, Sicarius stared at the words for a long moment.

"What does it say?" she finally asked.

Stiffly, Sicarius handed the note to her.

You killed my love. Before dawn, I shall burn your son alive.

"Son," Amaranthe croaked. "How could she know? How many people have you told?"

"Just you."

"That means...she was listening."

Sicarius's head jerked up, and his eyes scanned the ceiling, walls, and shadows. But there was no one else in the basement. With Arbitan dead, Larocka could not have access to the mental sciences, could she?

Sicarius grabbed a fallen brick and ran to the wall nearest the bleachers where they had been talking. He tapped the stone as he moved along it. Clanks echoed through the basement.

A more mundane possibility, Amaranthe realized. She grabbed a brick too. Soon the clanks turned to hollow thuds.

"There," she said.

She and Sicarius dropped the bricks and slid their hands along the cool stone. Rough and porous, it would conceal secret entrances well. Amaranthe almost missed the hairline crack running vertically up the wall.

"Over here," she said.

Sicarius shifted to her side, and he was the one to find the button. With a click, a portion of the wall swung backward. Inside was a chair, shelves, a tall cabinet, and a writing desk. On the back wall, a ladder rose into the upper levels of the house.

Amaranthe walked into the room. "How many secret passages does this place have?"

Standing mute at the entrance, Sicarius seemed stunned—or horrified.

Amaranthe touched the wooden seat in front of the desk. "She must have heard everything."

Sicarius slammed his fist into the cabinet. Amaranthe jumped. Wood splintered and gave, and his hand went straight through. Jaw clenched, he yanked his arm free. Blood ran down his fingers and dripped onto the stone floor.

Amaranthe stared, open-mouthed. His back was to her, and both hands curled into white-knuckled fists. She had never seen him lose his composure.

She licked her lips. "It's not too late, Sicarius. We can save him. We just have to figure out where she'd go to—"

Sicarius stalked out the door.

"Wait, please." Amaranthe followed him. "I'm sorry, but if you'd just listen to me—"

Sicarius spun on her, eyes raging. She skittered back and bumped into the wall.

"Listen to you?" he snarled. "This is *your* fault. All your questions. Why couldn't you leave me alone? Hollowcrest and Arbitan are dead. Everything would be fine now. But you had to pry. And, fool I am, I let you." Anguish warped his face. "Why couldn't you just leave me alone?"

Without waiting for an answer, he whirled and raced out of the basement. Shocked by his outburst, Amaranthe could not answer right away. Tears stung her eyes. Long after he disappeared up the stairs, she whispered, "Because I care."

* * * * *

Sespian wasn't sleeping when the knock came. Hollowcrest's threats kept repeating in his mind. Was there truly some assassination plot afoot, or had Hollowcrest simply been spinning hyperbole to make himself seem necessary? And what of that confrontation? Had Sespian

bested Hollowcrest too easily? Even now, Sespian could scarcely believe he had won.

He slid out of bed and headed for the door, but paused in the antechamber. "Who is it?"

"Lieutenant Dunn."

Uh oh. Hollowcrest was back. Or something else was up.

"Yes?" Sespian asked when he opened the door.

"Sire, I've been in contact with that renegade enforcer, Amaranthe Lokdon. I assumed you'd want to hear about it right away."

"Oh?" Sespian leaned forward. Since he had been drugged the few times he'd met her, he could hardly trust his judgment, but he so badly wanted to hear that Hollowcrest's words were lies.

"Yes, Sire. May I come in?"

"Of course."

A servant glided in on Dunn's heels to turn up the lamps and add coal to the stove. Sespian shifted his weight from one foot to the other, watching the process with ill-concealed impatience.

"What is it?" Sespian blurted as soon as the servant left.

Dunn wrung his hands and paced. "Before I tell you what she said, let me say that I think it's a very bad idea, and you shouldn't go off to meet her."

"She wants to meet? Me?" *Idiot, you sound like a love struck youth, not an emperor over millions.* Sespian cleared his throat and struggled for nonchalance. "I mean, what did she say?"

"What Hollowcrest said was true. Sicarius intends to assassinate you during your birthday celebration. Lokdon claims to have *pretended* to join forces with him to unearth his plans and feed the information back to Hollowcrest, but something went badly between them, and now she wants to share all her information with you."

Sespian paced. Spying on Sicarius? Could that be secret assignment Hollowcrest had given Amaranthe? The reason she had been in the Barracks to start with?

Disapproval pinched the lieutenant's face.

"You don't think I should go," Sespian said.

"It could be a trap. If she just wanted to relay information, she could come here to do it."

Sespian shook his head, recalling the last time he had seen Amaranthe—flying out a window to escape the guards. "For all she knows, we'd throw her in the dungeon. I can see why she'd prefer a neutral location."

"She could be working with Sicarius to lure you to your death," Dunn said.

"Did she stipulate I had to meet her alone?"

"No."

"Then you could come. And a couple carriage-loads of men. When does she want to meet?"

"Now. She fears Sicarius will find out about her double cross, so she insists on meeting tonight. She's waiting for you at Yestfer Smelter."

Sespian glanced at the black sky outside the window. This could be a mistake, a big mistake. But if he didn't go, and Amaranthe's body turned up in the lake later...

"Very well. Fire up the steam carriages and arrange the men."

CHAPTER 21

AMARANTHE CLIMBED DOWN THE LADDER AND returned to the hidden basement room. Several stories above, the passage ended at a trapdoor in the master suite, but there had been no sign of Larocka. Nor had Amaranthe spotted any clues that suggested where the woman had gone or where the assassination would take place.

She leaned her head against a metal rung. She *had* to figure this out. It wasn't just about helping the emperor and clearing her name any more. She *owed* Sicarius. He was right. This was her fault. Because of her incessant curiosity, she had been pestering him with questions since she met him, and now he was the one stuck with the consequences. Right now, he probably regretted not killing her that day on the trail. And why hadn't he? Because he thought he was helping his son's girlfriend. She groaned. All this time, she had been wondering if—hoping—Sicarius might possibly care for her. No, he had simply been tolerating her ludicrous scheme because Sespian gave her a bracelet.

"Amaranthe?" Books called from the spectator area.

She wiped her eyes. "In here."

A moment later, Books, Akstyr, Basilard, and Maldynado packed the tiny room.

"The servants have fled the house, and this mausoleum is gargantuan," Books said.

Akstyr wore a toothy smile and clutched a book the size of a small tabletop. "Look what I found." He danced forward, almost losing his balance due to the heavy tome. "It's Nurian. I'll have to find someone to help me translate—" he glanced at Books, "—but I could make scads of

progress studying their ways." He dumped the book on the desk, opened the first page, and didn't seem to notice his foot bumping something under the drawers.

A round, glowing purple object rolled across the concrete and clinked to a stop against the base of the ladder. The orb was smooth, flawless, and small enough to conceal in a pocket.

"Uhm," Amaranthe said.

"That doesn't appear natural," Books said.

"No, but it's a snazzy find," Maldynado said. "Cut it in half, and it'd make a fetching pocket watch fob."

"Somehow, I doubt it's for fashion," Amaranthe said. "Akstyr, do you—"

"Oh!" Akstyr had spotted it. He shut the book, hustled forward, and picked up the orb. "I've never seen a real one, but it looks like a communication jewel." He slid a finger along the top, and his eyes grew distant for a moment. "It's for talking to whoever else has the other one."

"Can it tell you who that might be?" Amaranthe asked.

"No." Akstyr handed the orb to her. "Only the ones it was tuned for can access it."

"It must have slipped out of Larocka's pocket," Amaranthe said. "She doubtlessly left in a hurry after..."

"After what?" Maldynado asked. "We looked all over the house for her, but the shifty broad just disappeared."

"I know." Amaranthe slid the orb into her pocket, not sure what she could do with it, but keeping it just in case. She led them out of the hidden room. "Larocka contacted us. She's...planning to kill the emperor as revenge for what happened to Arbitan. By dawn."

"That's not more than a couple hours off," Books said.

"She's just one woman," Maldynado said. "Are we worried about what one woman can do?"

Basilard looked pointedly from Amaranthe to the filled pit and back to Amaranthe.

"Oh, right," Maldynado said.

"Do you know where she'll strike?" Books asked. "She can't sneak into the Imperial Barracks, can she? Even if she could, we can't. How do we thwart her?"

Hands in her pockets, Amaranthe gazed at the pit for a long moment. Then she looked at each of them. "*We* don't. You've done enough. More than enough. I finagled you all into this, and yet you performed like empire-renowned champions in the rings. I can't ask for any more from you. The next step I take alone."

"What?" Maldynado propped his fists on his hips. "We've come this far with you, and we're not leaving now. I need a statue, remember?"

"We mean to see this through to the end," Books said. "Sespian is our emperor too."

Basilard nodded firmly.

"If they're going, I'm going too," Akstyr said. "Where are we going?"

"I'm going to the Barracks to turn myself in." Amaranthe jogged for the stairs.

"Upon reconsideration," Maldynado said, "I do wonder if this is something you should do alone."

"I have to try to talk to the emperor before Larocka strikes."

* * * * *

Sespian slipped a sheathed dagger into his boot and strode out of the Imperial Barracks. His guards trailed him to the outside stairs. Lieutenant Dunn, standing in the courtyard next to two armored steam carriages, waved them toward the second vehicle.

"Sire." Dunn held the door to the lead vehicle open, and a pool of light spilled out.

Sespian crossed to the driveway. A few soldiers clanked and clattered along the outer wall, but night was still deep. Few lights burned behind the dark windows of the Barracks. *Hardly anyone to see me leave.*

The thought made Sespian pause. He had one foot on the carriage step. The empty, blue velvet interior yawned before him. Shouldn't there be some guards accompanying his vehicle as well? The hackles of suspicion arose on his neck.

"Dunn..."

He started to lower his foot, to back away from the carriage, but Dunn shoved him. Surprised, Sespian pitched forward. Before he could catch himself and find a grip that would let him push back, Dunn rammed him all the way inside.

The door slammed shut.

Sespian rolled to the opposite side and scrambled to his feet. His shoulder clipped one of the wall lamps, and his head struck the low ceiling.

. "What are you...?"

A pistol pointed at his chest. Jaw set, Dunn thumped on the front wall. Steam whistled, and the carriage lurched forward. A familiar black dagger rested on one of the seats. Eyes widening, Sespian spun about, half expecting Sicarius to be lurking in the shadows.

"Sit down, Sespian." Dunn twitched the pistol toward the back bench.

"What happened to Sire?" Sespian thought about disobeying—it would be easier to attack from a standing position, but even if Dunn didn't fire, he could probably best Sespian in a wrestling match. Besides, Dunn would be ready for something now. Best to wait for a chance to come.

"You're not the man I thought you were. Sit."

Sespian eased over to the padded seat. The carriage chugged into motion, and a thick glass window displayed the front gate passing. If he yelled for help, the armored walls would muffle it. The gate guards were probably in on this anyway.

"Apparently, you're not the man I thought you were either." Sespian heard the sting of the betrayal in his voice. It wasn't as if people plotting against the throne—against him—was anything new, but he thought he had picked right with Dunn. "Why'd you pretend to be on my side if you meant to betray me to Hollowcrest in the end anyway? I assume you're taking him to me now."

"Hollowcrest is dead," Dunn said. "And when you selected me, I didn't know...I mean, I knew it was always a possibility I'd have to move against you, but..."

Dunn looked away, and Sespian tensed. If the pistol lowered...

As if reading his thoughts, Dunn snapped his attention back, and the barrel centered on Sespian's chest.

"If you're not working for Hollowcrest, then who?" Sespian asked.

"I'm not warrior caste, you know."

Sespian frowned. What kind of answer was that? "I know. I read your file."

"Most officers are. The Imperial Service Academy is costly, but I was fortunate enough to find someone to finance my education."

"Who might that be?" Sespian had read Dunn's service record before choosing him but hadn't thought to look into who paid for his education. A mistake, apparently.

"The same people who made it possible to blindside Hollowcrest. Did you honestly think some lowly lieutenant could get all the information you asked for so quickly? Half the intelligence department belongs to them."

"Who?"

The carriage turned and headed downhill. Where were they going? To the smelter Dunn mentioned, or had that been a lie?

Sespian bent forward slightly. His dagger was in his left boot. Since Dunn was to the right, maybe he could draw it without being noticed.

"I always knew there'd be favors expected later." Dunn sighed. "I didn't image they'd be treasonous, and I've been wrestling with that the last few days. I *liked* you. But then as it turns out, I'm not being treasonous at all here." He turned accusing eyes on Sespian.

"How not?"

"You know what I'm talking about—you must."

Sespian sighed deeply, using the expression to justify a slump. His forearms dropped onto his knees and his fingers dangled near his boots. "No, I'm quite lost in this entire conversation. Will you at least tell me what we're doing?" He let his left arm fall to his ankle.

"You're going to meet Sicarius," Dunn said.

Sespian winced. He had hoped that was a lie too. "The people who paid for your education hired Sicarius to kill me tonight?"

A few days ago, Dunn had seemed as chipper and willing to please as a puppy. Now he was as masked and guarded as every other lackey with an agenda.

"I'm sorry, but you're not going to live past dawn," Dunn said, probably the first straight answer of the ride.

Sespian's fingers fastened around the hilt of the dagger. Unfortunately, the cursed pistol was still pointing unerringly at him.

"People will miss me soon," he said. "Your employers couldn't have bought off everyone."

"They're not my employers, just people I owe. But I understand a confusing scene has been arranged to befuddle those who might follow."

Dunn shifted and slid a hand into his parka. The pistol never wavered as he pulled out a small brown bottle filled with liquid. He set it on the seat, withdrew a folded kerchief, and laid it down as well. With one hand, he unscrewed the cap of the bottle.

A grimness settled over Sespian as he watched. He suspected his time for wrestling his freedom from Dunn was coming to an end. He had to act soon.

"Dunn, I can appreciate your loyalty to those who paid for your school, but arranging my death?" Sespian eased the dagger out of the sheath. "It's...not a very nice thing to do. I liked you too. I thought I could trust you. Surely, you could have had everything you ever wanted working at my side."

"It would have been a lie." Dunn placed the kerchief atop the bottle and, one-handed, tipped it to soak the cloth. "You're not the rightful—"

Sespian lunged. Dunn saw him but hesitated before firing. He was probably supposed to deliver a living emperor.

Sespian's momentum took him into a tackle. He and Dunn slammed against the carriage door. The pistol struck the wall, then clattered to the floor. Sespian drew back his arm and stabbed, but Dunn dodged and the dagger clanked against the door. A boot hooked Sespian's legs and jerked him off his feet. He crashed into a bench. Before he could move, Dunn's weight leaned into his back. Cheek smashed against the velvet upholstery, Sespian pushed but could not budge. A hand snaked around his head and pressed the cloth to his face.

A sweet, cloying smell flooded his nostrils. He plunged his elbow behind him and caught ribs.

"Ooph!"

The grip relaxed for a moment, and Sespian tried to yank free. Dunn recovered and the kerchief smothered Sespian's face. The sweet smell invaded his lungs, and his heart thundered in his ears. Blackness encroached on his vision. The sound of the wheels chugging beneath the carriage changed; they were crossing a bridge. The last thing Sespian was aware of was brakes squealing.

* * * * *

A quick check of the carriage house out back proved Larocka, or perhaps the servants, had taken off with the steam vehicles. Arakan Hill and the Imperial Barracks loomed three or four miles away. With no other alternatives, Amaranthe loped off on foot. Despite her attempt to dismiss them, the others puffed along behind her.

The smell of wood smoke hung in the crisp air, and bare branches turned the moonlight into a latticework of shadows. Last time she walked this way, enforcers had ambushed her. Tonight, no one else lurked on the long street paralleling the Ridge. The city felt oddly quiet, as if it was holding its breath.

They had gone no more than a mile when an explosion boomed into the silence. The cracks of firearms followed, and Amaranthe halted to listen, trying to pinpoint the origins.

Maldynado stopped beside her. "It sounds like it's coming from the Midtown River."

The rest of the men caught up.

"They've already got Sespian," Amaranthe said.

Books bent over and sucked in a gulp of air. "It could...just be a... coincidence."

More firearms bawled in the distance. Up on Arakan Hill, an alarm bell pealed.

"Want to bet on it?" Amaranthe asked.

"No," Books said.

Running again, they turned west at the next street and raced off Mokath Ridge toward the river. She wished the trolleys were running, but it was too late at night.

Before they made it halfway there, the firing stopped, and only the alarm bell disturbed the silence. Amaranthe fought the urge to zip along faster, leaving the others behind. Her lungs were not yet burning, but she could hear the ragged wheezes of Books and Akstyr. She would probably need their help for whatever they stumbled across.

They rounded a corner, and the 52nd Street Bridge came into view. The street lamps illuminated a ghastly scene, and Amaranthe paused in the shadows.

Black smoke poured from a collision site. Two steam carriages had struck each other at the base of the bridge, one painted in imperial black and gold, the other nondescript. Another of the emperor's vehicles had crashed through the rail of the bridge, and wobbled tenuously, the front half hanging out over the frozen river twenty feet below. The bodies of imperial soldiers—no, the emperor's personal guard—littered the blood-smeared street.

"We're too late," Amaranthe whispered.

"What was the emperor doing out in the middle of the night?" Maldynado asked.

She touched the communication stone in her pocket. "I bet someone on Larocka's payroll talked him into coming out. Let's see if he's..." She gulped, unable to finish the sentence. She did not want to see Sespian's broken body on the street.

Despite the late hour, the noise had drawn a crowd from nearby tenements. A handful of enforcers struggled to establish barricades on either side of the bridge, but this had just happened and few men had arrived. Reinforcements would show up shortly, but perhaps Amaranthe could sneak close enough to investigate the crash first.

"Books, come with me, please. The rest of you, a distraction would be good."

"What kind of distraction?" Maldynado asked.

"The kind where you do something creative to keep the enforcers from noticing us snooping."

"Creative, eh?" Maldynado tossed a speculative look at his comrades.

Afraid to wonder, Amaranthe grabbed Books and angled toward the river. They passed between two street lamps and skidded down the snowy bank. She flailed but caught her balance on the ice. Books landed on his butt. She paused long enough to help him up, then ran and slid for the closest of the two piers anchored in the river.

Black against the starry sky, the truss bridge loomed overhead. Steam screeched, another vehicle approaching. A truck delivering more enforcers, probably.

Amaranthe clambered up the cement block, but hesitated when she looked up at the steel supports.

"Maybe you should wait down here," she told Books.

"I'm coming," he said.

She shrugged. One vertical and two diagonal steel beams rose from the concrete, and she took one of the diagonals. The angle made the climb doable, and she soon peered over the floor of the bridge. The tottering steam carriage wobbled to her left with the two crashed vehicles at the base to her right.

"Yo, when's this bridge gonna be cleared?" Maldynado's voice came from the crowd.

Feeling exposed under the starlight, Amaranthe hoped her distraction was forthcoming. She grabbed the rail and pulled herself over.

All the doors of the tottering carriage were open, and one hung from a sole hinge. The front of the vehicle was smashed. The driver had been thrown free.

Steel clashed at the base of the bridge. Maldynado had engaged a pair of enforcers in a sword fight. Amaranthe didn't see Basilard or Akstyr.

She knelt near the driver's body, her hand resting on the ground. Cooling blood puddled on the sand-covered ice and dampened her fingers. That didn't startle her, but the man's slit throat did. The crash hadn't killed him; a dagger had.

As she eased around him toward a second body, her fingers brushed broken glass. She plucked up several shards, some curved, some straight.

Behind her, Books lumbered onto the bridge.

"Stop them!" someone cried.

Amaranthe's head jerked up. Someone must have spotted them.

"They're stealing our truck!"

Steam squealed from the enforcer vehicle, and it lurched into motion. She almost laughed. She hadn't been spotted; the enforcers were yelling at Maldynado and the others. Metal crunched, the sound rising over the shouts of the enforcers and the crowd. Whoever was driving the stolen truck had crashed it into another arriving vehicle. Cries of "idiot!" punctuated baser profanities.

"We'll have to rescue them from jail in the morning," Books muttered.

Amaranthe slipped the glass shards into a pocket. "Look around. We won't have much time before someone notices us."

She slipped down the bridge where more inert bodies sprawled. The fallen all wore imperial uniforms. There was no sign of enemy dead. In

fact, there was hardly any sign of a fight at all. She checked body after body, each neatly dispatched. Despite the earlier gunfire she'd heard, these men had all been killed by blades.

It seemed inconceivable that even skilled assassins could so unequivocally dispatch Sespian's guard, who would have been doubly alert after a crash....

Amaranthe crouched beside one of the last bodies. Moisture— blood—saturated a guard's black uniform. A dagger stuck into the chest to the hilt.

After a moment of hesitation, Amaranthe tugged it free. Even coated in blood, even in the dim light from the street lamps, she recognized it. Sicarius's black dagger.

"Who's up there?" someone called.

This time, the enforcers *were* looking at her.

"Corporal Tennil," Books said.

"There's no..." Hand on the hilt of a sword, one of the enforcers stepped forward.

"Time to go," Amaranthe whispered.

She stuck the dagger in her belt and scrambled for the side of the bridge. This time, she made Books go first, afraid he would get caught if she didn't.

Two enforcers pounded toward them. Lamplight glinted on a steel blade.

"Hurry!" she urged.

As soon as Books's head dipped out of view, Amaranthe slithered over the side. A sword whistled down from above but glanced off the railing.

Her foot missed the beam on her first groping stab, and she almost fell. She found a foothold on the second attempt and released her hand just before an enforcer boot crushed it.

Sliding more than climbing, she made the bottom in seconds. Books landed at the same time with a grunt.

"Next time, I'll just wait on the—"

Crossbow quarrels clinked into the ice at their feet. She grabbed his arm, dragged him under the bridge, and raced out the other side. They clung to the deep shadows near the bank and didn't climb up until they were out of crossbow range.

Several blocks later, with the shouts fading behind, Amaranthe finally paused under a street lamp. She pulled out the dagger and held it beneath the light. Yes, it was definitely Sicarius's weapon, the one she had left in Hollowcrest's office. Someone was trying to frame him.

"I didn't see the emperor's body," Books said.

"No, there's still hope." Amaranthe removed the shards of glass from her pocket.

"Broken vials?" Books picked up a concave piece and sniffed. "Liquid smoke."

"What's that?"

"I remember a science professor trying to make some once. It's a Kendorian concoction that tears your eyes and makes it hard to breathe. They probably modified crossbows to shoot the vials. It's extremely expensive to make, but that wouldn't be a problem for Larocka."

"That's why the soldiers were dispatched so easily."

"They must have kidnapped Sespian," Books said.

"Yes, of course. The note said..." She stopped. Crazy times or not, she could not give away Sicarius's secret. "The emperor was to be taken somewhere and burned alive."

"But where?" Books asked.

"There's no way to..." A silvery bump on one of the shards of glass drew her eye. She squinted and rubbed it with her thumb. Molten steel that had hardened. She had seen it all over the scrapyard at the Oak Iron Smelter. She handed the piece to Books. "Looks like they prepped in a smelter. There was one on that list of businesses Larocka owns, wasn't there?"

"Yestfer," he said.

Amaranthe thought of the note, the threat to burn Sespian alive, and she gripped the lamppost as a vision rushed over her. Larocka dumping him in a vat of molten steel.

"That's where they'll be," she said. "I have to go."

"*We* have to go."

"*You* have to go back to the bridge. Try to extricate the others, but most importantly tell the enforcers to get men to Yestfer. If I get killed... someone else needs to know where Sespian is."

"They're not going to listen to me!"

"You have to try. Hurry, Books, there's no time to debate."

He lifted a hand. "Very well."

She sprinted down the street, heading for the industrial part of town.

"Be careful!" Books called after her.

The downhill grade made the run easier, but the blocks dragged past. Stars glittered in a dark sky framed by darker buildings.

She turned a corner onto a wide street heading down to the railroad and the lake. The massive chimney of the smelter came into view, black smoke pouring from its rim, blotting out stars. Someone was burning coal for the furnace. It was too early for normal work hours. A queasy lurch ran through her stomach. She was not sure whether to be elated or scared she had guessed right.

Beneath the chimney squatted a vast rectangular building with windows too high to peer through. A twenty-foot sliding door stood open two feet, and several steam carriages were parked out front. Guards surely waited to trap—or shoot—anyone who came through.

Keeping to the shadows, Amaranthe angled around the smelter. There had to be another entrance.

On the scrapyard side of the building, a roll-up door was shut. She jogged closer, but a huge lock secured it. Rounding another corner took her to railroad tracks coming up from the lake and the shipyards. The rails disappeared beneath double doors—also locked. Under them, a gap allowed the tracks to pass through with a couple inches to spare. A man would have a hard time squirming his way through the opening, but maybe she could fit.

Before she could talk herself out of it, Amaranthe flopped onto her belly in the gravel next to the tracks. She peered into the building, but saw only bins and stacks of ingots in the dim light.

She poked her head under the door, and heat washed over her face. She wriggled through the gap.

Once inside, she pushed into a crouch. A railroad car with a slag ladle blocked most of her view. A shoot perched above it, though no molten material poured down at the moment. Amaranthe listened for voices, but roaring fires and hot air pumping into furnaces drowned out lesser noises.

Catwalks overhead followed the walls, crisscrossed the interior, and met at the stories-high blast furnace dominating the building. Bins of iron ore, charcoal, and limestone cluttered the view at floor level.

Larocka could be hiding a battalion of soldiers—and her prisoner—in the enormous building.

The catwalks would provide the best view of the facility. Of course, it would also make it easier for people on the ground to view *her* too. No help for that.

She found a ladder and climbed. A diagonal track running from ore bins to the loading platform above the furnace offered her some cover. A cart waited at the top, but nobody stood up there manning it.

Thirty feet up, Amaranthe reached the catwalk. She still couldn't see anyone below, but the blast furnace blocked the front door area.

Heavy uniforms and shielded aprons hung on hooks, presumably to protect workers from the heat and molten detritus. Helmets and thick gloves perched on a shelf. On the chance she might need hand protection, Amaranthe grabbed a pair and stuck them in her belt.

Staying low, she crept toward the furnace. The open railings and metal grid flooring would only provide partial cover if someone started shooting.

Once she glimpsed movement below, but when she turned her head, she saw nothing. If someone dangerous and elusive was moving amongst the machinery, she hoped it was Sicarius. Dare she hope he was in the building? Only the metal splattered on the glass shard had made her think of the smelter. If it was up to her to save Sespian alone...

Daunted at the thought, she licked her lips and continued toward the blast furnace. The intensity of the heat increased. By the time she came abreast of the furnace, sweat bathed her torso and stung her eyes.

A ladder on the catwalk led up to the charging platform, where workers could shovel ore, coke, and limestone off the skip car and into the belly of the fifty-foot beast. When Amaranthe's sleeve brushed one of the metal rungs, the heat sprang through the cloth, and she jerked her arm away.

She inched forward and finally spotted men on the ground. A lot of men.

Between the front door and the base of the blast furnace stood at least twenty warriors. Clad in gray fatigues with no insignia, the broad, muscled men bore muskets, swords, or battle axes. A few men wore blood stains, but none appeared injured. This must be the party that slaughtered the emperor's guards.

A couple men watched the furnace where a worker in insulated uniform, gloves, and helmet stood. Most faced the perimeter, weapons ready. They were expecting someone.

"Time grows short, Sicarius," a muffled female voice called. Larocka?

Surprised, Amaranthe leaned through the railing. It seemed Larocka was the worker at the base of the furnace. From Amaranthe's angle, she could not see through the helmet's glass faceplate, but the voice had certainly come from within. That uniform would do a fine job of protecting her from a throwing knife as well as the heat.

"You tripped one of the magical alarms Arbitan set before—before..." Larocka clanked her hand against the face shield of her helmet, as if trying to wipe her eyes or nose but forgetting about the barrier. "If you think you'll sneak up on us, you're mistaken."

Uh oh. Amaranthe shifted back from the railing. What if *she* had tripped the trap? What if Sicarius wasn't there at all?

She had to find out. She eased farther along her perch, but when she passed a clump of piping two men came into view. They stood on the catwalk with her, stationed between her and the front door in a place they could see the entrance and also signal to Larocka. The intervening pipes and machinery had kept Amaranthe from seeing them—and thankfully them from seeing her. But all one would have to do was decide to take a walk, and her hiding place would be very open from their point of view.

Amaranthe crept back to hunker in the shadow of the blast furnace.

"It's time for the emperor to die," Larocka yelled. "I thought you'd want a front row seat, but I suppose knowing you're here is good enough." She placed one gloved hand on a lever, and Amaranthe imagined her vengeful smile behind that glass faceplate.

Not certain what the lever controlled, Amaranthe grabbed the hot metal rail and leaned as far past the edge of the catwalk as she could.

The sight below almost made her lose her grip. Sespian lay naked and spread-eagle, wrists and ankles bound by taut chains. He was under the spout that released molten iron. If Larocka pulled that lever, the floodgate would open, and Sespian would be seared alive. Even now, he was too close to the furnace with no protective clothing. His skin was red and dry. Heat stroke. He could die from that alone, even if the molten iron never came.

Larocka turned toward the lever and started to put weight on it.

Amaranthe tried to think of something to do, anything to buy time. She opened her mouth to yell.

"Wait!"

Sicarius.

He stepped out of the shadows, palms open, arms away from his weapons. Twenty men raised swords and muskets toward him.

"Whatever for?" Larocka asked sweetly.

Indeed, what for? What could he do? *What can I do?*

"I need the head," Sicarius said.

Sespian's head lolled to the side, dark eyes focusing on Sicarius, but only briefly before his chin slumped. He did not look good.

Amaranthe pulled herself back onto the catwalk. Sicarius was buying time. She needed to do something useful with it.

"What?" Larocka asked after a stunned moment.

"The head," Sicarius said. "My employer requires it as proof of an assignment completed."

Amaranthe groaned as she crawled toward the ladder leading to the top of the furnace. Of all the ways Sicarius could have bought time... surely that was the most condemning. Even if they made it out of this, Sicarius would be suspect in Sespian's eyes.

When she reached the ladder, she stuffed her hands into the gloves. They were far too large, and her fingers swam in them, but they let her grip the scorching rungs.

"You'd have me believe you're here to ensure the emperor is *killed*?" Larocka asked. "Do you think I'm stupid?"

Amaranthe climbed, hoping the new position would not let the guards on the catwalk see her. Her boots protected her feet from the rungs, and she made it to the charging platform.

"My opinion of you is irrelevant," Sicarius said. "If you kill him with lava, it'll sear his features to the point of being indistinguishable. It matters little to me if yours is the hand to slay him, but perhaps we can negotiate an alternative method."

"He's your son!" Larocka blurted.

Amaranthe leaned over the platform to judge Sespian's reaction. She was even higher now and could barely see him over the swell of the furnace. His face was too far down for her to read. The heat stroke had to be addling his mind. Maybe he was past understanding any of this.

The men watching weren't, and this was apparently new information for them. They looked about at each other, though their weapons never ceased aiming at Sicarius.

"Because the enforcer bitch believes that story doesn't make it so," Sicarius said coolly. "Even if it were, a contract is a contract."

Amaranthe studied the scant offerings of the charging platform. A shovel and the ore cart, which was about halfway unloaded.

"You should have kept the 'enforcer bitch' and her allies," Larocka said. "At least they weren't stupid enough to walk into a trap without backup."

Amaranthe snorted as she rummaged through the ore bin. Most of the pieces were only a couple inches diameter, not large enough to make devastating projectiles.

"But my spies saw you walk away from the house alone," Larocka said, "angry that your secret was out. You killed Arbitan, you bastard. Now you'll watch me kill your son."

"Arbitan was a traitor," Sicarius said. "A Nurian spy who used you to infiltrate Forge."

Amaranthe dug out a large piece of ore that must have weighed twelve or fifteen pounds. It would have to do.

"Nurian, yes," Larocka said, "but not a spy. He defected. He—"

"He talked you into assassinating the emperor, didn't he?" Sicarius said.

"No! I... You're lying. You're stalling, and—stay back!"

Amaranthe leaned over the rail. Sicarius had been advancing as he spoke, a fact Larocka had not missed. He was still too far away to do anything, and the team of hulking men stood between him and Sespian.

"Now you watch him die," she snarled and turned, putting both hands on the lever.

Amaranthe aimed.

Sicarius surged forward, but the men were expecting it, and they blocked him.

Amaranthe dropped the rock.

She held her breath. Its fall seemed so slow. The lever started downward in its track.

The rock struck the top of Larocka's helmet. Her hands flew up and she was hurled to her back. She flopped once and lay unmoving. The lever clunked back to its original position, and Amaranthe let out her breath.

Twenty sets of eyes looked up at her. A musket cracked, and a ball clanged off the metal railing.

Sicarius never paused. While everyone else was distracted, he drew a dagger and slashed the throats of the two men restraining him. He plunged through the rest and thrust the blade into Larocka's chest, taking no chances of her coming after him again.

By then the guards had recovered, and they surged around him.

The sound of boots on metal wrenched Amaranthe's attention from the scene below. She was about to have her own guards to deal with. The two men on the catwalk thundered toward her.

She should have felt terror, or at least a healthy dose of fear, but instead exhilaration thrummed through her. She ought to run, but she had time to get in a few more blows.

Amaranthe grabbed the shovel and threw ore over the side, taking care to aim away from Sicarius. The blond head was overwhelmed by the number of black and brown heads, but he did not try to escape. How could he? Sespian was still tied up and in danger from any of the men near the lever.

She hurled more ore. Any distraction she could provide to tilt the odds toward Sicarius she would. From this height, even the smaller pieces had to hurt when they hit flesh.

"Arwk!" came a cry from below the staging platform.

Amaranthe's lips flattened in a grim smile. One of the guards must have tried to grab the metal ladder with his bare hands.

Boots striking the rungs told her the men were coming up despite the discomfort. She abandoned the ore cart and took up a position at the top of the ladder, shovel raised over her shoulder.

One hand grabbed the top of the platform. She stomped on it with her heel. The man howled and let go but did not fall off the ladder. She swung the shovel. The metal head struck him in the nose. That time he let go.

He bounced off the railing and missed the catwalk, falling forty feet into the melee below. Three guards went down under him.

"What?" a voice protested in shock.

Amaranthe peered over the edge at the second man, who clung to the ladder, using his sleeves as protection from the hot metal rungs. He was still gawking at his comrade's rapid descent.

Amaranthe hefted the shovel. "Didn't your commander ever lecture you on the follies of assaulting a soldier with the high ground?"

The man refocused on her and threw a knife. Amaranthe jumped back, swinging up the shovel as a defense. The blade clanged off her tool, but the distraction gave the guard the time to climb to the top and lunge onto the platform with her.

Though she still had the shovel, it felt inadequate when the man yanked a double-headed axe off his back. The ringing of more boots on metal meant reinforcements were coming.

"Didn't your mother ever tell you men go to war while women mind the store?" The guard sneered and spun his axe.

Amaranthe retreated until her back bumped into the ore cart. "Didn't *your* mother ever tell you there's no point in fighting a war when your employer is dead?"

"We've already been paid, and we'll collect twice when we 'save' the emperor and bring in Sicarius's head." He took a step forward.

Amaranthe glanced over the railing. "Looks like your friends are losing that fight."

Actually, the brief look below told her little about who was wining. She did not even glimpse Sicarius, and only the seething chaos suggested he was still alive and fighting. Her words got the guard to look over the edge though.

She swung at the back of his head with the shovel.

His axe spun up and sliced through the wooden haft. The shovel head clattered onto the platform, leaving Amaranthe with a broken stick.

The guard lunged at her, axe raised for another swipe. She threw the haft at him and jumped into the ore cart. Her weight tipped it over the edge of the platform. She plunged down the steep track.

Too fast! was the only thought she had time for. Then she ran out of track.

The cart crashed into a solid bin, and she flew out. She bounced off a second bin, then smacked into the concrete floor. Her breath whooshed out, and black dots spun through her vision.

Disoriented, Amaranthe fumbled about and managed to rise to hands and knees. That's when movement from the front door caught her eye. She squinted and struggled to focus.

Soldiers wearing the emperor's black and gold were pouring inside. Her first reaction was to slump with relief, but then she went rigid. She and Sicarius had as much to worry about from soldiers as Larocka's guards did. Maybe more.

She lunged to her feet and raced toward the blast furnace. She dodged track, pipes, and bins and darted into the open area she had seen from above. The first body almost tripped her. Downed men littered the floor amongst pools of blood. Where was...

The lone standing figure amongst the carnage, Sicarius grabbed an axe. Black shirt ravaged, blood spattering him from hair to boots, he looked like—he *was*—the harbinger of death. He stepped to Sespian's side and lifted the dripping blade overhead to hack at the chains.

"Soldiers," Amaranthe barked. "We have to get out of—"

The first of the men plunged into the opening. They almost tripped over the bodies, too, but that did not keep them from seeing Sespian.

"Sire!" one blurted.

"Stop!" another shouted to Sicarius. "Don't hurt him!"

Arms raised, Sicarius hesitated. Less, Amaranthe guessed, because of the soldier's command and more because he was wondering if Sespian was safe now.

"They'll help him," she said, wincing at Sicarius's condemning pose. "We have to go."

A musketeer shouldered his way forward, weapon rising to take aim.

Sicarius threw the axe at the approaching men, though awkwardly, not with the intent to kill. They ducked the flying blade, and the musketeer dropped his weapon.

Amaranthe waved for Sicarius to follow and led him to the back door.

"Get them!" someone yelled.

Sicarius passed Amaranthe and kicked open the locked door. With night's darkness for cover, they raced through the scrapyard into the snow-draped city.

When Sicarius matched her pace instead of taking off on his own, she eyed him with hope. Was she forgiven? With the blood staining his

blond hair and eyebrows, smearing his neck, and dripping from his chin, he appeared even grimmer than usual, but he met her questioning gaze. As the shouts faded behind them, he nodded and patted her on the back.

EPILOGUE

T HAT AFTERNOON, AMARANTHE LEFT THE ICE-
house to find out what had happened to her men. On the way
back, she picked up a few supplies and a newspaper. The
front page story detailed the kidnapping, positing the "abhorrent and
degenerate Sicarius" as the perpetrator of the "unconscionably heinous
attack." Amaranthe was mentioned at the end as an accomplice—no
colorful adjectives for her.

She sighed. So much for getting her name cleared. At least the newspaper said Sespian had survived his injuries and was recovering.

When she returned to the icehouse, she found Sicarius still on the
cot in the office. Not surprising after the previous night's events. Her
shoulder ached from the ore car crash, but, between the creature and the
twenty guards, he had received a far worse battering than her. His eyes
were open, though, and he had bathed and changed clothes. His gaze
followed her into the room.

Not sure of his mood—they had not spoken more than two words
since fleeing the smelter—she set the newspaper, a couple of straw hats,
homespun shirts, and overalls on the desk. Remembering she still had
Sicarius's black dagger, she laid it on the pile of gear next to his cot. She
imagined it happy to once again be nestled amongst the throwing knives,
garrotes, poison vials, and other mortality-inducing appurtenances.

"You came back," Sicarius said.

"Yes." Amaranthe flipped over the empty chicken crate, sat before
the stove, and regarded him. Had he thought she wouldn't? Maybe
he was looking forward to returning to a solitary life free of pestering
womenfolk. "Guess I'm like a persistent toenail fungus, huh?"

"Hm." Sicarius sat up on the cot and dropped his feet to the floor. His face betrayed no pain, but stiffness marked his movements. "A stray cat perhaps."

"Adorable, loyal, and lovable?"

"Nosey, curious, and independent." His eyes crinkled. "Not something you plan to bring home."

Amaranthe found hope in his light tone. "But something you appreciate once it's there?"

Sicarius stood, grabbed the desk chair, and dragged it over to the stove. He sat close, looked her in the eye, and said, "Yes."

She held his gaze for a moment, then blushed and studied a whorl on a floorboard. It was silly she felt so pleased. It wasn't as if he had admitted some undying love—ancestors' eternal warts, he'd compared her to an alley cat. Still, she thought that yes might have also meant, "I'm sorry I lost my temper, and thanks for coming to help."

Sicarius picked up the newspaper and read the front page. Though his expression never changed, Amaranthe grimaced in sympathy.

"I'm sorry it didn't work out with Sespian," she said. "I'd hoped you would save him, and he would *see* you save him, and you two could..."

"We completed our mission. Hollowcrest, Larocka, and Arbitan are dead," Sicarius said, "and, outside the smelter, I found the lieutenant who betrayed Sespian. He had this." Sicarius showed her a glowing purple stone.

Amaranthe fished out its mate. "Larocka had the other in her office."

Sicarius nodded. "He won't be a problem again."

"That's good, but any chance you and Sespian had of forging a relationship was dashed. Those things you said to buy time... I don't know if he heard it all, but the papers make you out to be the mastermind behind the kidnapping. He'll only fear and hate you after this."

"Then it is how it's always been. He is safe for now. That's the only thing that matters."

Sicarius spoke as unemotionally and matter-of-factly as ever. And Amaranthe didn't believe him for a heartbeat. She lifted a hand, intending to pat him on the arm, but, in a fit of courage, she leaned over and hugged him. He did not return the embrace, but he did not pull away either. Though she had only meant to comfort him, she found herself noticing hard muscle beneath her arms, soft hair against her cheek, and the clean, masculine scent of warm skin washed with lye soap.

Amaranthe blushed and withdrew. The blond eyebrow he twitched at her was a little too knowing.

She cleared her throat. "How did you know Sespian was at that smelter anyway?"

"I remembered it from the list of properties we researched. Where else would you take someone to burn him alive?"

"Ah, quite." Amaranthe decided not to mention the intervening clue she had needed to make the deduction.

Sicarius lifted his chin toward the pile of farmer clothing on the desk. "What's the next scheme?"

"I need to get the men out of jail," she said. "They started a fight and stole an enforcer truck in order to provide a distraction for me. It seems they were incarcerated shortly after." She was not sure how Books had ended up in jail as well, but she had heard him throwing vocabulary words at Maldynado when she was scouting around the back of the building.

"Are you planning to plow them out?" Sicarius picked up one of the straw hats and turned it over in his hands.

"You could come along and find out."

With his goal accomplished, he had no reason to stay with them, but she hoped he would.

"To what ends?" he asked.

She opened her mouth to say getting the men out of jail was ends enough but smothered the words. Sicarius wouldn't care.

"I need them for my next plan," she said instead.

"What plan?"

What plan indeed. She thought of the last time she had hastily devised a scheme to pique his interest. This time, there was none of that blunt coldness in his inquiry. Maybe he didn't really want to leave.

To give herself time to think, Amaranthe opened the door to the cast-iron stove and shoveled in a heap of coal. She had burned the counterfeit bills as soon as she woke, and only piles of ash remained. She would clean the stove out before they left, which would be soon. It was time to find a new hideout, a place from which they could launch...

"Isn't it obvious?" she asked. "Sure, Larocka and Arbitan won't be problems again, but Forge was a coalition, not a person. Doesn't it seem likely others will pose a future threat to Sespian? And, of course, the nature of the progressive policies he wishes to instate will make him more enemies. He needs someone watching out for him. He needs..."

Amaranthe stood and paced the tiny room. As the old floorboards creaked beneath her boots, the rest of the plan formed. "The Emperor's Edge, a small but elite unit of specialists who can slip into places and situations where an army cannot. Though they are fugitives, they work for the good of the empire, a fact that—assuming their exploits are impressive and newsworthy—cannot go unnoticed by the emperor himself." As she imagined such future exploits, a sense of freedom came over her, something she had never felt as an enforcer. For the first time, she was crafting her own destiny instead of working within someone else's framework. "Since the principal members of this group are the same associated with Sespian's kidnapping and near death, he must eventually wonder if everything about that day was as it seemed. Why would people who'd meant him harm risk their lives working toward his interests? If he wants to investigate something, he has all the resources in the empire available to him. He'd find the truth eventually, all truths he sought. We just have to make him want to seek. And when he does, he should exonerate me, and I could vouch for you as...someone he should get to know. The Emperor's Edge is the path to what we both want."

By now she was expecting the stunned silence, and Sicarius did not disappoint her. A long moment passed before he spoke.

"To stay here in the capital, parading before enforcers, soldiers, bounty hunters, and Larocka's vengeful colleagues would be suicidal craziness."

"Yes. Are you in?"

He snorted and stared at her. Coals shifted in the stove. Somewhere outside, a whistle marked the end of the workday. As Sicarius's thoughtful silence continued, Amaranthe struggled to keep her patience. It was not as if she was asking for an oath in blood. He could stick around for a while, see how the operation went, and leave if it was not to his liking. Or simply say no and be done with it.

"Yes," Sicarius finally said. "I will follow you."

Amaranthe started to pump an exultant fist, but her jaw dropped as the entirety of his statement sank in. *Follow* her? "I wasn't looking for a subordinate, just a teammate, a co-conspirator."

"Teams need leaders to function." One eyebrow lifted. "Even small elite units of specialists."

"Yes, but you... You're more experienced, more worldly, stronger, faster, *deadlier*. If anybody should be leading this, it's you." She waved at the newspaper. "I'm just the accomplice."

"You don't believe that any more than I do."

"No," Amaranthe allowed after a moment. She had been the one to get a team together to pursue her vision. She had kept them together and working toward that end. Somehow she had even inspired enough loyalty for them to get thrown in jail on her behalf.

So why balk now?

Because it was *Sicarius*. Leading the other men, she could see, but leading him seemed presumptuous. No, she could do presumptuous, so that wasn't even it. It was...fear. It was walking through the world with a man-eating tiger on a leash, knowing she was accountable for its actions. One inattentive moment and that tiger could pull away and kill anytime it wanted or—worse—she could send it off to kill for her anytime she wanted. And what if she came to relish that feeling? That power? Would she become like Hollowcrest? She suppressed a shudder.

"Besides," Sicarius said, "I would create a team of assassins, because that is what I know how to do. That would not impress Sespian. You, however, will create a team of heroes."

She met his gaze and found only respect there. *If a man who has a mantra of trusting nobody has faith in me, shall I argue?*

She plopped her straw hat on her head. "We better get those future heroes out of prison then."

* * * * *

They waited until night, when there would be fewer men on duty. Amaranthe ambled into the enforcer station with the hat slung low over her face and one hand tucked into her overalls. If she could have found a stalk of wheat to chew on, it would be dangling from her mouth. Alas, it was not the right season.

Face shadowed by his hat, Sicarius waited at her back. The lone corporal manning the desk gave her a bemused smile.

"Help you?"

Rows of steel-barred jail cells stretched beyond an open doorway behind him. Amaranthe hoped, in the aftermath of the emperor's kidnapping, no one had found time to look up the new prisoners in the warrant book.

"Lost me a few runaways from my farm out yonder." She pointed vaguely in the direction of the lake, beyond which agriculture still dominated the lowlands. "Heard they was here."

"Describe them."

"Four strapping fellows, well except for old Hoss. He's a tall gangly one. Junior looks like he ought to be an officer in the army, 'cept the women and the drink keeps him under the table 'til noon if he ain't watched good. Surly used t' run with the gangs and looks it. Then there's Scar. Name speaks for itself, I reckon."

"Those aren't the names they gave me," the corporal said.

"Well, I figger not. Would you give up yer name if you was running from a work contract? I've got the doc'ments right here for 'em." She handed four bogus papers to the corporal. "They all signed on for two years in exchange for room and board and a share of the crops. I'd be in a right bind without them four hands. Planting season ain't that far off, y'know."

The corporal shrugged. "I'll get the paperwork. It's a hundred ranmyas apiece to free them."

"A hundred apiece! What'd they do?"

"Obstructed a crime scene investigation and stole one of our steam trucks. Then they resisted arrest. They've resisted *everything.*"

"Idiots!" Amaranthe slammed a fist into her palm and did her best to look infuriated. "Why couldn't they just run off and get drunk like you'd expect?"

"I don't know, ma'am." Amusement tugged at the corporal's lips. "Do you have the money to pay the fine?"

"No," she said glumly. "I reckon you'll have to keep them."

The corporal winced. She wondered just how troublesome her men were being.

"Don't they have anyone else who could pay the fine?" he asked. "The big one—"

"Junior," Amaranthe supplied.

"Er, Junior implied he had some family he might be able to get to come down."

"His family's all dead. Junior's so used to lying he couldn't tell the truth if his brandy supply hung on it."

The corporal rubbed his chin. "He did seem quite reluctant to contact his kin."

"What happens if no one can pay the fine?" Amaranthe asked as if she didn't know perfectly well.

The corporal slumped. "They stay here. One hundred eighty days in a cell."

"Well, I'm just a simple farmer, sir, and I'll never have that much money to spare, but if you'd release them and let me put them back to work, I'd sure be grateful."

"Can't let them go without a fitting punishment."

"Oh, they'll be punished." Amaranthe smiled and pointed at the heretofore silent Sicarius. "Pa here, he's the farm dis-ci-pli-nar-i-an. He was a soldier and he knows how to lay into a man an' make him wish he'd never thunk of running off. Ain't that right, Pa?" She smiled up at Sicarius.

"Yes," he said flatly. "Ma."

Hm, she would have to remember not to put him into positions that required acting flair in the future.

"I don't know, ma'am..." The corporal glanced over his shoulder toward the office. Wanting to get rid of the men but not sure his superiors would approve?

The enforcer that leaned through the doorway was not a superior though. He sported the rank of a raw recruit, and he had a swollen and likely broken nose.

"Want me to get those men for you, Corporal?" he asked in a nasal tone.

Amaranthe lifted her hand and pressed it to her lips to hide a smirk. How many enforcers had it taken to manhandle those four into cells?

"It makes sense," she said. "If they was to stay here six months, all four of 'em, that's a lot of meals you'd have to be feeding them,

and them doing no work in return, just lounging in them cells. I reckon that'd add up to a lot more than four hundred ranmyas over time. Seems like a better deal for the city if you let me take 'em back to the farm."

"I'm not the one paying for their meals," the corporal muttered, but he glanced at his subordinate, who waited hopefully in the doorway. "All right, get them out."

"That's kind of you, sir." Amaranthe smiled, and it was no act.

The corporal grumbled under his breath, disappeared into the office for a moment, and returned with paperwork. He laid the four sheets on the desk, stamped them closed, and scribbled something intentionally illegible in the box for recording the fine as paid. Illogically, the old enforcer in Amaranthe cringed at this ham-handed handling of the law.

Scuffles sounded beyond the doorway, and something crashed to the floor and broke.

"Rotten apples." The corporal pointed at Amaranthe. "Can you help, or will they just get worse when they see you?"

Sicarius strode through the doorway. Amaranthe hustled after. She had to speak first, before the men blew her story.

She need not have worried, for they halted and stared when they saw her and Sicarius. It was not disbelief at their arrival, she realized, but amusement at the farmer outfits. Maldynado managed to open his mouth at the same time as he smirked.

"Junior," Amaranthe blurted to beat him. "How could you leave the farm—leave my *sister*—like that? You plant your seed, then just run off to the city to get yourself wound up in antics that put you in jail. For six months! You expecting her to have the baby and care for it without no men-folk to help provide?"

Maldynado's mouth did not shut; rather his jaw dropped lower and hung there.

Books slapped him on the shoulder. "Lout."

"And the rest of you. There's work to be done, even if there's still snow on the ground. You forget your contracts? You forget your word what you gave me?"

Basilard appeared glad for his missing voice. An indignant expression lurched onto Akstyr's face, and he started to say something, but Books elbowed him.

"It was a mistake, ma'am," Books said. "We're ready to come back to work."

"Not soon enough." Maldynado issued a disparaging glare at the corridor of cells behind him.

Amaranthe led them out of the station before anybody could say anything that might give away her story. Outside, snow squeaked under their boots and black ice glinted beneath the street lamps, but gusts of wind from the south promised warmer weather coming.

"Thanks for springing us," Akstyr said.

"Indeed," Books said.

Basilard nodded.

"Not that we couldn't have gotten out on our own charms," Maldynado said.

"I saw your charms on a couple of enforcers' faces," Amaranthe said. "I'd call them contusions, but it's your story."

Maldynado grinned. "So, what's next, boss?"

"Since you asked..."

By the time they reached the icehouse, she had explained her plan.

"There's just one thing I want to know," Maldynado said at the end. He stabbed a finger at Amaranthe. "Is that the uniform?"

Smiling, she removed her straw farmer's cap. She stood on her tiptoes and plopped it on Maldynado's head.

"Only for you."

Maldynado started to reach up to remove it but paused. He wriggled his eyebrows at Amaranthe. "Does it look good on me?"

"You look like an illiterate buffoon," Books said.

"But does it look *good*?"

* * * * *

Sespian eyeballed the bowl of lotion his new valet had dropped off. The honey-and-cinnamon scent left him wondering if it was edible. He smeared some on his cracked cheeks and forehead.

Trog hopped onto the desk and swished his cobweb-draped tail.

"Yes, I know I look silly." Sespian smeared another glop on his burned skin, sat in the chair, and patted the cat. A couple of papers rested beneath Trog's paws. "You're just in time to help me with a decision."

Trog sniffed Sespian's chin, and the sandpaper tongue darted out to sample the lotion.

"I guess that answers the edible question," Sespian murmured. "We're here to decide something a little more momentous though."

He slid the wanted posters for Amaranthe and Sicarius out from beneath the cat. He picked up a pencil and sighed at the fresh feline tooth marks decorating it.

"Money alone doesn't seem to be enough of an incentive for someone to get rid of Sicarius." Sespian tapped the pen against his chin and then added the promise of a title and land to the reward money.

Next he considered Amaranthe's poster. Or at least he tried to. Trog flopped down and stretched out across it, inviting a belly rub.

"Don't worry, boy. I'm not going to upgrade her bounty." Sespian wished he remembered more of what happened in the smelter. The guards said Amaranthe had been there at the end, but he had no memory of anything after Sicarius demanding his head. No one had seen who killed Dunn. Sespian tapped the pencil thoughtfully. "I still have no idea what Lokdon has done and whether she's been acting of her own volition."

Trog meowed.

"Yes, yes, and I suppose there's the hope that maybe she..." He finished with a silly shrug.

On her poster, he crossed out the line about her being a magic user and simply wrote: "Wanted Alive — 10,000 ranmyas."

* * * * *

A young officer in the Imperial Intelligence Network intercepted the emperor's revisions before they could go to Enforcer Headquarters. The officer left Sicarius's poster alone, but he amended the one for Amaranthe Lokdon. "Wanted Dead — 10,000 ranmyas." Those with knowledge of Forge could not be allowed to walk the streets or contact the emperor.

THE END

CONNECT WITH THE AUTHOR

Have a comment? Question? Just want to say hi? Find me online at:

http://www.lindsayburoker.com

http://www.facebook.com/LindsayBuroker

http://twitter.com/GoblinWriter

Thanks for reading!

Printed in Germany
by Amazon Distribution
GmbH, Leipzig